THE STAR-CROSSED EMPIRE

A Whorl Chronicles novel

MAYA DARJANI

To the brown girls, to the dreamers, to the out-of-step girls, to the hidden warriors.

We can be heroes.

Copyright © 2024 by Maya Darjani

All rights reserved.

No part of this publication may be reproduced, distributed, or transmitted in any form or by any means, including photocopying, recording, or other electronic or mechanical methods, without the prior written permission of the publisher, except as permitted by U.S. copyright law.

The story, all names, characters, and incidents portrayed in this production are fictitious. No identification with actual persons (living or deceased), places, buildings, and products is intended or should be inferred.

Book cover design by Maya Darjani, using stock from DepositPhotos

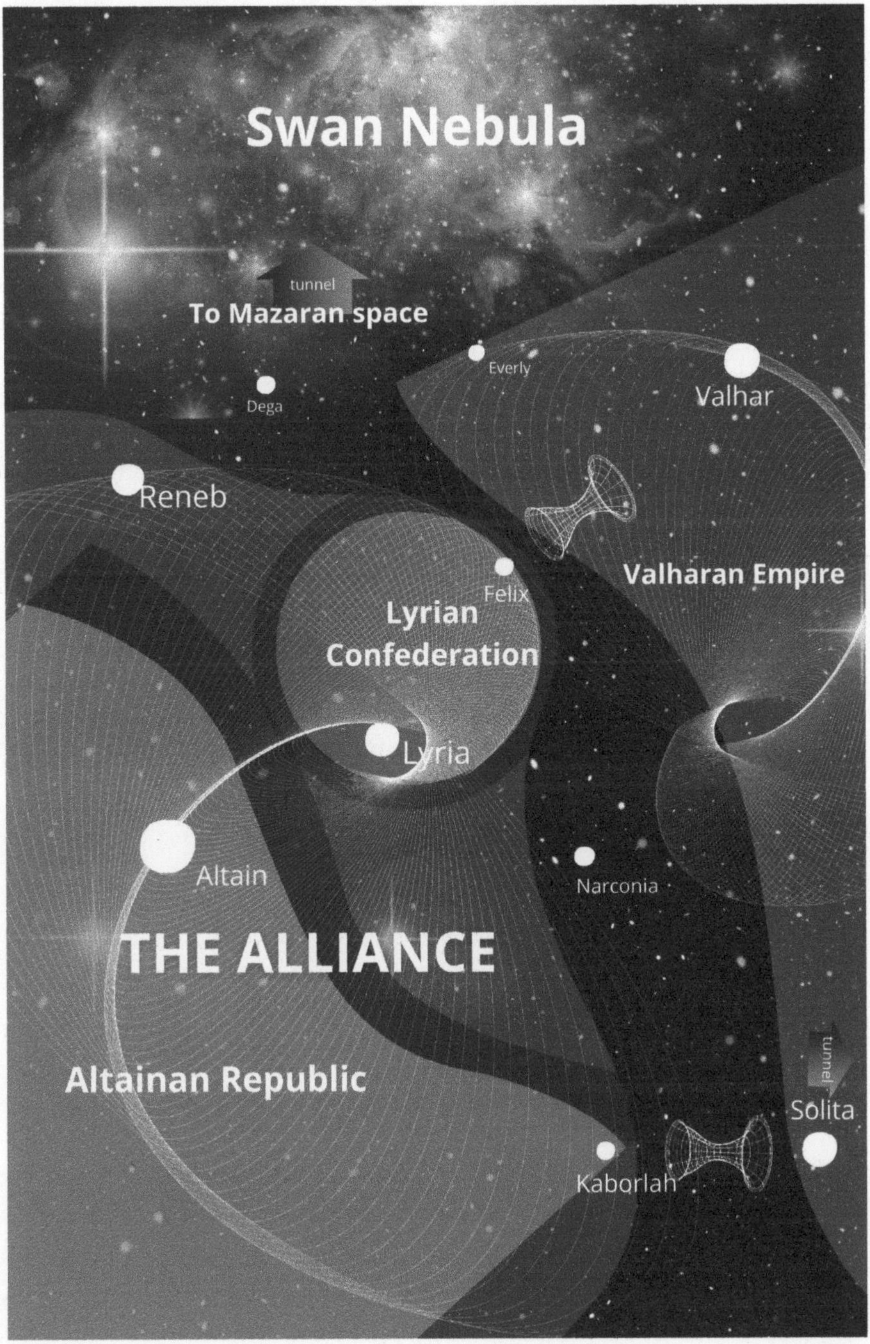
Swan Nebula
tunnel
To Mazaran space
Everly
Valhar
Dega
Reneb
Valharan Empire
Felix
Lyrian
Confederation
Lyria
Altain
Narconia
THE ALLIANCE
tunnel
Altainan Republic
Solita
Kaborlah

THEN

Then

Layla Kamil, Cygna City, Altain

16 Debedana 1125

"Tell me again," the security investigator says. His eyes hone in. I let my breathing slow, imagining cool water trickling down my back, just like Ignatius taught me.

A simple lie detector test is easy to beat, but I'm not trying today. Today, I have nothing to hide. Good thing, too. The cuffs on my hands measure my pulse, and *that's* the part I could cheat. But those eyes—those eyes are unrelenting.

He wears bionic contacts, all the better to measure any hesitation in my manner, or the slightest dissembling.

"Ignatius and I started writing two years ago," I repeat. "I've kept your office informed about the frequency and nature of the correspondence."

"No face-to-face calls?"

I start to shake my head but think better of it. "We know suspicions run high between Valhar and Altain. No reason to get ourselves into a situation where it's only our word we haven't been discussing anything inappropriate. A written trail, we believed, was best."

He narrows those eyes. The contacts make his irises gleam electric blue, and the lenses within whir about like clockwork gears. Something in the background clicks and ticks with steady precision, and though the light in the room is evenly distributed via inset bulb, I imagine one ponderously swinging lamp threatening to fall and crash onto my head.

Damn you, Ignatius. You get to live your life all lordful and high, and I'm always the one left scrambling to explain.

"What did he say about the new position?" he asks.

"His ascension? I had no idea it was happening. He said nothing at all, 'cept he'd need to stop writing for a while. Then Carlus abdicated, and ten days later, I saw the announcement."

The interrogator steeples his fingers, assessing me. "And then?"

"I haven't heard from him since. For the last six months." Fine. It's fine.

He scoffs and makes a note on his tablet.

"But I've told you all this already." I finally allow myself some irritation. "This is a scheduled counterintel screen. Why the drama?"

"Have somewhere to be?"

I grind my teeth. "Well the *President* of the entire Whorl-damned Altainan Republic has that Armistice Day speech to give tomorrow and if I don't get back to it—"

"Let me be clear, Ms. Kamil—"

"*Commander* Kamil."

He smiles toothily. In my imagination, miniature snakes slither out his mouth, chattering and hissing to go in for the kill.

"How Valharan of you." His voice oozes with derision.

I suppress the shiver, but of course he catches it.

"The chief of staff," he continues, "is the one who asked me to do a second level investigation, so I think he can forgive a slight amount of tardiness."

Chief of sta—Damnit, Srivani. "As long as I'm back by 1400." My hands clench and release. "I have a meeting with Roya herself."

"We wouldn't want you to be late for the President. I agree. Now, let's go over this again," he says. "When did you start fucking Emperor Ignatius I of Valhar?"

I leave, the claustrophobic room leading into a claustrophobic hallway, down in the ass pit of a shabby edifice: the People's House, the seat of power for the leader of the Free Whorl. It's as humble as possible, a nondescript brick squatting on a nondescript square. Typical Altain: down with the pomp and circumstance! Down with the gilded corridors and the stately busts. We're afraid to admit our predations, so invested we are in being the moral leaders of the Whorl.

I promptly run into Ransom, leaving the observation room to the south.

"You two never even *kissed*?" Ransom asks. Amazing, for how much he knows me, he can't understand how little physical intimacy matters.

"You were listening in?" Ugh. Of course he was, because—

"It's literally my job." He finishes what I assume is the rest of his lunch, grimacing as he picks at his teeth. "Haff a toofpick?"

I make an *urph* of disgust and hand him a neatly folded square of cloth. "Use this."

Ransom nods in thanks. His stubby fingers dive in and then he finishes up, stuffing the cloth into the pocket of his kurta. Looking over at me, he arches an eyebrow. "What?"

"I'm serious." I grimace. "Can we not talk about my unexciting romantic history when we get out in the open? I'd rather the general populace not know about, well, you know." We keep walking through the pit and emerge from the basement door into glorious sunshine. I bask in the gust of afternoon sea air, craygulls squawking in the distance.

Ransom pokes my shoulder. "What, that the joint heroes of the Mazaran invasion wanted to boink each other the entire war?"

I scan the plaza, noting the interns, journalists, and minor officials gathered nearby, and turn back to him glaring. "I'm open about it with my superiors, *because they need to know*." My tight whisper seems to ring out over the square. "Now, can you just shut it?"

"Yes, ma'am, Commander, ma'am." He salutes. "I guess that's what I call you now."

"Oh, stop." I roll my eyes. "That kid—"

"Already doing the 'kids these days' thing? You're not that old, little Layla."

Youngest O-5 in a generation, that's me. Aged 26 when I made rank, now 30. Hardly a pimple-scarred youth, but pimple cream and wine spritzer is the Republic Defense Force's stock in trade. At any rate, eventually they retired me, too, patting my back and telling me to stay close to the capital, while keeping me corked in case of emergency—and also for the occasional parade.

He spins off from me as we reenter the building from the street level, going wherever he goes to sit on his throne of lies and intrigue, cackling as he tweaks and pulls gossamer threads of intelligence and makes minions out of men.

Ransom's actually the deputy assistant national threats minister for counterespionage and leadership profiling, but I like to pretend he's a sinister puppeteer.

But in a way, it's true. Altain's leaders—those powerful, mighty leaders—use spymasters like Ransom to keep dissension in line, and scary bionic dudes to sniff out traitors. But then they turn around and talk about public trust. And maybe only I see it. I'm the only one who's been on the other side of the divide; the only one whose foreign experience spans beyond free states like Lyria and Reneb. Instead, I'm resident expert on the annoyingly militaristic Valharan Empire.

A few twists and turns later, I enter President Roya's austere office, which stands resolutely unadorned: generic meeting table with folding chairs on one end; her desk on the other. A plain black slab with a cushy-yet-functional overstuffed swiveling chair sits behind it.

Next to Roya sits the chief of staff, Srivani. He's the reason for my little security update-turned-interrogation.

I lower my voice as I pass: "Talk. Later."

Sri has the grace to look abashed. "Layls," he begins, "I know you're going to ask her—"

"Armistice Day," Roya interrupts in her throaty voice.

"We've got everything set up, ma'am," Sri answers, pivoting away.

"You've got those changes incorporated?" Roya asks me. Her only nod to ornamentation today is her shari-inspired skirt, a stiff gold-and-black sensation, the petticoat underneath flaring out dramatically to make the whole thing look like a Valharan ballgown.

Valhar's on my mind a lot, especially given the favor I'm about to ask the President.

"Ma'am, I changed most of them. But that phrase, 'requiem and remembrance,' had the highest engagement score of all our lyrical beats."

"Well, if the focus groups like it—" Roya sighs— "by all means, keep it in."

Chief speechwriter: *not* as glamorous as one would think. In fact, sometimes I feel no better than a vassal. Especially after the high of military leadership.

"We'll keep you off stage for this one," she continues. "Don't want my opponents to think I'm milking having a goddess-be-damned war hero on my staff. Now, about the state visit to Valhar next month—"

"I'm still waiting for my ticket," I jump in, then clamp my hand over my mouth. Oh, shoot. I literally just interrupted the President. Srivani puts his head in his hands, practically his default position when dealing with me.

But I haven't busted my ass for all these years to be tossed aside until I'm recast as a show pony. This is *Valhar* we're discussing. An empire, and Emperor, I have actual expertise on.

Thankfully, all I get from Roya is an indrawn sigh and one raised brow. "I'm sure Sri can handle any last minute changes to my remarks."

I continue with my push. She'll see right through me of course. Work be damned. I want to see *him*. "Madame President, humbly, you need to show your party you're serious about having good relations with Valhar. Especially with legislative elections coming up soon." I pause, gauging her response.

Her head cocks to the side, lips pursed in thought. Good. Since the end of the Mazaran war, the populace has worried about another threat. Valhar fits the bill.

"The more light you shine on the empire, the more we remind the voters they can be friends and allies," I resume. "I can help, ma'am. Not just last minute changes to *speeches*, but also if things go awry. And there's policy changes to boot, with the new regime. I don't understand them fully but I have more experience than—"

"Fine. Fine, Layla. But wear your uniform for the opening ceremony. They'll eat it up."

Victory. Of a sort.

"I aim to serve." I tense, anticipating a flurry of good-idea fairies capitalizing on the Emperor and I being old war buddies: joint appearances at a cemetery; thrown together in a ticker-tape parade.

But President Roya keeps going. It's curiously disappointing, despite the fact I loathe being shown off. Altainan performative pacifism at work, again. We Altainans are so far up our collective ass, we treat our soldiers like evil necessities, shameful secrets to tuck away in hope chests until the dowry comes due.

"All right," Roya says, "this is a formal state visit, not a working one. We'll avoid the heavy topics; the rumor they are constructing a tunnel in the empire's hinterlands is still very concerning, but my goal during this trip would be to gauge if it's even true. Regardless, other than that wrinkle, we're flying in, saying hi, dancing to some traditional songs, going home."

One month. In less than one month I'll see him for the first time in two years.

We've sent pictures in addition to our words, sometimes silly videos to convey what we couldn't otherwise, but we haven't talked in real-time. Now, after a couple weeks' travel, we're speeding our way toward Valhar. Toward *him*.

Just a friend now. Just a friend.

We fly past Felix through the Lyrian wormhole, and soon, we're on approach: ice-capped mountains, snow blanketing the ground. I quiver as if already cold. Cygna, Altain's capital, is temperate and by the sea, fueled by saltwater in the air and lush breeze. I've been to Novaria, the Valharan capital, only once before, when Gustav IV bestowed me damehood for my part in pushing Mazar back to its borders.

In the transfer shuttle down to the surface of Valhar, Sri shivers and messes with the cabin's environmental controls. "So. Previous relationship gonna be a problem on this trip?"

My eyes shift to him and I glare. "About that."

"Hari didn't give you too hard a time, did he? With his bionics?"

My teeth clench. "Not at all. It was a picnic." A picnic in *hell*.

"I *knew* you were going to push to come. Honestly, it was going to be a no. Anyway. We had to cover our asses. Yours too. Now that you've had a second level security review, no one is going to panic about your previous engagement to the Emperor of Valhar."

"We were *not* engaged."

"He asked you to marry him."

"And I said no!" Only because of Carlus II's stupid citizenship decree, which was the *first thing* Ignatius changed upon his ascension.

But I don't admit that. Nor do I admit the flutter it gives me to imagine Ignatius's satisfaction as he retracted that particular law.

"We were friends and colleagues," I say instead. "He can be a bit traditional, and pragmatic to boot. He thought we'd be a good match."

"You, a foreigner?"

"The commoners don't have a problem with outsiders. But the aristocracy is more..."

"Quaint?"

Provincial. Xenophobic. Atavistic.

"I'm glad they were able to bring some new attitudes to the throne in the last five years," I allow. Integrating the Valharan and Altainan elite out in the Swan Nebula helped…

My thoughts trail off. Then-candidate Roya had pushed hard to close that particular base, and succeeded too. Otherwise, would I still be out there? Would Ignatius be? What promises would he have made me then, knowing he had a chance to come into power?

The welcoming ceremony limps on, tedious as usual, but I gratefully tug my dress whites, warm and practical in the biting air. Sri clinches his brocade jacket tighter as the wind blows. Standing with her wife and the Emperor on the steps of the Imperial

Palace, President Roya resembles the Goddess Herself, wearing a serene expression even as soft flakes flurry around her.

We decamp to an inner foyer. Roya introduces our delegation: trade representatives, staffers, cultural attachés. The stoic Valharans regard our untidy gaggle of a delegation—with our rolled up sleeves and easy smiles—with barely disguised fascination. The Emperor's personal secretary, whom I know well, is in charge and handles the pleasantries. He has a polite nod for most and a genuine smile for me. But then—

Steps, sharp and measured. It's *him*: the uniform, rhythmic cadence of his footfall as familiar to me as my heartbeat. He enters: posture straight and tall, shoulders squared and back, head up, eyes forward, economical swing to his arm, heel-strike a rapped staccato on marble tile.

Clearly he's only passing through. His eyes rove over us as if reviewing troops, and he gives an impatient swing of his head when the secretary repeats the introductions. He pauses to speak with the President, and his brows knit together, lips in a thin line. He nods, and cuts his eyes at the secretary, who makes a note. Try as I might, I'm unable to achieve eye contact.

And I do try.

He then resumes walking toward the second exit, about to come near, and he's a rogue star attracting a flailing, wandering planet, capturing me in his orbit. My mind flashes to the Ignatius I know: the silly Ignatius, the loving one, the cut-clean soldier, drunk, lolling head spouting off some stupid theory, the one who held my hand and listened to my fears, the one who taught me to dance the calana, the one to whom I taught ancient mythology. The one who drew silly cartoons illustrating my silly thoughts. We bonded over frozen tundra and over our vows of service. We bonded over loyalty, over nation-above-all. Ignatius Kurestin. Esteemed son of a royal princess and a minor baron. War hero.

The love of my life.

"Of course," the secretary, Ephraim, says at last, "the Dame Commander Layla Kamil." Ignatius grunts in acknowledgement, never once looking at me.

And he walks right past me, out the door.

Then

He leaves, a supernova extinguishing all the light in the room, and I gasp in the vacuum. In his wake it's all business. The important delegates are taken to luxury accommodations. The rest of us schlep our way to the guest residence, tucked out of sight.

My stomach tightens, and I in turn clench my hands, close and open, over and over, as I work to keep the confusion and disorientation at bay. We're friends. Just friends. And when in professional situations, friends sometimes have to pretend not to be. That's all.

I've never been inside the palace before and therefore join my fellow staffers in their caught breaths and wide eyes. Majestic frescoes dot the landscape like signposts to a destination; here an origin tale, there a claim of divine rule, another commemorating glorious battle. All on the way to an ordered, disciplined society. What the Valharans must think of us! Freewheeling, bohemian laity all. Altain is soft words and kind hands—until our principles are squeezed, and then we lash out in protective anger.

Everything's gold. Everything shines. The palace smells of meticulous, antiseptic cleanliness. With their discipline, perhaps Valhar should be the culture of monastic simplicity and spartan pragmatism, and Altain should be slinging jewels and glitter. Instead, we're the ones gawking at the riches splayed out before us. Not so much as to be gaudy or gauche. Just the right touch for simple elegance.

For a moment, my step falters, thinking *this all belongs to him*. I'm heartsick. I can't even visualize a silly scene to will it all away.

"I thought you two were friends," my assistant whispers as we walk. I'm still smarting over Roya and Sri seeing that snub. Will it hurt my professional credibility?

Not for the first time, I think: *Goddamnit, Ignatius.*

In the morning, the common space in the guest residence sits covered in coffee mugs, tablets, and that desperate stench ten flunkies get when trying to keep their principal happy.

"She *had* to get snippy about the tunnel," Sri groans, face in hands. His bald pate sheens, but the luster disappears with an angry toss of his head. He subvocalizes what I assume are angry epithets against the President. She apparently made some waves in her private meeting with His Excellency.

"Well, she's right," my assistant offers. She's leaned back, bare feet on table, and I swallow my reproach. "There's a reason our pact of cooperation includes a clause about not building *an entire Whorl-damned expressway to the rest of the galaxy* in your backyard."

"He's not doing that though, is he?" Sri's plaintive. "Layla, tell me he's not that stupid."

Reclaim the narrative, Layls. This is exactly why I asked to come. "He's definitely not stupid. You know how insular the empire is. There's some reason they want to build a tunnel. Besides," I add, "doesn't it take generations to build one, much less figure out the physics?" There's a reason the Whorl only has one, in the Swan Nebula.

"Generations seem like a long time, until our grandkids are dealing with an invasion from yet another hostile people, on our flank this time."

I nod at Sri. Point taken. "So what's the deal right now? We think they're researching?"

Mena, my assistant, groans. "Blessed Lady, I *hope* it's just in the research stage. But here. Ransom's report came in this morning." She throws it at me. "Where were you?"

"Walking. Pretty view." The Republic forces made me an early riser, and the best thing to do from there is start the day right. And, maybe, getting a glimpse of a certain someone. But why do *I* care, anyway? I wanted to come on this trip for career purposes. Eyes on my old friend would've been nice, but apparently, for reasons I don't yet understand, I'm persona non grata. No communication since he became emperor. Completely ignoring me.

The flare of hurt at being disposable is something I try to eliminate. I visualize a trash stick grabbing the ball of pain like a wayward crumple of paper, stabbing it, then shoving it down deep inside me.

I scan the report. It appears there's a troubling amount of activity in the hinterlands of the Empire, in a location with known positive factors for tunnel creation. Hopefully it's nothing.

Is this a thing the Emperor would do? How would I know? I don't know the Emperor.

I don't mean this in some petulant way, as if I'm getting back at the man who pretended he didn't know me. Truly, I don't know the *Emperor*. I've never known him. I've never talked to him. I've never listened to him expound on the value of holding to promises versus acting in self-interest. Captain-General Lord Ignatius Kurestin, Viscount Aquil, Baronet Tyrii, is not the same as the man, the office, embodying the absolute power of the Ruler-Ascendant of the Valharan Empire.

Wherever Altain's faults lie regarding the treatment of our military, the fact remains that soldiers throughout the Whorl cleave to their respective oaths, a shared ideology in its own way. And because of those oaths of protection, Ignatius and I together were responsible for the pact of cooperation that catapulted our two superpowers into actual allies. Our nations fought together against the Mazaran Invasion, as opposed to being two comets passing in a starry sky.

Although perhaps that history no longer means anything to him.

To do anything to jeopardize either the pact *or* put the Whorl in danger of the Mazarans coming back would be anathema to the soldier I knew. But power changes people. And the first thing one learns in the officer corps is duty shapes people. The rank and position you hold is more important than what someone individually believes. Only those of lower rank have the luxury of holding on to principle. And so I don't know Emperor Ignatius I's decision tree. I don't know if his personal distaste for jeopardizing the Whorl factors into anything anymore.

The next day, Roya stands tall and proud, giving the traditional visitors' address in front of the Lords' Parliament. I mouth my own words along with the President, the universal tic of ghostwriters throughout the galaxy.

"And so, we find ourselves navigating the most complex of relationships: friendship. How much meaning pours into that simple word? Two nations set up so differently. No longer with a common enemy to fight. We've had peace, but can we learn to also grow close?

"I would like to thank the hospitality of Emperor Ignatius, the Right-and-Honorable-Lords, and the entire nation of Valhar," Roya continues.

She pauses for the intermittent applause and I smooth my burgundy skirt. No uniform. Today I blend into the comfortable anonymity of a background, anodyne, worker bee. My coworkers and I stand on the floor of the chamber, along a wall edge. Up in the observer galley are the well-to-do citizens of the Empire, plus their nascent press corps.

"He looks so intimidating," Mena whispers. I keep smiling and clapping while shifting my eyes to Mena, the President, and then to Ignatius: formidable, impeccable.

"He can be, yes," I offer, out the side of my mouth. It's funny; Mena works for me, but in the grand context of things, we're both nobodies. Somehow I occupy a prestigious position yet am also another cog in the wheel. Sometimes it grates.

"This Senate of Lords," Roya's speech goes on, "is different from the system we have in place on Altain. Hereditary. A position for life, a position borne out of privilege. Some in our republic look askance at the way you've ordered your society. But I say, after meeting with this man, your emperor, your leader, I have seen that you, the nobility, the electors in charge of choosing a new ruler, have done this entire Whorl an impeccable service."

That's off-script. But I don't begrudge her.

"He should probably have kids soon," Mena whispers, "or if something happens they'll have to do this all over again. Ooh, he needs a wife. Can you imagine?"

With effort, I temper my uncomfortable expression, contemplating that peculiar agony of not being able to confess one's heartbreak. But mostly, I want my friend back; I wish he'd look at me with just the tiniest lift of his eyebrow, so I know I'm not invisible.

"I wonder what his babies will look like," Mena adds, causing me to try to keep at bay the semi-hysterical, maniacal, panicked laughter bubbling in my throat. It's not Mena's fault. Most people don't know about the *relationship* part of our history. We loved each other, without ever allowing ourselves to be together.

Focus, Layls. I'm an officer and assistant to the President. Ignatius knows his duty. Which apparently means cutting ties with me. Which apparently means breaking treaties. Which apparently means jeopardizing this fragile peace we have in the Whorl. Now it's time to do my *own* damn job. I turn my full attention back to the speech.

"This formal state visit has been an inspiration, and what I hope is a continuation of a productive and beneficial relationship between our two nations," Roya says. "I would like to extend an invitation to Emperor Ignatius to come visit us on Altain within the next six months. I would like it to be a working visit, not a ceremonial one, so we can iron out larger issues and the elements of cooperation between us. Would you accept that, Your Excellency?"

My silent mouthing trips up at this point, because this is also off-script. It's about the subspace tunnel Valhar is rumored to be building, despite the treaties.

He has to accept. Roya's backed him into a corner.

I glance at Ignatius to observe his reaction, and he's looking straight at me. His jaws work silently. Apparently he's chewing over a response. *I had nothing to do with that part*, I convey with my widened eyes, and I am graced with the ghost of a smile.

Before he can answer Roya, a loud crack splits the room. Maybe the thundersnow forecasted this morning? But then comes the trickling awareness of shouting. The lights turn off.

Somebody screams.

"They have weapons!" one of the Lords calls. There emerges the rustle of one hundred men drawing their sidearms in response. Painfully aware we're fish in a shooting barrel, I tug at Mena and back us closer to the wall, grabbing an errant chair and place it in front of us, ineffectual as it may be. "Crouch down."

The wave breaks. My ears ring with the cacophony. Any minute I'm expecting the sound of arms fire. For now it's just a lot of yelling. "This is the Imperial Service. Stand down!" comes a voice. "This includes you, my Lords. We have the situation under control."

The running lights along the floor flicker on and in the ghostly shadows both the Emperor's and the President's personal security shepherd them out an inset door, the First Lady huddled alongside next to the President.

It's then Ignatius says, "Protect Dame Layla. She may be a target." His voice is deep, controlled, and authoritative, but in it beats the fear, the barely repressed terror hidden within a slight trill.

And all I can think is, *I knew it, you bastard. I knew you still loved me.*

I bend over Mena, who's curled up and shivering, panic radiating off of her in waves. "Deep breaths," I coach. "In and out. Still and controlled. I've got you." I miss having my sidearm, its hefty assuring weight digging into my hips.

A tap on my shoulder. "My lady," the man behind me says in an urgent whisper, "the Emperor has requested I bring you to safety."

I assess the chaos, then glare at him. "Let me stay with my colleagues."

"My lady, I'm afraid I cannot—"

"This is ridiculous," I snap. My lip pinches like an adolescent trying to have her way. I'm on shaky ground. In this place, I don't feel confident, or brave, or knowledgable. I shouldn't make waves. But the idea of just walking away goes against all my ingrained instincts.

The man—a security officer of significant rank—regards me with discomfort, but he doesn't look likely to give in. "Madam," he says, "this is a direct order from His Excellency."

I sigh. I'm an honorary noble, nothing more, nothing worth protecting, but Ignatius's word is law. I try again. "I'm not one to be coddled." But he ignores me.

I lean down near Mena. "Keep breathing," I whisper. "Nothing else is happening. Just a bit of chaos, and then it's done." With one last look back, I allow the man to lead me away.

With each step, I get myself more worked up, until I burst into the closet-sized space, my heart hammering angry spikes. "What's happening?" I demand, imagining my eyes burning holes into Ignatius. "Are those people armed? Are my colleagues in danger?" What I want to say is: *What's this hot-and-cold shit? Ignore me, then pull me away, like a lost earring picked off pavement?*

President Roya holds up a hand, warding off my tirade. "They're telling us it's just protesters. A large amount, but no danger. No attempt to harm."

"But is anyone taking care of our staff? They should have been able to come with us, ma'am. They're scared. Mena was hyperventilating!" I pace, tense, furious.

I'm probably making too big a deal out of this, but it's *unfair*. I don't deserve to be here more than anyone else.

"Peace, Layla." Roya has her arms around her wife, who also looks terrified. "Everyone will be okay. We're here as a precaution."

"Right." I whirl back on Ignatius, meeting his chestnut eyes. "So why the *hell* am I here, Your Excellency? No danger? Then let me be out there with my people."

"They're not *your* people—" the President attempts to interject, but I cut her off without acknowledgement. "So what do you say, Excellency? What's your excuse dragging me away from them? Surely your security has better things to do."

"Do not presume to lecture Us," he says, simply, voice cool and eyes glittering.

I'm not afraid of him. But I understand the office he holds—understand the need to clarify the ground rules of this interaction. I breathe deep, ball my fists down by my side, and nod once in acknowledgement.

Ignatius's lips quirk briefly. He walks toward me and bows. "Well met, my lady."

I curtsey in the Valharan style, almost by compulsion. "Well met, Your Excellency." Oh Ignatius, you've trained me well.

"Was that your speech?" Ignatius asks. "The President's?"

I clear my throat. "Some of it."

"Melodic," he says, turning to Roya.

"What can I say," Roya responds with a smile. "She's a superstar."

His eyes return to me, and mine to his.

I punch down the thoughts, the curiosity, the confusion. I don't want this. This is trouble.

Ignatius places a finger on his chin thoughtfully. "You have the soul of a leader," he finally declares. "I shall send a man to round up your people and spirit them to safety." His honey-coated cultured voice resounds in my ears.

He straightens and gives me a swift nod of respect. Now *that's* the way to my heart: praise my professionalism.

An entering Imperial general saves me from a literal swoon. "Sire," he intones. Ignatius strides over for a conference. President Roya hesitates but then asserts herself into the circle. Luckily they pitch their voices so I can hear.

"These folks have been agitating for the last year or so," Ignatius says. "Economic instability. The merchant and business class aren't happy about their standard of living going down and are asking for more civic freedoms to be able to vote in mitigating measures."

"I mean, they have a point," I mutter. The President turns to give me a withering glare.

Ignatius cranes his head and gives me an appraising look. "What do you think, Dame Layla? Shall we reward their tantrum?"

I resist the temptation to roll my eyes and approach. "Sire, if I may, this was a whole lot of noise for show. If you ignore them, it might be the opposite of what they want. I expect you've been cracking down when they try things like this?"

At this, he smiles thinly.

"Well, that might actually galvanize them," I continue and then hesitate. How to word this? "The Empire has strength in its spine. Between your fearsome reputation, and your secret police, letting them go may actually cause more unease."

"If you let them free, sire," the general warns, "they will just be emboldened to increase pressure. This wasn't a mere *protest*. Weapons, in the Senate! Storming and shouting during a foreign visit. This was a *threat*."

"Don't your own Lords have weapons in the Senate?" I can't resist.

Ignatius speaks into a comm and turns back to me. "All well, my lady. This is the first time they've amassed on this level and done something so disruptive. But they are guilty of no more than embarrassing us in front of our visitors and frightening our people. They have been let go, with a strong rebuke and warning that further activities will be closely surveilled."

Roya gives him a nod of impressed surprise. I close my eyes in relief.

The general glares.

Ignatius's personal secretary chooses this moment to interject. "We have all clear, sire. President Roya, Madame First Lady, I'll take you and Dame Layla to your people."

Ignatius stands back as he guides us out the small room, but reaches for me as I pass. "Layla, lady and commander, jewel of my heart: you contain multitudes," he says, jagged whisper leaving hot breath in my ear.

Then

During the heyday of Emperor Gustav's rule, Ignatius was, in some respects, "eighth" in the line of succession. But the line of succession runs only through the current monarch's immediate family. Eventually, other eligible members of the family passed away, and when Gustav IV died, Carlus, his son, became emperor. The only ones automatically eligible for succession after that were his children. And when, in turn, Carlus II abdicated, he took his children with him. Suddenly the Lords had a decision to make. Ignatius was one of the possible candidates. So was his mother, in fact, although it was highly unlikely they'd pick a woman barring other extraordinary circumstances. But they could have gone in a very different direction. I'm guessing no one was surprised more than Ignatius that they eventually chose him.

Layla Kamil's update to Ransom Ghain, re: Valharan succession, sent from Valhar

The day after the Senate incursion, I read Ransom's latest message to me and respond.

<Ransom>: How was his mood? What do you think his next steps are?

<Layla>: He seemed to take it as a matter of course, once things calmed. And I can see him imposing more stringent laws relating to disruption of the peace, without overall infringing on the right of assembly. Wait, do they have a right to assembly?

After afternoon tea, I receive this:

<Ransom>: Under Ignatius they do. Not sure if they did under Carlus. That's the thing with these absolute dictatorships. They can change laws like they've changed pants. A veneer of legality to underline what is really personal dictum.

<Layla>: Fucked up

Our conversation continues over the hours.

<Ransom>: Quite.

<Layla>: You sure we're secure here? I'm literally bad mouthing an imperial government while sitting in their palace.

Every government experiments with various encryption protocols. Reneb is the best. Altain prefers hidden text in innocuous files, which Ransom asked me to try this morning. It's 0400 hours my time when I check for Ransom's response, and I stifle a yawn as I read.

<Ransom>: Trust the spaidara. You're my way into that place girl. You know the Emperor better than most. So keep using this channel. And we'll do a full debrief when we get back. All approved by Roya of course.

Later in the morning, I make my bed to military specifications, ignoring the amused snort from Mena, who keeps her sheets crumpled on the floor. I stare her down mockingly, making my corners crisp and precise. No early morning walk today. I stayed up all night checking the chat.

"Are you okay after what happened?" I ask.

The guest house is two to a room, and my second floor berth overlooks a frozen lake surrounded by tall firs, Mount Palatina in the far distance. The heat from the air vents lend a soft, warm, breeze that complements the sharp chill from the window, even when closed.

Mena plops down on my perfectly made bed. "Srivana was pretty pissed off. He was worried about the President and the First Lady." She grins, despite the tension. "I guess you're all-important, being taken away."

I bring my hand to my face. "It's stupid—"

"You're an honorary peer. That's wicked," she continues over me. "That captain of the guard was pretty cute. After he took you wherever, he came back to check on me."

"Lord, Mena. Is that all you ever think about? Men?"

"I'm equal opportunity. Don't have to be a man."

I nod. Fair.

Mena changes tack. "The Valharans might be building a new tunnel. Ingrates!" She shakes her head. "You were on Dega, right? How could you even handle being stationed there? I would die."

"Some people couldn't handle it." *It* being the cold, and the fear, and the isolation, and the endless waiting, *waiting* for the Mazarans to come back. I'd barely made it myself. "We were so alone? If they flooded through that tunnel, I'm not sure we could've stopped them. They could have burst through and laid waste to the entire base."

"It's really irresponsible to open us up to that danger in another part of the Whorl." But her face breaks into yet another grin. "Two years isolated on that hellhole. Hope you at least got some deep dicking in there."

I choke.

"Are you all right?" she asks innocently.

"You're incorrigible."

"I mean, come on," Mena protests. "Isn't it a basic human need?"

"Not for me."

Maybe there's a whole part of human existence I'm missing, but sometimes it's a superpower. Maybe it's how I've handled being in love for the last five years with the man who's now just a few huge residences over from me. I don't need the physical to feel close.

And we always pulled away because it didn't feel right: the fraternization across ranks, the collusion with maybe not an enemy, but not a close ally either.

We pulled away because duty is king.

We're relegated to the butt-bin of the palace for breakfast again today—the help, while the important delegates dine above us in splendor. Sri panics about the President's schedule changing; an early evening visit to an educational center will no longer be a photo op, as the Emperor has elected not to attend. I flinch as well; hopefully the President hasn't offended him.

At breakfast, a woman in palace livery appears beside me. She gives me an almost imperceptible skeptical look-over as I bus my tray. I pretend not to notice. Today, no military uniform. No brown pencil skirt either. I'm dressed for comfort.

"Minister Raderfy would like to see you," she says.

Ephraim? Ignatius's secretary? What for? I look my own self over. "Shall I dress?"

"You are suitable."

Ephraim's office is through an internecine set of hallways, deeper and deeper into the palace. And ... shit. He's effectively Ignatius's right-hand man. Perhaps Ransom wasn't as suave as he thought he was? Neither he nor I did anything wrong, but holding an ostensibly secure conversation hidden from palace authorities in a culture obsessed with loyalty maybe wasn't the best idea. Is Ephraim also the Emperor's personal hatchet man? Have I caused a diplomatic incident? How long would it take for Roya to shake her head at me and for Sri to fire me, pretending they didn't approve this?

Ephraim evidently has his own secretary who likewise has *her* own secretary. We walk through multiple rooms until getting to his inner sanctum, well-appointed like the rest of the palace, maps of the Empire on the wall sharing space with ceremonial military artifacts.

"Ah, Dame Layla," he says, smiling as he stands to greet me. I am immediately becalmed.

"Cha, made in the style of Altain," he says graciously, indicating the tea.

I gratefully grab a teacup and take a few biscuits.

"Thank you Minister. You wanted to see me? How may I assist you today?"

"The person who wants to see you," he says, "is the Emperor."

Blood pounds in my ears. "Ah."

"Ah," he agrees. His nose crinkles as he looks at me, a slight crack in the foundation of formality permeating this visit. It gives me an uptick of joy and nostalgia. My shoulders lower.

"Well. I'm certainly not dressed for an audience with His Excellency."

He smiles. "This evening. An after-dinner tour of the gardens."

"I can make that work."

Ephraim gets up and walks over to his door and closes it, before approaching me. "Layla, I don't need to impress on you the need for discretion."

"Ephraim, whenever have I not been discreet? When it comes to him? If you're asking whether or not I'm going to inform my own superiors..." I take a sip of cha and control my face at the overly milky, bland taste.

He holds up a hand. "I understand that need. Select trusted superiors, that's fine. Just remember any word that you had a personal conference with the Emperor would set this palace off in a flurry of speculation we do not need right now."

"And this personal conference is about?"

"I honestly don't know," he says. "Let's both assume he's trying to catch up with an old friend. But given your history together it may be more. He has not seen fit to confide in me."

More.

A wave of dizziness hits me that undercuts the camaraderie of the discussion. I don't know what I'm walking into this evening. And I don't like not being in charge of my destiny.

Ignatius has spent this entire visit in military dress: stiff white high-necked collar, shoulder epaulets, tabs and braided cord. But as I approach tonight, he's in simple wear: a pressed but loose linen buttoned shirt, dark slacks, casual loafers, and my heart leaps high, high into the air and bursts into fireworks at the sight of this man, this man I thought I had lost forever, my kind, solid Nate. He still stands stiff, posture eternally correct, as he bids me welcome, but as the doors close the steel melts off him and he grins easily at me.

"Hey," he says, voice soft, the amber of his eyes so different from my black.

"Hi, you," I respond, almost in a whisper. His hands reach out to touch my face, one finger gently running down my cheek, and then he backs up again, demonstrating the expanse of this quiet room with his hands.

"Behold, my lady," he says, with a touch of formality, "my gardens. Climate-controlled, a greenhouse to protect during our harsh winter." He makes to reach for my hand, thinks better of it, and clasps his behind his back. "Shall we?"

Just that vacillation between giddy remembrance and courtly etiquette makes my heart thump into my ears. That accursed barrier of his, that *voice*, the poise, all of—

All of him. Every frustrating, infuriating scrap of his damned elegant self makes me flail like a schoolgirl.

Fine. I'll play.

"Finally decided ignoring me wasn't worth it?"

He startles, the tart note in my voice apparently putting him on alert. A grimace. "I wished to spare you ... this. Me. Our feelings."

"We can be just friends without you having to pretend you don't know me."

"No, we can't."

"We did it for two years on Dega."

"No, we didn't."

Right. We may not have acted on it, but we were definitely not "just friends."

(When I informed Sri about this invitation, he sighed and said, "Promise me to resign before you actually become Empress, okay?"

I fired back: "Promise *me* you'll never become a betting man.")

Ignatius narrates for me, pointing out every species of flower and ivy. I listen politely and ask the right questions, though botany has never been an interest. Then he grins and whirls me off onto another path. "Watch this."

A beetle lazes on a fat leaf. He plucks it from its perch and flings it at a large plant in the distance, which proceeds to open its maw and swallow the hapless insect whole. "Holy shit!" I exclaim and then clap my hand to my mouth. "Sorry, Excellency."

He gives me a *pssh* of disbelief. "Don't be sorry. I like it when you're you. Isn't it great?"

"It's barbaric, Nate, c'mon."

His grin grows larger, giving me a glimpse of his silly interior. "You mean *awesome*."

We both do our peculiar version of cracking up, wherein we are intensely amused by something but try, try with all our might, to control the hysterics. A side effect of military leadership, that. I love that it's a trait we share. I love that he's still *Ignatius*, underneath the pomp.

"It really is terrible, condemning that poor ladybug as sport," I reiterate. "Damn violent Valharan, emperor of them all, you are."

"Beetle, not ladybug."

"This is not a distinction that lends itself to protesting no 'ladies' were harmed," I counter.

Our faces are flushed, sweating in the heat of the conservatory. We look at each other a shade too long.

Ignatius straightens up yet again, this time even tugging self-consciously on his shirt.

A silence looms between us, the go-between crackling energy sparking.

"I wish to have you," he announces, after a while.

And I stare, and I blink, and stare some more, and I smooth the velvet on my jacket, leaving little uneven lines.

"Wait, what?" I manage, finally.

"I can have it arranged, discreetly."

My blinking has become more rapid now, an impressive feat, what with my eyes wide and my brows climbing higher and higher.

"Did you just proposition me? For sex?"

"I perceive this is an undesirable request?"

My mind flashes to images of the two of us tearing off our clothes and then a flying handmaiden flitting around fanning my face.

"It's a no-go, for oh-so-many reasons." (The emotional cost, my *career* ... Oh great Goddess, I'd have to report back to Sri who would tell Ransom and then send me to Hari and his bionic eyes and then I'd never work in the government again. And for what? *Sex?*)

"What the actual hell, Your Excellency?" I continue.

"Ah." Ignatius finally appears to process his uncouth request. "I am, truly, sorry. I don't know what I was thinking." He sneaks a glance at me and then turns his head almost as quickly. "I can't stop thinking about you," he finally admits, in a whisper.

I twist the folds of my dress, cursing the embarrassed heat on my cheeks.

"Ignatius," I begin cautiously, "I know you're used to being the all-important Emperor and all, but that's just not how you pursue a woman." I scrunch my face at him. "C'mon, Nate. You used to woo women left and right. Don't tell me you don't know how to do that less awkwardly."

"I had a different plan in mind," he admits.

"Which was?"

He's silent for a time.

"I want to have you forever." He stops short, and his stance is open, yet lost at the same time. "That's what I want. You. But I don't know—" he falters. "I don't know what you want."

My ears flood with static, and it's almost as if Ignatius's words have become garbled underwater gurglings. Important. What he has just said is important. Defining. Real.

What *do* I want?

The question throws me off. I continue on our walk, hands clenching by my side as if I'm holding Ignatius's hand, feeling the weight of him looking at me.

What do you want, Layla?

I never get to pick. I have a chance to change the course of my entire life. I have a chance to take the love that's supposed to be mine. Is that why I came?

Oh. Yes. It is.

Do I dare?

"Marry me," he says, as if echoing my thoughts. The words seem to slide out of him, a tremor in his voice I have so rarely heard.

Even though I was thinking the same thing, even though I was about to blurt it out myself, for the second time in two days, a burst of disbelieving, hysterical laughter bubbles in my throat. My traitorous thoughts whisper, *damn, maybe Sri should play the slots after all.*

"That's—that's your *second* choice? Like, you're thinking, 'Oh great, now I have to buy the damn bovine? Are you trying to prank me?"

"No," he breathes. He turns to me and *oh* his face. Open. Sincere. Vulnerable. Schoolboy-earnest, despite being weathered and pale. "I mean," he stumbles, hesitates. "Why the hell not? Why do we do this to ourselves? Why don't we get to be happy? Would you want to?" he continues. "Marry me?"

He casts a shy grin, making my heart flip.

"I—I need to sit."

I stumble to a bench and breathe deep. Ignatius kneels in front of me and grabs my hand.

But I stand, removing his hand, and pace. "Ignatius, you're the *Emperor*. And you need to marry, and have heirs, and why me? What about all those women you courted before?"

"They're not you."

"That's kinda the point I'm making." Again, I sit.

He chides my self-deprecation with the smallest purse to his lips. "The first time I asked you to marry me, with Carlus's Law, I could understand why it wasn't feasible. But, Layla, I changed that law."

"I saw."

"It's the first thing I did."

"I *know*, Ignatius." I expect he didn't do it for me; maybe for the memory of what we could have been. But now, I reconsider. Maybe he *did* do it for me. For us. For possibility.

I put my hand on his, and smile, ignoring the sudden urge to hyperventilate into a paper bag.

Ignatius's eyes soften. "Would you reconsider? Now? You would keep dual citizenship. And Layla, please, let me be clear, you change your mind, you could leave me, leave all this, decide to go back to Altain any time, always."

"I have to resign my commission as a Republic officer." The moment I accept, I'm done.

(What do I *want*? The career? The love? I'd have to pick. How absurd, in the year 1125, I have to choose.)

He starts to pace. "I know. You don't want any of this. Pomp and circumstance and being under a microscope, being *royalty* for the Falcon's sake."

False choice. False dichotomy. Not because I *can* have both, but because the rat race is a lie. Live to work. Work to live. All in the service of others. Nothing in service to myself.

"Ignatius," I begin.

"I shouldn't have asked for you tonight. I'd be asking you to uproot your entire life and your entire way of being for *me*."

"*Nate*."

"I'm an idiot. I mix signals. I say one thing, I say another. Obviously you're going to say no. I'm so sorry. Maybe, just maybe, we can start slow if we're interested in each other. Or maybe friends? Then more?"

Enough of this. "Captain-General Lord Kurestin," I say, more sharply than intended.

He looks up. "Yes, my dear?"

I steel myself and say what I'd been intending all along. "Marry me, for the deity's sake."

His face splits into a huge smile.

Oh, *oh*. *This* is love.

All that worry I have, changing the course of my entire life, jumping headlong into something when I've always been so cautious, so careful—none of that matters in the face of his happiness.

I would move mountains for that smile.

And so I lean in and grab his face between my hands. He kisses me, and this is it. This is the culmination of everything we've been feeling for five years. Suddenly it's too overwhelming and I pull away. Rather than protest, Ignatius puts one chaste hand on my shoulder.

I've fallen completely, inexorably in love.

"What are you imagining now?" he asks.

I bite back a laugh. "Heart bubbles. From our kiss. It's stupid."

"Wait right here." He lopes off toward a nearby wall cabinet, hidden among vines and thorns, and returns with a single-use tablet and a stylus.

I watch as he draws, his lips pursed and eyebrows knotted in concentration. With a flourish, he whips it through the air toward me. "Hearts and kisses. Just for you. And, um—" he digs through his pocket— "this."

It's a ring. I raise my eyebrows. Sneaky man.

I begin to put it on my finger but hesitate. I'm not ready for any of this to be public. When I instead slide it onto my necklace, he nods as if he gets it. Because this is weird. This is new.

We sit and talk for hours. We relearn each other, tentative pulses leading to bursts of electricity. As the night ends, I tiptoe into my shared room at the guest house, sending a note to Sri to come speak to me in the morning. I pause in the stillness, Mena's rhythmic notes of sleep rustling the room in time with the fluttering of the gauzy curtains. On the single-use tablet, the image springs to life in front of me. I pick a command and the pixels coalesce into something tangible, a 5 x 8 cm square I can fold and place into my slim black journal.

Then

From the writings of former Dame Layla Kamil, City of Novaria, Valhar

19 Faylan 25

Five years ago, the Mazarans screamed out of the Swan Nebula tunnel and pummeled Dega Station, its only orbiting human outpost.

The Mazarans took the nations of the Free Whorl—the Altain Republic, Lyria, Reneb, and a host of other small planets—completely by surprise. Two of Reneb's colonies had been the first to fall, paving the way for a domino effect. The Mazarans split: one way down the first Whorl spiral, toward the heart of the Altainan Republic, a second, smaller force heading to Lyria, and onward to Felix. Felix, at the mouth of the Lyrian wormhole. Felix, one small wormhole jump to the imperial planet of Valhar. There, was the first stand of the Mazaran war. And the Valharans sat and *observed* (those bastards) while Lyrian and Altainan forces fought the Mazarans and died.

I fought in the Battle of Felix as a Republic lieutenant, close quarters low-orbital combat, railguns ripping holes through canopy, I in my snub fighter juking and dodging and preparing to die. And then, it happened: the blast force as my engine exploded, a sudden twirling tumble down, a final autumnal fall from one beautiful, devoted leaf on the Republic's tree. My eject button was stuck, and I, hypoxic, noticed on the edges of my vision a lone fighter following me down.

The bastard that shot me. Trying to finish the job, then.

With mission parameters changed, in a last-ditch effort of revenge, I aimed my railgun and fired. Then, anger giving me one final adrenaline push, I slammed on that eject button with all my might and went hurtling through the air.

When I was growing up on the small Altainan territory planet Kaborlah, I was terrified of heights. I still am, to this day: a funny phobia for a pilot. I never did do well in paratrooper training.

On Kaborlah was a swimming hole I detested. To me, it was brackish and murky and the idea of *jumping into* that mess was anathema. I didn't learn how to swim until I had no choice in the Academy; my instructor had screamed at me to jump, *jump*, lest I wash out and where would that leave me? I had wanted to leave Kaborlah. I had wanted to be a poet, actually, but in my world, with my prospects, leaving Kaborlah meant joining up. By the grace of my brains, and maybe a bit of that poet's soul, I at least had a chance at the officer corps.

And this time, my snubfighter gave me no choice but to jump, *jump* as the ejection mechanism shot me into the air, and then freefall, and then, the worst over, the cord pulled and parachute deployed. I was clear of the wreckage, thankfully, as my fighter finally gave up the ghost but below me was—

—was, damnit, the enemy starfighter. The *Valharan* fighter. Those bastards. Those slaughter-observing bastards.

As I landed, I expected to be taken prisoner. Alas, no hidden weapons on my person, not like the Valharans, who carried blades and little hold-out pistols in even the most pedestrian situations. Instead, the ogre came up to me and started *yelling* at me, for shooting him.

"You shot me first," I screamed back.

"I was aiming at the Mazaran behind you, who was about to *smoke* you."

"Well, then you're a really crap shot."

Between all his snarking (*Well, excuse me for following you down to make sure you were okay*), and my recriminations (*You lot just sat there and watched*), my disdain (*Who the fuck carries around a paper map?*) and his smug superiority (*So where's your tablet then? Oh yes, it has exploded*), we managed to find the following:

1.) Our tablets and communications equipment were all fried; 2.) In the heat of battle, my command probably had me listed as lost in action; 3.) *His* people would search for him, or at the very least strive to recover his body, but actually getting access to Felix through the Lyrians would be difficult; 4.) My adversary-turned-hero had adequate rations and water packed away in his starfighter and; 5.) There was a communications tower (*yes, the map is helpful*, I agreed grudgingly), 100 kilometers northeast of us.

That distance in a forced march would normally take us a day at the very most, and rather more quickly as determined as we were, but alas, we were in a desert. Between the heavy packs filled with food bars and water (*Always be prepared*, the Valharan smirked), the need for shelter during the hottest and coldest parts of the day, and various injuries we suffered from our ungainly descents into the desert, it took us two and a half.

Valhar is a notoriously self-interested empire, although, thankfully, not aggressively expansionist against other populations. But that game of not-allies, not-enemies, defending our own flanks, met its match when Ignatius and I met ours.

After we had gotten to know each other on our long walk on the hot sands, after we linked up with our own people, Ignatius and I pushed and pulled to get our governments to work together and force the Mazarans back. Over those initial weeks of tense diplomatic effort, there was no question where our duty lay. Our responsibilities were to our nations. Nothing would compare to that duty, even the feelings we were starting to have for each other. And somehow we managed to parlay those feelings into a full alliance. Ignatius and I were heralded as heroes. Later, we headed up a joint base at Dega for two years, after we had driven the Mazarans back but before the official armistice, watching and patrolling the Swan Nebula subspace tunnel: a new era of cooperation for our respective nations.

All because two people fell in love.

I find Sri in the morning after my surprise engagement in the unyielding mess of coffee cups and despair, and stare at him until he acknowledges me. When he looks up, I give him a teeth-baring, full-faced cringe, and he groans in defeat, slamming his head down on the table.

"Goddess damnit, Kamil," he says.

"Sorry?" I wince again.

He shudders with his whole body and massages his forehead. "Holy Mother Lord Herself," he says. "You know I was joking, right? You didn't need to actually go out and *do* it."

He admonishes me to speak with Roya well before an announcement, but the idea of formally announcing makes my head spin again with the reality of what I have just agreed to.

I need to talk to Ignatius. All of this, so sudden. What happens next? What am I supposed to do when I get home? *What have I done?*

I've found eternal happiness, that's what I've done. But it's utterly terrifying.

I end up spending the entire rest of the day with my feet on springs and then with moments of slammed helplessness. What the hell am I thinking? And then the jetpacks fire again and off I go, walking on air. My hands scrolling through my tablets, last minute edits for President Roya, my fingers on my lips, replaying our first kiss, my eyes on my new ring—unobtrusive, quiet, and modest, just like us. My ears newly attuned to the silent tension in the capital, the cilia of my arms straightening at the quiet, watchful calm before explosive social change. I resolve: if I am to become part of this society, I need to know what's going on, what's in *his* head, because the times, they are a-changing.

In the torrid whiplash of a woman trying to do her job while being so very much in love, my attention turns again to my ring. Ruby red on a simple band. He had it with him. He had it ready.

Get your head out of the clouds, Layls.

But at the intersection of *big complicated feelings* and *mindless drudge work* lies this: the heady excitement of going to a state dinner, in the guise of an Imperial *ball*, no less, gorgeous dresses like clouds floating on the chill air, soft lights echoing the twinkle of stars—and being the person in charge of coordinating the security arrangements and making sure things run on time. Regardless, I'm rather pleased with the opportunity to *do*, which keeps me from the pingpong thoughts bouncing about my brain.

Here, at the dinner, I'm cold. *Dega* was cold, of course, but due to the extreme temperatures I was always dressed in a winter wear uniform. Tonight, I'm in a sleeveless outfit. I eye with jealousy the substantial skirts, too ostentatious for my status; my own slinky dress is vented too high for this air, and the shrug covering my shoulders too thin.

Sri checks in on us from time to time, but he's part of the important people, in the inner circle. And he and I both share a smile, knowing what most people in this room don't know.

That secret drumbeat: I'm engaged. I'm engaged to *that* man. The one over there, in his impeccably tailored formal uniform, literally fit for an emperor, shine of medals and ribbons and heavy, *heavy*-laden with power and history.

One word from me either to the President or to Ignatius, and I'd be sitting at that table with them, or, if the watchword is discretion, at least helping Sri out in the more high-level wrangling of our diplomatic delegation. But I resist; I need to be me for the moment. I need to assert my independence from this momentous life alteration. For someone outwardly devoted to duty, I am always in rebellion, and on this night, being subordinate to everyone in the room, waiting hand and foot on the principals: this is me with my eyes blacked with kohl, ready to fight. I feel more powerful with my clipboard and earpiece than I have since taking command on Dega Base.

You will not define me, Ignatius Kurestin. *This* will not define me.

I look 'round for people I will have to know in short order, whenever our engagement becomes formal. Ephraim is there with his soldier wife, whom I've never met. There's that general from the Parliament disaster—Turine, is it? And in the corner closest to us, Lord Berilus, Earl of Dracini, who supported Ignatius's first cousin once removed, Lord Abilio, for the throne.

"This is good," Sri says, coming to check on us again. "Events like this are usually filled with nobles." Indeed, a prominent minority of invitees are proles, mostly merchants and businessmen from what I understand, a nod to Altain's desire to become a robust trade partner with the Empire.

"It'll mollify the business elite, too, with their financial woes."

"The government's still getting a huge cut," he counters.

Sri ambles back to his spot of honor, and I return to my favorite current pastime: watching Ignatius, watching the way he moves, watching how people react to him, how they yield to him. And it's not just because he's the Emperor; I watched it when he was Commander Lord Kurestin, after we were rescued by the Lyrians; I watched it for two years on Dega—he the Captain-General, leader of men and women of virtue; I watched it during my own peerage ceremony, his countrymen surrounding him with quiet deference.

He dances the first dance with President Roya; out of courtesy to her, it's something familiar and easy for anyone in the Whorl. As Ignatius is escortless, out of courtesy to *him*, the dance is between the two rulers: no separate couples dance between Shondi and Victoria Roya. He gives the welcome toast. I critique Roya's facility with the Altainan waltz the same as I scrutinize Ignatius's speechifying.

My eyes yet again scan the assemblage. Ransom sent a chat this morning, asking me to report on the crowd, including possible pressure points for Altain to exploit. Suddenly, it bumped against a different, deeper loyalty, to the man with whom I want to spend my life. Something didn't sit right with me about transmissions in the palace behind his back. Something didn't sit right about pressure points and intrigue.

So I deleted the file holding the encrypted message. Ransom will see I've done so. Ransom won't like it one bit. There may be consequences. But if marriage—and the promise of marriage—changes nothing of our actions, what is the point of it?

Oaths govern my life. Oaths and fidelity are ironically the key to freedom. To *choice*. Because if you stay true to the people to whom you're pledged, then you're able to return to them when you need shelter. This is why I didn't accept Ignatius's first proposal, years ago. I could never give up my Altainan citizenship.

But oaths and fidelity also apply to marriage. And so my carefully constructed morality begins to fall apart. Will I be able to keep two diametrically opposed vows?

As if summoned, Ignatius materializes in front of me. "Well met, my lady." He bows. Oh, this canard again. Some attendees look on in curiosity.

"Well met, my lord." I curtsey.

"Dance with me."

I look at him askance. "We're old friends," he insists. "Everyone knows that. You should have at least been in dress uniform today."

"The uniform would've called too much attention. I'm working tonight."

Ignatius shakes his head and catches Sri's eye. "Mr. Reva," he calls softly. "Take over for Dame Layla for a bit, will you?" He takes the clipboard from my hand and shoves it in between Sri's, not thinking twice about issuing orders to a foreign representative. Sri smirks at me.

Ignatius gives an almost-imperceptible nod to Ephraim, who turns toward the orchestra, which then begins the low tones of the traditional calana.

Oh, you showoff. *Honestly.*

The calana: a romantic dance, long leg sweeps, controlled shoulders, hands swiping in invisible caress. We move in precision, and I'm an ugly duckling in a princess story, *I'm literally a fairy tale*, what in my life has led me here, of all places?

"Come see me tonight," he whispers.

"The infamous plan of discretion?" I ask, with a suppressed grin.

The air stills, as if in silent import, and then like a flash, it crackles.

His smile blooms and then he fights it down; *there*, the beginnings of a blush, a subtle clearing of the throat, his hand momentarily sliding through his hair. It is beyond endearing. My heart leaps again. My Nate. My Nate is in there, slotted between the uniform and his metaphorical crown.

He rewards me—yes, it is a *reward*, for him to allow such an unguarded expression on his face—with a lopsided grin.

"If you would like," he says, with studied casualness. "If not, I at least would like to show you my personal apartments. After all, it'll be your home as well."

Simulated snow falls in a soft shower. The delicate flakes glint in the quiet light.

Right now, I wish my skirt swirled.

We aren't perfect. We stumble and giggle in the middle of our pas de deux. His beautiful eyes soften as he looks at me, such a change from his normal public stern look that I blanch.

"We're being way too obvious," I warn.

"Who cares," he says, mouth near my ear.

The music changes. Ignatius signals to Sri. "Hold," he says to me, "let me introduce you to a few people. You should have been an honored guest, completely removed from your relationship to me. Your nation will never cease to surprise me in how they discount the preeminence of a soldier. At the very least, they should realize when in Valhar—"

"Hey, they put me in uniform the first day. That was their nod."

"Rubbish."

So I acquiesce. I make the perfect Valharan curtsies, bow when necessary, sometimes snap a salute, depending on the station of the person to whom Ignatius has introduced me, which he manages to convey in the fewest words possible.

I'm a curiosity in this Valharan space, yet honored. When I attend similar functions on Altain Prime, I'm dismissed, overlooked, or thought of as less-than, all by virtue of my Kaborlahi dark-and-stout features. There, it is when I am introduced by name that eyes snap forward and the demeanor becomes respectful and solicitous. Here, I'm another Altainan, not an outsider play-acting as a Primie, though it's obvious my connection to the Emperor is of value.

I had received some etiquette training when Gustav elevated me to an honorary peerage but, truly, a lot of this, especially knowing the calana, was from my friendship with Ignatius on that isolated base. "How—damnit Ignatius, how long have you been preparing me for this?" I ask at one point. His responding smile is enigmatic.

After a terse exchange with a Mr. Malachi Finley, who trades in ores and metals, we enjoy a lovely discussion with Lord Benedik, Viscount Gruesse, Ignatius's second cousin.

He would have been next in line to the throne had Dracini succeeded in getting Benedik's father chosen. Then I get a glimpse of Roya's bemused smile.

"Your Excellency," I say out the corner of my mouth, "we need to wrap it up, lest it looks as though I'm upstaging the President." He lets out a long breath, but he understands.

When I return to my post, Mena eyes me and lets out a long, low laugh. "Sure, boss, I see how it is."

I follow Ignatius's instructions and find an assistant, who leads me to his apartments. A simple sweater and trousers for me. Maybe not the best look for meeting him, but it won't do to be wandering later that night in my slinky formalwear.

A library, a musty sitting room, a fireplace, rug. I'm in sensory overload, not just from *stuff*, but from this whole situation. Later, I will be able to analyze the setup and layout, the number of servants, the way they move and talk and how Ignatius deems to interact with them. Maybe I'll be able to ruminate on the subtle shedding of layers he makes at every footfall toward his sanctuary: from stiff and stern to watchful and quiet and beyond; from charming and suave to the slight stutter in his step signaling nervousness; icy control to sincere warmth.

I sit on the couch, stiff posture, contemplating the warm fire.

"Nervous?" he asks, amusement in his voice.

"This is weird," I finally admit.

"Hey." He reaches out and lightly strokes my hair. "It's *me,* Layls." A hint of hurt mars the undertones.

"It's just..." I bite my lip. "We've known each other for so long."

He wrinkles his brow. "Right. So why is this so nerve-inducing?"

"It makes it weirder."

"But, we love each other?" His sideways grin makes it clear his feelings aren't hurt. Thank the Goddess.

"Ahem. Loving each other and making out are two totally different things."

"Totally different," he repeats. He chuckles and pulls me to him. I lean into his strong chest and tickly beard. He tips up my chin.

My eyes shift away from his. "Is it going to be a problem? My reluctance? Or, to be clearer—disinterest?" My heart hammers and my palms sweat. Damnit. I am who I am, but sometimes *who I am* causes so many problems.

"Of course not," he says, quick to reassure me. Does he mean that?

I smile through the awkwardness. "Thank you. And it's not fear or anything like that. Balance, that's all. It's like ... running."

"Running." He raises his eyebrows. "You hate running."

"I don't *hate* running," I counter. "I run. I don't usually do it for *fun*, not like some people. I do it, though. And when I'm done, on those days at least, I revel in the sweat and the runners high, and think, 'Well, I did it. That was nice, I guess.' But then the next time when it's between running and chocolate cake, the pull of the cake is just as strong, and I'll be short with someone cajoling me to lace up my shoes. And avid runners are always so offended and worried about my milquetoast reaction to running. *Run more, run often, run better! You haven't tried this race, this shoe, this technique. You're not using your goddess-given calves to their full talents. Such a shame.* And here I am saying, 'Guys, it's not like I never run. I do. It's okay. But it's not my *favorite*.'"

I don't mention the rest of it. How hard it is to even feel much of anything other than bored and uncomfortable. The times I'm so unenamored with the idea that I go into a minor panic attack. The pressure to *do* and *be* and *want* and the feeling of wanting to throw up and hide forever that accompanies it. The revelation I'm perfectly happy to imagine sex in my mind and that's all the satisfaction I'll ever need. That stuff stays secret. Revealing those types of things never ends well.

He puts his arms around me, kisses my ear. "You know yourself. I like that," he whispers. "I've always loved that about you. Your confidence."

Confidence? I suppress a disbelieving snort and snuggle in closer to him. The warm fire and the spreading pleasantness from the wine lead me into sleep.

Then

I get home to Altain and all hell breaks loose.

I'm in the middle of announcing my eventual departure from the administration without explaining why ("*Ms. Kamil,*" the note says, "*is off to pursue new opportunities*") and getting the turnover documents ready for my deputy, who is looking at me in mute horror at the thought of having to take all *this* over. Ephraim has already hooked me up with the palace's social secretary—a prim woman named Beatrix who is giving me *all* the details on what each next step is going to entail, proper etiquette, and of what, if anything, I need to divest myself. I'm writing after action reports of our state visit as well as undergoing regular debriefings with Ransom about what I saw over there, and oh yeah, there was the deep tissue massage of a debrief I had with Hari and his bionic eyes regarding my freaking *engagement* to the freaking *Emperor of Valhar*.

Then Sri shows up at my door and says, "Roya's office, *now,*" and I'm caught between "What blew up now?" and "Oh, no, did *I* do something?" So I take my short legs and move them fast to keep up with his long strides, and we engage in our favorite pastime: walk and talk.

"Lyria," Sri says, handing me a few flimsies, "has confirmed it. Valhar is actually beginning construction on a subspace tunnel."

My step falters and I almost fall into a corner as we turn. "By the Goddess."

"They're screaming," Sri confirms. "And they want a statement from us."

"Right." I throw a mock salute. "I'm your gal. But Sri..."

"Is working on this gonna be a problem?"

"No! But you want me to analyze Lyrian intelligence reports? You sure? I mean,

Ransom..."

We turn into Roya's office. He claps his hand on my shoulder. "Ransom said you swore you would never give up our secrets."

"Of course." I mentally add an asterisk. I have no particular loyalty to *Lyria*. Their secrets aren't safe with me.

"Layla," the President says as I enter, "I need your words. Lyrians say the Valharans broke the treaty clause, but they're not making the information public. Our government isn't convinced. I need to send a public message to complement some private shuttle diplomacy, but it needs to be a public message that somehow avoids letting the *public* actually know what's going on."

"Right, ma'am. Totally makes sense."

"Don't be cheeky, Kamil." A smile spoils her deadpan delivery. "The Whorl as a whole is war-weary. I'd like to avoid any provocation to violence, nor do I want to alert our citizenry to the prospect of another subspace tunnel being open to the galaxy. And not to be too indelicate, but as you've pointed out, legislative elections are up soon. I'd sooner not make any grand declarations about red lines we won't allow Valhar to cross, but I also can't afford to look *too* dovish."

"Are the Valharans aware the Lyrians know?"

"The Valharans likely found out the night of the state dinner," Roya answers.

Oh. A mini-me in my brain screams in embarrassment. I *could* confirm Ignatius got some sort of important call in the middle of the night after the state dinner, and he was serious and grave and had to leave.

But I'll just keep that to myself.

Figures. I *would* reconnect with my erstwhile ex right before a major interplanetary incident, and now I'm in a launch tube already on my way to a battle I can't hope to win. If this had come up before we left for the state visit, what would have happened? It would no longer have been ceremonial, for sure. Adversarial. Barbs no longer veiled, but brandished.

I probably wouldn't have been allowed to come. And even if I had, would I have chosen Altain? Or *him*?

A few weeks later, I receive orders for 0700 the next morning. Report to Ransom, in uniform. Before I retire that night, I send notes to old colleagues to see if they, too, have been activated, and I wake at 0500 to a flurry of confirmations.

A feisty eel undulates in my belly as I think it through. So far, this is standard procedure. When diplomatic tensions escalate to a certain level, we increase military patrols within the Republic; a precaution, nothing more, and in effect we treat it as equal parts shakedown cruise and reunion, the clearing of throats before a pantomime we hope never to perform.

But my position is excepted. I'm not supposed to be called in. Forget whether I *want* to be or not. And further, I'm not assigned to a capital ship, and that sits wrong.

I might be asked to be a consultant, advisor, agent. But somehow, I don't think that's quite the case.

Any hope of a cushy staffer job was dashed this morning, all spit and shine, as I entered the complex and was told to report to Ransom. I tap on his door in the rustbucket backyard rambler of a building tucked in behind the main government complex. One of Ransom's many doors, within many buildings, allowing him to wear his many hats. I'm not sure which headgear he will sport today.

"Ah yes, Commander Kamil," Ransom calls out to me, this time without a trace of his normal irony. "Sit with me a spell."

I see. The spaidara, indeed.

His look is cool and professional, but not cordial. More assessing and shrewd, if anything.

"I'd like to pick your brain," he says.

A knock on the door, a box handed over. Ransom peeks in it and sits in front of me. He pulls out a squat bottle and syringe.

"Aw, *hell*," I breathe.

Ransom doesn't even bother to say sorry as he sets up my chair, pulling down hidden armrests and unfurling restraining straps. My heartbeat zooms. He prepares the truth serum wearing a blank expression.

"There's not even going to be some fucking oversight here?" I ask, on attack. He gives me a sideways glance and keeps going.

"Uniformed personnel," he finally mutters. "Regs less stringent."

"Great, *that's* why I got recalled into active duty?"

No more answers. Ransom remains expressionless, save a slight curling of his lips.

He places my arms into the apparatus. I breathe in and out, the sound noticeably loud to my ears, my exhales raspy and uncontrolled. And I don't like needles, don't like them at all, even beyond this complete violation of my bodily autonomy thank you very much and being strapped down is even more nightmare fuel. I'm helpless and vulnerable in this room with a person I'm supposed to trust.

The needle is now in, pushing down inside me, the buspirathol serum injected. I'm imagining it's fire, and I'm visualizing it ripping through me, burning molton heat throughout my circulatory system.

"Fuck you, Ransom," I gasp loudly. "*Fuck you fuck youfuckyou...*"

I'm heavy, groggy, laden.

"Please state your name and rank," Ransom begins dispassionately, and the distant part of me remembers to think of cool water, but the immediate part of me answers, unbidden.

Ransom bodily rips information out of me. The eel in my gut uncoils and spools again in endless rhythm, and I cry.

THEN

26 Amadi 1125

My dearest Layla:

You're but a nebula away, but it might as well be a galaxy.

I want to apologize again, about the ladybug and the carnivorous plant. I hope it didn't scare you. I don't like being so cavalier with a life. Sometimes I feel like I'm continuously learning, from you.

Mother has been agitating to meet you, at least once before the formal announcement. She's rather cross with me since I've never once shown you to her, after all these years—yes, of course I've spoken of you, for long now, dreamt aloud of our possible union. You'd like her, that saucy bird. Can't imagine she wasn't chosen for Empress over me, but you know these old lords. Why prevail upon an old woman to rule when one can make her the dowager instead, placing the crown on her young, hot-headed son?

Yours always,
Me

Nate:
Re: ladybugs
I'm used to being the spoilsport in any given social situation. Please don't consider this a case for self-flagellation.
-Just Miss Kamil, for now, Cygna City, Altain

This is not the first time I'd experienced the serum. In the military we were trained on it, in a controlled environment. Trained not in order to *resist*—because one can't resist the power of the buspirathol—but instead trained to recover. You see, the serum invades you. Colonizes your amygdala. Burrows into your darkest fears and says to them *welcome to your new playground.*

It stays with you. When the injection is consensual, like in training, it can lead to a nightmare or two, and knock you on your ass for an impromptu nap.

But when it goes like it did in Ransom's office, the effect can reverberate into every interaction. Every harsh look. Every possible vector of danger and insecurity.

I, for one, slept all day, after Ransom's guys carried me out on a stretcher and dumped me in my apartment.

I peel into Ransom's office two mornings later, recovered—if one can call it that—from my ordeal: one full day of sleep, another day of shakes and hallucinations, and a lifetime of freakouts looming before me.

Forget betrayed. I've been *forsaken*, removed from the rolls of someone of worth, someone deserving consideration and grace, and it *hurts*, burns worse than the serum coursing through my veins.

"What in the fucking seven hells was *that* for?" I ask Ransom. I make my face stern, as if I'm a general dressing down troops, but it's no good. My voice shakes, my body trembling on a quiver. Ransom. *Ransom.* We bonded by being outsiders in the Altain Prime cultural landscape: me, a Kaborlahi as dark as its famed mud, he a squat man from a nomadic peoples. We were supposed to be united against this world.

Ransom sighs, puts down his tablet, and tips his chair back, arms behind his head. "It's nothing personal, Layls."

"Nothing *personal?*"

"It's a standard precaution."

"I've been cooperative—hell, I've been *more* than cooperative. I've staked my entire system of honor on being open and transparent to all levels of the entire damn government and this, *this* is the thanks I get? Because I have the *audacity* to have feelings for someone inconvenient?"

"Layla, I'm truly sorry."

"Didn't say that two days ago," I mutter.

"Wasn't the time, two days ago," he says. "Duty, you know? Objectivity? I'm sorry to put you through that, but now you're cleared—"

"—oh fuck off, Ransom. That excuse is getting old. How many times do I have to be *cleared* this millennium? Are you actually going to *honor* my rank and let me contribute something using my Goddess-given talent and skills instead of being relegated to a honey-trap? Or shall I never return from that week's leave you promised me? Since, you know, I can't go finish up my turnover with my deputy speechwriter considering you got my civilian pass *revoked*."

"Done?" he asks mildly.

I cross my arms.

He shoots out of his chair and stalks forward, and I, to my utter chagrin, back away. "You want to know why you're always pulled for secondary screenings? Why I jabbed you? It's not because of your boyfriend."

My arms fold again, this time to hide my thudding heart, as if it could give me away by beating out of my chest. I know. I just didn't know *he* knew. I've been less-than-forthcoming about the beginning of the reign of Carlus II of Valhar. Oaths may govern my life, but I hid something major from my government, years ago. Because I promised. Because I *vowed*.

Thump. Thump. Thud.

"You've been lying. We both know it. And I'm going to let it go now. But—" and Ransom advances further. This time I hold my ground— "if you take overt action against the Altainan Republic, *ever*, powerful empress or not, I'll see to it we strip you of citizenship."

He didn't ask. He could have asked in interrogation. The lie of Carlus's reign and Gustav's end: it seems like such a little thing now. Little, yet scandalous by virtue of my complicity.

I am forever in your debt, Commander, Carlus had said, and it wasn't mere words. It was promissory.

And as for Ransom stripping me of citizenship, he can do that. He's got hidden power. Systemic, burrowed-in-deep power. And for how much the planets of the Whorl are trying to lift their veils of secrecy, Altain doesn't just let anyone in its borders. And without citizenship, I am no one.

"Come with me," he says. The change in tone gives me whiplash.

I glare.

"C'mon," he says. "Let me buy you a beer. Well, not really *buy*. There's a secure lounge just a few floors down, but since our taxes are paying for it and you're about to become a non-tax-paying citizen, in a way, I'm buying."

I intensify my glare, hoping to curdle his brilliant brain, but when he leaves, I follow.

"It's not long anyway," Ransom says, as he plops a foaming cup into my hands, throwing some samosas on a plate for good measure. "You'll have your week's pass, spend another week here with us while the Imperial minions pack you up, and then you're off to Valhar in advance of the official announcement. We suspend your orders then and you're a private citizen. You can decide then whether or not you're coming back to live here, though I expect you'd rather avoid the press scrutiny."

"Probably the first time I appreciate a nation without a vibrant press. No tabloids."

"Speaking of information."

"Ransom," I say, "I'm not going to be your fucking informant."

"I didn't ask you to be. You know we have—"

I hold up my hand. "I don't know the details. Don't tell me."

"You could be helpful. I can tell you how to reach me." He pulls a note out of his pocket, much like I pulled my handkerchief a lifetime ago. "Memorize this, then destroy."

I hold it between my fingers, refusing to look. He pulls it back out of my hand and flashes it at my face. "Just. Look." Then he rips it up.

I make no comment.

"Valhar." Ransom shakes his head. "Still want to go through with this?"

"Uh, yeah. I mean, when my friends treat me like this…" I wave my hand, encompassing him in the gesture.

"I'm sorry. I am still your friend."

"Really?" I ask. "Or am I a means to an end? Don't answer," I amend, shaking my head. "Duty. I know. Doesn't mean I like it."

"Valhar," Ransom repeats, a note of incredulity in his voice.

"I've been molding myself for other people my entire life," I finally answer, looking down at my cup. "I'm ready to be with someone who sees *me*." My voice breaks at this last, a final shattering of the catechisms of my life.

"What are you going to *do* there, Layla? Be pampered and eat mangoes all day?" He hesitates. "Do they even *have* mangoes?"

I pause, contemplating. "I'll make my own way. I'll figure it out."

"Ok..."

"I'll figure it out."

"Figure it out," he repeats, skeptical. "*You*. No plan, no line of attack."

I finally summon a grin. "Liberating ain't it."

Nate,

The love of my life once told me he'd need to be radio-silent for awhile; things were afoot. Ten days later, he became the Emperor of Valhar...and here we are...gone to outright monitoring of our communications...not sure what's going on with our foreign relations. I have to admit, Ignatius, I feel queasy, sick at the thought our nations are at odds right now, and I know you can't explain the whole picture to me, not when anything we write each other is going straight into the coffers of...analysts and into Ransom's greedy little arms...a snake.

Ransom, whom I know is reading and redacting this, will likely find me tomorrow and remind me snakes don't have arms. Regardless, I've never felt more in the dark. You can't tell me, no one in the Roya administration can tell me—I'm just watching the vidfeed like every other Altainan citizen seeing this diplomatic tension and it sucks, Ignatius.

And what makes it worse is that I don't care. I'm the silly bint in this tale, counting down the days until I can get on a shuttle and speed through three wormholes to get to your arms. I know you care. I know you have the weight of an Empire on your shoulders but when I think that, all I can imagine are those shoulders, wanting to massage them for you and carry some of your load. Is this what devotion feels like? It's dizzy-making. I've never felt this single-minded drumbeat toward a person before; I may be brash sometimes or quick with my words but overall, I'm rational, I'm pragmatic, I think before I leap but then...then there's you.

Re: your mother's hot-headed son—I can't imagine anyone describing you as 'hot-headed.' To me, you're the icy north breeze shaming us all with your dignity and forthrightness.

Yours,

Commander Kamil, from her cleared-out desk

Layls, Layls, Layls:

Of course I'm hot-headed. You've heard stories of my temper. What, you think I intimidate the piss out of people because I stare at them coolly? That stare is backed up by some pretty epic tales of brawls with peers and the sorrows of insubordinate corporals facing my inexorable wrath.

That icy north breeze is the overreaction to the molten lava in my veins. Control, control, that's all my father says to me. You can't be a leader of men, he says, unless you tamp down that fire. But, he says sometimes it's good for your people to know the fire exists, and to know that sometimes it will emerge. The secret, of course, is to have the wisdom to know when that time is. I hope, as I age, I can make him proud.

—Your Nate

It's a funny thing, patriotism. My allegiances are now based on previous oaths, but once, long ago, I was on fire for my nation. I thought we were the best in all things. The most virtuous. And the reason was probably that innate desire to fit in, to no longer be the backwoods hick from Kaborlah, who had no reason to care for Whorl politics. As with all things, the zealousness of a convert—of an assimilator—often far outmatched that of natives.

That vision of Altain died long ago. And I'm not sure I've ever given myself time to grieve.

Maybe now. Maybe as I prepare to not necessarily *cut* my ties, but rather, extend them. Maybe time for reflection, now.

Home leave, that's what I'm approved for, in the end, and it'll double as the moment I look my mother in the eye and tell her what I'm about to do.

The trip to Kaborlah is always an exercise in small humiliations. The spaceport on Altain Prime is a shiny marvel of modernity: ceiling to floor vistas; limited AIs in every alcove providing services, information, and even advice on travel itineraries; massages and spa services to recover from days- and weeks-long flights. But every time I head to Kaborlah, I need to do a hop, skip, and jump down a-ways to the second terminal, the one that features broken lighting, not to mention every other broken piece of technology. The personnel are harried and short, problems harder to resolve, creature comforts few and far between, and most destinations take two or three transfer points. It's all understandable, of course; not as many people travel between Altain and the Whorl Rim, so why expend the cost? But even with the understandable money-saving measures, I always feel exposed, sized up, and resented when I enter Terminal Two. Altain Prime and Kaborlah share a common ethnicity, but over the centuries, much has diverged. Prime acts like we're their ugly stepcousins.

Whenever I tell Amma this, she says I'm projecting my own embarrassment of my homeland onto others, now that I consider myself too good for it, and that just about sums up the relationship between my mother and me.

In the main terminal, my uniform causes others to give me a wide berth, as if people can tell I'm lower class by the fact I'm a servicemember, because the elite find this sort of service beneath them. In Terminal Two, I'm mercifully one of the crowd of military heading for short hops home, especially now that a bunch of reservists have been activated and need to settle their affairs.

Regardless, the uniform is rare in the spaceport on Kaborlah, and it comes in handy after the two day trip, allowing me to skip ahead in the ingress line and step out into the melee. The arrivals area is always a cacophony of sound. Family members press up against glass dividers trying to wave down their kin. People fight over baggage and taxiflyers, which sputter and chug and honk to get the attention of passersby.

I exit and see nothing but beautiful landscape. The territorial government decided to clean up areas of the city most seen by inner-Whorlers, but the actual lack of beggars seems wrong somehow. I blink a few times, as if checking to see if I somehow missed the sea of humanity thronging at the port gates, caterwauling and trying to grab the notice of emigrés coming home. Where do the undesirables go, when they are pushed away and hidden?

And there but for the lack of four stable walls around my family home, go I. Few people on Kaborlah live in luxury, but my family is near the bottom of society's rungs.

The compound where I grew up sits not too far from the port, so I walk, inhaling the petrichor permeating every pore of flora. My boots sink into the tell-tale burnt umber dirt and I enjoy the small rebellion of uncleanliness. In my home language, *lah*, of Kaborlah, means land, but not just land. It's the soil of the land, it's the *soul* of the land, the people, the kinships, the food that comes from it and the journey of those who leave.

Honestly, sometimes I despise the lah. I look like lah, I'm dark like the lah, I'm surrounded by lah and I don't know what it wants from me.

My community compound, rundown and spare, is surrounded by tent cities, with people bathing in the muddy water, hanging threadbare strips of cloth that men and women alike drape around them as clothing, men squatting down shirtless and in skirt-like lunghis clipping their nails, banners and silk flowers waving in the wind, the garish colors masking abject poverty.

I arrive in our small room-cum-home. My mother is holding one of my nieces against her hip, bouncing and singing softly in that absentminded way mothers have, and I'm struck by thought of her holding her own babies and now her grandbabies and the endless chain of time that extends down from mother to mother and back again to the dawn of humankind, all bouncing and singing and rocking and burping, the utter muscle memory that comes from long hours in the night, the remembrances that must accompany her every time she smells their soft heads. It must happen only to parents; Goddess knows, I spent countless hours myself taking care of children, my mother working long hours to allow us to survive and then, in her free time, zoning out on smoke and pills and lashing out in anger. I, the second-eldest, was tasked to raise my siblings. I can rock a baby with the best of them, but I don't get that feeling of *beyond* and onward through time that she and my sisters have spoken of.

I quell the resentment of seeing Amma caring for my nieces and nephews more than she cared for her own children, leaving it to me instead; after all, she had no choice. For life here on Kaborlah, choice is an illusion, a preset menu of options that say "do *this* or this will happen," "don't do *that* or you'll deserve what befalls you." Personal responsibility and civic duty are presented as virtues that lead to endless wealth and fulfillment and pride when really, what we do on this planet is survive. *I* joined the Republic forces to survive, the minute I saved up enough funds for a trip off-planet, to escape being consigned to tilling a land that could no longer provide for all of us. Patriotism and duty came later. My only duty, in the beginning, was just to live on and on and on.

Amma is looking at me with a cocked brow, still shushing in time as my fat niece snores. "The great hero comes home, I see," she says, and I ready myself for combat.

"Ma," I say, "I'm getting married."

My brother is home now, and he scoffs as he sloshes his cup of beer. "Gonna be some fancy whore, then," he says. " 'spect you'll get all that respect and honor you think you've been due for years now."

I used to change this kid's diapers. "Big man, huh?" I say. "I don't need others to give me honor." That's my gift to myself. It's what I hold onto in the storm.

If we understand anything here on Kaborlah, we understand storms.

"I see nothing wrong with it," Amma chides my brother. She settles into the one stuffed chair in the place, leaning back in heavenly respite as the smoke wafts from her fingers. "You take what you can, and in this case, your Apa has taken a hefty chunk. But don't forget your family, right, shona?" She directs this last to me.

"I'll still send funds home," I assure her. "Obviously bigger than before. But I can't—" I hesitate and wave my hands around. "I can't have the whole compound ask me for—Ma, you know. Money. Resources."

She nods once, sharply. "We tell them," she says, punctuating the air with her rolled leaves, "there are laws. Private citizen of another country can only give so much to foreigners, yeah?"

"That ... works," I say, reluctantly. "Amma, but the whole family can come to the wedding, of course. Cousins, you know? They can come."

Amma clucks, a sharp *tcch* sound against her teeth. "We have no need for that," she says, dismissive. "Those people, they aren't our people. They are bilahi, not of our land. We don't need to go visit some big planet with big people and have them sniff at us and look down."

"Wait, you're not coming?"

She grunts, looks off. "We'll see."

30/13/25

Layla:
I would understand if the appointed day arrives and you're not here on

Valhar. If I could run away from all this too, I would.

———∼∼∼———

A fortnight later, I take a commercial ship to Valhar, reveling in the last time I'll have anonymity. My last debriefs are discharged, my life packed up (such as it is, my tiny apartment holding only necessities and the odd bit of memorabilia, a consequence of growing up with no possessions and then entering the military—with no possessions.)

I managed to visit most of my other siblings, but not my eldest sister, Zaya. We don't see her anymore. Zaya ran off and married a soldier. And *she* was the first of us to leave, not me, but now she lives on another backwater far away and her husband doesn't let her talk to us, or leave, or do anything to get help and escape the shitstorm of a marriage she found herself in. And Zaya has decided to accept it. Fidelity. Oaths. Again the paradox rears its head.

I have almost no examples of marriage from Kaborlah, which the elite like to blame on our supposed brokenness, or a fault in our morals, but is really a consequence of the ruinous policies that keep my people under Altain's heel. They destroy our families via predatory consumerism and overwork and the carceral state. My main model of matrimony is Zaya's hell of a marriage.

And she never left breadcrumbs to find her way home.

My mother was happy with the prospect of my marriage in general, raised with the sense that young people should pair up and make babies, although in Amma's case the "pairing up" wasn't very permanent with any of her men. But that's being a teenager on Kaborlah in a nutshell: drink and drugs and sex and wait to die. Create new life while you're at it.

My brothers and sisters did just that. I, on the other hand, was an oddball. Sure, I liked to *look*. But I had no desire to accommodate the boys that sniffed about. Even the times I was pushed up against a wall and forced to *try*, I'd push them off instead of acquiesce out of shame. I had a few girls make subtle passes at me, sure I was hiding my orientation. But no. It's not like I didn't like the attention...well, initially, that is. But I would almost throw up at the idea of being *wanted*.

I don't know if I even believe in romance, in the traditional sense. Funny thing to say for someone who is giving up her whole life for a man. But there's a weird sense of pragmatism in it. Whether that comes from mother's influence or if it's yet another orientation of my own, I can't be sure

I thought I was broken, until I finally had the words to describe it.

In my youth, especially in that hellscape of a community, I despaired at never finding someone who maybe could understand. I've found the closest thing in Ignatius—not that he *really* does, and that fear settles in the pit of my belly as I imagine the reaction previous boyfriends have given me when they finally realize the extent of my non-enthusiasm.

But with Ignatius, I believe we can work it out.

Amma was *more* than pleased, I suspect, because she began calculating how much my marriage was worth to her. Not just monetary gain. And that's just the way things go with me. I'm useful to people. But I don't want to be *used*. For information, or for money, or for my body, or for prestige. I want to be *loved*. Loved beyond all reason. Beyond borders.

I move my ring off my chain to my finger, because I'm off Altain. I think on what Ransom asked me as we shared that beer, about if I was sure, about *why*, why throw away the familiar for such a drastic action. But those few days at home, visiting my mother, was a proving ground, solidifying my resolve. My entire life, I've followed duty and order. But I'm tired of the rules, I'm tired of being the daughter who picks up the pieces of my broken family over and over and over again. I wanted to escape Kaborlah, but now it's my time to escape my entire life and way of being.

I'm probably making a terrible mistake. Will I find myself a place there, or will I be a spectacular failure?

The long-ago voices of my fellow cadets whisper to me furiously, cajoling, *Jump. Just jump!*

So as we reach the Lyrian wormhole, I imagine catapulting myself into the breach, into the void, into something akin to the swirly evanescence of a subspace tunnel.

And I think: Onward.

Now
Two Years Later

* Now

"Onward."

Layla tucked away the slim volume she'd been perusing. Password protected it so no one else could read her recollections. Locked it back away in her soul, sealed with a kiss.

It had been over two years since she and Ignatius had proposed to each other in a steamy Imperial Palace garden. Two years since giddily hurtling herself off a carefully constructed path, a tuck and roll through a forest of stinging nettle and poison clover, arriving disheveled on someone else's road. The life meant for some Valharan noblewoman, groomed and prepared for the hazards in her way.

Her road, now. But it still resembled a fever dream.

Poor girls from the slums of Kaborlah did not grow up to be empresses. Sworn military officers from a democratic republic didn't fly off and pledge allegiance to an empire. And strong women didn't define themselves based on who they married.

And yet.

"Your Grace," Ephraim said, bowing, "His Excellency is sorry to keep you waiting. He's ready for you now but ...well, not in here."

"Where?"

"War Room."

War Room. That didn't bode well. Usually, when Ignatius needed her advice, they met here, in his private study. What crisis would she be dealing with now?

"All right, Ephraim. I can make my own way there. Thanks."

Ephraim, the perfect, hyper-competent majordomo, gave her one sharp nod, turned on his heel, and headed out of the door.

She patted the journal in her pocket. Sometimes, she needed to look back and trace the folds of her life, as if she were a delicate paper crane with pedestrian origins. Because here she was: fragile. Precious. And oh-so-sculpted.

Just like this study. Though this was Ignatius's inner sanctum, it, like the rest of the rooms in the Imperial Palace, stood ostentatious, majestic, overwrought. So unlike Altain. So unlike *home*.

One day, perhaps, she'd achieve the serenity that came from total alignment of life-spheres: love and family, ambition, integrity, faith, political belief. Her fervent desire. Would it ever happen?

Flinging herself off a path indeed. Or was there a hidden catapult?

She walked along the well-trodden pathway to power—Emperor's study to War Room—her indelicate, non-Empress-like strides landing upon the gleaming floor like the drums of war calling out its violent cadence. War had been brewing her entire tenure here. In fact, it defined their entire *relationship*. They had met during the Mazaran invasion of their little Whorl of systems. They had fallen in love after they'd each crash-landed Felix. So on, and so forth.

And the crises did not abate with marriage.

Now she was pregnant. Which was a different sort of crisis on its own.

Striding into the war room at her husband's summons, she banished the combination of secret joy and instant regret defining her reaction to the pregnancy. She and Ignatius hadn't yet announced, though she was a few weeks in, and it was worth holding onto the respect and deference she had fought and clawed to get from the assorted admirals and generals in the room.

Providing an heir. Wasn't that her primary function? Not diplomatic counselor to the emperor-her-husband. Not quiet reformer, trying to push the Valharan Empire closer to a constitutional monarchy.

Broodmare.

They stood as she entered, everyone except Ignatius. She waved them down and glanced in amusement at her husband, her beloved. He hadn't even noticed her arrival.

"So?" she asked. "What's on fire today?"

"Felix," Ignatius said, looking up. He pushed the image of the Lyrian colony planet from his tablet to the air, tiny pixels reassembling into a holographic display.

Literally on fire. Well, then.

"Felix," Layla repeated faintly. She located a beautifully appointed upholstered chair and sank, biting her lip and panning around the room, deciding what to say next. Ignatius, knowing her way, waited in silence.

"And are we," she resumed carefully, "the cause of Felix being on fire?"

Not an idle question. Lyria, Felix's mother planet, was now in a war of attrition against Valhar over the Empire's construction of their new subspace tunnel, which they feared would bring in new invaders.

In response, Ignatius gestured to General Huxley Turine, seated at her left.

The tough-jawed man inclined his head. "The Lyrians have signaled they are tiring of a proxy war, Your Grace. Our intelligence indicates they're making preparations for a direct assault on Valhar itself. Hence, a preemptive strike on Felix, to prevent them from coming straight toward us through the Lyrian wormhole."

She nodded, because that was all she could do in the moment. A preemptive strike. Oh, Goddess. The war with Lyria just got worse. Meaning Altain, a Lyrian ally, could any day decide to jump in themselves. And Felix, the planet that had facilitated their first encounter, would play a further role in their lives.

And it was Ignatius's doing.

Layla took a breath to center herself. "What do you need me to do?"

Ignatius steepled his hands. "Insight. How is the Altainan Republic going to react?"

She gave him a look, which hopefully translated to *they're going to flip their shit, what do you think?* but verbally played the part of dignified monarch consort. "Altain had wanted to avoid a shooting war. That's why their president has been so careful not to announce any red lines that would trigger a response." This was true even when the first rumbles and rumors were occurring. "But a strike against a Lyrian colony? Altain and the rest of the Alliance may view that as an unprovoked attack on Lyria, which could very well compel them to come to Lyria's defense."

"And lead to a Whorl-spanning war," Ignatius concluded.

She dipped her head in assent. Ignatius sighed. "Can't be helped, I suppose. I'll reach out to Benedik and see if he can get in one last meeting with the Altainans before he ships out toward home tonight. Gentlemen, my lady, thank you."

He rose, they rose. And Layla followed her husband back to his study in order to give him a piece of her mind.

They walked in companionable silence, two people accustomed to each other and their foibles. Her fingers splayed on her outstretched hand as she walked, nearly brushing his, the acknowledgement of love and fidelity hidden by layers of formality. His head almost unconsciously tilted toward her, a green sprout straining toward his sun, even as he marched with majestic precision.

Arriving at his office, however, the low gurgle of frustration deep within her belly had space free to roam, and it licked impatiently against her shores of reserve, pausing only long enough to notice Ephraim sitting in Ignatius's guest chair when they entered.

She shot the man an apologetic look. "Hi, Ephraim. You might want to leave."

"You can yell at me in front of Ephraim, dear," Ignatius said, a weary note in his voice. "Great Bird knows, I feel a bit like stomping my feet myself."

Ephraim looked back and forth between them and made his decision. "I think I'll come back later, sire, grace. It's not important in the slightest."

"I'm sorry for kicking you out," Layla called as he made his hasty exit.

"I don't think I've ever seen Ephraim call one of his agenda items 'not important'." Ignatius chuckled. "Being married to Mariah must give him a finely honed danger sense."

Layla kept her arms crossed, not inclined in the slightest to give Ignatius any ground. The sea foam of resentment overflowed its banks.

"*Can't be helped*, husband? Are we now denying our hand in starting this whole mess?"

"*We*," Ignatius said, pointing to himself to emphasize the Imperial pronoun, "are continually ensuring the stability of Our Empire."

Yes, because nothing spelled stability like war. Layla emitted a low growl of frustration. Probably not prudent to open up *that* line of argument yet again, thank you very much.

"Ignatius. It's *Felix*." She hated her plaintive tone but wouldn't shy away from it either. They had met on Felix. They had changed the course of a war on Felix.

"It's not like you to be prone to sentiment," he rumbled.

She threw open her hands. "It's not sentiment, Nate. It's an indication of how far gone we are now. We fought to *save* that world from the Mazarans. Remember? That was only seven years ago."

"We're not going to harm Felix."

"Bull. This is going to be a humanitarian disaster and you know it."

"We need to protect the Valharan home world, Layla," Ignatius said quietly. "The only way to do that is to control the Lyrian wormhole, and it runs right through their colony."

They stared at each other, at an impasse. The same argument over and over again, one they've been having for years, like a call-and-response cadence. *Valhar needs to build a tunnel to open up exploration into new systems and rescue its economy,* he would say.

Is that worth a treaty violation? Punitive action from the other powers in the Whorl? Is it worth the danger of letting another invading force into the Whorl, just like the Mazarans? she would ask.

Ignatius sat on the chair Ephraim had vacated, and as if they actually had had that conversation, he reached over and pulled her down to him. "How are you feeling?" His low timbre produced shivers down her spine.

She folded into him, resting her face in that small place between collarbone and shoulder. "People tell me horror stories about puking. No one warned me about the utter *exhaustion.*"

"The puking," he said, stumbling over the slang, "may come, in time."

"Thanks. Very helpful, Nate."

He traced his fingers on her belly, deft light touches almost imitating the little bubbles she knew she'd feel at quickening. "I know you don't approve of my decisions—"

"I don't presume to rule in your stead. But I *am* an advisor, and I will speak as I see fit."

Obligatory words said, they settled once more into quiet.

This new role, that of Empress Layla of Valhar, had shrunk her. Temporarily, of course. Just the realities of adjusting to a new world, new mores, new pressures and scrutiny. But over time, she had been reborn into a fully realized human being, like a wobblebug liquified inside a chrysalis, emerging finally into flight. Someone beyond the identity of brand-new immigrant wife, thrust into a prominent position out of circumstance more than intent. Someone holding her own as a woman in a society that ostensibly gave her equal rights, but was still wary of actually handing her power. Someone who thought her husband hung the moon but did not drown in his considerable shadow.

Layla again contemplated the baroque furnishings. Ignatius's study likely looked the same as it had during Carlus's reign, abbreviated as it was, and maybe Gustav before him. This is how Ignatius was; he settled into his unexpected role as Emperor as if he had always meant to be there, as part of the milieu as any overwrought staircase or petrified artifact.

But for Layla, she had been herded into this position, every turn taken ending in barriers on three sides, forcing her this way and that, boxing her in until, at the end, she was here, on a foreign planet, consort to the monarch, incubating his heir, and you could call it *choice.*

And now her birth nation was likely to declare war on her adopted home. She technically had dual citizenship. She was still bound by oaths she had taken when she first joined the Altainan Republic forces. But time and time again she had drawn on her insider knowledge working for Roya to assist Valhar's diplomatic forays. How far would she go to help them wage war?

***

A week later, the senior Valharan leadership crowded around in the situation room, watching the Altainan vid feed as President Roya declared war.

Altain was broadcasting in the clear. No need to hide this from anyone in the Whorl. No need to obscure the fact her two homes were at war with each other. No need to shy from a war-weary populace as things were about to, again, become terrible. Lord Benedik's last attempt at negotiation had failed.

(They hadn't heard from Benedik in a while. Wasn't he due for a check-in? She made a mental note to bring it up.)

Her home. Her people, that she abandoned. The bonds she held with her husband and his loved ones warred with this sense, this inner *condemnation*, of her abrogation of duty. Those were her soldiers. Officers and enlisted she fought beside, led, inspired, and because of her adopted home's actions—her *husband's* actions—they were once again called to fight.

The duality of her loyalty waged its own little war. If only that stupid tunnel—the threat of a Mazaran reappearance, really—didn't loom over every interaction: the tension between Valhar and the Alliance, and now open war; every painful event over the last two years; her own tug-and-pull of honoring her marriage vows first, but remembering her oaths as a soldier. If only she could end this. She was the diplomatic counselor. She was the empress. She *had* to find a solution, somehow, because she couldn't keep doing this for the rest of her life.

But she swallowed the rising bile and breathed calm and surety, as befitted her station.

Ephraim, whom she had so rudely kicked out a mere week before, stood on Layla's right, putting a hand on her shoulder in comfort. She clasped one brown hand over his bronzed one gratefully. He knew what this moment was costing her. This hour was the culmination of all the events that had led her to Valhar, beginning with crash landing on

Felix and encountering a dashing Valharan soldier.

Ignatius, poised on her left, set himself apart, resolute and stern. No weakness here, not when he was the ultimate leader of the men and women who now would be facing a far stronger and more intractable foe.

General Turine turned away from the vid, resignation clouding his features.

"It's done, sire. The rest of the Alliance will follow suit. We must be prepared to defend multiple fronts. Your orders?"

"Felix," Ignatius replied, hands clasped. "We need to hold Felix. But we can't expend all our forces to do so. Our priority on Felix is to ameliorate the humanitarian conditions. Drop the siege barriers and ship in food. Restore order but do so under the aegis of community policing. Make it clear this is a temporary holding and they will revert back to Lyria at the end of the war. The more stability we give Felix, the less the populace will resist and the less time the Alliance will spend on freeing it." Ignatius spared a glance at Layla, and she gave him a small nod of approval.

"Very good sire," said Turine.

Ignatius signaled, and anyone sitting stood. "We'll reconvene in our war room, 2200 hours. Get to work." He grabbed a flimsy displaying fleet movements and bent to study it.

"Benedik," Layla murmured.

Ignatius's head snapped up. He signaled to the officer manning mission control. "Viscount Gruesse left Altain a few days ago. I need the location of his transport."

The young officer swiped through the projected screens at his station, finally zooming in on an area beyond the planet of Reneb. "Sire," he said, shakily, "we lost his signal near the nebula."

"The Swan Nebula?" General Turine strode over to the station. "What in the devil possessed them to go that way? That wasn't on the filed flight plan."

"Shit," Ignatius muttered, soft enough so only Layla could hear.

She touched her hand to his arm, briefly and lightly. "I'd been hoping to have tea with Alina soon. I'll visit with her tomorrow about Benedik." Alina and Benedik were still newlyweds. Alina was strong, *Valharan* strong, taught to bear hardship with stoicism. That didn't mean she shouldn't have comfort.

Ignatius's eyes darted over to her. He and Layla had extensive practice in having entire conversations through the microchanges in their expressions: her slow blinks, his quirked smile, her stilled breaths, his tilted head. When they were stationed together on Dega, commanding their respective nations' forces, she would find meaning in one flutter of his impossibly long eyelashes. The intimidating, terrifying, humorless Captain-General of the Valharan Force, putting his people through maneuvers beneath the dome of a rogue planet, would slowly turn his head in her direction as she went by, and in that outwardly severe countenance she would read it: *I see you. I love you.*

And now, while his face betrayed nothing, she was close enough to see the tightening of his throat. In Ignatius terms, that was pure anguish. Lord Benedik, Viscount Gruesse, was a second cousin but near-brother to Ignatius, one of his few close confidantes and someone who remembered and related to him as the person he was pre-Ascension. One of an ever-shrinking generation of a family touched by early death and other misfortune.

"Please do see Alina," he said, outwardly calm. "And, my lady, caution her not to worry. We'll find him."

*
Now

On the inner edge of a long sweep of a galactic arm lay a tight stellar cluster, stars arranged only a few light years apart in a lazy spiral, another spiral offshooting from the center at a reckless angle. A bright nebula, a stellar nursery, abutted the twin spirals, squeezed between them at some points, and bisected each near their tails. All these together formed their Whorl, a mini-galaxy of their own. One republic, one empire, some colonial confabs and a few independent planets, all traveling along a galactic orbit as cordial, yet wary, neighbors. At least, that's how it was, before this new initiation of hostilities.

The Whorl was lousy with tiny wormholes that allowed traffic between close systems with only a negligible nod to time dilation when traveling to their mouths. And then in the Swan Nebula dwelled a human-made subspace tunnel, a gateway to the far reaches of the galaxy, from whence the Mazarans came and changed the course of Layla's life.

Somewhere, across the Whorl, forces mustered against her new country, against Ignatius's subjects. Somewhere, on the edges of the Swan Nebula, Benedik was ... what? Safe? Captured? Lost? Dead? Somewhere, through the only completed man-made subspace tunnel, guarded only by scant leftover Valharan forces on the rogue planet Dega, the Mazarans lay in wait, abiding by the armistice treaty Ignatius and Layla had helped broker. For now.

Layla liked to think of Valhar and Altain, separated only by a swath of the Swan Nebula, as two planets orbiting the same gravitational object, mirror images, the two strongest powers in the space, spanning between them multiple planets and moons.

Homeworld-to-homeworld, it was the Altainan ally Lyria that had the straight shot to

Valhar, just a blip through their wormhole near Felix. But Benedik would have meant to take the back way, through the hinterlands of the Valharan Empire.

Flying through the Midtown Hills Tunnel in her armored transport toward Finley Court, where Alina and Benedik made their home, reminded her of the subspace Solita Tunnel in the imperial hinterlands, the construction of which started this war. Once, bypassing the hills of Novaria—hills being quite a misnomer for the surrounding mountains—was as arduous a task as building a gateway to the rest of the galaxy.

"Welcome back, Lady Layla," said the doorman, with the customary casual appellation she treasured. Layla dismissed her guards, enjoying the momentary feeling of being *alone*. She allowed herself a discreet yawn, before heading up the stairs to the drawing room where Alina—Viscountess Gruesse—was already waiting.

"Tough day?" Alina asked. Arched eyebrows offset an impeccable face, her long tight braids framing her as if she were a prized portrait.

"Me? How're *you* doing?" Layla asked, allowing her Altainan drawl to emerge over the usual clipped Valharan accent.

"Ephraim called me and told me," she said. "Yes, I'm worried. How could I not be? But, come on, Layla, have you *met* Benedik?"

Layla considered. "Good point, that." Benedik could charm his way out of a horse's ass. He could face one hundred murderous Narconians and talk his way through. And if all else failed, he could logic the shit out of the situation.

Wherever he was, he had better give 'em hell.

"Anyway," Alina continued, "I think we're better served discussing this over tea."

At that moment, the butler arrived with the repast. Alina sprung up, as official hostess, to pour the drink into her guest's mug, per Valharan tradition.

Layla waved her off the initial selection.

"I think I'm *actually* going with tea this time," she said. Alina gave her a curious look but went over to the trolley and selected Altainan cha. Layla let the heavy spiced smell waft over her. If only she could just suck the caffeine up through her nostrils.

She rose to pour for her host, also per tradition. "And which brewery is your father-in-law supporting these days, anyway?" Layla asked, noting the pale amber of the beer she had poured for Alina. The intended 'tea,' natch.

"Think something from one of the colony planets. Gracy, was it?" Alina said, wiping froth from her lips. "I admit I have something else on my mind. Probably focusing on it to keep my mind off Benedik, but isn't that the way of things sometimes?"

Alina was putting on a brave front, but she must have been terrified. "Is your runway show coming together nicely?" Layla asked.

"Oh, that." Alina waved the thought away. "I have that well in hand. Although," she said, pausing, "we're suddenly at war. I might have to reassess whether this is the right time for luxuries. No, this is about Dracini. He's been yapping at Benedik's father again about the succession. Abilio wouldn't get caught up in that type of mess but I'm afraid of some sort of by-association blowback."

Sedition. The word was sedition, and what a loaded word that was, on Valhar. Benedik's father Abilio had been a top choice for emperor after the abdication of Carlus II. Meanwhile, the yapping Earl of Dracini had never made it a secret that he preferred Abilio on the throne and found Ignatius lacking. Abilio wouldn't take action against Ignatius—the thought was inconceivable—but he was close to Dracini, and Dracini was someone to monitor.

"We trust the Dargas family, Alina," Layla said, softly but firmly. "Ignatius wouldn't think any of you would cast aspersions against him."

"But you don't speak for Ignatius, no matter how much you would like to think you do," Alina countered. "So, since my husband isn't here to plead his father's case, I'm coming to you. Not to pass judgment yourself, but to *pass it on*."

"Right. Roger," Layla said. Alina frowned at the vernacular but shook her head, as if to rid herself of it.

***

Mariah, Ephraim's wife and Layla's personal bodyguard, often joined them at their socials, switching tracks from protector to friend, although when she was on duty she didn't partake in drinking the *fun* tea. This day, she instead had the morning off, choosing to meet Layla at the imperial gates when she returned from Alina's home. Tall and auburn-haired, Mariah inhibited such deadly grace one had to wonder if perhaps she felt shortchanged by having one short, quiet empress as an assignment.

"You don't always have to be on high alert," Layla offered, as Mariah shadowed her through the public areas of the palace. "We're in the Palace, for stars' sake."

Mariah's head swiveled in a detection pattern. "People get too complacent. Did you tell

Alina?" Mariah continued on without looking at her, still scanning.

Layla pressed her hand to her stomach, then, conscious of being in public, moved it and rubbed her arms. "Didn't seem like the time. You know, with Benedik and all."

"Mmhmm."

"I'm really excited. Can't wait to tell everyone."

"That," Mariah said, "is such bullshit. Your Grace," she added belatedly.

"It's still early, Mariah." So early. Unfortunate things could happen that early on, as she well knew.

Mariah graced her with a small smile.

Layla looked over at the woman guarding her and had a vision of the past: Mariah, nervous energy emanating in waves, leading her through a tapestry and into a basement, her lantern-illuminated alabaster skin almost glowing with heraldic doom. The parallels in Mariah's manner stole Layla's breath, and she worked her mouth to regain her air and ask the percolating question.

"Mariah, did you get any new orders? Now that Altain is in the fight?" Mariah didn't technically work for General Turine—she answered to no one, really, except for Ignatius—but Turine had the ultimate say in security arrangements in the Palace.

Arrangements that accounted for one Altainan empress, whom Turine feared going rogue.

Mariah paused and looked at her carefully. The silence stretched a little too long, its viscosity almost at the breaking point, and Layla charged in with words just to put the tension back in its neat and organized place.

"It's all right," she said softly. "You have a job to do. I understand duty."

"That's part of what I'm worried about, Your Grace," Mariah said, opening the door to the restricted section of the palace.

As they arrived just outside the residence, Mariah stopped scanning, and her shoulders slowly came down. The hardened bodyguard graced Ephraim, standing at the edge of the royal apartments, with a genuinely loving smile, though it quickly faltered.

"Your Grace," Ephraim greeted Layla. "The Emperor wants to meet with you."

Ephraim, ever the professional, betrayed nothing but faint concern in his close-set eyes, but *Mariah*—Mariah obviously saw something deeper in her spouse's countenance, because she immediately cut in. "What's wrong?"

He shook his head at Mariah, the action causing his straight jet-black hair to fall over his eyes. "It's not as bad as—well, come along, both of you. Please."

They decamped to the private library in the residence, Layla plopping down on the couch, taking off her absurd heels and rubbing her feet, waiting for Ignatius. As he entered, the hard set to his shoulders and his pale face told the same story Mariah must have read in Ephraim. Layla popped up and walked quickly to him, grabbing his arms in alarm.

"Nate—"

"Nothing solid on Benedik," he said, distracted. He cleared his throat and then looked at her straight on, his brows furrowed. "Ah, but my lady—our resources out in the nebula got to his shuttle and found his pilot and his guard killed. No trace, though, of..." he rubbed his eyes and groaned. Blessed Lady, he had never before looked this tired.

"Take a break, Ignatius," she said, trying to put some of her old military steel in her voice.

Even exhausted, even scared, Ignatius radiated intensity. The first time she had met him on Felix, he lit up the hot sands with his sincerity, his earnestness, his depth of feeling on doing what was right and what was honorable.

That Ignatius retreated long ago, a tender seed curled up deep inside in a tiny protective shell. The man in front of her, the ruler of fifteen worlds, didn't have the time to sink into her arms and allow her to stroke his hair. The man in front of her faced a war on multiple fronts, an existential threat to his system of government, and a missing loved one.

Still, she asked.

As expected, Ignatius shook his head sadly, but then he took her face in his hands.

"I'd like your help," he said. "The nebula. If you have any contacts out there that aren't officially attached to the Altainan Republic, please reach out. And of course, warn them Valhar has people in play too, although I doubt they'd coordinate. I know it's a tough line to walk, with Altain now an enemy, but if anyone can thread that needle, it's you."

He left with the same guarded air with which he arrived, and then it was all business. Layla turned to Mariah and braced herself.

Ephraim took one look at the women, obviously felt the crackling tension, and turned on his heel to exit.

The silence roared in Layla's ears, but finally Mariah spoke.

"I'm going to stand right here and assume you will not contact Ransom."

Layla wrung her hands briefly, then paced, looking wistfully at the bedchamber just off the study: firm mattress, soft pillows. Why did this all have to go to hell when she couldn't even stay awake for four hours straight?

"Why would I do that? I don't even see how that would work," she responded.

Ransom. Even his name sent shivers up her spine.

Mariah clenched her hands by her sides. "Sure. And it has nothing to do with the fact you don't want to expose any assets he might have in the palace."

"I keep my oaths," Layla said sharply. "I'm a dual citizen."

"You're the *Empress*. Ignatius—"

"*Emperor* Ignatius understands and supports my position on this, Mariah. *And* I reject your accusation. I know nothing about any Altainan assets. So drop it."

"Just a precaution. Ma'am."

"General Turine is up to his nonsense again, I bet," Layla grumbled under her breath. Her stomach tightened with the memory of the fallout the last time this discussion had occurred. "Mariah—" She went to put an arm on Mariah's shoulder, and to her surprise, Mariah let her.

"Yeah, yeah, I love you too," Mariah sighed. "You get where I'm coming from, though, right? We're not all that different."

"No, I don't think I was ever Emperor Gustav's personal—"

"Fixer. Elite fixer."

Layla opened her palm in a *whatever you say* gesture. "Think we'll get to go on some grand mission to rescue Benedik, wherever he is? Make use of some of our combat training for once?"

Mariah grinned, at last. "Not you, preggo. You're benched." She threw a jaunty salute and left.

Layla smiled ruefully and rubbed her stomach again, this time not bothering to hide the action.

***

As Layla tried to sleep that night, she twisted and turned, her discomfort nothing to do with the physical changes in her body. Her dreams flittered in and out and then took on the sharp edge of memory.

"Tell me again," the security investigator said. And then it shifted to Ransom's office, and her hands being clamped down, and fire in her veins, and she woke with a start, stumbled into the bathroom, and promptly threw up.

Ignatius was waiting for her as she emerged. "Pregnancy sickness?" he asked.

"Yes," she lied.

She sat on the bed and heaved a sigh. Ignatius moved to encircle her with his arms.

"So," he said as she rested against him, "Commander. Now that our nations are at war. You think the Republic is going to activate you and send you off to fight?"

"Hah," she said. "It's not a joking matter. I've already experienced what they'd do in a situation like that."

"Would you have made a different choice?" he asked. "All those years ago. All the way back in the beginning, when we first met and knew?"

"What choice?" she asked then, turning to him. "Tell me one thing we could've done differently." They had never acted on their feelings. Not during their stranding on Felix. Not while they petitioned their governments for a cooperation pact. Not the years they were stationed together. They never wavered. All their connection consisted of looking into each other's eyes and talking, dreaming together. The occasional hand running down her face. Her fingers in his hair.

It was probably much easier for her than it was for him. Although there were other women, at times, for him.

"I *did* propose to you."

"Even if you hadn't."

There were sims she'd play as a kid, where she could choose different directions for the story to go. And it was a very Altainan game: individualism and choice, freedom. It was supposed to teach them they all had the freedom to choose the paths their lives would take. But the sim was preprogrammed. The player didn't have a whole universe of choices—just a few, sometimes only two. It was a false dichotomy, with careful structured paths her adventure could trod.

Life was like that. There were unseen architects that created the structures that constrained choice. At a certain point, it became that being here with him was the only choice she could make.

"Well," Ignatius acknowledged, "you forced your way past my defenses and wouldn't let go. I couldn't resist you. You were an attractive nuisance."

She groaned at the pun and leaned into him, shivering as he kissed her shoulder. A stirring of interest, a rare enough happenstance she now reveled in it. She kissed him back.

Soft lips, prickly beard. Questing hands. A nibble on her ear, her legs wrapped round. Her mind wandered. Benedik. How would she start researching how to help Benedik?

He backed up off her, gently running his fingers from nose to chin, and lower, still lower. She barely noticed. She had contacts out in the wilds of the Whorl, but she hadn't used them in...years. Too many years. Could she just waltz up and—

The absence of touch, where there used to be some, light and feathery. Right. *Focus*, Layls. She glanced up to see her husband standing in front of her, winking. "The Emperor has no clothes," he said in a deep seductive voice, and she burst out laughing.

"Damnit," he said, ruefully. He kissed the top of her head and pulled her to him, and she rested again in her favorite spot, against his shoulder.

She loved him so. And his strong hands, warm chest. His baby-soft hair with flecks of silver, the crinkle of eyes on fair skin.

Layla's personal office, unlike most of the palace, reflected her taste. The floors, hardwood. The desk a beautiful red cherry, in front of windows overlooking the frozen lake. An overstuffed chair. The front of the room featured a couch and tea table, with a vase of fresh flowers replaced daily. It was a functional, useful space as well, with a holomap showing the homeworld, colonies, and territories of the Valharan Empire. Near the desk was her information center, and here she padded to, in stocking feet, after some requisite snuggle time with Nate—more for his sake than hers.

She only briefly skimmed the classified reports to which she was entitled—mostly unsubstantiated missives on a large ship construction out in Altainan territory. She instead went over to the interplanetary news feeds, using her eye to track and pick her selections.

No surprises there. Lyrian media was full of war stories. Altain's was rife with think pieces. And yes. The gossip rags were out in full force. All about her, of course. Even the slightly more reputable pubs had headlines like *The Traitor Empress: From Hero to Zero* and *The Temptress-in-Chief.* Wonderful.

Enough of that. Her concern was the nebula, and a missing Benedik. Ignatius's had faith in her abilities, but this was a tangle. She mentally listed her tasks. Find individuals out in the nebula who could go where Valharan intelligence couldn't, even under cover. Make sure they didn't step on the toes of any assets Valhar did have out there. Ensure they understood the gravity of the situation and the need for discretion.

And finally, figure out how she, an empress with no chance of anonymity, could even get in contact with people like that.

She'd have dispatched Mariah, but Mariah had her own tangled web of enemies looking for revenge or leverage against her, given her previous occupation as a 'fixer'. But who else could act as Layla's proxy?

She tapped her stylus on the desk in a steady rhythm. She had an idea. A very bad one.

After another moment of hesitation, she toggled her comm. "Ephraim. I need you to connect me with Ambassador Park at the Renebian Embassy. Please."

Ephraim's breezy voice came through immediately, amusement vibrating through the speaker. "Your Grace, you know it's close to midnight. Most normal people won't be answering their comms."

"*You* did."

"I think we've established long ago that neither you nor I are normal." But he had already taken a brusque tone. All business, ready to serve. "What shall I tell him is the nature of the discussion?"

"I need him to hand-deliver a note, eyes-only, to our good ol' war buddy Charles."

It was rare she could render Ephraim speechless. 'Charles' was formerly Carlus II, the deposed Emperor of Valhar.

Contacting him could backfire. Badly. Ambassador Park of Reneb was untrustworthy. Carlus had a tense relationship with the Valharan regime. This may not be worth it. A shot in the dark to find Benedik, something unlikely to bear fruit. But if anyone could honor Ignatius's request to find contacts in the nebula, it would be him.

Ephraim finally found his voice. "Layla," he said quietly, "are you sure?"

"Erm..."

She sat frozen with indecision, her eyes distant as she flashed through the possibilities. Park blabbing, in his very Park way. General Turine, thinking her contact with a former emperor was some sort of precursor to treason. The personal consequences, if this should go sideways, could get her cast off from Valhar—no, that wasn't true. Her husband wouldn't allow that, for sure. But absolute rule or not—

Benedik. *Benedik*, she repeated in her mind. Alina, trying to play off her worry and concern. If she didn't do this, and something happened to that sweet man, she wouldn't be able to bear it. Crawling tension going up her spine notwithstanding.

"Ephraim? The answer is yes." *For Benedik*, she resolved.

Benedik!
Now

4.5 weeks after the beginning of the Alliance-Valharan War

Lord Benedik, Viscount Gruesse, son of an earl and cousin to His Imperial Excellency, was tied up shirtless to a soft bed and he did not like it, not one little bit.

Certainly, if this little display had anything to do with his lady wife, then it would be quite all right. But between the travel to Altain and the time spent trying to make progress on the diplomatic front, he had been gone from her for weeks. And the way home would take weeks longer—

Focus, Benedik.

As usual, the admonition sprung to his mind as if his beloved wife were speaking the words. But she was right. Wouldn't do to have his brain jump around like a jackrabbit, now. First, where was he? Tied up to a bed shirtless, yes. His hands, to be exact, were cuffed together to a bedpost. Benedik tugged experimentally and found a slight give. It was also rather gently done, giving his arms enough slack that he wasn't in a stress position.

His eyes adjusted to the dim light and he perceived he was in a pink pony bedroom.

"Yeech," he said.

This was either an amateur hour situation or the creepiest brothel ever. Either way, it was time to collect more data.

Benedik modulated his voice to one of mild concern. "Ahem. Uh. Hey! Anyone out there?" Sometimes the direct approach was best.

The door opened and two lean, sour looking people entered. They carried themselves like they had military experience. Benedik squinted. Militia, maybe. Either way, one had a sidearm and both looked confident and controlled.

Well, damnation. They looked competent. Benedik eliminated the hopeful puppy look from his face and replaced it with wary curiosity. This had been fun. Now, business.

The blond one, with the sidearm, took up position by the door and the dark-haired, lanky beanpole approached Benedik with a placid expression.

"Lord Benedik," the lanky one greeted. Benedik suppressed a groan. He didn't know if his identity would be of help or harm, but he'd hoped to have a chance to make that choice.

He didn't allow his dismay to show and instead gave the person an ironic look. "In the flesh. I seem to be at a disadvantage."

"Yeah," the stringbean said. "You are."

"And I'm a prisoner?"

"A rescue, actually. We saved you from having your innards gutted."

"Thanks?" Some rescue. Benedik gathered these two weren't the actual rescuers. Something about them made them seem they weren't captains of their own destiny...

Captains. *Pilots*.

Benedik started, pulling himself upward, clanging the handcuffs on the post. (The blond shifted his weight forward in response to the perceived threat.) "Pilot. I had a pilot and a guard. Where are they? Are they well?" How could he have forgotten? Great Clawed God, he was an ass.

Blondie shook his head. "Whoever tried to get to you succeeded in getting to them. And no, I don't know many details."

Benedik closed his eyes in regret. His father—one of them, at any rate—had drilled into him that with privilege came responsibility. What that meant for the entire system was something on which he and Father disagreed, but regardless. People were dead, and it was in service to him.

He was suddenly too tired to put on an act. "Okay. Now, where am I?"

His two captors exchanged a look. "Solita," Beanpole said. "But they found your ship a day or two out from Dega."

Benedik shifted again. Solita and Dega were nowhere near each other. "How long have I been out? And what in the name of the Great Bird was my ship doing near the Swan Nebula?"

His brain caught up to his surprise. "Oh, and who's *they?* And who're you? Maybe I should have started with that," he added weakly. Mush. His diction already sounded like mush, and his brain, too, apparently.

The lean duo exchanged another look, and finally, Blondie nodded.

Beanpole turned back to Benedik. "You're not gonna bolt if we free your arms, are you?"

Benedik shook his head. "Let's say you provide me with something to eat. And, erm," he said, looking at himself, "some clothes, then I think we're in business."

"You were delivered to us in a Mazaran stasis unit. By our benefactors. They had gotten word you were missing and found you." Beanpole, who had introduced themself as Fern, stoked the fire and sent off a shower of sparks. "The details are fuzzy. But they brought you to us. You've apparently been frozen for a few weeks. They popped the lid and let you thaw out here."

"Mazaran tech," Benedik mused. "Can't say I've ever experienced *that* quite before."

They appeared to be at a lakehouse of some sort, rural enough that the stars numbered in the millions, much like Valhar's capital of Novaria. The subspace tunnel the Empire was building wasn't visible, unlike the Swan Nebula tunnel over Dega. Made sense; Dega orbited its tunnel, but the Solita one had to be outside the system.

Some sort of rodent roasted on a makeshift spit. Benedik's stomach quailed at the thought. Did Mazaran stasis units alleviate the need for food, or were nutrients fed through tubes? He certainly didn't feel hungry anymore. But he wasn't about to let on.

People sometimes called him prissy, which Benedik found mightily unfair, as most of those people knew of his "in-Novaria" personality. Well, of course he'd act like a popinjay in the capital. That's what the capital was *for*. His shipmates in the Fleet hadn't thought he was foppish or weak, had they? Of *course* Benedik would eat the animal. After he made sure his captors had had their fill—to be polite, of course.

There's nothing you're too good for, Dad always said.

"Solita. Well, at least I'm back in the Empire," Benedik said. "If you folk can help me get back to Valhar, I'll see you receive an Imperial Order of Merit for your good turn."

"Yeeaaah, about that." Blondie—Jax was his name—unconsciously tapped his sidearm.

"You're not going to let me go, are you?"

Fern scratched their head. "We're still not sure what to do with you. Thing is, we're not in charge. Need to hear from the big guy first." They shrugged apologetically. "If you wanna run, you can, but it's pretty remote here. We don't have transportation either, so you're kinda stranded here with us."

"I'm on Solita."

"Yep."

"And so you're Solita revolutionaries, aren't you."

Fern put out a palm. "Got it in one."

Benedik brightened. "Well, that's *great*! Maybe we can work something out, after all."

Again, *again*, they exchanged looks. Maybe they were actually having full mental conversations through those looks, like his fathers did, or how he and Ephraim did when Ignatius was in one of his moods. Didn't seem likely, that. Which begged the question of the point of those looks. Gratuitous signaling of confusion, perhaps.

"Work something...out?" Jax asked.

"Perhaps," Benedik said judiciously, "I should wait until your superiors get here."

Maybe then he'd have more of a plan.

Solita. Solita was on the back way toward Valhar proper, which was the way Benedik was to have gone anyway. "Back way" being a misnomer, of course, because wormhole travel in the Whorl was not like a simple freeway between contiguous systems but a dazzling crisscrossing in, out, and around the spirals. Political borders could not be drawn as boxes on a map and instead were a function of the sequence in which one could leapfrog through the wormholes. So the back way, in this parlance, was two small wormhole hops to an area near the Empress's home Altainan colony of Kaborlah, and one more large wormhole jump that would have taken him inside the Empire's borders.

Benedik sat on the rickety back porch of the shamble shack by the lake, enjoying a smoke proffered by Jax, cloud Os lazing through the air as he tapped his foot with agitation. Regardless of what was coming in an hour, maybe he could get a message to his lady wife—an apology, perhaps, if this was going to end badly for him. *Dearest Alina,* he mentally composed, *sorry I got myself stuffed into a metal tube and frozen and then kidnapped by incompetent militamembers and shot. They were rather nice, though, at least until the shooting...*

Revolutionaries. Benedik knew what they were on about; they wanted no more than home rule, a chance to reap the economic benefits of being a waystop to the soon-constructed tunnel without serving as subjects of an Imperial governor, a chance to invest their monies as they saw fit, or to organize their society in a way that reflected the mores of a backwater-turned-express station. Benedik didn't mind the idea of limited self-rule as much, not that he argued for it in front of Ignatius. Advocating the overthrow of a Viceroy to his-cousin-the-Emperor would be sedition, plain and simple, childhood bosom buddies or not. Ignatius was a reformer himself, but a silent one, and it didn't take away from the fact it was Just Not Discussed. Leave that discussion between him and Layla. Although Layla would be thrilled if the entire system were overhauled.

As for Benedik, he may have thought the march of progress to be a good in itself, but he loved his Empire; he was bred to serve it. It still rankled that he'd had to retire his commission after Carlus abdicated. When Carlus took his three children with him into hiding, Benedik was on the list of people that could be chosen at any time to be Emperor. Until Ignatius went and begat himself an *heir*, Benedik would remain on that list and not be permitted to endanger himself in military service.

Benedik pondered his current tenuous safety. What was *this*, then?

That was Ignatius for you. Benedik had groused at being sent on a simple unskilled *courier* mission, and then war suddenly became imminent and he had to play diplomat with Roya—not that he quite enjoyed that task either, but at least it was something *important*, and now he was some sort of bargaining chip. Damn that Ignatius. The Emperor never let on, but he always planned ahead, maneuvering other people to fulfill his goals. And he had sent *Benedik* to Altain, knowing he was about to authorize a strike on Felix, piss off the entire Alliance, and expand the war.

And now Benedik was in limbo, about to face the leaders of a revolutionary militia and what? Be killed? Ransomed? Dissected to see how nobles ticked?

Betcha feel bad now, Iggy.

All too soon, the sound of a shuttle filled the air, and Fern ran out in a panic. "Lord Benedik! We need to return you to the holding room!"

Ah, yes, the pink pony bedroom. Benedik now remembered some hasty promise, extracted after a long night and some sort of rye drink, to pretend the two militiapersons had been competent, strict jailers of the revolution's prized aristocrat. He heaved a sigh and trudged up to the pink abomination, bringing his hands forward together in order to be manacled.

"I might say," Jax mumbled as he maneuvered Benedik into position, "you don't seem like any nobles we've met before."

"Well, now, can't hurt to be polite. Would you have shared your table with me if I had sneered and demanded to be let free, and asked if you realized how important I was?"

"Not a chance. That's, uh, what we were expecting though."

"Treat everyone you meet with respect, that's what my Dad says. Father believes it too, but he somewhat comes at it from a high-bred etiquette angle."

"Maybe we can—"

Then: heavy footsteps on the stairs. Jax clammed up.

The woman who entered had a scar running from eye to cheek on her left side, an unkempt mass of short curls, and a scowl. Benedik's blood ran cold. He could handle shortsighted men hopped up on their own invincibility, but women were usually the real deal.

"Lord Benedik Dargas. *The* Viscount Gruesse," she said, observing him. "How kind of you to drop into our laps."

"I guess you should thank my rescuers," Benedik said with caution. He added an imperial lift to his chin for effect "You are...?"

"None of your concern." How was she going to play it? Was she one of those women leaders who liked to play up her sexuality, leaning in, sitting on his bed coquettishly, like a black widow inviting a fly into her web? Or was she forward, direct, take-no-prisoners, and generally scarier and more competent than all the men surrounding her, because of all the bullshit she likely had to put up with to rise through the ranks?

She wore a calculating look, and casually leaned back against the wall, arms crossed. The take-no-prisoners type, then. Benedik suddenly didn't like *that* phrase. She may have been leaning, but her body coiled, tense, like a snake ready to strike at any moment.

"I have been advised," she said, studying him, "that taking you for a hostage would be most effective."

Hostage? For what? Best keep that question to himself and allow her to talk. So he merely raised his eyebrows and waited for her to continue.

"Holding the Emperor's favorite cousin to convince him to sack the Viceroy," she said, "will be the best use of the boon that has come to us so unexpectedly. At least, again, that's what I've been told. His Imperial Excellency does what we say, or we execute you."

"Well, *that* won't work," Benedik said, unfortunately giving in to his tendency to think out loud. He mentally smacked himself and then resolved to use his mistake to his own ends.

"Oh?" She appeared calmly curious, like a crocodile.

A plan began to form in his head, although at the moment it wobbled around like a gelatin monster. But improvisation was his strong suit.

She didn't like "being advised." Benedik could see that immediately, could see that if he pushed whatever tale he was about to spin (for he didn't quite know what he was going to say) too hard, she would immediately discard it.

So he instead demonstrably clamped his lips shut and looked away.

"You have something to say," she said, sharply, "then say it."

Benedik sighed, and answered truthfully. "Ignatius is a man of honor and duty. He would rather let me die than negotiate with terrorists."

"We're not terrorists, we're—"

"Freedom fighters. I know. But if you take a hostage and threaten to kill him, that's terrorism. If you want your revolution to succeed, I'm afraid you have to take a much higher road."

"And what do you care," she asked softly, stepping closer to him, "if our revolution succeeds?"

"Check your sources," he said. "I'm a progressive. I believe in the Empire, but I'm an advocate for experimental self-rule. *Especially* for the new territories we'll unlock once the tunnel is completed, but I could be convinced Solita should have the first chance."

"You're telling me you could convince your cousin of that?"

Benedik shook his head *no*, the best he could, at least, while his head lay against a pillow. "He won't be convinced. But," he hesitated. So far, everything he said had been true. But this last would be a lie. Did he dare?

He decided to hold on to that hesitation for a bit.

The woman narrowed her eyes.

"I could get hanged for saying this out loud," he finally allowed, weakly. "But if I were Emperor, I could possibly make a deal amenable to your ends."

"A reformer willing to dethrone a sovereign?"

"You and I, we're not that far apart, after all," Benedik said. "Why do you think Ignatius sent me away?"(*Oh* but his heart ached with that statement. Why indeed, dear cousin?) "And without any additional information on what happened to me out there, I can't help but wonder if he was the hand behind my initial, er, incapacitation."

"But why? He's your cousin."

"Not really," he sniffed. "Second cousin, first of all."

"And you're next in line for the throne?" she asked, not without skepticism.

"There is no 'next in line' in this case," Benedik said, beginning to warm up to his subject. "If Ignatius had children, they'd be in the succession. But otherwise, Parliament elects someone. It's about the only real duty they have. And Parliament, conservative as it is, usually sticks to the royal familial line, the closer to the previous emperor the better."

"And, how do we know you'd give us home rule? After you ended up in power?"

He shrugged, again, best he could. "How do I know you won't try to take the entire Imperium down once you achieve your first goal? Look, all I know is that Ignatius wouldn't give in to your demands. Ever. I'm as good as dead. I want to live, and you want freedom. We can worry about betrayals and reprisals down the line, hmm? The question I have, is how exactly would a ragtag group of militants like yourselves help me overthrow an emperor?"

Her eyes glittered. "We have our ways. And sources." She undid his locks and stuck out her hand. "I don't quite like my 'advisor' anyway. Let's try it your way."

His skin crawled. It was to be treason, then. And then somehow turn the tables on his captors before he turned myth into reality. Even uttering the words he had was grounds for execution.

Clawed grits, Benedik. You aren't some sort of secret agent.

May-be I am, he defiantly muttered to his inner Alina-voice in defiance. Gallivanting throughout the Whorl, women and men falling to his considerable charm, his lady wife on his arm...

He frowned. The wife and the assorted falling humans didn't seem to mesh, at least in reality. In his fantasies, maybe, Alina wouldn't quite mind...

Focus, Benedik, his wife's voice scolded yet again.

Benedik swallowed, and moved to a sitting position gingerly, as if he had been prone and manacled for an extended period of time. He took her hand to shake. "I think you'll find," he said with manufactured alacrity, "that I will usher in a new era of enlightenment for our Empire. It's a deal."

*
Now

Layla

If Layla could draw the perfect ballgown, it would be what she was wearing today: a substantial skirt, flaring out from a tight corset, long sleeves, perfect for the Valharan winter, the red brocade pattern a subtle nod to her heritage while confirming to Valharan standards.

The corset was a bad idea.

Layla made another entry in her mental tally of *things they never tell you about falling pregnant*, and this one was the false notion she wouldn't have any demonstrative physical changes until she began to show. What a bunch of crap. Her lower belly jutted out with bloat and gas and a newly hardening lump. Layla tugged at her dress, willing herself to *breathe*, shifted the corset a bit higher so it didn't sit on the most sensitive spot. Unlike her first ball, where her stealth engagement spelled delicious anticipation, this little secret was really, really uncomfortable.

Ignatius looked her over with an arched eye. "You should have had that let out, my lady."

"I did," Layla said, blowing hair out of her face. "But I think we underestimated how much more I'd get bloated in just a few days. I had another dress—but the skirt on this one hides things better."

"There's nothing to hide, you know. *You* can feel it, I'm sure, but no one else is going to notice. But I do like the dress."

"Thanks," Layla said. "It has pockets."

Ignatius gave her a bemused look and then straightened as the attendees began filing in for the receiving line.

Layla had expected her diplomatic duties to lessen as the Whorl geared up for violence, but canceling the Winter Ball was never going to happen. Most of Valharan society was to be there—not just from the home planet itself, but the viceroys of the colonies and the governors of the subsidiaries and territories, and maybe a few prominent families from both. And as much as it felt like this war was between Valhar and *everyone else*, there were enough unaffiliated entities that there were foreigners here as well.

She glanced down the line toward Alina, by tradition the most junior member of the family present, and smiled encouragingly as the first of the guests approached her. Benedik had been missing for a few weeks now. A few weeks—just the right travel time back to Valhar, accounting for an unanticipated trip to the Nebula and back. Layla kept expecting Benedik to rush in, travel clothes dirty and hair all askew, simply for the drama of the moment.

It was patently unfair to expect Alina's participation in the festivities, but the fact they had misplaced Benedik, Lord Chaos was virtually unknown. The family had to keep up appearances, after all.

Alina, she of a career in fashion design, looked *perfect*, her skin, darker than Layla's, fresh and gleaming, *glowing* in the way Layla's, in early pregnancy, was supposed to but didn't. All grace and etiquette as she began greeting.

The receiving line made it past Alina, Benedik's fathers Abilio and Henri, and Ignatius's parents Anastasia and Tonin. Layla accepted the bow from the squinty-eyed man in front of her and gently touched his shoulder in greeting. Dracini. Of course he'd be at the head of the line.

"Well met, Empress."

"Well met," she replied.

"Congratulations," he said, inclining his head and giving her a meaningful look. He moved on to speak with Ignatius.

Her eyebrows climbed. What had he meant by *that*? Ignatius hadn't seemed to have heard, but Anastasia, on Layla's other side, returned her confused look.

He said nothing additional to Ignatius, other than traditional greeting, as he came forward and bent on one knee. "My liege," Dracini said. "Thank you for honoring me with an invitation."

Despite the press of attention the empress drew at an event like this, the revelers were kind enough to leave her be when she took a much needed break to rest her feet. She always imagined she was erecting a bubble around her at those moments. Pop at your own risk.

Princess Anastasia was one of the few people who could join her in the bubble without destroying it, and here she was, pulling up a chair and handing her a fizzy drink.

"Non-alcoholic," she said. "I noticed there weren't many choices of that except water, so I prevailed upon the wait staff without mentioning your name. Who planned this thing? They should have taken your condition into account."

"You make it sound like a disease."

Anastasia looked at her with true fondness. "Oh sweetheart. Being a *woman* is a disease on this accursed planet."

"Thought you should know," Anastasia added. "Dracini is at it again."

"What now?" Layla groaned.

"Still with the congratulations. Walked up to me and asked if I was happy my daughter-in-law finally did her duty. Hinted that he had thought you were celibate. I damn near punched him."

"Wha—ok, how does he even know?"

Anastasia gestured to her. "That dress hides it well, but there are enough outfits with enough showing that eagle-eyed obsessives could generally figure it out. As for the celibacy thing, I think he's been reading those rags out of Altain." She held up her hands. "And none of my business on your personal life. I think it's unconscionable Dracini would even pry. Thank goodness tabloids aren't a thing here. You don't need more of that."

"The Altainan gossip headlines are getting worse," Layla said. "And whenever we announce, trust my family to jump in on *that*. They're the force behind the celibacy crap too."

Altainan infotainment coverage about her had been mostly positive over the years. They had a fascination with royalty, for how much they disdained it in practice. The main exception were the tabloids that had gone digging in Kaborlah. Here they had found her family, who obliged with tales of how she had neglected them and left them in poverty. She was a diva, a social climber, a whore in search of a meal ticket.

Anastasia sat in silence for a moment, then turned back to Layla. "Don't worry about Dracini too much. I mean, yes, he's a corrugated moron, but I don't think there's anything sinister behind his insinuations." True. Probably still upset his 'candidate' lost the throne and therefore any chance of Parliament getting statutory responsibility. Dracini's choice,

Abilio, always did have a heart for shared power.

"He's not the only one," Layla muttered, watching who Dracini was speaking to at the moment: the Earl of Corval, who also wanted more Parliamentary say-so, but less for reform reasons and more to check the Emperor's prerogative to bring in undesirable outside influences and ideas. Like Layla.

"Yeah, I don't like the idea of the two of them talking. If you'll excuse me, love." Anastasia rose and walked toward the men, doing what she did best: disrupt and destroy. With elegance.

Corval had been one of Carlus's closest friends. Although Carlus was reform-minded in some aspects, he and Corval shared an appreciation for mild xenophobia and isolationism.

Had Carlus been in contact with anyone here on Valhar? The list wouldn't—*couldn't*—be long; the real reason for his abdication, for one, was a closely held secret. Almost everyone believed the beloved emperor was pushed out because of an accident of birth. The truth was more explosive, but it would never be shared. Even Layla didn't know the truth until after she was married and had a frank conversation with Carlus himself.

She'd thought she held all the secrets about Carlus. She'd been wrong.

Speaking of Carlus—

She caught the eye of Ronin Park, the Renebian ambassador. He nodded once and inclined his head toward the lakeside doors. Layla stood, slowly, smiled for the benefit of the partygoers, and then ambled her way to the back. She patted her midsection for good measure. If people were going to gossip, she would make use of it. It *was* muggy in that room, and anyone, especially one with child, would need some fresh air.

She stood on the balcony over the frozen lake, the guesthouse in which she had stayed on that fateful state visit just visible in the fog.

"Carousing while Partha sinks."

Layla turned at the voice. Park held out a drink for her. She took a minute sip, politely, and then casually placed it on the rail.

"The war hasn't asked us to sacrifice yet," she said. Despite how it was portrayed in popular entertainment on Altain, the speed of war was slow. Space was big. Close quarters battle proved rare. With everything moving like a snail's pace sync swim presentation, it was easy to forget the Whorl had a lit match under a tinderbox.

The longer this war went on, the less likely lasting peace. Which meant she wasn't safe anymore. She *should* feel safe here, with her husband by her side. But she could never forget.

"Besides," she added, "being here, it's not just frivolity. There's a method behind the madness. Pledging fealty to the Emperor during uncertain times. Bringing news from the colonies. Demonstrating the confidence and might of the Empire. This too, is duty."

Park nodded thoughtfully. "I guess most of those folks have kids in the military as well. Not like you damn Altainans. Ma'am. Or Your Excellency. Whatever."

"Always enjoyed your lack of obsequiousness, Park."

"Only because of Dega. You were so easy going about things. I mean, the Captain-General over there"—he chucked his finger back toward the ballroom—"has always been terrifying, so his becoming Emperor? Let's just say I show him the proper respect."

Layla took a moment to breathe in, reveling in the smoky, crisp smell for fir; yes, apparently crisp had a *smell*, not something they had had on Dega Base, with its spare landscape. The light from the gloaming reflected on little icicles on the trees; Layla imagined them tinkling like little bells.

"I'm amazed you're still here, given the commencement of hostilities," she said at last. "When I dashed off that note to you I expected you'd be returning to Reneb and delivering my message in person."

"Most of the embassy staff has gone home. My government has requested I stay in case I stumble upon diplomatic solutions to this war."

Read: Reneb had always wanted to play both sides of a fight. They weren't usually so obvious about it, but come to think of it, they had had no choice once the Alliance member planets had a majority vote to honor their defense pact with Lyria. What could Reneb have done, other than sit back, hedge their bets, and hope for the best?

"I'm not happy with that, Park," she said. "I had expected privacy, not you opening up the note and reading it to our friend Charles, no matter how secure your communications are." Which they really *were*. Reneb was the leader in real time point-to-point, in a way Valhar couldn't hope to emulate.

"Look, you got a message to him, just like you asked. And he said to tell you: he planned to take a *gander* at it."

Layla rolled her eyes. The Screaming Goose wasn't the most scrupulous mercenary unit operating in the nebula, but at least Carlus had done the job; there was no way she could have reached out to them surreptitiously. Outside Reneb, on the border of the nebula, space proved wild, individualist, lawless. Not a place for an empress, even virtually.

"I know I can't ask you to keep things from your government, but I'm assuming they now know our dilemma with Benedik, just as you do."

Park shrugged unrepentantly.

"I need a way to reach Charles myself," she insisted.

"You can come over to my office anytime—"

"Not good enough."

He grumbled to himself. "Fine." He pulled out an infostick. "One-time encryption stick. Virtually unbreakable. We *can't* listen in. This I swear on our shared service together. We usually use it for emergencies, but if you insist."

She took it and dutifully placed it in her useful dress pocket, not trusting Park one iota.

She had told Park the war hadn't yet asked them to sacrifice. It would, eventually. What sacrifice would be required of her?

Carlus had sacrificed for the sake of peace. Maybe he had gone about it the wrong way, but there was no doubt he took the drastic actions he had for the safety of Valhar. And he eventually lost his birthright, as well as his home. Thankfully not his good name.

Or thinking about it the other way, Carlus lost everything when he violated his oaths. Would she, one day, violate oaths for peace? Would she sacrifice the thing she held sacrosanct above all else?

Approaching the doors, she spotted her husband surrounded by admirers. She had done one job, and now it was time for the other: being on Ignatius's arm, gently directing the conversation and acting as a buffer, allowing him freedom of movement and privacy while keeping him accessible to his subjects. She breathed the air in one more time while gazing at the dancing sky, and reentered the fray.

***

She should probably receive a medal for the number of yawns she had managed to suppress as the night waned. This was getting to be too much: the public appearances, worrying over Benedik, fretting about war.

Ah, yes, poor you. The Empress tires of social engagements.

Of course, at times, the quiet khed game they were playing with the political tensions in the Empire seemed as fraught as a predawn raid on a Mazaran stronghold. This time, no one was going to die in front of her, but when one followed the chain of reason through the universe of possibilities, well...

"I can't believe we invited Finley." Abilio Dargas pinched his face at the thought.

"Hey, you want more Parliamentary power," said Henri.

"For us, not for the merchants!"

Henri snorted, swirled the amber liquid in his glass, and looked over at Layla, silently daring her to weigh in on *that* statement. Layla merely shook her head. Malachi Finley, the minerals trader who headed the pro-representation Volg Coalition, was a strategic choice, an invitation designed to mollify: *look, we bring you to the unofficial halls of power; witness, we smile as we risk war just to open resources for your ilk.*

"They were perfectly happy," Abilio said, "when they were fat and rich off the nobility."

"Even potatoes grow eyes when they are let out into the light," said Henri, amiably.

Abilio glanced at Layla now, brow creased. "Any news?" he asked, hopeful tremor barely detectable in his controlled manner.

"Nothing yet," she replied.

Henri put his arm around him and Abilio grasped his hand gratefully.

The snide tones of Viceroy Stanlo carried toward the trio, bidding all three to grimace simultaneously into their drinks. The viceroys always seemed outside the Valhar noble ecosystem, little monarchs of their own that in *theory* were loyal to the Falcon Throne but conveniently forgot the home planet existed when they were ensconced in their own court. Layla much preferred the administrators and governors of the territory planets, which served like extensions of the homeworld, and found them more humble, loyal, and competent. Some of the viceroys were perfectly fine, but others were sad little kings of their sad little planets. Stanlo, however, was a sad little king of a now very important planet: Solita.

Ignatius, for how much he played up his fearsome and stern reputation, was actually quite the politician and charmer when he needed to be, and now he was tolerating Stanlo's monopolization of his attention; Stanlo, for his part, was being downright obsequious, which was unusual given his outsized ego. Arrogant arse. He had much to be thankful for, of course: a new area of trade opening up right outside his system's heliopause, the lure of import and export taxes flowing into Solita, the boon from the numerous scientists and engineers that were crowding around making the first manmade subspace tunnel the Whorl had seen in *centuries*.

"Your Excellency," he was now wheedling, "those rebels—they are nothing, my liege, not right now. Mere gnats. But we all know how small problems can become large faster than one expects. If they have their way, they would *collapse* the tunnel. I simply need more resources."

Hmm. Layla always thought the push for the Solita revolutionary militia was the *success* of the tunnel and the ensuing desire to benefit more fully from it.

Her husband placated Stanlo and dismissed him with a few well-placed words and hands. So much mollification, now that real war had come to Valhar. So much obfuscation, so no one would notice a missing young viscount. So much posturing, so the vultures wouldn't attack.

Oh, the intrigue. The jockeying for position. The arrogance. All while above them, the Whorl battled for its future.

What could she do that she hadn't done all along? An advisor, a reformer, an information-gatherer: all of it seemed so useless. So trite. Performative.

Maybe to help end this war, maybe to protect the entire Whorl, she should make more waves. Loud. Obnoxious. Like a Kaborlah summer squall. Like an Altainan craygull. Maybe she should be willing to sacrifice, despite the fear of losing this home, too, a thought that clogged her throat and made her palms sweat.

Ignatius turned to his family, who were unconsciously drifting near each other, as if a secret signal had gone off: assemble. Ephraim read the mood and nodded to Ignatius's personal security. They took up formation as Ignatius gestured expansively to the group, signaling his retinue was about to depart.

She joined along silently, not able to shake the feeling of foreboding as they all engaged in a pantomime of normality.

She cursed this war. She cursed politics. She was good at it and she knew the territory, especially compared to feeling lost and unsure when she first arrived here in Novaria. But what would she say now, looking back, to that star-eyed woman who thought she could shed her old life like a skin? Who believed love and family and warmth would sidestep ghosts of old wars, old wounds? Pretty words and succulent thoughts were so useless. So trite. Naive. Sometimes she wanted to take that stupid journal of hers and toss it into the frozen lake, letting all the sweet poetry float belly-up in the water like stinking dead fish representing war and lost family and petty dynastic disputes.

Then

Layla's Memoirs

Then

It's still winter in Novaria, a capital city nestled in a cozy crook curling around the northeast corner of the northwest continent on Valhar, and it will be for a few more months yet. It's night when the personal transport approaches the Imperial Palace, looming high in the mountains of Novaria, emerging from the clouds. The palace has a small footprint but goes up and up, the tallest spire emanating a cyan glow at night that reaches into the heavens, complementing the aurora borealis twisting and snarling in the sky.

And then we're on the ground. I'm hustled through the windy maze of the palace. As I enter Ignatius's apartments, I look around at the furnishing and decor. How much of this is his? Probably few; maybe he has more at his family holdings out in Corval, where his parents still live. Well, regardless, my meager possessions and I: we will hardly make a dent on the household. Just *blip*, like a dark spot disappearing into the sun.

And what a peculiarly upper middle class dream: being able to pick where one lives and make it a reflection of oneself. I couldn't do that, growing up poor, and then in the military. The closest I've ever gotten was my apartment in Cygna, on Altain. And perhaps Ignatius, on the other end of the spectrum, can't do it either.

I imagine running through the residence, satchel over one shoulder, valise in the other hand, flinging them both aside as I simultaneously thrust apart the double doors guarding a cozy room and launch myself into Ignatius's arms, saying, I'm home, I'm *home!*

But, of course, my luggage has been seen to, and I am led serenely to Ignatius's private study and shown in with a discreet duck-in-and-withdraw. And I expect we will bow and curtsey and *oh my stars is this my life*, but he surprises me by rushing toward me and swinging me in the air.

"You *came*," he says in that delicious baritone. "You're actually here."

My new life begins almost immediately, and belatedly I understand the wonderment in my fiancé's voice. Who would want *this*? This endless parade of appointments and fittings and pictures and lessons and scrutiny?

And of course, most of these are things I do *alone*, not with Ignatius. At least *this* particular appointment—our engagement portrait, far out back on the palace's winding winter garden path—requires both our presences.

Although honestly, until Ignatius shows up, I won't put it past Ephraim to commission some sort of holo-stand-in for him so it wouldn't crowd out more important things on his precious calendar.

Now that I'm here, I can stop *thinking* about him all the time. Stop with the girlish obsession.

Starting now.

Right now.

Get it together, Kamil, you're marrying the man; you don't have to preciously hoard every minute with him.

Eventually, the second presence—His Imperial Presence, to be formal about it—shows up. I *feel* him before he appears. Always, even in the beginning of our acquaintance, I could pick him out by his voice or his stride or his posture.

Now, I can pick him out by the way the air sizzles.

"Sorry I'm late," he whispers, planting a peck on my ear. "We had a bit of a beetle-related issue."

I resist the urge to turn my body to him in shock, and instead slowly incline my head. "A what?"

"I'll explain later." Ignatius flashes me a grin.

The photographer directs us into more and more contorted positions, evoking a feel of two adolescents awkwardly posing for a formal.

"Relax," he mouths. I shiver against him; it's hard to relax when I'm freezing. I lovingly look at my coat, being held by an attendant.

Ephraim stands off to the side, a nervous eye on the time, foot-tapping and pent-up energy in one pint-size package. His wife Mariah has been assigned as my personal guard and so she's here as well. They're a study of contrasts: Ephraim's earnest loyalty; Mariah's stock-still, glitter-eyed, dangerous calm.

"Sire," Ephraim finally says, "we need to wrap it up." He accompanies this statement by a finger spiral motion directed toward the photographer.

The photographer nods, suddenly nervous, and straightens. "Well, um, Your Excellency, Dame Layla, maybe we have time for one candid? Something to show this is a love match, instead of arranged." She winces, like she's spoken out of turn. Ephraim certainly thinks so, with that scowl suddenly blooming on his face.

Ignatius placates both of them with a small smile. "Excellent idea," he booms, his voice resonating through the snow-capped trees. Without warning I'm scooped up and dipped. I'm shrieking as he plants a kiss.

An audible *woosh* as the holocam engages. Then he lovingly straightens me and I put his face in between my hands—my favorite move, apparently—and we gaze at each other.

Ephraim coughs discreetly and we whirl apart, here to play our roles again.

"I should be done early enough tonight to dine with you," Ignatius says, as we walk back to the palace. "*Right*, Ephraim?"

"It's all up to you, sire. If you can stop yourself from enraging the Merchants' Council, maybe we'll actually end on time."

"Ingrate," Ignatius mutters. "You'll see," Ignatius adds to me. "You think you're being herded about now, wait until the announcement hits and Beatrix starts setting up teas with the ladies of Novaria."

I've privately taken to calling Beatrix, the palace's secretary, our "cruise director," but this is too much. "Tea? Can't we just guzzle pints of beer?"

"My entire Empire to see you ask Beatrix that."

I resist the urge to stick my tongue out at the ruler of over fifteen systems; instead I look over at the vision of feminine statuesque warrior perfection guarding me and choose to pivot. Surely Mariah can provide an antidote to the absurd gynoterrorism I'm about to be subjected to.

"So, hey," I begin, "I know you've served some exciting roles in the military. Anything you can tell me about? Soldier-to-soldier?"

Mariah keeps scanning the area around us, as if an assailant is going to pop out of nowhere in the most secure backyard in the Valharan Empire. "I was Emperor Gustav's personal assassin," she says, coolly.

Um.

Ignatius's lips twist in amusement and Ephraim's heart-shaped face is a study in neutrality. I glance back and forth in quick succession to determine whether she's telling the truth. Ignatius finally catches my eye and gives me a swift micron nod.

"Right," I say breathlessly. We reach the doors and the two men peel off.

Damnit, I forgot to ask about the beetles.

One of the consequences of winter on Valhar is an early sunset; I'm already feeling the emotional draw-down from shorter days and longer nights. I've spent most of my evenings this past week in my well-appointed guest room within the Residence, researching all the intricacies of Valharan history and culture I'll need to know to succeed here, plus the reams of etiquette information the cruise director has forwarded to me. I see Ignatius every evening, but often it's an invitation for a late nightcap in the living spaces of his rooms, and even when I stay over, he's gone by early light.

Inside the Residence, the barrier between Ignatius's rooms and his personal guest space is a mere formality, and I often pad my way over to his space in slippers and nightwear, ready to share stories of our day beside the fire. For her part, Mariah and the côterie of Imperial guards generally stay out of our intimate spaces, which helps make their presence more tolerable.

We've hardly been in this routine long, yet it's still a surprise when Ignatius softly raps on the threshold of his library, where I'm lounging and catching up on galactic news feeds.

"You can't possibly be done for the day," I say.

"I wasn't going to be finished by dinner. Decided to have an early repast with you and head back for the night."

I look ruefully at my lounge pants but Ignatius shakes his head. "No one will be there. Not even the guards." I cock my eyebrow at him but he smiles enigmatically.

"Time for adventure," he whispers. He leads me out of the library, down two halls to a spare closet.

And then he yelps in surprise, a sound so un-Ignatius-like that I'm dumbed into silence a moment and then moved to yelp as well, because if something can make Ignatius Kurestin cry out in surprise, it must be—

—a beetle.

A big, fat-ass beetle.

I take my finger off the emergency beacon—inset on my Goddess medallion locket—just in time.

"Ahem," Ignatius says and rummages around the closet's extraneous supplies until he produces a flimsy and a cup-like object.

"Surprised with that reaction you weren't just gonna stomp it."

He shakes his head ruefully. "Don't want to give them more reason for revenge."

"Re-revenge?"

"The beetle emergency," he explains. "We have a wee infestation. I'm quite taken with the idea it's because I murdered one of its kin in the gardens to impress you."

"You," I say, "are ridiculous."

"It's *looking* at me."

"Oh great meaty warrior, *save* me from the fucking *beetle*."

"Surely you mean mighty."

"You heard me."

"Right then." He straightens, and pointedly ignores me when I start laughing. "On to the show."

He produces a portable cooler with a flourish. Gathering it and the trapped beetle, he moves aside a few coats and sundries. He then leads me into a bolt-hole Mariah already indicated to me during my orientation.

"A dank musty corridor? Oh Ignatius, how ever did you know?"

"Hush, you."

"Hold this for a sec," he continues, handing me his bug contraption, and I look at the beetle through the clear cup and give it *I'm watching you* eyes. Ignatius grabs a tool out of his pocket and pries apart a panel in the small room, exposing daylight. On the other side is a small outcropping, just large enough for two to sit and stretch comfortably and safely. A simple handmade fence surrounds the ledge, which is good, because it saves me from acrophobia.

As I watch, he gently releases the bug with a flick and directs it to climb on the exterior wall. "How do you know about all this?"

"I used to play here as a child. Grandson of the emperor and all that."

"...and have you told your Imperial Guard about all this?"

"It doesn't compromise security. Only a member of the family can get in here. I want my kids to discover it one day."

"Mmm," I say non-committedly, both about the fact he didn't answer my question and, of course, *kids*. The kids. Those kids. Which we will be having. Probably soon, since an emperor needs an heir and—

—the momentary vertigo likely has nothing to do with heights, but I recover quickly.

"Benedik hated our little unspoken rule that we would only show family this. He wanted to bring girls up here to schtup."

"Schtup?" I giggle.

"His words." He digs through the cooler. "About that repast..." He pulls out some crackers and holds up two bottled beers. "Figures it counteracts the endless tea dates you're about to experience."

I shake my head at him but reach to take one. "How did the meeting with the merchants go?"

"Well, I didn't enrage them."

"That's good."

"But they enraged me. The entire reason for the meeting was a ruse to argue once again they need spots on the Lords' Parliament. Not a dedicated, quota spot either, mind you. They want anyone with a certain amount of influence and net worth to receive the same benefits as a noble and to be granted full voting rights."

"Oof. That's not gonna work."

"No, not like this." He grunts and leans back. "Not by shoving entitled grubbers at the nobility and just making *more* nobility. That's what they want. And as long as they have influence and power and *money*, they are fine with the state of things in the Empire. It's the money that is the sticking point right now."

I bite my lip as I contemplate the political atmosphere. Between the tariffs, and the taxes, and the regulatory restrictions, and the eminent domain, and *now* threatened sanctions from the Alliance, there's no way for the businessmen to recoup their losses. The system used to work for them, so they didn't make waves; now suddenly they're losing money and they understand what real disenfranchisement feels like. Revolutions have started for less. Empires have *toppled* for less.

Valhar is going to be in trouble unless it makes a change. But where to begin?

Step one: survey the land. "Do you think, maybe, over time, you can open things up for everyone, not just the influential merchants? I gather they won't be happy about that, but I bet you'd enjoy the irony."

"You mean, expose their hypocrisy?" Ignatius snorts. "Yes. I like that. One day I'll do that. Unfortunately, I'm not quite in the position to pull that off yet."

Maybe I can make that *one day* my life's work. "What are the issues?"

"Very basic. We can't rush things. Too much change at once is dangerous. Stability is important, or people die. And take care, Layla," he adds. "The merchants aren't lambs. They are wolves, with teeth. I know something is stirring in that head of yours."

We sit in silence for a spell. I contemplate the idea of *stability*, and how it *is* the most important in all things, but how it can also cover for all manner of ills. "Did you want to be Emperor?" I ask, finally.

"Oh. Great Claws. No. This was never supposed to happen. Carlus had—*has*," he amends, "three kids. They should have been next in the line of succession, but when he left, they went too. If I see him again, I might just punch him."

"You're still not going to tell me what happened there are you?"

"He was illegitimate. A bastard."

Why don't I believe that's it?

He looks at me and dips his head in salute, as if he knows what I'm thinking. "Regardless, the throne was never a heartbeat away. Maybe there were moments, before Carlus had kids, that I would have conceivably been next in line, but I was pretty young and stupid, so in that case I really do think they would have gone with my mother first. She's sorry she won't actually be able to meet you before the announcement after all," he adds. "I waited too long to schedule an appointment and she's full up."

"You have to make an appointment to see your own mother?"

"You'll understand when you meet her. Whirlwind of energy. Brilliant, at that. She collects people; I rather imagine she'll be collecting you."

"Why the hell wasn't *she* named Empress-Ruler?"

He takes a swig. "Too radical."

"What: having a woman on the throne when there's a perfectly good male available, or that she herself is radical?"

He considers. "Yes."

"You'll love her," he assures me.

He holds me, his arm curled around in a swan-hug, as we watch the sun set on the jewel of the Valharan Empire.

Then

"Just to warn you," Ignatius says in the transport, as we make our way to his mother in Corval, "my mother and the cruise director will be working together to put on an extravagant wedding. I know that's probably not what you want."

I've been expecting this. "I prefer something small and intimate, but I know I won't get that. If that's the custom required, I'll submit for the cause."

Ignatius lets out an undignified snort. "Rather likely the only time in your life you'll submit to anything."

I'm not sure if I can swat the Person of the Emperor in front of his driver so I demur. "How does it all get paid for? Taxpayers?"

"We do have some state funds, but most of the extravagant expenditures will come from my mother's purse."

"Must be nice."

He glances at me but refrains from commenting. I know he has an ungodly amount of riches, but to me, money is something to hold onto. Store away. A little coin is the difference between getting regular meals and having to steal from the food stores destined for Altain Prime. And to someone raised like me, meeting people with money elicits a vast churn of conflicting emotions: anger, envy, scorn, desire.

By habit and out of a need to deflect, I make to grab my handheld tablet, but of course it's not there. Beatrix and Ephraim effectively wrested it from me, as now the announcement is live I'm getting personal messages coming out of my ears. Makes sense. Let them handle it, and they can forward the important ones on to me. Already I feel a disconnect from that old life. I think of Mena, and how gobsmacked she must be right now, and she appears as an afterimage in my memory.

"Welcome back, Lord Ignatius," the manor's house guard—a sergeant by his tabs—says as he bows low. As has been explained to me, he calls Ignatius by his lesser title to befit the casual nature of this visit.

The guard looks familiar. The credit drops suddenly. I look to Ignatius and receive confirmation. This is Ephraim's father.

I look around in interest as we climb the stairs. If things had been normal, this is where I would be living. If I had accepted Nate's offer all those years ago before we left Dega. If the previous emperor hadn't abdicated and taken his whole family with him. Lady Layla, of Kurestin Manor.

It's a rather simple house, all told. My Altainan sensibilities approve as my eyes slide over the tasteful, modest furnishings. Not as ridiculously austere as Roya's People's House, but classic and bold without being ostentatious. Wealth without excess. Although the house passed through Ignatius's father's family, it is out of the bounds of the former Tyrii barony. Regardless, it exists not only in the Corval earldom but also in the duchy that includes Novaria: Aquil, Princess Anastasia's duchy, actually. Because in addition to being a princess—the daughter of a late Emperor—and a baroness by marriage, she's styled Duchess Aquil.

These people collect titles the way Kaborlah collects mud.

"It's a smaller house than I expected," I say, hoping he won't take offense.

He stops, turns, and smiles at me. "The Kurestin family, for generations, has been the forefront of distributing our wealth to our vassals as well as other charity efforts. Though Mother *has* expanded our residence for more room to entertain."

The butler announces us as we enter the upstairs drawing room. Ignatius takes my hand, squeezing it tight. I look at him gratefully a moment before he leads me forward.

"Mother," he says formally, "I'd like to introduce Dame Layla Kamil, Commander in the Altainan Republic F—"

He doesn't get to finish the introduction before his mother, wild curls and all, leaps toward me, squealing and enveloping me in a large hug. "Finally!" she says, squeezing me. "I've been wanting to meet you for *so long*."

"—and did I mention my mother is a hugger?" Ignatius finishes weakly.

"No," I squeak, and she finally releases me.

"Sit, sit!" she exclaims. "We have cha, Layla. I hope I wasn't presumptuous."

I shoot her a genuine smile of thanks.

She beams. "Good. Now. You sit here, you, Ignatius, sit *here*. So," she says briskly, grabbing the tea pot and pouring, "your announcement picture. It was perfect."

"Thank you, Your Highness."

She shushes me. "The name is Anastasia."

"Dad calls her Stacey," Ignatius cuts in.

"*That* I won't answer to," she replies with a glare.

Tonin Kurestin, the esteemed baron, isn't on Valhar. Some sort of stubborn adherence to propriety, because heavens forbid a low noble have undue influence on the Emperor.

Anastasia fills the silence accompanying the mention of Tonin with what seems like customary cheer. "That picture! Do you know how many calls I've received today that mention *the picture?*"

"Erm, good or bad?" Ignatius asks.

"Good in all the best ways, dear heart."

"That means that the people she likes love it and the people she thinks are idiots had something cutting to say about it," Ignatius says to me in a stage whisper.

My face is warm. Thank the Goddess for dark skin.

Ignatius stands to pour his mother's tea. Another Valharan tradition I only recently learned. During meals centered on drinks, like a tea, the host, no matter how high the rank, pours. Then a guest pours for the host.

"I'm surprised the cruise—err, Beatrix, allowed us to pick that one," I say, when everyone is served and Anastasia has taken her first sip.

In that last moment—when he and I were looking at each other, smoldering, his face in my hands—unbeknownst to us, the photographer clicked. And included it in our options. And Nate and I, we looked at it, and we knew.

"Beatrix is shrewder than you think." Anastasia chuckles. "Bucking convention from time to time, especially on small matters like this, has a net positive in the long run."

"Mother wants to wish away Valharan society."

"I'm a reformer dear. As are you."

"The Emperor has no political opinions."

Both Anastasia and I roll our eyes at this. Then we look at each other, delighted.

"Could you two not," he says, "be a combined bad influence on my future children?"

"Kids? Bah. There's time enough for that. Get to relearn each other first."

"Mother, I have no obvious heirs. If something happens to me—"

"If something happens to you, there will be an election. Maybe then Cousin Abilio would get elected, or Benedik. We're not a violent society—no matter what the rest of the Whorl seems to think." She directs this last to me. "We reformed past that centuries and centuries ago. There's not going to be some mad Duke from out of nowhere raising arms, claiming the throne. The Parliament will nominate some choices, vote, and that's that. You have enough on your shoulders. Don't put that on them too."

"You have a rosier view of our stability than I do," Ignatius says.

I glance at him, concerned. He waves it away.

"In any case," she says, "you're *my* child, and it's time for you to run along." She makes shooing motions.

He rises with a rueful smile. "I do have some manor duties to discuss with Sergeant Raderfy, on Father's behalf." He gives his mother a kiss on the cheek and me a peck on the lips and leaves.

Anastasia settles into her chair with a wiggle. "Did Ignatius ever tell you I was part of the Narconian Military Exchange?"

"It's where you met Baron Tyrii. Right in the middle of the Narconian uprising, I hear."

She stands again and offers more tea. I'm unsure which is more polite: accept or decline? Offer to pour myself, or do the hostess rules still apply?

She smirks at me. "Just be yourself, Layla. Do you want some tea or not?"

I indicate I do, and she pours.

"You've got to stop this," she says, as she pours herself a cup as well, waving me down as I rise to fulfill the guest obligation. "The whole *being in awe of him* thing."

She puts her palm up at my look. "Oh, I know it's not the whole emperor thing. If you were the type of girl that started squealing about the fact that she was marrying into royalty, you'd hardly be the right girl for Ignatius. He needs normalcy in his life, and that's you, my dear, but still. You're looking up to him. Like for all the world he's wiser or more capable. You're not treating him like he's your equal."

I think fast in the sudden silence. She seems to expect a response. "I'm just in love," I say.

"And you two have been in love for years. Didn't you treat him like an equal back then? On Dega? And on Felix? That's what he loves about you. If you don't claim your power in this relationship, Layla, you'll be doing him a disservice. Sure, moon over him a little. But after a while this place will eat you up. You have to get control of this place. And of the situation."

"But it's just new," I protest.

"You're a Republic commander, aren't you? I might not have had the opportunity to command, but I know a little about being a soldier. Did you walk up to your troops on your first command with chattering teeth and bitten fingernails? I will bet you projected confidence no matter how you really felt. This is no different. You need to march right back into the Imperial Palace and make it your bitch."

She laughs at my shocked look. "Didn't expect a bona fide princess to start swearing, did you? Well, I only do it with family." She pats my knee. "And you're family now."

Returning in late afternoon, I get Mariah back from whatever Mariah does when her services aren't needed.

"Do you and Ephraim get any time off together?" I ask as she shadows me through the public areas of the palace.

"Sometimes. We live to serve, my lady."

How she manages to pack a masterful razor's-edge FU in such an innocuous statement, I don't know, and I'm also not sure what brings it on.

I search for something else to say. "I know there are Valharan women in the military. Princess Anastasia said she did a few years, but they all seem like generally safer non-combat positions. How'd you buck the trend and find an operational position?"

"Look," Mariah says, with a polite edge, "when I'm working, I'm working. Maybe we can try being friends or whatever you want to do sometime when I'm not your bodyguard."

"I'm sorry." My smile is sheepish. "I'm trying to connect with someone without it being all about Ignatius."

"You want to be independent, strong, and fierce, and you see me as an aspirational goal?" she asks, giving me a quick glance.

I nod.

"And you don't want to be treated like the future Empress."

I nod again.

"Then," she says, "you shouldn't have gotten betrothed to the Emperor."

She leaves me to the safety of the private wing and I gape for a moment in appreciation of her unassailable logic.

Ignatius planned this quiet dinner with his cousin—second cousin to be exact—and his lady friend Alina to give me some more time with his relatives in a calm environment. Maybe this is how I'll find my place here. I've met Benedik before, but I don't feel I know him.

I wait with Mariah in the anteroom as Ephraim ushers in Benedik and Alina and gets them settled. I turn, and here comes Ignatius and his quick measured strides, never looking like he's rushing, always in control. I look down at my timepiece pointedly. Ignatius isn't *late*, of course. Ignatius is almost never late. But he's perfected this *just-in-time* dance with all our joint social obligations.

He gives me only a wan smile in response to my theatrics and I look him over, concerned.

"Later," Ignatius promises quietly. He reaches over and lifts my hand to kiss it. "My lady."

"Shall we?" I ask in response.

All three in the room are still standing as we enter, and when we both fully cross the threshold, Benedik comes forward and bends on one knee. "My liege," he greets. "Thank you for honoring me with an invitation."

"Rise, my servant," Ignatius says. "And thanks for coming, Benedik," he adds in a lighter casual tone.

Benedik grins boyishly and turns to the beautiful dark-haired woman at his side. "Sire, may I present again Lady Alina."

Alina curtseys, also murmuring thanks to His Excellency for the invitation, and Ignatius claps his hands as Ephraim makes to leave.

"Ephraim. Hold one second. We're dining deep in the Residence. You and Mariah join us?"

It sure sounds like an order, not a request, so on they join. I glance at the two guests to gauge their response, and Benedik's smiling broadly, so I suppose this alteration's all right with them.

"Just one more thing," Ignatius says, as we wind our way through his apartments. "I was visiting my Duchess mother today as mere *Lord* Ignatius. It was a welcome change. And Alina and Layla are new enough—well, let's just drop the pretensions for tonight, shall we?"

Benedik stops short and glares. "Wait, you decided that *after* I sank down onto one knee in fealty?"

Ignatius clasps his shoulder. "Just payback for all those times you made me do the same when playing emperors and knights as kids."

I've seen how Ignatius sheds his layers every night when he comes home, but now I carefully watch how it's done with his social set. There's still some sort of quiet watchfulness among all of them, like everything about the sudden parity is just a polite fiction and in reality he's still lord ascendant.

"Hi, I'm Layla," I whisper to the leggy woman on my right as we walk, sticking out my hand. She'll be nice, won't she? Hopefully? I'm so awkward and new and she's this gorgeous, self-contained—

"Er," Alina, Benedik's prospective bride, says, staring at the proffered limb as though she doesn't know whether to shake it or kiss it, "Your Majesty. Or Grace. Which do you prefer?"

Oh thank the Goddess, she's as much of a mess as I am. "Layla," I say firmly. "I'm not even married yet, for the Goddess's sake. Can I call you Alina? Or do you prefer Lady—"

"Alina, of course," she says, finally taking my hand and giving a business-like shake. Firm grip. Nice contrast with her jitteriness. I certainly can relate to feeling out of depth.

"Nice to meet you. You said you've met Ignatius before?"

"Igna-? Oh, the Emperor!" Alina colors. "Yes, Benedik formally presented me at the Trooping Revue a few months ago. I—sorry. This is all very new to me."

"Yeah, I hear ya," I say, pure Altain drawl. "Didya know—" and here, I bend my head toward Alina's, the effect slightly ruined by how *tall* Alina is compared to me, "the *Emperor* once gave me a belly-dancing doll from Narconia as a birthday gift, and it became a years-long game of who could sneak it back into each other's possession." Alina gapes, then giggles. Mariah looks back at the disruption and though her expression is stern at first, it softens.

Then

The dinner has devolved into some sort of reunion-*cum*-skills competition, and Alina and I are left flabbergasted, while Mariah does her scary Mariah thing, perched on a stool in the corner with eyebrows raised, filing her nails.

"Ignatius, my cuz," Benedik says, weaving, "you're pissed off your Imperial Arse."

"Our Imperial Arse is perky, taut, and decidedly keen to whip yours, cousin."

"Neither one of you lordly sirs is in a shape to win this particular feat of wizardry," Ephraim interjects, cooly sipping water as he watches Ignatius aim his coin at a distant glass. "I pledge fealty to you for the rest of our natural lives, my liege, but you're going down. You couldn't even pull this off sober."

"We're not *that* hard up," Ignatius protests, still aiming and re-aiming the coin. "Reports of Our drunkenness are highly exaggerated." He finally lines up the shot, launches, and misses. "Ergh!" he opines, flopping back down to the settee. Benedik crows.

After Benedik successfully makes *his* shot, he saunters over to Alina like a knight banneret, presenting her with a beer stein as a chivalric token.

"Oh yes," Alina says. "Well done my warrior. Come back from the battlefront drinking your ale or drowned in it."

At Benedik's wounded look, I turn my face away, hiding my snort with a delicate sneeze.

Benedik glares. "Cuz, she's corrupting my lady love," he calls, glancing backward.

"Me?" I ask in outrage. Ignatius waves us off with both hands, as if to wash himself of it. Ephraim merely sighs, and surveys the room with a pinched nose.

Then Benedik screeches as he lifts his bare foot. "What in the seven hells was that?!?"

Ignatius lifts his drink in salute. "You squished a footsoldier of our beetle enemy, my cousin. Welcome to the war."

Ephraim snorts. "Better than eating them, sire."

I boggle. "Excuse me, what?"

"Oh yes." Benedik clasps his hands together with relish. "Ignatius was lost in the Corval Mountains you see. Backwards place, really. Land of 10,000 mountain goats, not like my ancestral home by the sea..."

"The point, Benedik," admonishes Ephraim. Then he shakes his head in defeat. "Ah, never mind."

Just a week-and-change here on Valhar, and I'm learning Nate's family and friends, decimated as it may have been over the years and tragedies. As kids, as expected, Ephraim was scholarly, quiet, and pragmatic. Ignatius? He was brooding, intense, and passionate. Benedik used to be the ringleader of their triumvirate, even though he was the youngest, the runt, the squirt. Yes, Benedik: chaos personified, good-hearted, and full of backfiring schemes. Slowly it changed. Now Ignatius is the gravitational force and they are his satellites.

Benedik glares at the interruption and continues. "Sulked away after failing to impress some girl. His temper got away from him. Took us the better part of a day to find him. He was none the worse for wear except for an epic stomachache from the countless beetles he ate since he was *starving*, a growing boy after all. Anyway, he was a hormonal mess back then, Layla. *I* was the level headed planner, and I was only, what ... twelve at the time? Sometimes I can't believe *this guy* is—er ... anyway, it's amazing how we all ended up." Benedik fizzles out his sentence and takes a nervous swallow of his drink. Alina grips Benedik's arm.

Ignatius raises his eyebrows, part irony, part amusement, part mild rebuke. Suddenly, I'm sick to my own stomach. *Can't believe this guy is Emperor* is what Benedik was about to say. Insulting the Emperor's fitness to rule. *Sedition. Treason.* Not just buzzwords, here in the grand Empire.

Awkward chitchat, smiles of forgiveness, clasps on the back. Mariah even descends from her perch and loops her arm around Ephraim's, placing head on shoulder and smiling serenely as he pecks the top of her head.

And then a runner brings a whispered message to Ignatius, and the color draining from his face makes everything shatter.

The other men stand, noting the watershed. "Sire," says Ephraim. Simultaneously from Benedik: "My liege."

Ignatius shakes out his hand once, twice, then clears his throat as his eyes turn glitter. Was he ever even drunk?

"Lyria," he says, "has severed diplomatic relations."

With that, some bustle and arrangements made, belongings retrieved, spent drinks hastily arranged on a waiting tray.

"You don't seem surprised," I say, as the others take their leave. Benedik and Alina shuffle out, Ephraim straightens his collar and waits right outside the door. Mariah takes her sweet time walking toward the threshold.

"We've been getting rumbles," Ignatius answers. "I'll probably be back late, love. You don't have to wait up for me."

"Can I come?"

He hesitates.

Mariah overhears. "Sire..." A note of warning is in her voice.

"You might be able to provide some insight," Ignatius says to me. He nods to himself in affirmation.

Mariah puts herself in Ignatius's path, respectfully and at a distance, of course. "Excellency, if we may talk about this—"

"Mariah," Ignatius says, exasperation overlaying steel, "Lady Layla has more than earned her place at the table. She has insight into contemporary Whorl politics few others do. Gustav and Carlus trusted her. I'd see you do the same."

That's probably a stretch, especially the Gustav angle, but invoking his name appears to have a conciliatory effect on Mariah. *I was Gustav's personal assassin*, is what she had said the other day. I suppress a twitch. Mariah mumbles a "yes, sire" and sweeps by.

Ignatius's hand finally connects with mine, and he lightly squeezes it before letting go, indicating the door. "Ephraim, by now, has surely garnered enough details to brief us as we walk, dear. Shall we?"

"Lyria has completely pulled out," Ephraim says as we approach. "Lyrian officials leaving now in the cover of night. I expect we're not to stop them?" At Ignatius's curt nod, he continues. "The generals expect any day now Lyria will begin attacks—short of declaring a formal war, of course. We've already planned defensive counters and will be happy to brief you when you arrive in the war room." He peers curiously at me, but doesn't ask. "Altain," he continues, giving me another glance, "is rejecting non-official travel to Valhar, but I expect they'll keep up a diplomatic presence. Reneb, of course, is choosing not to get involved—spineless cowards," he adds as an aside, "—as are some of the smaller worlds."

Ignatius stops short. "Planning defenses and counter-attacks. My lady, I'm sorry to retract my offer, but—"

"Can't invade the boys club, got it." At Ignatius's chagrined look, I amend. "I was joking, Ignatius. I understand. You thought we'd just be talking strategy and politics. I'm not going to interrupt operational level planning. Not my forte, in any case."

Ignatius squeezes my hand one last time as Ephraim leads him away. And I'm left with a scowling Mariah, who leads me back to the residential wing.

It is, indeed, late before Ignatius returns, but I'm still awake in the library, trying valiantly to break Valharan firewalls and get some information on what is going *on*, damnit. I turn my irritation on him, shrouded in the doorway, with nary a hello.

"Lyrians found incontrovertible proof of the tunnel, huh," I say by way of greeting.

Ignatius sighs. "Yes. Have I spoken to you about the tunnel yet? You should be fully briefed."

"Funny that, Nate. No. I think we've both been avoiding the topic. *I* certainly didn't want to ask if it was true your empire was violating a Whorl-wide treaty."

"Ah, yes," he says, clearing his throat. "I imagine you have questions." At my crossed arms he continues, traversing the room to sit next to me. "We were working on it way back in the reign of Empress Hadria. Decades *before* the treaty, obviously. Before the Mazarans, before Carlus, everything."

"Building or researching?"

"Researching, while sending a generation ship to the proposed terminus. But that research started escalating to construction before Carlus abdicated. Because right about then, our scouts on the other side would have hopefully reached their destination and begun building their end. This isn't some new whim of mine. It's been steady constant progress since then. I just have elected not to halt it."

"What's so important as to risk war?"

"Economic stability, Layla," he says. "Our subjects are happy. We provide: stability, tradition, creature comfort. Yes, there have been rumbles about political modernization here or there but as a whole, when people are confronted with a buffet of options of where to live, what to do, how to consume entertainment and food, they stop worrying so much about governance. But now we're facing recession, Layls. A big one. Economic downturn." Ah. The merchants. It all makes sense now.

"The fact is," he continues, "we need to open up some economic opportunity and exploring new parts of the galaxy is the way to do it, and so we're moving forward, treaty or not. *Misguided* treaty or not, but that's a discussion for another day."

There's *a lot* to discuss for another day. But I bide my time, and my tongue. "Didn't you ever think this was going to be a massive conflict of interest for me?" I ask instead.

"Why do you think I walked by you that first day? I didn't want you to have to choose."

"Well," I say, scoffing, "that ship has sailed, hasn't it. What would you think was going to happen when the Alliance found out?"

"They were never meant to. This was a highly secret project. They've got specs. Planning documents. Private discussions." He slams one fist into an open hand, and repeats the action with the other hand. "We have some sort of mole in the government," he declares, then hesitates. "I'm sorry to put you in this position, dear, but do you know if Altain has any eyes and ears inside the palace?"

I think back to only a couple weeks before, debating Ransom on my future utility within the palace. Utility to Ignatius *and* to Ransom. It was, it seems, so long ago.

To avoid the topic of Altainan ears, I pivot. Because he's right about a mole, if not an Altainan one. "I can confirm the *Lyrians* have a well-placed person giving them intelligence."

Ignatius gives a start, obviously not having expected any answer from me. He frowns too, as if he knows I'm deflecting "The Lyrians. But who?"

I shake my head. I don't know the players in the aristocracy well, except one

"Ignatius, do you think it could be Carlus? Providing intel to the Lyrians?"

Ignatius almost pushes himself away in shock. "Carlus wouldn't do that," he says firmly.

I shrug. "I don't mean to disparage a former emperor. I *like* the guy. I'm just thinking of people who would have access to this sort of information and who are no longer part of the Valharan ecosystem."

Ignatius has a look that can only be described as *queasy*. "Former Emperor Carlus is a patriot," he says weakly. "He didn't even want to sign the Mazaran deal because he thought it advantaged them too much. Remember..."

Oh yes. I remember. The first and only time I met Carlus, then-crown prince. During the same negotiations, I, along with Park and Ignatius, had inadvertently found out Emperor Gustav had fallen seriously ill. We knew that any news of Emperor Gustav's incapacitation would blow up the Mazaran talks, and possibly, too, break the cooperation between the Empire and the Alliance. So Carlus and Nate vowed to keep it a secret. And somehow convinced the two non-Valharans, myself and Park, to stay quiet too.

Happenings that later reverberated throughout my life, including Ransom's continued distrust of me. Less than one year later, Emperor Gustav was dead and Carlus installed. And just one year after that, a scandal about his parentage erupted. Gustav's son, yes, but out of wedlock with another woman.

And months after that, here we are.

"Reneb *did* give Carlus asylum," I point out. "After the whole legitimacy scandal. I can see them working him, and then turning around and selling the information to Lyria. It doesn't have to be *malice*, Nate. But who's to say well over six months—eight months, now?—worth of gratitude to Reneb for taking him in won't lead to his being *some* sort of information conduit."

"Eight months. I'm only eight months into my rule."

"And look," I say, turning expansively, as if to encompass the room, "at all you've wrought. Already."

"So much more chaos incoming." He crooks a grin at me, then sobers. "I'm only eight months in. I have so much to learn."

Now

* NOW

After the Winter's Ball

Layla sat, exhausted, deep in the residence for the private family after-gathering. In the same place she had first bonded with Benedik and Alina, what seemed a lifetime ago.

Would it be rude to head to bed? Likely. And it looked like her husband-the-emperor wasn't flagging one bit.

"Lyrian sovereignty? What about *our* sovereignty?" Ignatius said, raising his voice a hair. "We want to expand the borders of *our* Empire. We want to be able to travel through a tunnel on *our* terms, not beholden to Mazaran interests. We want to further economic development with *our* culture and mores intact, not contorting ourselves to become palatable to the Whorl Free Trade Alliance."

"Was that the Imperial We and Our or *normal* pronouns?" asked Tonin.

Ignatius took a deep breath, let it out, and then grinned boyishly at his father. Tonin looked over at Layla and winked.

The room, just as grand and sumptuous as the rest of the palace, featured stiff-backed chairs boasting columnar legs with fluting ridges, as well as fussy occasional tables with an arabesque scallop. Layla missed Altainan clean lines, the only nod to ornamentation being bevels and the occasional rebellious curvature.

"Damn Altainans think they're the policemen for the entire galaxy," Abilio said into the silence. "No offense, dear," he added, patting Layla's knee.

She gave him a none-too-impressed look, and chose to make good on her promise to herself. Time to stir the pot. "You all do realize, there's this thing called a *treaty* that Gustav signed about not building a tunnel...?"

Interesting to watch how each member of the group reacted. Ignatius kept a neutral expression, like he hadn't heard her. Alina folded into herself, as if it could shield her from conflict. Abilio wore a patronizing look. Henri leaned forward in interest. Ephraim took a sharp intake of breath and nervously looked over at his Emperor. Mariah prowled; she had served Gustav and clearly wanted to honor his legacy, but Layla didn't know what side of the debate that put her on. Tonin looked amused. Anastasia shrugged, as if to say, *well, she has a point.*

"Maybe," Layla added, feeling reckless, "if you looked at the root causes of why this tunnel thing is so important to the Empire, you can find a non-treaty-breaking solution that doesn't lead to war. Just a thought."

"Like what?" Henri asked. "Are you talking about keeping the business class happy?"

"Exactly," Layla said. She looked over at Ignatius. He kept that neutral look, staring off into the distance, never at her. "They've been saying it all along. The taxes and the eminent domain and the tariffs are killing them and depressing the economy."

Henri nodded. "But as Prime Minister, I have some insight into how that would work. And it would drain our coffers."

"So tax the nobility. You know all their loopholes." She folded her arms. "They put their wealth into trusts that aren't touched. They sell ancient properties as leaseholds instead of freeholds, so they still generate income off of them. They rent out land as event space and historical curiosities, but receive tax benefits because they are landmarks. And don't forget the taille, a tax only generated against non-nobles. And why is that law still on the books? Because the only form of representative government available in the empire is concentrated on the Lords' Parliament, which in turn only includes the Earls and Countesses, unless you add in designated representatives and"—she nodded to Henri—"their commoner PM. And the only thing *they* can do, statutorily, is approve and impose taxes. In every other respect, this is an absolute monarchy. Why wouldn't they hold on to the only piece of influence they have?"

Ignatius grunted into his empty cup and stood. "I'm getting a refill," he said, voice like gravel. Ephraim went with him, likely to pour his drink for him, per tradition.

Benedik would have found a way to loosen the mood, right about then. She felt the absence of him more than ever. Everything seemed incomplete, a pantomime without his presence.

"You can't change our entire system," Abilio said with a scoff. "As for your more radical ideas, the people of this Empire don't want elections. Or for the nobles to cede ground. We are the moral leaders of our nation."

"Yeah? Look at what you all have been doing the last eighty years. Your own husband is a commoner and is Prime Minister. Ephraim is the Minister of the Interior. The military has become a meritocracy, with proles being elevated over the sons of dukes. Half of things becoming acceptable is people insisting on treating them as if they are, and bending reality to fit."

"Not that I completely disagree," Tonin said with a cough, "but you have to realize things don't work out in idealistic ways. The merchants don't want self-determination for all. They want the same power as the nobility, something they've found their wealth can't buy. Effectively, an oligarchy, like those blasted Renebians. And those stressors, too, what would that do to the power of the throne? They don't have the same ancient notions of fealty the aristocracy has. We couldn't risk the Office of the Emperor."

Ignatius was back now, and she couldn't say what she wanted to say. So she threw up her hands. "Yep. All true."

After all, she shant disparage the divine right of His Excellency to rule.

Later, as they retired to their chambers, Ignatius finally spoke up.

"You can't sit there among my family and push for democracy."

Layla paused mid-undress, eyebrow arched. She exhaled. Ah. Here it was.

"You know how I feel about this," she said, doffing her stockings. "We've talked about it for years."

"To me, yes," he huffed. "But not in front of everyone!" Ignatius had his arms crossed, leaning against the wardrobe, the only true evidence of his anger and frustration being the slow, calming breaths he was now taking.

"I mean, I *did* vow once to uphold democratic ideals," she said, not able to hold back the snark.

Now he gritted his teeth and faced away from her. "That's before you were the empress. Why would you marry me if you can't accept our culture?"

Layla rolled her eyes and threw the last of her clothes into the laundry. "Repression isn't a culture!" Her voice muffled as she grabbed her nightdress and worked it over her head. "And because I love you, you colossal oaf."

"Our system," Ignatius bit, "isn't perfect." He seemed to belatedly register her declaration of love, and his voice softened as he brought his arms to his side and began pacing.

"I want more parliamentary power. I want self-rule for the colonies. I want elections. But we're—"

"—we're not ready for it. Yeah. I know. I truly understand. But you can't get angry with me for even discussing it!"

"I can't be seen to be pushing for it. Nor can you. It's a delicate balance, Layls."

"We were among family."

"Even then, love. Family includes prominent Parliament members. And Parliament, ironically, will be a problem. They want more power. But they don't want the proles to have power. This type of thing … I fear a showdown one day soon. Between me and the Lords. It's not going to be pretty."

Layla sat on the side of the bed. "You all act like I'm pushing for a fully representative democracy. I'm not! I'm saying give the business class more say-so in Parliament, and, in turn, give Parliament more power. It's not the same as overthrowing your entire system. I'm not an *idiot*."

Ignatius paused in his pacing and gave her a quiet smile. He approached, putting his arms around her. "I've been Emperor for less than three years," he admitted. "I don't know how stable you imagine my position to be, but it's not. Not to make big sweeping changes. Not to anger the nobility."

She didn't pull away at that, even though she wanted to. Instead, she placed a calm hand on his chest. "You said that two years ago. *It's only been eight months.* Next you'll say, *I've only been emperor for twenty years.* Who cares if they get angry?" she ventured. "So, there's some upheaval."

"And then the Mazarans strike!" He said this in an agitated growl, and Layla knew that if she were anyone else, it would have been a roar. "Do you not think they are lying in wait? Exploiting the first chance? My job as Emperor is to keep stability."

Her voice went tart yet again. "So you are about protecting the Whorl from the Mazarans…but you're building a subspace tunnel that can allow them to attack us on our flank?"

"Are you," he bit, still putting in effort to remain calm, she saw, "being thick on purpose? They control the Swan Tunnel on their side. This is folly! More than just economic escape, we need strategic escape—the ability to travel! And before you say it, that's exactly what we've been arguing to the Alliance. That, and the stability of Valhar is a common good. But they don't listen. Bah! They prattle on about courting self-determination even if it means revolution, but they don't understand the cost. They are like children! They won't experience the civil war that would be to come. They didn't experience the Mazaran war, and they won't this new Whorl war—because they send their less privileged to fight and die for them. I understand your Altainan ideals, my lady, but how can you defend them, knowing all you know? *You*, my dear, pragmatic empress-wife, where is your rationality and realism now?"

"Then why don't *you* go fight, yourself," she asked, unmoved, "against the men and women who stood with you against the Mazaran threat?"

Fighting those who had stood with them. That would include the Felicians as well, whom the Valhar Empire had so recently attacked.

"If I could go to battle," he said, "I would."

"Me, too," she responded, challenge in her voice. Her sincerity surprised her, and scared her, but still she held his eyes, making sure he knew exactly what she meant.

* NOW

Sitting in her lonely office in the early dawn, Layla groaned and massaged her temples. The initial high of justified anger at her husband wore thin in the morning light. Her message console blinked in urgent staccato and she stared at it, confused. She had checked all her feeds and portals. Nothing new had popped up in front of her. What had she missed?

Probably a glitch.

Her gaze drifted to the encryption stick Park had given her, which ostensibly would allow her to contact Carlus undetected. She needed to get that over to someone trustworthy to analyze for bugs, as well as to assess the mechanics of how the program worked. Reneb was more technologically advanced than Valhar, and likely, it had some sort of steganographic protocol.

The blinking console caught her eye yet again. Usually someone sending an encoded message wouldn't want any external indicator of an unreceived message, but if the recipient was in a relatively secure location and didn't know to expect something...

Ransom. The day they shared that beer. Image files, right? There had been only one image recently sent to her: a constituent (*subject*, she reminded herself) who had expressed gratitude for matching funds for an all-girl's school. Let's see. It hadn't been *that* long ago. Her eyes tracked to the upper right corner of the picture of smiling children in smartly pressed uniforms, and she blinked once, activating a hidden pixel. Then she inputted a long-ago memorized hex-string.

One message received.

Kaborlah. Take care.
— *Spaidara.*

As if by instinct, Layla quickly closed the message and erased every trace of it. She started sweating.

Oh, no no no. That was *so* inconvenient. No. What did that mean? *What did that mean?*

Kaborlah, her home, was near a far Valharan "border," or more accurately the closest populated Altainan territory to the Redma wormhole leading into the outskirts of Valharan space. Was Kaborlah in danger? From what? Valhar? Something else: pestilence, climate, poverty?

Whatever Ransom had meant by sending this to her, it would, eventually, provide intelligence to Valharan forces if she reported it, once they managed to suss out all the possibilities. No doubt, Ransom *didn't* expect her to report it. It didn't track with her personality, as he knew it—and he knew her personality very well, not only from their personal and professional acquaintance but also from all manner of psychological testing, both overt and covert. No, he expected her to keep this in her pocket and do whatever she needed to protect Kaborlah, for whatever reason. He wouldn't have sent it to her otherwise.

So she could sit on it, knowing she wouldn't be found out. This wasn't some sort of trick. Not with that signoff, *spaidara*. Or was it? Had her old communications with Ransom been compromised?

No. She wasn't going to go down that road again. That last time, it was practically broadcasted in the clear. This, however—this *was* Ransom's style.

She had already erased it. Move on, pretending she had never seen it? Keep an ear out, in case she needed to act on her homeland's behalf? Be that cautious, plodding self Ransom knew, the one with an almost-pathological devotion to promises kept? Because if she told Valharan intelligence about it, Altain was about to have one of its encryption methods exposed.

General Turine had asked Mariah to keep an eye on her, in the initiation of this war. Empress or not, she was suspected of divided loyalties. Mariah knew. Mariah worried.

Intrigue. The day after a ball no less. When Layla was young, she'd fantasize about becoming a character in one of her beloved spy novels, dancing while handing off coded messages, all glitz and glam and hooded eyes.

Not all it was cracked up to be. Much like becoming royalty, for that matter.

The last time a ball had been *magical* and made her walk on air was that State Dinner, oh so long ago, and then she had gone home and reality hit. As for what had happened after she had gotten home to Altain...

She fought the encroaching vomit. Ransom had been doing his job, but that *job*, his actions, had been a watershed, wherein she could divide her life into *before* searing fire in her veins and *after*.

But this wouldn't have to be the sacrifice she feared making. Ransom didn't have to know she sold him out. In fact, what she could do was acknowledge receipt. Play along. Be the dutiful soldier. Not give him any reason to take away her citizenship. And report it all the same.

This was it. This was the point of no return. The hellgate. She had to make a choice. Apportion her loyalties or go all in.

She scrambled to reconstruct the message and then put out a call for Mariah to join her in her office.

***

It had been only three hours since Layla had seen the message, but the situation already had taken on the quality of hazy afterimage. Ransom, out of nowhere, contacting her, just like she seemingly experienced two years before. Kaborlah, in the midst of a wartime tug-the-rope.

Now mid-morning, sun rays streamed through the windows in the private dining nook, enveloping the late breakfast crew in a glow that rendered them all angelic.

"That's incredibly cryptic, Layla. Are you sure it's something we need to concern ourselves with? Or that your Ransom isn't peddling misinformation?"

Her Ransom, he wasn't. "I have a reputation for a slavish devotion to duty, don't I?" she asked, responding to her husband's question. "No matter how many twists and turns I need to make to make it make sense? Ransom knows me. He knows I wouldn't bring this to you." She swept her arm toward Ignatius and Mariah, acknowledging the irony. "I'm not saying he *doesn't* have an agenda. He wants me to worry about Kaborlah and take some sort of action, but he wants me to do it without your participation. So now I need to unravel the riddle."

"Kaborlah." Mariah paced, her favorite 'thinking lollipop' in her mouth an adorable foil to her lethality. "Kaborlah is in some sort of danger. Not from the Altainans but from us."

Ephraim, the fourth member of their crew, watched his wife as a ligra tamer would watch a stalking cat: equal parts wary, awed, and worshipful. He caught Layla's eyes and straightened as if caught skiving school.

Her internal smile at the byplay gave way to furrowed confusion. "Like Felix. Another place symbolic for me. You," she said, pointing at Ignatius, "will attempt to take Kaborlah. Even if you don't know it yet. And he ... what? Wants me to prevent it? How could I do that?"

"By warning Ransom when His Excellency is about to do it," Ephraim said, glancing sideways at Ignatius. "So they can mobilize, but not too soon. They need that intel from you, so they can act at the last possible moment. *We* don't know we're going to make some future play for Kaborlah, because we don't yet have some crucial piece of information. If they mobilize *now* to prevent a hypothetical future Valharan invasion, we'll wonder why, and we'll know to look there. And if we look there..."

"We'd figure out what the Altainans are up to," Ignatius concluded. "So instead of tipping us off by mobilizing now, they keep a look out, and when we independently discover whatever prompts us to invade, you will hue and cry to Ransom and then Altain will pivot to just-in-time defense."

"So, what *are* they up to? Why would you all—*our* Empire want to protect that flank?" Layla asked. *Your slip is showing, Empress.*

"The tunnel, naturally," Ignatius responded.

That damn tunnel. Just like the argument they had had the night before. Worried about the stresses on the Empire, the simmering tension...

It's a pressure valve. Ignatius had said in the night. *The entire Empire. The tunnel will release some of it.*

Releasing energy. The tunnel. Her eyes widened. "Oh, shit."

"Her Grace is right," General Turine said, reporting to Ignatius's study in early afternoon. "We've been receiving reports for a while hinting at some large production in the Altainan Republic, out in space. Particular construction intended for containment. Rumors of the development of supersized particle accelerators."

"A fucking antimatter weapon," growled Ignatius. He slammed his tablet down in frustration.

Layla only rarely heard Ignatius swear, but Turine didn't bat an eyelash. Not a surprise; Turine's square jaw and leather neck made him perfect casting for some Altainan action flick featuring piss-mouthed spitting antiheroes, a very *othering* way of glorifying proverbial gods of war that would never share space with the average Republic citizen. Turine, for his part, was smarter than the generic jackdaw of popular imagination, given his degree in nuclear astrophysics. Although, achievement could set one up for a larger fall; Turine was both apoplectic and apologetic that he had missed the significance of the Altainan efforts given his academic and research background.

Layla knew far less about science, and wouldn't have noticed the signs of weapons creation on the part of her former masters, but every schoolchild in the Whorl learned the basic mechanics of both natural wormholes and man-made subspace tunnels. Completed tunnels had charged black holes on either side connected by vibrating cosmic strings, kept open by constant negative energy shooting through. Increase positive-energy particles and over-oscillate the strings, and siphon enough energy away...

That was as far as she got on the particulars, but a tunnel only half-created without a full loop intertwining both strings, with only one Whorl-side charged hole completed, *had* to be relatively easy to collapse. An antimatter weapon had to be detonated, in this case, Whorl-side, at a certain point before the event horizon. Likely a remote detonation. Little risk to anyone involved.

It was absurdly simple.

"I'm not comfortable with how much guesswork is going on here," Ignatius mused, "based on a four-word message. We need corroboration."

Layla spared a quick glance at Turine, who was waiting at modified parade rest for further instruction.

"You've done well, General," Ignatius said magnanimously, advancing closer to bid him goodbye. "Keep working your angles. I'll see what I can do on my end."

With a sketched salute and muttered thanks, Turine departed and Ignatius turned to Layla, eyebrows raised. "Well, dear? What idea has popped into that head of yours?"

She twiddled her fingers. "Park," she finally admitted. "I was just thinking. It was looking at that encrypted drive he gave me."

"You think Park had something to do with this? Ransom contacting you?"

She shook her head. "No. I mean, maybe. They get their sticky fingers into everything. But what I mean is, those sneaky assholes trade in information. And Reneb is an Alliance member by rights. They might be willing to confirm what Altain is up to. That they've truly developed an antimatter weapon large enough to take out the Solita Tunnel."

"Ask Reneb to sell out the Alliance." Ignatius shook his head. "Well, it's certainly possible. But I don't trust that guy."

"Naturally. But he did recently reach out to Carlus for us. He didn't have to do that."

"Somehow, dear, that makes me trust him less." Ignatius slammed his fist down on his desk, hard, and Layla jumped. She stilled as she noted his head was now in his hands. "Sorry," Ignatius muttered. "Temper. Not you. I just—I miss Benedik."

"He *would* be able to smell Park's bullshit a mile away," she acknowledged, not putting voice to Ignatius's real worry. Ignatius smiled at her gratefully, confirming she had made the right choice.

Layla tugged him down to his desk chair. "You always stand when your subordinates visit. You can sit, you know, after you greet them. Hell, it gives *them* a chance to sit, too."

"Look at you," he said fondly. "Always looking out for the little guy."

She snorted. "I *am* the little guy. Never forgotten it." She rubbed his back and he groaned.

"So," she said after a while, "we confirm Altain is going to collapse the Solita Tunnel. So we stop them. Does that actually involve taking Kaborlah?"

Ignatius clasped her hand and looked up at her. "It makes tactical sense, my lady. Our flank is woefully underprotected. If we can take the chokepoint—"

"It's not going to go well for them. Kaborlah, I mean."

"We've done all right on Felix."

"That's *Felix*. Kaborlah is already a logistical nightmare. We're one natural disaster from complete collapse, always and continuously. Any military action that impacts the territory ... there's no food or water surplus. Essential medicines. Hygiene. It's all borked."

"We can activate some covert elements near the edge of the Empire. Have them spirit your family to safety before we act."

"I don't give a flying—it's not really my family I'm worried about, Nate," she amended. "They wouldn't go with anyone anyway." They wouldn't leave. Too prideful. Or, on the other end, word would get out and they'd have to shoot the masses of people mobbing their transport intended for ten-and-twenty, all demanding berth. "It's the people as a whole that has me bothered. Little boys and girls like me, just wanting to escape into a better life, but who will end up trapped in the ensuing chaos."

"You hate that place."

"I was born from the dirt and sweat and tears of that place. It's my home, not Altain Prime. It's the place that made me. Surely you can understand that. The mountains of Corval made *you*, and that was no picnic in the park, either."

"There's nothing more important than beating the Alliance back, Layla. They aren't the thought-leaders for this Whorl. They aren't the shining police force, serving nobly and proudly to keep the evil imperialists in check. The Alliance single-handedly decided the prohibition against tunnel construction extended beyond the Mazaran war. That's not what Emperor Gustav originally agreed to. You know it! You were there at the negotiation! The security of this entire Whorl depends on the opposite. We cannot be dependent on the Mazarans for access to the greater galaxy. And we cannot cede our sovereignty to a bunch of hopped-up elitist neo-interventionists."

"Even if it means risking my home?" she asked. Her forehead creased in disappointment. "You're so focused on being *right* that you're no better than Altain."

He looked at her. Really *looked* at her.

"We won't do anything rash. I don't just mean until we get confirmation. Even after, we'll see if we have enough time to try alternatives." He pulled her close. "I really *do* miss Benedik. I could have sent him to the Altain Republic to do a little reconnaissance."

"Surely you have people."

"Benedik has a unique advantage in that no one would see him and think he's being covert at all. He can just swash and buckle a swath through the center of the Whorl and be as brightfully obtuse as the Swan Nebula, and for most people, that is that. Hiding in plain sight, you see?"

"Hmm," she agreed. She sighed. "I don't like this, Nate. We're lighting up the entire Whorl. Why wouldn't the Mazarans invade right now? While we are distracted and divided? Or have they truly decided for peace?"

Ignatius snorted. "I don't believe that for a hot Narconian second."

"I mean," she considered, stretching, "they have new leadership, democratically elected, and have their own internal problems that preclude war, especially after that costly misadventure here in the Whorl. They're not some sort of unknowing evil."

"They're an expansionist Empire. Democracy by fiat, with not so much as a *how-do-you-do* before they pivot to dictatorship when it conveniences them. Expansionist in the conquering and pillaging sense, not the way we are here, expanding to worlds unknown but leaving settled peoples alone."

She raised her eyebrows. "Felix and Kaborlah notwithstanding?"

"Hush, you. Holding territory and later reverting it back to its rightful master is far different from subjugating entire civilizations. No, they aren't an *unknowing* evil. They know what they do. We saw the face of it, seven years ago. I rather fear we've forgotten."

***

Ronin Park shuffled into Ignatius's formal receiving room without his usual haughty calm. If Layla could detect auras, she imagined his would be pulsating puke-green, with tentacles of nerves flung about every which way.

She narrowed her eyes. What had he done to warrant that nervousness?

After being announced, Park cleared his throat and stayed standing, respectfully. A wavy strand of dark brown hair fell over russet colored-eyes, and his hands, entwined behind his back, twitched in impatience. Ignatius took a moment to finish reading his feeds and glanced up at him, and, still sitting, leaned forward with his arms on the tea table. Layla expected him to extend an invitation to sit, but it never came, an apparent intentional omission.

My. She didn't realize there was that much tension between the two. Certainly explained Park's demeanor.

"Erm," she started out hesitantly into the silence, wary of speaking out of turn. Great Goddess, she was an empress. She straightened and tried again. "Ambassador Park," she said, glancing quickly at Ignatius to ensure he wasn't upset with her for jumping in, "I assume you received my questions? *And* investigated in a discreet manner?"

"It was a doozy," Park admitted. "I think you're right, Lay—Your Grace. Apparently the Altainans are making plans to attack your rear flank. The only reason they'd want to hit that border is to get to Solita. They must have something."

"And where did you receive this information?" Ignatius asked, voice cool but courteous.

"Our chief executive authorized me to tell you, Your Excellency. Altain has been keeping the rest of the Alliance in the dark. This seems to be a purely Altainan plan. So she's not betraying the tripartite agreement by passing this along. We have our own sources of intel."

He most definitely did not answer the question. "Can I get my hands on those reports, Park?" she asked instead, solicitously.

He waffled. "They aren't reports, per se. Just contact with a third party who is in on the plan." Uncomfortable pause. "And that third party didn't freely give all that information, in any case. It was something our operative had to deduce between the lines. Although it's not as hard as one would think. Guy thinks he's smarter than he is."

"And?" she prompted.

"I'm sorry, Excellency, Layla. That's all I can tell you. But I think you have enough actionable information at this point, right?"

"It'll do," she said in her most imperious tone. "But what do you get out of this, Ambassador?"

"Pardon?"

"It must be in your interest to sell out your ally. So, why?"

"Doing a favor for an old friend—for old *friends*," he amended, "isn't enough?"

Layla waited. Ignatius gave a small snort and picked up his tablet to continue going through feeds. *Rude, husband.*

Park made a motion to sit but appeared to belatedly realize he still hadn't been invited. Sheepishly, he straightened. Layla looked over at Ignatius and mentally rolled her eyes.

"Sit, Park," she said.

"Ah, thank you, Your Grace," he said, alighting delicately on the edge of the chesterfield, as if still unsure. "War injury flaring up. Erm," he said, as Ignatius raised his eyes at the perceived rebuke and then put aside the tablet once more. "What were you asking? Your Grace?"

"What's in it for you, Park." She let her Altainan accent slip through.

He looked her straight in the eye. "The tunnel," he said, strong and sure. "The Alliance wants it destroyed. We on Reneb have no choice but to join our allies opposing the tunnel under our collective defense agreement. But, for Reneb specifically, we think the tunnel could provide an opportunity. For trade, perhaps. Most Favored Nation status, between Reneb and Valhar."

"So why don't you make honest women out of yourselves and leave the Alliance to join us?" Ignatius asked, voice flat. "*We*," he continued, emphasizing the imperial pronoun, "are not interested if you insist on playing the neighborhood strumpet." Layla pursed her lips at the sexist terminology but resisted comment.

"And have Altain and Lyria and all their sycophants attack *us*? I'm sorry, Excellency, but our power lies in our purse, not in our might. But we'd be willing to be a backchannel as much as we can, as long as we don't outright break any of our agreements. Please feel free, Excellency, to call on me if you need assistance or information. Our executive wants to maintain normal relations with you. Even though Altain is decidedly *not* impressed that I'm still on-planet."

Ignatius nodded and stood. Layla and Park both joined him, Park springing up so fast he winced, perhaps from that old injury. Ignatius reached out his hand. "Thank you, Ambassador. You're dismissed now." Park hesitated a moment, seemingly contemplating asking something—likely an answer on the implied diplomatic trade—but thought better of it and took the proffered hand, bending low in benediction and allowing the steward to see him out.

"Is that confirmation enough?" Layla asked, settling into one of the ornate settees littering the room. She took Ignatius's hand as she lowered herself and rearranged her full skirt to cover her cold legs.

"Maybe." Ignatius glanced at her hunched frame and went to stoke the fire burning off to her left. "Unless this is another angle those shifty-eyed fuckers are running."

"Two curses in one day?" Layla reached out and stroked her husband's arm in appreciation, nodding at the fire. "I thought you left all that prole vulgarity to the likes of me."

"I was a soldier." Ignatius almost looked wounded.

"I remember you as a soldier. You used to specify the exact temperature and composition of your afternoon tea."

"Still do."

"Yeah, but now you have an *excuse*. Your Worshipful Imperialness."

"Must you be so impertinent?" he mock-growled.

"Whaddya gonna do about it?" she challenged, going full Kaborlah.

He harrumphed, and then leaned in to tickle her. She shrieked and smacked him away, and he relented immediately, raising his hands in supplication.

"Ugh," she said. "Hooligan." He sat next to her and she drew up closer to him. "So, what's the verdict on Kaborlah?"

He sobered. "Assembling a fleet, quietly, will take a while, then we head to the border, again surreptitiously. We'll be in position in a few weeks. I promise to revisit the idea of actually taking the settlement, Layla, but we can't waste time in case my answer is no." She muffled a noise of assent. "Meanwhile, we need to follow the trail of that purported antimatter weapon and see if we can confirm and disrupt."

"So," she said, stroking his beard, "contacting me was an insurance plan, so they know if they need to protect the settlement. But otherwise, obviously they're hoping to just sneak in. How, Ignatius? How are they planning on crossing our border without our noticing?"

Ignatius frowned. "I feel if we can answer *that* question, we can solve all manner of mysteries prompted by this war."

Benedik!
Now

Benedik had passed the point of no return and now was endlessly tumbling into a black hole of fuckery.

This is sedition. This is LITERALLY sedition. It's the thrice-damned definition of sedition, you soggy lump of curdled eggs, Benedik. You fool. I hope you enjoy the few weeks of life you bought yourself before your second cousin hangs you in the Imperial Square.

Despite his mental screaming, Benedik spoke with all the haughtiness and surety he could muster as he explained the intricacies of Valharan succession to the scary woman. Honestly, as an Imperial subject, she should have been more aware of the system of rule under which she lived, but Benedik was fast learning things on the reaches of the Empire didn't always work as they should.

The scary woman—who called herself Delilah—was much nicer to him when she mentally recast him as a useful puppet, but Benedik still regarded her with the wariness a frog would visit upon a scorpion.

"So," he said, "when Gustav was Emperor, the only official successors were his immediate children. That's it. Carlus was the second child, actually. And yes, if we had our old system of succession, that would have made Ignatius much lower in line, but in practical terms, that's not how it works anymore. Then Carlus's big brother died, then his father, and he became Emperor, and *his* kids were his only named successors, but when he left he took his kids with him and bam! You have a succession crisis. But this is where our system works, ya see? Because there aren't too many options for the Parliament to choose between."

"That's on purpose?"

"Oh yeah, for sure. Ya wanna keep the numbers low. Just enough heirs that you have someone able to step in, but not so much that there's a clown car. Emperor Titus had two kids: Empress Hadria and then later in life, Philomenus, my grandfather. Empress Hadria had three kids, which is about standard and advisable for the actual Royal line, including Gustav and Anastasia. The other, Augustin, died in the Samdha crisis of '85. Two heirs and a dead spare, seems to work out that way a lot. Gustav had two, again, not ideal for the royal line. Carlus's older brother Jules died in a shuttle accident and then we have that nasty business with Carlus, who at least had the sense to have three, though I guess that's moot. But notice Anastasia only had one, so did my parents. Which is right and proper for the periphery of the line, to show no intent to challenge the throne. So when it came to an election, it was really only between four people, two in each generation, so really only between two once you decide if you want to go young or go old. Old folk: Anastasia or my father Abilio, and young: me or Ignatius. Hey," he said, lifting his mug and shaking it a bit, "you got any more of that jungle juice?"

Delilah signaled to her bland-faced assistant with a sharp dip of her chin, and he took the mug from Benedik, bowing obsequiously and backing away. Benedik, free-handed at last, leaned back languorously and stretched, surveying the room as he did. Still on Solita, they were, still far removed from the colonial capital—Benedik dreamed of ways he could garner the attention of Viceroy Stanlo, but alas, it looked like it was still up to him to rescue himself—but the furnishings spoke to a location that was much less removed from society than the cabin-with-the-pony-bedroom. It was utilitarian, for sure, but well-equipped with whatever Benedik put his mind to ask for, with increasing levels of entitlement, which he creatively applied to plant the suggestion they offer him the aforementioned drink concoction. Luckily Fern and Jax were out of the picture—packed up and sent back to the outskirts, with a pat on the back and an atta-y'all for their work in securing the prisoner—or they'd have a devil of a time reconciling this new imperious lordling with the kind, handsome, perfect, witty man with whom they had broken bread.

Delilah looked upon Benedik's ripped arms with interest and raised her eyebrows. Ah, good. She was switching tactics from being an utterly terrifying front-line commander to playing black widow. A sign Benedik's ploys were working. Benedik gave her that earnest dimple-deepening grin, allowed a slight blush to creep up his neck (he did so by imagining his wedding night with his scrumptious, delectable...ah, blast it, the pleasant warmness in his nether regions might be overkill, possibly), and he switched his gaze to confident smolder and then, studied disinterest.

Lord Dreamboat, they called him in Novaria.

Literally no one calls you that, his inner Alina scolded. *Lord Prisspants, maybe.*

The assistant returned with another mug full of very alcoholic jungle juice, and Benedik took a long draught, allowing some dribbles to traitorously escape onto his chin.

"Ah, yes, the good juice," he sloshed. "Luxurious libations! Well, let us continue. If you want me to be Emperor, we would need to delegitimize the other three options. Not *eliminate*, mind you; if we harm or kill anyone and there's suspicion I had anything to do with it, it would be very hard for me to have a legitimate rule myself. So you'll need a clever way to take them out without obvious foul play. That's near impossible to do. You'd need a systems-wide revolt against Iggy boy, with the Parliament convinced neither he nor his mother could rule effectively. I wouldn't worry about my father though. I can find ways to deal with *him*."

"Would a rising-up throughout the empire calling for self-rule in each colony help?" she asked.

Eh. No democratic revolutions if he could help it, even if he *was* sympathetic. Might be hard to put that imp back in the snifter. "Maybe, if it looked like he couldn't contain them," he allowed. "But I propose"—he lifted his drink again, as if calling for a toast—"instead of advocating for self-rule, it should be something that still augurs for the continuity of the Empire. Something like ... ah, like he isn't prosecuting the war effectively. First he gets us into a war that we can't possibly win, and now he's making it worse. Blah, blah, et cetera, and so on."

"I wasn't aware you can impeach the Emperor." Delilah frowned at him.

"No, my dear, not at all. But Carlus left, didn't he? Got himself outed as a bastard." Benedik didn't bother to hide his wince. He was closer to Ignatius, certainly, *loved* him, but losing Carlus still left an imperial-shaped hole in his heart. Benedik had looked up to Carlus so very much. Why couldn't Carlus have stuck around in some form? Where *was* he? Or, the question that truly kept Benedik messy and bothered: why wouldn't he even just keep in contact? Benedik *needed* the big lug.

He shook it away and kept up his part. "Keep in mind, Parliament doesn't have the ability to actually *remove* anyone, but Cousin Iggy may be convinced the Lords would take up arms against him and cause civil war. A good leader would want to avoid that and decide to abdicate." Like Carlus. Two emperors in a row being forced to abdicate; now *that* was never going to happen. And likely scary boss-lady was aware of that too, but really, what other options did she have? Benedik gave her the lopsided smile again and ruffled his blond hair.

Perhaps his heart-stopping grin was what finally put her over the edge. Delilah cocked her head and nodded to herself. "So," she said in contemplation, "uprisings. And making it look like he's losing the war. The Altainans would *love* to help with that." She rubbed her hands together excitedly.

Wha—"Altainans!" he yelped. "There's a war on. I will *not* be beholden to the Republic—" For a moment Benedik forgot he was playacting. Imagine if a Valharan emperor was found to have been colluding with the enemy!

"They don't have to know they're putting you on the throne," she soothed. "They just know they're supporting freedom fighters. Besides, you're already beholden to them. They're the ones who rescued you."

Finally. Some damn information. "How'd they even know I was out there?" he asked, trying to look bored, hoping the slight start he gave could be attributed to drunken twitchiness. He wasn't twitchy, of course. Benedik was immune to jungle juice; its active intoxicant was cousin to a particularly nasty poison against which most people in the putative line of succession were given injections to create a tolerance. Yet another example of things his captors didn't know. How far in above their heads these rebels be.

Delilah looked smug. "Actually," she said, leaning in, "I heard the Empress herself reached out and told them to look for you, but when they found you, they decided to use you to help *us* instead." Oh, how important she must feel, being worthy of consideration from those *insufferable* republicans.

Alas, that didn't seem right. If Layla had reached out to any of the Alliance powers, it wouldn't be her former countrymen, not with a war on. It would be Reneb. They were shifty enough to play both sides. Sacred Falcon, Delilah's contacts were probably Renebians *posing* as Altainans. Benedik decided to keep that insight to himself.

"Well," he said instead, "that certainly sheds a new appreciation on the situation." Meaning, of course, the Renebians sold him out, those flopping oligarchal masters of perfidy. Now, what did Reneb want with Solita militants? Benedik turned that thought over and then tossed it to the back of his mind; he had more immediate problems with which to deal.

He steepled his fingers and looked at Delilah intently. "Well, the Altainans probably will have ideas of their own; likely some hidden agents of theirs can drum up the necessary anti-war sentiments from certain segments of the population while stoking the fires of nationalism among the populace most likely to critique the manner in which Ignatius is prosecuting the war. You all, I assume, have methods of communication and dissemination that have eluded the imperial censors and can spread messages of my cousin's incompetence. And what do you need from me?" Belatedly aware he had sounded too lucid, he made sure to add a burp as a coda.

Delilah squinted at him but then gave herself a shrug. "Watch our efforts, be sure we're on the right track. Other than that, just be ready to step in, love. You know, I've been told the Altainans might even bend on the whole tunnel situation and let it go forward, which would really help our economy."

Now that *really* didn't seem right. The Altainans wanted that tunnel collapsed, no matter how one did it. Definitely Renebians. The Renebians *would* work an angle to turn the issue of the tunnel to their fortune. Benedik would need to remember to warn Ignatius the plutocrats were swimming in the Empire's waters. But first things first. A rebelling populace to engender instability: how would he stop this plan from actually going into motion? He wasn't worried about Ignatius's prospects or popularity, of course, but again, the outcome didn't matter as much as the *actions* taken against the Divine Command, and in that, he was very guilty. His delicate neck would look so terrible from being bruised-via-hanging. Perhaps they could put a kerchief around him for his wake. Ah, a traitor wouldn't have a wake, now would he?

His fathers would be devastated. Abilio had just wanted him to settle down more. He had shorn fat grateful tears at Benedik's wedding, certain it would lead to his son having a homestead right outside the city, a passel of kids, a cushy imperial government position. The fact Alina was actually okay with Benedik gallivanting around the Whorl at Ignatius's discretion ground heavily at Abilio.

Henri didn't care. Henri just wanted him to be happy. But being hanged so ignominiously would *not* make Benedik happy. So he imagined Henri, too, would mourn. If he were to die doing what he loved, maybe, perhaps, death by snu snu, then Henri may throw a clawed-damned celebration.

A radical. He was about to take up the actions, if not the ideology, of a radical. Forget the rebels, he himself was far above his head. Typical Benedik, et cetera and so on.

Whatever. Ignatius was a radical in his own way.

But, if the tables were turned and *Benedik* had been Emperor (he shivered at the thought), Ignatius would have borne the plight of a hostage with dignity, willing them to execute him for his ideals. But Benedik wouldn't have, *couldn't* have, given that order.

Benedik probably would throw away the entire empire rather than consign his beloved cousin to his death.

Not for the first time, he was glad the Lord's Parliament didn't think to elect him.

"Who is your advisor? Not the Altainans?" he asked.

"Someone the Altainans put me in touch with. Said he had expertise in societal change. I don't really care for him. He's too arrogant. And his eyes creep me out."

"Well, now," Benedik said with a swagger, "I'm arrogant, dontcha think?" He pushed his chest out, as if it were a badge of honor.

She gave him a lascivious grin. "*You're* commanding. It's sexy."

Benedik was certain Delilah wasn't actually the type of woman attracted to some archaic archetype of male power and prowess, but the persona he was playing wouldn't be able to detect the lie, so firmly entrenched in his alpha male nonsense ways, so he grinned back at her and let his eyes rake over her body. And then tried to change the subject.

"My cousin likely wanted me dead. Guess I should stay dead, for now. And after we destabilize his rule, and then I show up out of nowhere ... well, I wouldn't make any accusations, but Parliament will be able to put it all together."

His family. Oh, blessed bird, his family was probably so worried. He needed to find a way to contact them, warn them, and also stop this revolution he was about to start. Maybe this was too much. Maybe he should let himself be a hostage, let the demands be made, then, of course, denied, therefore sealing his fate. Better than what he was doing now.

But no. There was more to this than he understood. He needed to stay alive, and investigate. Ignatius would understand, wouldn't he?

Ignatius would also probably be better at this than him. Despite all Benedik's posturing, Ignatius was better at *everything*. Even matters of love. Ignatius was the one who exuded the broody charm that in their youth had women falling over him in droves. (Benedik liked to call him *Ignasty* when the situation got particularly debauched). Meanwhile, Benedik stumbled through life lusting over unattainable people of all genders until one took pity or saw his over-compensation as *dashing*.

As if to dispute his self-evaluation, Delilah climbed on top of him. Oh, oh *no*. Oh, in his wayward youth he would have let her ride him till the dawn came, himself thrusting with all his might to alleviate the utter frustration and disdain he was feeling at the moment. Maybe he'd even feel a sort of tenderness for her; after all, you couldn't swap bodily fluids with someone without having *some* sort of pang in your heart, not unless you were a monster. But he was a faithfully married man, damnit. Benedik groaned, his natural reaction overlaying his utter panic. His inner Alina, his lodestar, had her arms crossed and her eyebrows raised, as if to say, *well, what <u>now</u>, you utter lout? After all, you encouraged this.*

Lean in, he thought to himself, still in his wife's voice. He pulled the witch to him—oh, that very *sexy* witch that was gyrating on him with such skill—and gave her a long, slow kiss, while simultaneously using that *other* trick they learned to protect themselves from poison. He opened his mouth wider to allow her tongue to push down hard on the back of *his* tongue, thought long and hard about the rotten-egg smell of his great-grandmother's dried cod casserole, and promptly threw up all over her.

Now

Layla
Six weeks after the beginning of the Valhar-Alliance war

The first dewdrops of spring brought with it the scent of pressed petals, like lightly perfumed oil touched lovingly behind a woman's ears. Warm weather, but with a slight chill in the breeze, not humid despite the sunshowers that broke every morning. Winter snowstorms were common on the northeast continent. Spring thunderstorms were rare, unlike on Kaborlah, which brooked bracing hailstorms and tornadoes with regularity.

The Winter Ball may have been the biggest ceremonial event of the calendar, but with spring came the Valharan festival days, religious celebrations serving as formal thanks for warmer days ahead. With required royal appearances at a significant number of benedictions and worship services, Layla's schedule was again full.

There was no national religion on either Altain or Valhar—officially, of course. But in both nations, the majority dictated official practice: bank holidays, broadcasted services, oaths given, secular celebrations overlayed on the ecclesiastical. For all their calls of ecumenical unity, Valhar was the nation of the Falcon and Altain the realm of the Goddess, and not coincidentally, the majority religions of the Empire and Republic were first created on the actual planets of Valhar proper and Altain Prime. What would have happened if humanity had evolved on only one planet—old Earth, perhaps, the cradle of so much of the sprawling human populace—as opposed to throughout the galaxy? Would all of Earth—and therefore, all of humanity—have eventually adopted one religion? Certainly much of Valhar's language of elitism came from that planet, a testament to its far reaches.

As it was, the nations had significant liturgical differences. The Altainan dominant culture, the Goddess-worshippers, were the more religious of the two, believing in an intercessory force that required worship and devotion, although by this point in history, the elites of that culture considered themselves socially evolved and saw religion as a pastiche of reality. In contrast, it was the rank-and-file Valharans who were not religious in the slightest. According to lore, the Great Falcon created the world and then left, a grand watchmaker who left humanity to tick and tock on their own. But as with all religion, contradiction and crossed-wires were paramount. Uninterested force or not, the Falcon of Valharan myth still somehow blessed every emperor, giving him or her the powers of God-made-flesh. And where Altain worship was a riot of color—a stark contrast to their cultural practice of minimalist and inconspicuous design—Valharan praise came in the form of abnegation. A typical chapel was blinding white, no chairs or pews to be found, worshippers on hard floors sitting in silence and meditation until the cleric ascended the pulpit, when the congregation then stood, hands clasped behind their backs as they contemplated the lesson given. Layla didn't enjoy the long services on a good day, but on a tired *I feel very pregnant* day, it was beyond dreaded.

Beatrix, the palace social secretary, had pointedly reminded her she could have begged off her ceremonial duties if she had made public her *condition*, but the conversation made Layla's stomach roil in a way quite unassociated with the gas bubbles that normally plagued her. A few more weeks. Just a few more weeks, and she would be far enough into her pregnancy that it would be absurd to not announce.

It was still so early in the gestational period. Time slowed down when one was pregnant. The rest of the galaxy went on double-time: Benedik had been missing for six weeks now (his fathers and his wife, after some hard conversations about how long to keep his disappearance quiet, had finally released the news in hope of eliciting information); the mission to quietly create a force poised to take Kaborlah progressed; and the drumbeats of war thud closer and closer to home. At the Winter Ball it still hadn't felt real. It was something happening over *there*, out in the Whorl. There was nothing visible about it on the homeworld; families had sons sent off but most had been on offworld duty anyway. And then isolated deaths occurred, and then more. And suddenly the economic and societal implications hit. Cessation of trade and out-of-Empire travel. Grumbles of unrest as families lost scions. And soon it would get worse. War was funny like that sometimes:

nothing, then a little bit of something, then more implications, until it all snowballed.

Also multiplicative: the gathering of Imperial subjects finding the courage to gather together to demand change. The news reels were censored, of course, but Layla got the undiluted feed, vacillating between pride and dread at the peaceful marches, the creative signs, the chants. Pride, because freedom always found a way. Dread, because she didn't know how this all would end.

"These protests are bullshit," came a voice, interrupting the reverie. "Subjects don't deserve the right of assembly if they use it to be so damned unpatriotic." Mariah lounged in an uncomfortable accent chair in Layla's private dressing room while the Empress's lady's maid, Paula, flittered around fitting a modest flowing pantsuit fit for worship to Layla's form, or vice versa. At this point, poked and prodded and stuffed, she really couldn't tell the difference.

"Are we so insecure in our government that we can't handle a few upset subjects?" Layla asked. She winced as a straight pin missed its mark.

"*We* are protecting them. *We* are doing this for them. I'd like to see *them* run an empire. Fuckwits. Remember when this was all a hoorah rally 'round the flag endeavor? Remember when the Emperor was feted and adored for defending the realm?" Mariah had raised herself up to an alert position during this rant and then flopped back down, sucking on that silly popstick. Surprising, in that Mariah was always alert, always on-call. The tailoring maid wasn't much of a threat, but then again, those damned pins were tiny torture devices.

"Paula? Could you excuse us for a sec?" she asked her attendant. Paula bowed low. If a bow could be sarcastic, this was it, and Layla loved her for it. Bowing and scraping, genuflection and adoration: after two years, it was still odd, and Layla specifically cultivated staff who felt okay letting their personalities shine through.

Exhibit: Mariah.

"That pantsuit's material is too thick," Mariah observed. "It's sweltering outside. You're going to burn up."

"It is decidedly *not* sweltering, you winter-borne soldier. Even with me running more hot than usual. Also, spill. What am I missing?"

At her *pardon?* look, Layla clarified. "It's more than a protest, isn't it."

Mariah squinted at her. "The Free Press Coalition is serving up some barmy nonsense. Ugh, the press. One of your inalienable rights. More freedoms demanded, all on the path to overthrowing our rightful emperor."

"Giving people positive rights doesn't lead to democracy, Mariah. Democracy is what creates freedom. We can have concessions here or there without threatening our system or our liege."

"Wrong. Unlike you, I actually have a degree in political theory." At Layla's startled look, Mariah rolled her eyes. "Yeah, you don't know everything about me. Anyway, no. Freedoms lead to democracy, more often than not. More and more demands. A taste for certain sociopolitical conditions that they want to replicate and reproduce en masse. You want to protect your husband's rule, you keep people in their place. We have an order and a system and it *works*."

"So," Layla said, changing the subject to avoid the topic of *her husband's rule*, "what are they doing?"

"We think they're recruiting. Trying to instigate mass unrest. Probably co-opting these anti-war twerps but keeping their role hidden. Organizing an entire shadow government, ready to take over on notice. But it's all ephemeral. Done under the cover of free discourse. In chatrooms, academic conferences, teahouses. Too subtle for them alone to pull off, of course. I swear if any of them are being supported by those damned Altainan nonprofits I'll have them round up and executed for treason. Cavorting with the enemy. During *wartime*, no less. Selfishness personified." Unspoken: *is that the society you want? Miss Duty-Above-All?*

During *wartime*, Layla's mind echoed. That endless, depressive weight with the unbreakable chain, dragging their entire society underwater. It had that positive spin at first, beginning with a general shrug in the direction of the Lyrian smash-and-grab attacks over the last few years, and then leading to a surge of optimism as Altain enjoined earnestly and made this an actual damn *war*, a fight that had been coming for some time between the ancient Empire and the three republics of the Whorl, the vacillation of Reneb notwithstanding. There existed a sense of *go get 'em. Don't let the ballot-worshippers push us around.*

Valhar had just gotten to the hard part. The *this is real* part. The *this is actually war* part. And the populace could do nothing but watch as their countrymen died. Frivolity seemed immoral. Her friends were restless and uncertain and unable to concentrate, in distress but feeling guilty that the same anxiety affected their productivity and ability to make any sort of difference. They, as a populace, were unmoored, claustrophobic.

It was exposing the cracks. Rebellion? On Valhar? Shocking to some, but what was the Valharan Empire but a sprawling paper tiger, held together with spit and whistle and myth?

Altainans: a monotheistic female Lord ruling above space and time. Valharans: A great clawed bird that set off creation and then ran away.

As for Layla, she worshiped her mother-in-law.

"You look like cake icing," Anastasia said, inspecting her getup.

"Still have to exude elegance, even when sitting cross-legged in a meditative pose," Layla responded, allowing Anastasia to enter the transport first and then sliding in herself. With elegance.

"I was a literal *Princess* and I didn't have to subject myself to this fashion monstrosity. But no, I understand. You have three times the scrutiny: being married-in, a commoner, and a *foreigner*. They've have to make you perfect."

"Four times. Heathen, too, Princess."

"Ever wish you were home?"

Layla snorted. "Have you seen how *they* treat me?"

The small craft flew slowly above the ancient road, the better to process in front of tens of thousands of adoring subjects standing on floating platforms, waiting for a glimpse of their empress and the former princess on this festival day. The transport hardtop winked out of existence and in its place, a protective shield bubble.

And the crowd roared.

Their conversation cut short by the necessity of waving and smiling and turning back and forth like animatronic dolls, Layla and Anastasia switched to "on" mode as the procession rolled along. In *on mode*, Layla retreated into herself, replaced by plastic pomp and circumstance. In *on mode*, Mariah perched on top the follow craft, pulse weapon at the ready. In *on mode*, Layla couldn't dwell on the frustrations of Anastasia's life, full of promise and spitfire but held back by circumstance. In *on mode*, as they inched along toward the Little Chapel of Winged Desires, the crowd was just a crowd, not an ironic simulacrum of how a Victory Day parade would look.

In *on mode*, Layla ignored that she wrote her mother a letter begging her to stop violating her privacy, and that her mother turned around and published it. In *on mode*, she pushed away the most recent tabloids out of Kaborlah proclaiming she was heartless, a traitor to her country, because her sexuality didn't allow her to love. Fucking Karbolah, that she was trying to save.

Smile. Wave. Twirl. Repeat.

Bubble lowered, hardtop back on. Anastasia relaxed fractionally, sitting back in that still-refined courtly manner she had. She took Layla's hand.

"There's honor in this work," she said after a moment.

Layla looked over. "Pardon?"

"You see me as a kindred spirit, and I am! I love you, Layla. We see so much with the same eye. What you have trouble seeing is the logic behind our culture. I may want to change it and refine it and make it *better*, but I was raised in it. Maybe it's easier to understand the Valharan perspective if you remember the ancient adage: with great power comes great responsibility. We're born to it. We're bred for it. A class of people charged with loving and protecting our citizens. Even the most strident noble wouldn't be as arrogant to say our class has unique capability or intellect for it. Anyone *can*. But not everyone will, responsibly."

"...and nobles are more responsible?"

"Government by humanity is fallible, by nature. Even the best of intentions can eventually lead to a massacre. But the overinvolvement of the noble families in each others' lives balances out. Training to avoid rookie mistakes. Shunning those who overstep. Honestly, some of this explains those three, four strikes against you."

As the chapel came into view, the throng waiting for them remained solemn, as befitted the parishioners on this holy day. A fake sort of solemn, playacting for an absent god.

"This whole system your class has idealized, with hereditary power and adoring subjects," Layla asked, as they prepared to exit the transport and enter their period of silence. "What comes of it?"

Anastasia patted her hand. "Why, my dear, an empire, if we can keep it."

Two hours of peace and quiet. Not bad, actually, in the sense a rucksack march during basic wasn't *bad* and kissing slobbering boys on Kaborlah wasn't *bad*. Time for her mind to wander, to be idle, to breathe, even if the forced stillness caused an overwhelming need to shake and move and juke, as if little electrical shocks were jittering up her spine, while other forces compelled her to be as silent as the quiver of an arrow.

Foreign as stillness was to her, it would have been unknown more to Amma, who despite her faults did backbreaking work for a bunch of shitty landlords just for the honor of *survival*. Free time was for entertaining, or sexing, which despite the non-work aspects were both still a mode of social survival. The more contacts, the more interrelatedness, the more her mother not only warded off loneliness and despair but also cultivated a stable of folk willing to help her out in hard times.

In the stillness, Layla condemned the idealistic elitism of the Altainan government, so proud of the utopia of enfranchisement they had built, yet so ignorant of the reality of billions of their citizens. In the stillness, Layla contemplated the shibboleths of Valharan culture: the notion of order and stability inextricably tied to tradition and purpose, a closed-off system admitting only a select few newcomers, and devotion not to only a set of patriotic ideals but also to a small set of families. In the stillness, Layla feared the impact of upheaval. Parliament and Ignatius were already heading toward a showdown. And Valharan institutions were strong, but were they strong enough? Enough agitation, and would her husband's life be in danger? Her life? One of the nicest things about egalitarian societies was their stability didn't depend on the lives of a handful of people. In a non-egalitarian one, would they need to rid themselves of those handfuls to enact a new start?

In the stillness, Layla fretted about her circle of loved ones, which had always been small: in turn, her mother and siblings; her squad-mates; Ignatius. Small meant she could protect them. Small meant as long as her little circle was intact, anything could happen in the galaxy and it would be okay, because she had her people and they had her. But now, the galaxy intruded, and the reach of what she could affect was not long enough. Her husband and his family were larger than themselves. For she didn't marry a man. She married an empire.

A melodious bell sounded, signaling the end of meditation, and the congregation rose for the sermon. Layla thumbed her Goddess medallion, currently safely hidden in her pocket lest it cause offense. At this point in Altainan worship, there would be music. But here, on Valhar, the wind chimes outside tinkled as if continuing the call of the signaling bell, and an imagined melody washed over her as her soul swayed in time. The Goddess Herself was speaking to Layla in the middle of this other god's worship, and She was whispering of the blessings She had given her. For one: new life, graven in her womb, a precious fluttering Layla held close, not ready to share with this craven world.

I can protect you, she promised her little one. But she had said that the first time, and—

Well, damn. She had dropped the locket. Aside from the scandal of another religion's iconography falling to the ground in a temple of the Falcon, it *was* also her panic button. *Idiot.* Layla inched her bare feet near it, hoping to snag it on her toes. A wriggle, and success. Her head bent slightly as she went to retrieve it, and as she did, a *pffft* went over her head.

The man in front of her twitched and collapsed to the ground.

His partner screamed. Layla gasped and fell to him. Anastasia yanked the necklace out of Layla's hands and squeezed it tight. Why hadn't she used her own ... right. Layla's would garner a faster response.

Helpless. She was helpless. A de-armed soldier in a fight she couldn't understand.

The man would be okay. Wouldn't he? A woman had gently moved Layla away, stating she was a doctor. The man appeared to be having some sort of seizure. Some of the congregants milled around, in a loose circle, watching and murmuring. Anastasia was holding the man's wailing husband.

No one was looking for the assailant.

Where the *fuck* were her guards?

Where was Mariah?

Strong hands gripped Layla's shoulders and ripped her away from her charge.

"It's me. It's *me!*" Mariah yelled as Layla kicked and flailed and cursed.

"Medics..." she gasped. "That man over there—"

"Leave that to everyone else. Let's go." Mariah pulled her along. Anastasia, free of her charge, was already heading to the armored transport, not one hair out of place.

Layla spun around. "This wasn't an isolated medical event. Something *happened* to that man."

"I'm aware."

"Is anyone else?"

Mariah spared her a minute glance of acknowledgement. "Our guards are trying to track down the intruder ... if there was one. And I agree there must have been one. Awful coincidence that the person in front of you started spasming."

"But if no one else knows there might have been foul play, they might not have the right treatment for him. We have to go back—"

"No time," Mariah said, propelling her farther and farther away from the scene.

"Is my life more important than his?"

One hand still gripping Layla's shirt, Mariah grabbed a passerby and spun him toward the chapel. "Inform emergency services that this might be an assault and not a preexisting medical condition." She shoved him forward and then let Layla go, getting in her face. "Move, soldier," she barked, and Layla moved on instinct, closing the last few meters to the waiting vehicle.

"Fucking finally," Mariah muttered. "Worst protectee ever." The shove into the transport was anything but gentle. Mariah squeezed in next to them. "Aleph protocol," she ordered the driver.

Layla turned to her bodyguard. "The precious minutes I spent arguing with you could have sealed his fate, Mariah." Mariah, entering commands into her tablet, ignored her.

The transport bounced in the turbulence, raising the passengers briefly into the air. Anastasia calmly fastened her restraints and looked to Mariah. "Aleph Protocol? That's usually for a demonstrated, verified threat. Which I agree, but will Imperial Security see it that way?"

"I make in-field decisions, Highness. I don't worry about what call the armchairs will make."

"Ah." Anastasia leaned back on her seat with pursed lips and just a hint of tension written on her face. She reached over and patted Layla's hand, as she often did, but with it came a slight squeeze. Layla understood the subtext: *the authorities believing the seriousness of this threat? Don't fucking count on it.*

* * *

"It was an attack, General."

"I know you feel like it was, Ms. Raderfy, but we're in the business of facts—"

Mariah leaned in close, not so close to be threatening, but close enough that *intention* vibrated up and down her spine.

"General Turine. You know what I am. Believe me when I say I recognize an attempt against my charge's life."

Ignatius held up his hand to forestall Turine's retort. "My lady," he said, turning to Layla. "What did you observe?" His eyes squinted in concentration but they lingered on her a mite too long, widening briefly in abject terror for her. She stroked his arm briefly and he regained his composure.

She described the whistling sensation passing above her. "Next thing I know, the guy's seizing."

"Are you sure you didn't imagine—" Turine began to ask.

"I'm sure."

"So why did he miss?" Where Mariah was tense and stiff, Ignatius was cool, leaning.

Layla thought a moment. "I think I must have briefly bent down. Bad luck. Well, good luck for me. The man in front of me was very tall, where I'm short. They were probably aiming for my head."

"Not just an isolated attempt, a fucking execution. With your pardon, sire," Mariah added at Ignatius's look.

"Did you see any evidence, Mariah?" Ignatius asked softly.

"Other than my own eyes?" She shook her head, lolling a candy stick 'round her tongue. "I believe her, although I didn't see anything other than the twitching. But you know the drill, sire. We treat any unusual event like this—"

"You did the right thing, Mariah. Dispersing the guard to search, covering the Empress. Ephraim," he called, turning to the majordomo, getting off a call, "what's the latest on the patient?"

"He'll live," he said simply. "No evidence of foul play."

At that, Turine put one hand up as in vindication, but kept up his look of professional curiosity. "Any history of seizures?" he asked.

"No, but apparently he was on medication that could cause them if used improperly."

"That doesn't prove anything!" Mariah said. "Your Grace, surely you still think—"

"How about you not tell me what I think," Layla offered. "I heard what I heard. But the jury's out on this one."

"What's a jury?"

Layla looked at Ephraim—and his interjection—with wonder, but Ephraim just chuckled, though mirthlessly. "Pulling your leg, Empress."

"I say we dispense with Aleph protocol. Let the Empress come out of hiding," Turine offered. "Sire?"

Ignatius hesitated, and looked Layla's way. "What do you think, dear?"

"I agree with coming out of hiding," Layla offered. "I'm not going to be cowed into submission."

"Let me think on it," Ignatius said. "But regardless, I still want increased force protection. I'm not willing to stake your life on this being a coincidence."

"You shouldn't be willing to stake your *baby's* life on it," came an interjection.

Ignatius turned his dangerous eyes on Mariah, and she stopped her tirade short. "Sire," she said, bowing in supplication.

Ephraim put his arm on his wife's shoulder. "Come. She's safe here." Ignatius threw Ephraim a mini salute as he led her away.

Safe. Safe at home. Two years after, was this palace *yet* her home?

And then she felt a fluttering in her belly, or, more like the popping of bubbles. Was that...? She froze, then let out a small, secret smile. And she looked at Ignatius, his brows pinched in concern, and took his hand. Home. Home wasn't a place. Home was people.

"Mariah's right," Ignatius said to Layla as Turine too went on his way. "About this being a credible threat."

Layla shivered. "What do you think it was?"

"Some sort of neural disrupter, likely. Got the guy in his spinal cord, but may have caused you a stroke had it hit your skull."

Layla shook her head. "I'm not going into hiding. Baby or not."

Ignatius sighed. "Layla, I don't like the unknowns here. We don't know what, if anything, we're facing."

"So let's find out. We need intel, Ignatius," she said as he attempted to interject. "We've got nothing to go on this time. Let me go about my business, albeit with extra protection, and maybe we'll draw them out."

"I refuse to use you as bait!"

"I'm not just the bait. I'm the prize itself, Ignatius." She sped on to belay his objection. "If we lock down, it'll give them time to regroup, to try again once we lower our guard. But if we parade around now, maybe, just maybe, it may make them move sooner than expected, lest we change our minds. See if something similar happens. That way, we can at least establish there's a credible threat. Otherwise, we'll convince ourselves this was nothing, to our detriment."

He cleared his throat and placed both hands behind his back in a formal stance. Layla presumed that hidden from view, those hands were clenching and unclenching in agitation. "May I forever be labeled a fool, for agreeing to this," Ignatius murmured, mostly to himself. "You will not be convincing me with this *drawing them out* nonsense. But," he acknowledged, "I also fear a lockdown might be too much too soon, leading to later complacency." He stroked his chin, humming discontentedly to himself.

You shouldn't be willing to stake your baby's life on it, Mariah had said. Was she the worst mother ever, thinking more about grand plans to catch a criminal than hiding away, keeping her child safe? If something happened to the baby, because Layla was bullheaded, she would have utterly failed in her first, foremost duty. Keep safe the ones she called her own. She'd already lost one child, certainly through no fault of her own, but how much mourning could one heart bear?

But as she said to herself, before everything changed: she didn't marry a man. She married an Empire. And the problems of the Empire were intruding in her circle of domestic tranquility.

"Hiding away would just lead to *more* hiding. That's how these things work," she said, eventually.

They shared a look, Ignatius then closing his eyes in silent prayer. "None of this is going to be over soon, is it?" he asked.

She leaned in to him, head on his shoulder, hand snaking up to caress his beard. "No. But we're together. And we're not running scared. We've always said that's all we ever needed."

He kissed her forehead. "Okay, my love. Go be a hero. Stand tall, show your face. My stubborn soldier."

She smiled wanly. Stubbornness had brought her here, years before, to a nation on the brink of war. And everything had been on a circling holding pattern ever since. Cryptic notes on tablets. Loyalty and fidelity at odds. And intrigue. Whoever had done this to her—she sensed they'd been at this game just as long. This was nothing new. The answers were somewhere in the past.

THEN

Then

6 Shuktan 1126

This week, after severing diplomatic relations, Lyria officially declared war on the Valharan Empire. Because of the Alliance's treaty organization, every other government in the Free Whorl will have to follow suit. Including mine.

Maybe. Maybe not, if I can help it.

I've seriously underestimated this situation. What I thought initially was a cut-and-dry diplomatic snarl is growing, and I fear it won't be over anytime soon.

We've finally given up on propriety and moved my things into Ignatius's bedroom. Beatrix, the Cruise Director, has begun to populate my closet with clothing appropriate to a Valharan noblewoman; every day I open the door to the wardrobe in the guestroom, and *poof!* like a magic trick out of a hat or a portal into an ethereal world of fashion, beautiful dresses appear. Most of these I don't move into Ignatius's room, unless it's the rare casual, comfortable, yet approved outfit.

Apparently, as there are many different "apartments" in the residence, we're expected to move to a more appropriate, sprawling, overwhelmingly huge set of rooms after marriage. But Ignatius's current space suits me just fine. And unlike the rest of the palace, it isn't filled with scrollwork furniture and brass accents. Just simple. Spare. Like me.

But my lady, Beatrix fretted yesterday, *you will need a suitable dressing room and closet.*

Why can't the little guest room serve as that? I asked, perplexed.

Regardless of that point of contention, his room is currently *our* room, and that makes me feel a little less like a stranger, foreigner, interloper, *guest*.

This is becoming real.

Ignatius, in his—*our*—bedroom rubs his face and groans. I've never seen him so tired. "I still wish I knew the Lyrians' source of information. The palace seems unlikely."

"Maybe it's a Solitan. They would have all the documents too."

Ignatius frowns in thought. "I'll ask Viceroy Stanlo about it. I'm not sure I can stop all this," he adds. "The rest of the Alliance is looking for an excuse to declare. Soon enough, they'll follow the Lyrians."

I shake my head, trying to swallow away the visceral *fear* that follows that statement. What will happen to me if Altain declares war? I'm not a citizen of Valhar, not yet. In fact, technically, I'm still a Republic officer, with no documented loyalty to the Empire.

I look around this royal bedroom, in a royal palace, warily. A lamb in a lion's den.

"They don't want war," I reiterate, as if stating it could ensure truth. "Look, elections are coming up soon. Not for President, but legislative seats. And actual war would *not* help Roya's party. She won the presidency by promising to withdraw from Dega! Altain will jump in if they feel they have no choice, whether because they're compelled to enforce the tunnel treaty, or because of their collective defense agreement with the rest of the Alliance, or because they think the cost of inaction is great. But Roya, at least, will be looking for a way out. Not to mention Reneb. C'mon. They hate taking a stand."

I draw my legs up on the bed, already in comfortable nightwear: flannel PJs with little unicorns all over them, thick socks. A robe would probably help too, in this Valharan chill. Ignatius reaches into the wardrobe to grab more sartorially-appropriate silken duds. Maybe one day I'll get him a onesie with wind-up waterfowl all over it. Or, at the very least, a comfortable panjabi.

"So, how do we ensure it's worth it for Altain and Reneb to stay out of it?" he asks.

I tilt my head. "Someone would have to convince them this doesn't trigger their collective defense agreement with Lyria. *Lyria* is doing the attacking. They aren't the ones needing protection. Altain can't be expected to jump into action every time a member of the Alliance decides to rattle sabres. There's a chance they're already using that justification and aren't planning to enter the war. I just don't know." I cross my arms in frustration. Lyrians are long-lived. Their patented and top-secret biotech allowing them to slow aging keeps them alive nearly *twice* as long as the rest of the Whorl denizens, but they also are living proof that old age doesn't alleviate utter stupidity.

"And if Altain stays out of it, Reneb will follow."

"And vice versa," I say.

"*Someone* has to convince them," Ignatius echoes thoughtfully, looking at me.

I shake my head sharply, the squeeze in my throat possibly a symptom of my heart leaping into it. "Oh no. No. That wouldn't work."

"Why?"

I breathe deep, in and out, in order to clear out of the air even the *possibility* of this happening. "Let me count the ways," I say, ticking off on my fingers. "First, plain and simple: I don't know if I want to be the spokesman for Valhar. I just *got here*. To speak on the interests of Valhar seems rushed. Second, you know your security detachment doesn't trust me. There's no way they'd be okay with sending me off alone back to Altain on the eve of war to engage in shuttle diplomacy on Valhar's behalf. And third, Altain. They—" I pause, cutting my recitation short. "No, Ignatius," I insist instead. "I need to stay put."

"Do you want to go back?"

"What?"

"Back to Altain. I meant what I said. You can leave at any time. You know, fight in the Republic Forces."

Oh, Ignatius. I spool a strand of hair on my index finger, buying myself time with the fidget. "You know," I begin softly, then breathe in to still the gyroscope battering my insides, "if I thought I could go home and actually fight for my country, I probably would." I jump in my seat as I realize what I'm implying. "Look, Nate, what I *want* to do regardless is stay here with you! Saying I want to go back—"

Ignatius holds up his hand. "I know exactly what you mean. It's *me* you're talking to. I'd be the same way." We look at each other, those vows of duty binding us yet again. We *get* each other, in ways no one else can probably ever comprehend. He plops down next to me on the bed with an audible groan, then grabs my hand.

"But," I say, "that's rather moot isn't it. I won't ever be trusted again. I can't do anything to fight for my country. They'd never give me a position where I can make a difference. Not anymore." And that's what has me out of sorts. Well, other than war, other than the feeling of both halves of my soul being drawn and quartered. It's the futility of it all. The finality.

All I ever wanted to do was serve my nation. They—Ransom, the entire paranoid establishment—took that away from me.

That's not saying I'd *never* go back. I still keep that mantra, as if chanting it will ward away all ills. *You can always go home. You can always go home.*

I'll never do anything to eliminate that choice.

"Quite." He scoots in closer to me and my head fits neatly on to his shoulder. "If you stay here," he begins, and then he pauses as if to reconsider. "Our nations aren't at war. Hopefully they never will be. But, if it comes to that, I would like us to consider moving up the wedding. I'd hate to rush you into something like that, like a wartime elopement—"

"Ignatius," I say, "I'm not exactly the *big wedding* type anyway. We could go get married tomorrow. I don't care."

He raises his eyebrows, lips twisted in thought, combined with a pleased glint in his eyes. "Well, then that's an option. Let's not—there's no reason for that yet, although I have to admit a giddiness at the idea of just going for it." He pauses, running a hand through his hair, and gives me a shy grin, and my heart explodes. "But it is something I wanted to raise. If we go to war, your status is unclear. Harboring an enemy combatant without any external vows of loyalty to myself or to the regime might be too far for some of the nobility. Marrying would allow me to protect you."

Read: *I may have absolute power, but that power has hidden limits.*

Protective custody at home, protective custody here. I know which one's more comfortable.

"Ugh. Politics." I roll my neck, trying to will the tension out. "Being in the middle of this maelstrom."

"Nothing new."

"The emperor thing, though. Ruler-ascendent of the Valharan Empire. *That* is new to me."

"It is for me too," he says plaintively.

"Hmm," I respond. Ignatius is as duty-bound and honor-coded and careful and planning as I am, but this isn't the jump for him that it is for me. I can see the thread of his reasoning in marrying me. What he needs: a line of succession, plump new babes pumped out of a hearty, warrior wife, maybe one who can capture the imagination of a nation, perhaps with a tale of star-crossed lovers, a woman crossing the Whorl to be with the emperor, a foreigner who conveniently enough had been named honorary nobility before it was even thought Ignatius would be emperor. Tailor-made. Not new and scary, not in the way it is for me.

There's no good answer here. I'm forever torn between these two worlds. But there was that day mere months ago, when I looked at Ignatius and chose to leap.

"You're stubborn. When you come up against Valharan society, they're going to be the ones to break, aren't they?"

I shake my head again, an eerie restlessness and frustration prickling my senses. "If your mother couldn't do it, how could I?"

Then

I sit in Ignatius's personal library, wondering. Writing. Thinking.

Is Altain wrong to worry the Mazarans would come through the Valharan tunnel? Maybe. Probably. It takes decades to go from Mazaran space to the area where the Valharans are building. But the Mazarans have become the bogeyman of the Whorl, for good reason, too. The Mazarans don't even seem entirely *human*; as an expansionist space-faring society, they've evolved to longer, leaner bodies, and large wobbly heads. Though weak-boned at birth, most train extensively to be able to survive on gravity-laden planets, and in any case, conquering armies wear mecha suits that make them seem like robotic giants holding the line while their ships smite down destruction and death. And even though we had an armistice, those bobble-headed dicknuggets held the upper hand in negotiations. When the Whorl finally stood together to repel their invasion, it wasn't superior military might that pushed them back. The little gnats of the Whorl fighting back finally made Mazaran expansion a bit too costly for them. But the scrappy kid standing up to the schoolyard bully doesn't usually earn respect, or fear. Just disinterest and dismissal. Bigger fish to fry.

And Mazarans or not, what other invading nations are out there that could find their way to our quiet, isolated Whorl and wreak the same havoc? Obviously, the Whorl knows about other human societies, but we're mostly off on our own. We get the occasional traveler or generational ship coming through the nebula, though not often. It's a year-long journey through that tunnel. From what I've heard, most of the galaxy doesn't have the wormholes the Whorl is blessed with, although some civilizations, like the Mazarans, have perfected faster than light travel. The Whorl planets have FTL, but not in the same measure. But the Mazarans, all the while, were expanding their borders until they got to the ancient man-made tunnel in the nebula. Goddess alive, it would probably take them much less than decades to get to the Valharan tunnel when complete. Two entrances into the Whorl, surrounding us on both ends, and maybe other invaders to boot.

I shiver. Maybe I *shouldn't* be helping Valhar avoid this war. Maybe my duty is to defeat this threat to my people.

And then: the note from Ransom arrives on my tablet.

Layls, it says, *Sorry about the jab of fire. Let's talk. -R*

Then a string of numbers. If I put in the effort, I can probably figure out how he wants me to contact him.

Shit. *Shit.*

The message wasn't sent using the secure system Ransom hacked back when I was here for the state visit. Maybe it's been compromised. Nor is it via the process he asked me to memorize during our last conversation.

No good way to verify his identity. *Jab of fire.* The buspirathol. It's probably not someone else in the Altain government. With time and distance, I've begun to suspect Ransom's little interrogation was off the books.

How did he get access to this tablet?

Could this be a trick by the palace? A way to see my fealty to Valhar, or if nothing else, my fealty to Ignatius?

The more I think about it, the more I'm convinced this is a plant. I'm under so much security, there's no way this could've shown up so easily onto my tablet. I don't care how skilled Ransom is, or how many tendrils he has.

Who would know about the buspirathol? Ignatius does. But it's private. He wouldn't share that information. He knows not to. And he wouldn't be involved in a phishing expedition.

But if I'm right that this is a trick, and I report the contact, I'll elevate myself in their eyes as a loyal person. Maybe I'll be able to keep my freedoms even if Altain declares war. Maybe it'll give me the ability later on to help my country. But what if I'm wrong, and this really is from home? The only way Altain could get the message to the palace would be by using a human source. By sharing the message, I'd put that person in danger.

My thoughts whirl round and round, without a set form or structure. Loyalty. Duty.

What are those things? Do I owe anything to my home nation?

Who do I owe? I'm a military officer, but I joined the Republic forces because where else could I go? For Altain, I gave and gave until there was nothing left.

They gave me an education. A place to belong. Something to fight for. Is it a case where they put enough coins in the *education* and *housing* and *friendship* vending machine and loyalty falls out?

What Valhar's doing with the tunnel is wrong. It will endanger the entire Whorl. But I'm not a spy, damnit. Turncoat. Double agent. I've staked my career, my *honor*, on being honest to a fault. Always above board. Dutiful.

What I'm not going to do is run to them and tell them Altain tried to reach out to me. I'm not going to risk exposing a source. A real person, who could be hanged for treason.

That'll mark the first time in my life I haven't been completely transparent to the authority figures that run my life. Maybe second, if you count Carlus's situation. Whatever. And whoever that authority may be, right now.

If this is real, I wouldn't give information to Ransom anyway. That'd be a betrayal of Ignatius. And I can't do that. I can't do that to him.

…

I erase it all.

Then

Per my suggestion, Ignatius sent Benedik to smooch up to Altain. He's been received cautiously but, as Benedik puts it, with a twinkle of relief. Seems like unless all hell breaks loose, the Whorl has a reprieve from the onset of war. Lyria, yes, but alone, they are needling gnats.

But this is Valhar, so they still have a standing "war room." It's not the high-tech vault I expect. It's a small, fancy space, like any other in the palace, more suitable for visiting dignitaries and victuals than up-to-the-minute reporting or late-night strategy sessions. The only difference between the so-called war room and a tea room is the disposition of its inhabitants—crusty old men in starched uniforms—and the type of refreshment: straight vodka.

Of *course* the Empire thinks it's acceptable to make military decisions affecting millions of lives while hammered.

Ignatius holds my hand as we enter, and the frown-lined men deepen their scowls as they lay eyes on the slip of a girl who's been allowed in this hallowed realm, even as they stand for their Emperor. I take my hand back with a start, and Ignatius gives me a bemused look, as if he has no idea what my reaction is about. As for me, I think, *Great. A hostile environment.*

"Ahem. As you were, gentlemen. I just needed to show Lady Layla something." He leads me over to the east wall.

"Can you at least refer to me as Dame Layla in situations like this?" I whisper. "I mean, it's kinda an honor and stuff."

Ignatius's low chuckle reverberates in my soul.

He activates the inset screen to display a familiar map: the Swan Nebula in the vicinity of the subspace tunnel, the rogue planet Dega just beyond it, as if the tunnel is a sun for Dega to orbit.

"My father sent me an update from Dega Station. Someone's been scouting Mazara's defunct relays." Ignatius's face as he mentions his father holds that same sad distance it always does, when it comes to Tonin Kurestin.

"Scavengers?"

He shakes his head. "Whoever it is didn't actually get caught. Routine patrols found some tampering, after-the-fact. Very slight, unavoidable indications of repair attempts. Whoever these are, they're professionals."

I worry my lip as I think. "Special Forces or a third party? And regardless, on behalf of what government? And why?"

"Exactly," he says.

"The Tarlanian family, from Reneb, they have that mining project out there. I'm not a comms expert by any means, but if they can somehow control lines of communication in the nebula ... hmm." A future Empress doesn't stomp in frustration, at least not in public, so I settle for biting the inside of my cheek. "I'm talking out of my ass, Ignatius. Hell, someone could be trying to contact the Mazarans without having to do the year-long journey through the tunnel. Goddess knows why anyone would do that."

"Not Altain?"

"Who the hell knows anymore. Would be weird. Those Tarlanians though? Last I checked, they were the ruling family on Reneb. Which means it wouldn't be prudent to ask Park. He'd probably be wary of talking." The Renebian government ostensibly has free and fair elections, but in truth, family conglomerates run the whole place. Politicians and officials: bought and sold. "But there are some mercs out there. Maybe they know something."

"How do *you* know all this, Lady Layla?" comes a cool voice behind me.

I turn to find a heavy-set, square-jawed man evaluating me. General Huxley Turine. Head of Imperial security, with an expansive portfolio covering regime protection and incursions into Imperial space. If it occurs within the bounds of the Empire, it falls, in some fashion, under Turine.

And now Turine examines me like I'm a particularly interesting butterfly, one that's intended to be decorative but instead is performing differential equations.

Or maybe I'm projecting.

"Dame Layla has some useful contacts out in the Nebula," Ignatius responds, taking my hand once more.

"Oh?" Turine hesitates, looking at his emperor, seemingly worried about a misstep. "Forgive me, Lady—er, Dame Layla. I had thought you were a speechwriter. Back on your home planet."

"Yes, sir," I respond. His eyebrows draw together at my *sir*. "But I was also Republic military." *As you well know.*

"Ah," he says, acting still confused. Oh, come *on*.

I move to turn back to the display, puzzling over this unusual activity out in the Nebula, when Turine mutters to Ignatius, "No offense intended, sire. It is not the military experience I was questioning. It's the easy comfort with espionage."

I stop short. Oh, hell. He's the one who sent the ersatz message from Ransom, isn't he. I remove my hand from Ignatius's once more, shaking out suddenly-clammy fingers.

Just then, a younger man takes Turine aside and I strain to listen. What will it be, then? *Arrest the wench now!* Or *off with her head!* But thankfully, the conversation appears to do nothing with me. Instead, the soldier is showing General Turine a small, flat, disc. *Our only prototype, sir,* he says. *A paired set. You wanted to be the beta tester?* Turine nods briskly.

This damnable palace is turning me paranoid.

Ignatius continues to regard the screen with the relays overlaid. "I wonder," he says, stroking his beard. "Huxley," he calls to General Turine, turning around in confusion when Turine is no longer next to him. "Ah," he says, waving him over. "Since my normal contacts on Reneb would be loathe to go against a powerful ruling family, is there a safe way to contact our man Charles? I don't know—he's only been there for nine or so months—but perhaps he has some insight."

Turine startles, glancing at me with something akin to dread, and then turns back to Ignatius and shakes his head. "I'm sorry, sire, but there's no good way to reach him without effectively broadcasting in the clear, with goodness-knows-who listening and discerning things we don't want them to discern." He spares another discreet (or so he thinks) look at me.

Poor General Turine. He doesn't know *I* know about Carlus being on Reneb.

"All right, all right," Ignatius says. "Good point. We'll just have to file this as an unsolved mystery, for now." Turine nods and walks away, looking disturbed.

I awake languorously from a subsequent nap, on a couch, a blanket tucked around me carefully. Ignatius sits next to me, peering at his tablet, sleeves rolled up and a stylus tapping thoughtfully against his chin.

Maybe my mind doesn't perceive desire the way other people's do, but I can appreciate the aesthetically pleasing. And Ignatius at work is an incredibly attractive specimen.

He notices me, and his look of concentration eases into something so soft, so kind, eyes crinkling and tiny quirked smile, that my heart soars.

"Hope I didn't wake you," he murmurs. "You were so peaceful." He reaches out his hand.

"What are you working on?"

"Budgets."

"Budgets," I repeat skeptically. "Didn't know the Emperor is also a CFO."

He shrugs. "You know how it is. I delegate, of course. Ephraim's the star in sorting all this out and liaising with the appropriate agencies and ministers. But I still need to have a general idea of what's going on."

"I missed you," he continues. "Doing all this without you..." he trails off, and begins anew. "I kept thinking what you'd say. How you'd advise me to act. We went from sending vids to each other to nothing, and I was adrift. And I *need* you. Someone who's an equal. I can't even be free with Ephraim, and I've known him since we were three. I mean, you're more attractive as well," he adds with a crooked grin.

I giggle.

"My fault, I know, that we didn't talk," he adds quickly. "Back then. After my ascension, before we saw each other again. I hope you didn't feel abandoned. I was trying to avoid causing you problems."

"Believe me, I appreciate it. They were so *suspicious*, Ignatius. The Roya administration. They looked at me like I was about to declare myself a royalist and go annex all of us to the Empire."

He sits back, in a mock huff. "Wait, I thought that's what this was. A formal marriage-of-alliance."

"Hah."

"Aren't you some sort of war hero? Can't you seize power and then hand the reins over?"

"You joke, but I honestly think that's what Ransom was worried about." My shoulders lower. "So, any news?"

"Benedik says his wooing and genuflection is still paying dividends."

"You mean I don't have to fear being reclassified as an enemy combatant? Thank goodness. Though your general may be disappointed. Mariah too."

Ignatius chortles. "Ah, yes, the tangled web we weave. I probably panicked that poor man in there, didn't I?"

"Indeed." I grip Ignatius's arm lightly in affectionate remembrance of one of our shared memories, one waypoint in our journey of trust and love in each other, when Ignatius bound me to secrecy in the wake of Gustav's incapacitation. I worked with him in the days following, all the little tips and tricks to avoid spiking a lie-detecting machine, in the case my interrogation-happy government decided to ask details of my interactions with the Valharan monarchy. The negotiations went on as scheduled and the Whorl was officially at peace with the Mazarans.

Park's the one who years later squirreled Carlus and his family to Reneb when Carlus wanted to leave and hide away forever, and Park reached out to both Ignatius and me at the time. So of course I knew. But explaining all that to Turine doesn't seem like it's in the cards.

"Turine *does* know he's on Reneb, right?" I ask.

"He does, but not the details of how he got there and exactly where he is. You're one of the few keepers of that particular secret. One secret among many." A rueful smile on his face. I yet again get a sense they're are even more secrets that I too do not know.

"I'm still worried," he admits. "I feel like I should send you home—"

"Cold feet?"

He takes my hand and squeezes tight. "Never ever ever. If I could choose, I'd marry you right this second. Pledge fealty to you. From now on, in fact, my main loyalty is to *you*, more than anything else. If you're willing to take the journey with me..."

I think on my satisfaction months ago as I effectively told Ransom to go fuck himself. "Well then," I say, squeezing back, "we're doing this. Together. No take-backs. You might have to convince your advisors though.." My face sours.

"You might be the stubborn one, but I do a passable imitation of an immovable object. Don't you worry. You're the one light in my life I will never ever give up. Like you said." He pecks my cheek. "No take backs.."

Now

* Now

NOVARIA GAZETTE

BREAKING NEWS

Emperor Ignatius I suspends Parliament, institutes self-rule. How will this affect the war effort?

***

Layla shielded her eyes against the morning sun as her husband's oldest friend cajoled him to give up on his cousin, forever.

"You know I love Benedik as a brother, sire," Ephram said. "But the trickle of information we've gotten in investigating his disappearance has dried up completely. And the Free Press Coalition is convinced you have him locked somewhere in a basement, and are just *daring* you to shut them down so they can hue and cry oppression."

Ignatius grimaced. "And if we declare him dead, they won't just cry murder?"

"All the broadcasts are crowing about the Empress's recent pregnancy announcement. Including the nascent independent papers. *And* the outfits that are bold enough to raise a stink about your declaration of personal rule have no time for a new conspiracy theory. Now is the perfect time to bite the bullet, pay our respects, and let your family move on." Ephraim removed his spectacles and cleared the condensation. That little gulp at the end told Layla more about how Ephraim *really* felt about the fate of one of his closest friends.

"It would also help with the investigation, sire, if we can call it a suspected assassination rather than a missing persons case. Because, sire, you and I both know this was no accident. He had been driven off-course. His bondsmen were found dead. There are larger forces at work."

Ignatius crossed his arms over his chest in a way that would have looked defiant and petulant had Layla attempted it, but on him looked commanding. "I'm not doing anything without talking to Alina or my uncles. I don't like the idea of announcing my cousin's death as something I can slide in between news channels, but maybe Abilio would have some thoughts on how he'd like it to be done."

"You just dissolved Parliament, sire. I'm not sure the most prominent member of that Senate and his husband, the Prime Minister, would be keen to discuss mitigation strategies with you."

"No need to be snide, Ephraim."

The protests and unrest had infiltrated the Lords' Parliament. No pacifists there, of course. No, the specific grievance uttered by Parliament was Ignatius not prosecuting the war effectively. They demanded less gentleness with the Felix occupation. Less war of attrition and more aggressive action against the Alliance. If they had known about the threat to the Solita tunnel, certainly there would be outrage the Navy hadn't yet taken Kaborlah to cut off access. As it was, the Fleet had been prepped and was creeping toward the border, as Ignatius dithered on whether to open yet another front in the war.

Dissolving Parliament. By the Goddess. Layla couldn't help but worry about how this was affecting Ignatius. He was at his worst when his authority was being challenged. It would be up to her to leash him.

She hadn't yet taken the initiative to comm Carlus directly, but Park had couriered messages from him via diplomatic pouch. She could tell Carlus was being circumspect, with the Renebians listening in, but she could almost hear the gravelly, worried voice via text. *Tell Him to take care. The best of men can make grave mistakes in the quest to protect His people.*

What a mess. She was frightfully aware of her heavy influence on Ignatius's measured response to both Felix and Kaborlah. She didn't want to be known to history as the failure behind the throne. The thought of being *wrong* made her palms itch. There was a reason she had played it safe for most of her life. And if she were wrong, if Felix fell, war would come to Valhar proper. No one knew exactly what would happen next. Surely, though, if the heart of the Valharan Empire were to find itself on a spike, she'd be holding the spear.

Would this war ever end? And *how*?

"All right, Ephraim," Ignatius conceded. "Talk it over with Turine—and with Mariah—to see if there are any royal protection angles we may have missed, but after that, have a draft statement sent to me." He bowed his head and swallowed. A quick blink-and-you-miss-it glance toward Layla revealed a crooked smile and sad eyes. She lightly touched her hand to his arm in support, regal-style.

"I should be off, Ignatius," she said gently. "The schedule for this afternoon is tight." Ignatius nodded.

Ephraim cleared his throat. "Right. Ma'am. Your chariot awaits. The suggested plan is for me to ride in the back with you, if that's okay?"

She raised her eyebrows and gestured to the transport. "Why in heavens not? Onward, soldier."

The glut of spring festival days had abated; Layla had managed to squirrel out of further appearances after the incident at the temple (her heart quickened at the thought of what might have happened, if the fear even was *real;* the doctors had ruled the man's collapse a medication-induced seizure with no threat to the Empress). But her schedule had ticked up with her pregnancy announcement. Goodwill, and all that. Perform for the masses. And, the reasoning apparently went, now that she was *with child* certainly no one would think to put her in danger. Ridiculous assertion, by Layla's count. Why not? If the goal was to rid themselves of Ignatius—although, who even knew who was doing the targeting and what their goals were—why not eliminate a future heir?

The thought turned her stomach. She still felt disconnected from the little mite, but the notion of her child in danger was almost paralyzing. Despite Layla's general belief that she should not run, nor hide, from whomever wished her harm, hopefully she wasn't being careless.

"Today's just a sweet, easy day touring the former Tyrii barony, Your Grace," Ephraim siad, pulling up a timetable on his tablet. "You're touring a new school specifically for young girls, trying out some local delicacies and hearing some folklore. How's the exhaustion?"

"Much better," she affirmed. "I shall be able to smile and curtsy with the best of them."

"Your Grace, it's not your place to curtsy—oh, never mind. You know all this."

"What do you want, Ephraim?" At his jerked head, she clarified. "Love spending time with you, but you usually travel in the follow car. I know when you're maneuvering. And don't even think about hiding behind formalities or I might choke you."

Ephraim chuckled. "All right ma'am...Layla," he amended. "I wanted to talk to you about our relationship with the Dargas family."

The Dargas family. The esteemed earldom of Gruesse. Benedik. Alina. Henri. Abilio. *Ignatius's* family. How could Ephraim speak of them so coolly? They were Ephraim's family, too, after a fashion, given he, the son of Kurestin Manor's head of security, was raised alongside Ignatius, who had in turn been raised alongside the younger Benedik. Three in a pod.

After this Tyrii trip, would her next appearance be in Gruesse for Benedik's funeral?

"Whose relationship?" she asked instead. "And to what end?"

"The Palace's. Specifically, the Emperor's, but from the ruler side. His personal affiliation with the Dargas family is not at issue."

"Can you really separate the two?"

"In truth? No." Ephraim bit his lip, an uncharacteristic gesture. "Look. Speaking plainly, Layla, everything is going to shit. The populist revolt is bad enough. And no," he said, holding up his hand, "I decidedly do not want to hear your opinion on *that* thankyouverymuch. Small mercies that our planet of Valhar proper follows social order and only a small faction *here* is protesting. But within the colonies and territories, we're facing an unprecedented level of unrest. They're agitating about internal taxes and those on imports. In the past, we could argue our Lords' Senate is the virtual representative body for all of the Empire and is charged with generating funds, so they could petition *them*."

"But now—"

"Parliament's *separate* actions have taken apart the argument that we have sufficient virtual representation, and that's how we've found ourselves in the situation we have today with respect to the colonies. That in itself makes Parliament's actions downright seditious."

Sedition again, damnit. "They didn't disband *themselves*, Ephraim. Ignatius did that."

"Yes, because some core group of Lords decided they knew better than their emperor on how to prosecute a war. So, *completely logically*," here, his eyes rolled, "they decided to stop levying taxes in support of that war? As long as Parliament was in session, the emperor couldn't get war funding. With it disbanded, he has options."

"But Abilio didn't have anything to do with that. Nor Henri." They were, in fact, on the side of following Ignatius's wishes. Layla resisted throwing her hands up in frustration. "Why are our relations with them strained? Why are we tarring them with the same brush?"

"Because—and this is not entirely their fault, Layla, it's the nature of the beast—they cannot support self-rule. By tradition, they have to oppose disbanding Parliament. Which means, however, that they are now in opposition with their emperor, despite their original support. They cannot be trusted."

"So, what? They are persona non grata within our family now? We're doing this in the wake of everything going on with Benedik?"

"They aren't going to be part of the Privy Council. They aren't going to have free access to the royal family. And this, Layla, is where you come in, because that includes access to *you*."

Layla sat back and the transport rolled on. Because of the altitude in the Corval Mountains, traditional speeders wouldn't fly safely, so antiquated modes of locomotion were required, and therefore they traveled on wheels, on the ground. Not many of these in the royal fleet; in fact, this car wasn't armored. Goddess, when was the last time she was in an unarmored vehicle?

"It's surprising there's been this much dissent from the nobility," she said.

"Indeed," said Ephraim. "Someone—or a group of someones—is egging them on. Organizing them. Whispering in their ears. Same thing with the colonies."

"Same someones?"

"I don't know," he said darkly, "but I intend to find out. I can't rule out Alliance propaganda and covert action. Does that sound like them?"

She nodded. "Oh yes it does, Altain specifically. Wonder if unrest is the back door way they expect to sneak to the Solita Tunnel?"

Ephraim gave her a long glance. "Aaah, I hadn't thought of that. I wonder if General Turine has."

Their transport reached the mountains and slowed to a crawl. *Valhar* was slowing to crawl. No, that wasn't quite right. Valhar was holding its collective breath. At last count, the forces opposing Ignatius were thus: the entire Whorl Alliance; the Volg coalition, led by Malachi Finley, made up of merchants and businessmen who wanted a seat at the political table; the Free Press Coalition, which was bundling up demands for positive rights—free speech, et al—with a call for wholesale systemic upheaval; the anti-war commoners, a minor subset of angry subjects but who had outsized voices; the populist colonists, much larger, more dangerous, and prominent on Solita, a rather strategic location indeed; the parliamentary war hawks, led by Corval, wanting harsher measures;

the traditionalists, led by Dracini, horrified by the disbanding of Parliament and self-rule. Plus: freedom fighters on Felix, attempting to throw off the Valharan occupation; Altain, planning to sneak to Solita—were they being supported by the Solita rebels as Stanlo had claimed, despite her skepticism?; and, Kaborlah. Not opposing yet, as it hadn't yet been conquered, but suddenly, it was clear as day: of *course* Ignatius had to take Kaborlah.

With what funds, though?

"Ephraim," Layla asked, "with Parliament disbanded, how is he getting the money for the war?"

"We're using the nobility's loopholes against them, just like you suggested." Ephraim grinned. "Some creative accounting. All feudal holdovers are grants from the king and can technically revert to the crown. Also, an old law about ship mone-"

The transport lurched. Thank goodness they were still in the foothills or Layla's fear of heights would have panicked her. She craned her neck forward to speak to the driver. "What was that?"

The driver shook his head. "I'm sorry, Your Grace. Felt like some pebbles hitting us off course."

Ephraim craned his neck around. "Wait, where in the ever-loving Falcon is your security escort?"

Another motor transport pulled up beside them and trilled its horn. The driver opened the window—

—and a shot rang out. Layla and Ephraim's transport accelerated, leaving the other behind, a cloud of dust permeating the vehicle. Layla climbed over to the driver's seat, where her chauffeur was spasming—no blood, was this the neural disruptor Ignatius theorized?—and attempted to kick his foot off the accelerator.

"Use the restraints to arrest his movements!" she called back at Ephraim. She took the controls, sitting on the wounded man's lap.

"Layla, what the hell—this isn't your job. I was a soldier too!"

"Yes, but you have medic training. I don't. I drive. Control the fucking restraints so I can control this cab. And then get him out from under me."

Ephraim cursed but did as she said, pulling the restraints in the driver's seat taut, and Layla finally had complete access. She shifted as Ephraim grabbed at the man to pull him into the backseat—forget medic training, she couldn't have done even *that* if Ephraim had moved to drive. And then: three vehicles, on this empty dusty road, careening toward her. From different vectors.

"Hold on!" she yelled. She coaxed her engines to go faster and shot forward. Then she took her foot off the gas, reversed her thrusters, and flipped the transport around in a lightning-quick J-turn.

One of the enemy vehicles was catching up to her, and as it approached, she slowed so it was just a hair behind. The window was still open. She could get shot with a disruptor too. Sending a prayer up to the Goddess, she aimed the front axle of her transport to the opposing one's back axle, and spun it out.

Her groundcar sped as fast as it could on its antiquated suspension. The situation rather resembled those sims she had done in basic training, down to making sure she followed a racing line; thankfully driving antiquated transports was part of the curriculum. Goddess help her if there was some sort of barricade to overcome next, because she didn't think this shitty little vehicle could handle another intentional collision.

Shots. Projectiles? Did these damn attackers have fucking rail guns on their ancient motors? A hiss. Layla cursed. "Losing thrusters," she called.

"They got our comms, too. Somehow," said Ephraim. "I've been trying to reach backup..."

"Who in the living *fuck* is trying to kill me?" And her baby too. This was getting real old real fast.

In the distance, in the deserted valley ... no. It really *was* a barricade? Should she spin around again? No, the additional sounds of shooting put that plan to rest real quick. She sped up, mentally calculating the points she'd have to hit to break through ... if the transport could handle it ... if her *body* could handle the jostling without hurting her child, and then she recognized the cars in front of her.

"Ephraim," she called, "we're coming in hot. Is that our team?" A lone warrior up top held an epically large rifle. "*Is that Mariah?*"

Ephraim propelled himself to the front and stared. "Yes. Yes!" he called. "Slow down. It's them. Flash some signal or something so they know it's us."

Safety signal sent back and then two of the flanking vehicles in front of her shot past her, guns blazing.

Safety. Protection. Layla coasted to a stop and then stumbled out.

Mariah rushed to her. "What. And I cannot stress this enough. The *fuck*."

Layla looked up at her in agreement, then bent down and threw up.

It was evenfall by the time they returned to the capital and to the palace, and the golden light seemed to wink at her as if everything was amazing and shiny and she hadn't almost been assassinated. Her driver had died; whatever had hit him had gone straight to his brain, and so there was no question what would have happened if the shot against her at the chapel had rung true.

"Corval, that fucking snake," Mariah fumed. "It had to have been him. He's trying to bring back Carlus's reign, or something like that. Cut off your heirs, then kill you, then bring the former emperor back, swooping in to save the day."

"You've known Carlus almost your entire life, Mariah," Ignatius chided. "You served his father faithfully. You know Carlus would have no part in that."

"I don't know anymore what Carlus would take part in. I pledged fealty to him and he broke my fucking heart. Besides," Mariah continued, "this doesn't necessarily need Carlus's approval or knowledge. Corval could be making a play on behalf of him."

"I'm not going to jump to accusing the Earl of Corval of treason just because Layla got attacked in his earldom. Are you accusing my father because it was near Tyrii barony? Or my mother because it's within her duchy?" He threw up his hands. "Investigation by throwing darts at a map isn't prudent, and it destroys lives, Mariah."

Mariah opened her mouth and Layla fervently hoped she wasn't about to say, *Your wife's life was almost destroyed, Excellency.*

As if Layla's furious mental signals worked, Mariah closed her mouth, sighed, and spoke again. "You're right, sire. We need some intelligence. Permission to devote all necessary resources toward information-gathering?"

"As long as we aren't violating any civil liberties, as outlined in my imperial decrees."

She nodded and bowed.

Layla prodded Ignatius's side with her shoulders as Mariah headed out, closing the door behind her. "You needed an imperial decree to ensure civil liberties?" she asked, out the side of her mouth.

"Everyone's definition of civil liberty is different," he murmured. "I just codified my own."

She winced at a sharp cramp in her side and gestured for a chair. *Hold on, kid. Just a few jostles today. We're okay now.* As Ignatius helped her over, he bent on one knee and grabbed her hand. She calmed at his upturned face. "They really were trying to kill me. Back at the chapel. That shot was supposed to hit home." She gave a small soft smile at his quick intake of breath.

"I'm sorry," he said. "I'm so sorry for bringing you into this."

She shook her head, trying to will away her unease. "It's funny. It's not like my life hasn't been on the line before. We've fought in wars..."

"War is easier. You know who's shooting at you and why, and you can fight back."

"I was a stagnant waterfowl. In that chapel that day. And today, my driver too." He had two little girls and a newborn son. She made a mental note to visit with his wife. "Whose bright idea was it to draw them out?"

Ignatius snorted. "Got what you asked for, did you?"

She shook her head. "No. No, I didn't." Foolish her. She didn't expect something this coordinated. This choreographed.

This changed everything.

"We need to get you into hiding."

Except that. No. "And let those assholes win?" She crossed her arms.

In fact, that was her problem, wasn't it? She had been afraid of risk. It was time to take a chance. Ironically, it might be the only way to be safe.

Now to convince Nate.

"This isn't something we can be cavalier about, Layls. I fear..." Ignatius stroked his short beard. "Are we on the brink of revolution? Layla, this is worse than I thought. And what I thought has been pretty bad."

"But it doesn't make *sense*, Nate. Most of your opposition isn't trying to usurp the *throne*. Mariah sees plots everywhere, but I can't say she's paranoid. There obviously *is* some sort of concerted effort to remove me from the equation. Or, more to the point, the baby."

Ignatius closed his eyes. "Do you think, maybe, it's the same people who went after Benedik?"

Was someone gunning them down one by one, like the end of a billybird hunt? "If whoever went after Benedik is the same person going after me, they'd still need inside help, which goes to exactly what Mariah was saying. I don't like fingering Corval either, just because we were technically in his territory. But it could be him. Or maybe Dracini. Or anyone against self-rule, or the war hawks. But even if they want to remove you, they shouldn't have any issue with your *heir*." *Or me*, she wanted to add.

"You're right." Ignatius sighed. "Merely wanting to remove *me* shouldn't endanger the rest of my family. Which still points to this situation as someone wanting the throne for *themself*, Layla. Which would mean..." Ignatius's voice trailed off weakly. "Oh God. My mind almost went immediately to Carlus." Before she could respond, a curious sound emanated from Ignatius, like a tiny growl. "Don't worry. I'm not entertaining this notion. Carlus loves Benedik as much as I do. He *wouldn't*." He grabbed her hands. "I learned a valuable lesson about trust when we were engaged. I had let the fear inherent in being a new emperor sway me. It made me forget my ideals. And I almost lost you. Never again."

Carlus would forever be in the mix in this sort of conversation, and it wasn't necessarily an undeserved reputation. Layla stood, then paced. "Maybe there's someone else out there who thinks he deserves the throne. This is ridiculous, this going in circles." She planted her feet, refusing even her body to continue the circle. She put her hands on her hips, silently preparing the point she was about to argue. "And I agree it's not Carlus." Hopefully. Dear Goddess.

The little encryption stick burned a hole in her pocket.

She had only met Carlus face-to-face twice: once, during the Mazaran negotiations; the second, when she was working to keep Reneb from joining Lyria in war against Valhar. Both times, despite the circumstances, despite what she learned about him, she loved him. Carlus did that to people. He was noble and generous, gregarious and insightful. One could see a man who had taken a misguided action, but thousands of times otherwise had done the right thing.

Ephraim was pushing Ignatius to have Benedik declared legally dead. She wasn't comfortable with doing that without at least checking in one more time on information out in the nebula. And while she was at it, she could gauge the former emperor's intentions. Just in case. She had the encryption key. Time to cash it in.

*
Now

In the end, Ignatius had agreed she should contact Carlus, despite his fear she would somehow alert the forces behind her attack. Now, a rush of sentimentality hit her as she spoke to the husky man, the sound of his kids' laughter echoing in the background.

"Oh, Carlus, it's so good to see your face again. Is this line secure?"

Carlus gave her a large, gap-toothed grin. "Secure as it'll ever be. It's Renebian tech, so there's no guarantee they aren't snooping."

Well, no matter. When Layla had first reached out to Carlus, with Park as middleman, it was as furtive as it was because she didn't want to announce Benedik's disappearance to the entire Whorl. Apart from the PR disaster of losing a whole person, there were the details of flight and diplomatic procedures to consider. But Reneb knew all anyway, by this point, and even if they were listening in, the encryption meant it wasn't an open broadcast.

Layla said as much to Carlus, who scoffed, making his bushy mustache jump. "Never trust a Renebian, that's what my father used to say." His eyes flashed, regal bearing intact even after the preceding tumultuous years. Did he still think of himself as rightful Emperor? Was his little cousin Ignatius just an upstart to him? A failure, perhaps?

No. This wasn't the face of a man who would kill a pregnant woman in a first step toward retaking the throne, and believing that sort of thing was an insidious cancer.

"I did as you asked Lady Royal. I contracted with Screaming Goose and told them where to look. Nothing. There is no way Reneb didn't put their own sources on it as well, as if I wouldn't guess. Having the Valharan Empire indebted to them, perfect for those opportunists. After all," he smiled coolly, "the power of indebtedness is assuredly why they granted me asylum years ago."

"But Screaming Goose didn't find anything."

Carlus shook his head. "Not a thing. And if *they* didn't find him, I'm not sure what to think. I know you don't think that much of them," he added

"They're a bit mercenary, naturally. But moreover, their sense of fair play is more lacking than the other groups I used to contract on Altain's behalf."

"Yes, but they're the absolute best at tracking people down. Even have some fancy Mazaran tech, for tracking *and* storing. I laughed at the thought of Reneb sending their people out, because the Goose would assuredly get there first."

Interesting. The expert trackers just happened to find nothing. As it was, though, Benedik didn't just evaporate. The only reason the Goose wouldn't have reported at least *one* lead to Carlus would be...

Oh, shit.

Well.

"Carlus, just how shifty are the Screaming Goose group? Could they have sold you out? Or rather, given the info on Benedik to the highest bidder, not you?"

Carlus's eyes widened, an incongruent look on a man who carried himself with entitlement and assuredness. "But who would know to even bid..."

"Reneb," they both said, simultaneously. Reneb, who was probably listening in on this damn conversation.

But to what end? Reneb would want Valhar to owe them. But they *hadn't* passed on any information about Benedik, even as Park gave him info on Altain's antimatter weapon.

As if piggybacking on Layla's thoughts, Carlus murmured, "Maybe they found evidence he was already dead. That's not really being the bearer of good news."

"But then they could have just let the Goose report to you regardless. Unless covering up was in their interest. Who would want to assassinate a Valharan royal anyway?"

Altain?

Reneb was not like that, but was Altain that bloodthirsty?

Altain stood for freedom and liberty. Integrity. Peace. The idea they would assassinate an innocent figure, sweet *Benedik* at that, who had spent so much time in Cygna City as Ignatius's personal envoy to the Republic, was almost unthinkable. And why? Even if they could, why would they?

It couldn't be Altain. Therein lay madness. Just like the madness that had made Ignatius suspect Carlus. That had made Mariah look at a map and decide Corval was the perpetrator.

But just in case, if Altain had been the ones to go after Benedik, would they go after her too? Were they behind the attempts on her life? Despite Ransom's apparent contingency plan dependent on her ratting Valharan military movements out to him?

She was one of theirs. A citizen. Would they strip her of that right for the sake of expediency? Were her oaths and citizenship a lie, her plan for safety and security a lie? If the very thing she counted on to protect herself—her citizenship—was actually a fiction that Altain could just up and throw away, then what was it worth?

And no matter who it was, who the hell on Valhar was partnering with them?

She wanted to ask Carlus. Carlus was her friend, he had unique insight, and she trusted him, no matter where the discussions with Ignatius and Mariah had taken them. But Reneb might have ears in this conversation. She didn't give a shit if they had heard her speculate malfeasance on their part regarding the Benedik situation, but the attempts on her life were need-to-know.

So she continued to stare at Carlus over the screen, and him at her, each lost in thought. She appreciated this about Carlus; his mind was always going, but he didn't feel the need to think out loud.

He smiled, wryly. "Tough stuff, Lady Royal," he said, again employing his fond nickname for her. "This war. Not great, feeling caught in the middle, is it?"

"It's better than it was after the Lyrian declaration of hostilities," she said. "When we thought Altain and Reneb might jump in. Obviously actually being at war now makes everything difficult, but at least I know where I stand. Who I *am*. Two years ago, I didn't have that luxury."

Carlus nodded, again silent. They had bonded over this feeling of being adrift, years ago when she had first visited him on Reneb. He wasn't Renebian, wasn't quite Valharan anymore either. He was regarded with a certain deference, but also had no power. The Layla of old could relate.

"How're the kids? And Nadia?"

He sighed, suddenly heavy. "They're good, Layla. They're good. Homesick. Maybe they can come home one day. But not until that kid of yours is born, just to ease any thoughts of usurpation. Erm, congratulations, by the way. I should've said something earlier."

She waved him away. "After last time, it's not something I talk about a lot anyway."

He frowned. "I was so sorry to hear about that the last time. I wish you could've at least flown back here afterward. Access to facilities and the like. I'm suddenly appreciative of their health system right now." He fell silent, tugging absently at his mustache, which sprawled out over his full beard like a cowled shawl.

She frowned in turn. "What are you saying, Carlus?"

"I'm dying, Layla."

No.

"A late-stage metastatic cancer. Not much longer now. That's why I think—I hope—Nadia and the kids can come home. With the Emperor's leave, of course."

"Is there nothing...?"

Carlus shook his head. "Told you. Reneb is among the forefront of medical technology. Look, Layla, the Blessed Falcon has marked me for His own. I ruled in His name. And then I betrayed that name."

"Surely you can't believe this is a down payment on your sin, Carlus. Tell me you don't think like that."

He looked away, contemplation written on his face. "You think about that stuff, when you're close to the end. Events evolve in the most unexpected fashion. I refuse to, or the very least, it *troubles* me to believe there isn't some reason behind it all." His eyes returned to the screen, flicking to and fro as if they were searching her out. "I'm a villain. Never thought it would be me, but truly, do villains ever think they are? And now redemption is out of my grasp. But think on you. Who are you? Why are you there, of all places, in Novaria, in the Valharan Empire? What has called you to be there, in that place at this time?"

"The bit player who keeps getting caught up in huge things," she said, dryly. "The commoner-turned-royal. How useless can you get?" She waved off Carlus's incoming objection. "I hear you. It's just a lot."

"Mere chance didn't turn you into our Empress."

Our Empress, he had said. Oh, Carlus. "You can't die." Layla bit her lips and fiddled with her fingers.

He smiled and shook his head. "Would it be thy will could stopper death, Lady Royal."

***

Ignatius stood at his window, muscles high and taut. He didn't turn to look at her. Layla went to him, intent on massaging his shoulders, but the height difference was too awkward and instead she squeezed his arms. "It's not Carlus."

"Pardon?" He looked down at her then, soft smile and all, but his eyes looked like they were somewhere else.

"I spoke to Carlus," she specified. "As expected, he was sincere over his bafflement over getting nothing in the search for Benedik. Remind me to share some theories later. As for the Valharan throne..." She paused. "He says he's terminal."

Ignatius's eyes snapped to her. "What?"

She nodded. "We should confirm that but..."

"Blessed Falcon." Ignatius rubbed his face with his hands. "This all just gets better and better, doesn't it. God. *Carlus.*"

"He says the Renebian medical establishment is really good, so I guess there's nothing we can do from here." She slumped into his desk chair, looking at her husband, who had resumed staring out a window.

"You know," he started, "when we were kids, Benedik and I would look up to Carlus so much, since he was older. And I would get upset that Benedik didn't think I was cool, since I was older than *him*, and he'd tell me Carlus was his idol, but I was his sweet big brother." His hands clenched into fists.

"We'll find Benedik, Nate. Even if the worst happened. We'll still *find* him."

"It's not that."

"No?" She waited, but when no answer came, she continued. "Didn't you have a full day of events, by the way? How are you *here*, with no one harassing you to do something?" She smiled, trying to add levity. "I've been told for years your schedule is micromanaged to the second, and here you are, all alone, just mooning out a window."

"I canceled everything. It's actually related to—"

Ignatius shook his head, but fell silent yet again.

"Nate?"

When he spoke, it was as if from far away. "With all the things arrayed against me—the hawks in the Senate, the conservatives opposed to self-rule, the popular uprisings, the Volg—that's an awful lot of coincidence, don't you think? What if it's all being instigated by an agent of chaos?"

"Could be," Layla conceded. "But sometimes things go to shit all at the same time. Especially politically. Like sea changes in attitudes."

"And then there's the matter of the attempts on your life. And Benedik's. If, we assume, it isn't someone related to him doing all this."

"Yep—wait, what? Are you seriously—"

"No. No. I'm not accusing the Dargas family. I'm thinking like Mariah." he sighed. "But that's neither here nor there. We return to the idea of someone trying to usurp the throne and also taking out possible heirs and electable candidates."

"We should just tell them they can have it. Who the hell *wants* to be Emperor anyway?"

He chuckled and gently flicked a hair off her forehead. "Agreed, but the type of person who'd do this is not who I want running my empire." He cleared his throat. "They're trying to take out the heir. We should go ahead and take the heir out for them."

A beat. Layla furrowed her brows so hard she could sense the beginning of a headache.

"You...want me to get rid of the baby?" She massaged the glabellar area right above her nose, trying for serenity.

"In a sense." He looked her up and down. "You're not showing yet, so it may not be a ploy that bears fruit in the short run. But, I was thinking a womb transplant. And then announcing a miscarriage. Maybe even imply it was due to the actions of the assassins without making those incidents public."

Layla stood, the action rattling the desk, making his mementos clatter. "Have you gone *mad*?"

"This is about keeping you and the baby safe."

"I'm not faking a miscarriage." She spat the words out. "Could you actually *be* that insensitive?"

"Then we won't announce it. Just create rumors."

"That's not the point. Ignatius, a *womb transplant?*"

Ignatius looked frustrated, which couldn't be right, because *he* was the frustrating one. He was the oaf with the plan of ripping her child from her out of fear. Ignatius gave her a placating smile as he spoke, which infuriated her more, because that was the smile men gave people who had the audacity to have emotions. "Lots of people do that, dear. It's become rather fashionable in the aristocracy. Find a donor and she can be anonymous and sent to a safe place. Or he, for that matter. But I think picking a woman would attract the least attention."

"And who would we force to do that?" She leaned against the wall, not entirely sure why she felt so breathless.

"It's not *forcing*. I feel like you're just shooting things down just to shoot them down at this point."

"No, I'm saying there are so many problems with this outlandish plan of yours. I haven't even gotten through all the issues yet."

Ignatius's lips quirked. "Shall we invite Mariah to this discussion?"

"Mariah would agree with you. I don't need her particular brand of overzealousness in my life right now."

"All right." Ignatius spread his hands and headed for his seating area, indicating a spot next to him as he settled. He cupped his chin and looked at her as she sat. "Tell me why hiring a surrogate is forcing."

Fool man. So attentive to her, so loving. How did a man like that create such idiotic schemes?

"You are the *Emperor*. You have an extraordinary amount of power and influence. No one would feel comfortable saying no to you. It's exploitative."

"They get paid an extraordinary amount! Anyone would be honored to carry the Empress's child."

"Honor doesn't cover bodily autonomy." She put her hands on her hips, best she could whilst seated.

Ignatius massaged his temples. "Let's agree to disagree on that point, dear. But if I can convince you of this, I acknowledge there are a few more hurdles. I don't want any political opponents to call our child's legitimacy into question."

"Because what?" She crossed her arms. "People think I was never pregnant? Like Dracini and his obnoxiousness about my perceived celibacy?"

"Not even because of that, but yes, that could add fuel to the fire. I think we should take precautions. Video the transfer. Maybe even sign some papers after birth to formally acknowledge the child as our own. Biologically ours or not, then, the baby will be a rightful heir."

"I'm not signing some ridiculous adoption papers."

"You have an issue with adoption?"

"No! What the shit, Ignatius? It's just *all of it*. No. Just no. I'm not faking a miscarriage. I'm not forcing someone else to carry my child. I'm not videotaping the transfer. I'm not adopting my biological baby. *None* of this."

"I just don't want a Carlus situation, legitimacy-wise."

"The *fake* Carlus situation?" She would scream in frustration if only it didn't guarantee an embarrassment of guards.

"It was all-too-real. You know that. Even if it was just an excuse for his departure in the end." Ignatius frowned. "Maybe it should be standard no matter what that any monarch's child should be legally declared an heir instead of it being automatic birthright."

"You'd think they would have thought ahead."

"Well, he wasn't first in line anyway."

"Fine." She threw up a hand. "Make a change in Valharan succession law. Whatever. But I think you need the Senate for that so..." She swallowed her snarky comment. "Regardless. I'm not doing this. I'm not transplanting my child."

"Just think about it, my lady—" he paused at a staccato rap. "I know we're not finished. Do you mind?"

She jerked her head toward the door. Saved by the proverbial falcon's head doorknocker. "Go on. I didn't think you could keep hiding out much longer."

He stood. "Come in," he commanded.

General Turine entered, stood at attention, and saluted. "Sire!" he said. "We have news on the attack in the Corval Mountains." He looked at Layla hesitantly.

"Relax, Huxley. And this concerns Layla, before you ask, as you well know. She's staying." First names. Ignatius was really putting on the charm. Did wee ickle Huxley hate her so much that this level of schmooze was needed?

"Right, Excellency. Of course. We caught one of the drivers. Based on Minister Raderfy's descriptions. And Empress Layla's, of course. He's down in the basement."

"Interrogation?"

"No drastic measures needed. He's singing like a willowlark. Said—" Turine cleared his throat, again looking at the two of them with hesitation. "Said," he continued, clearing his throat, "he was contracted by the Free Press Coalition, and he says he thinks they're doing this on behalf of the Volg."

"The merchants? And the journalists?" Ignatius shook his head. "General, that makes no sense. Why attack Layla? And they seriously were able to hire a native Corvali for that?" He paced. "Was he from the Corval Mountains? He would have to be to know his way around like that, but that would make him from my family's Tyrii barony."

"I thought the same thing, sire," Turine stated. "That's why I went digging into his background. Turns out, he's not Corvali. He's from Dracini. To the south." He waited a beat. "He also, decades ago, used to work in the Dargas household. As a driver. And as you know, that family did a lot of traveling to the Corval mountains to vacation with your family, sire."

Layla could read the addendum as plain on his face: *And the Earl of Dracini has never shut up about his belief that Abilio Dargas, Earl of Gruesse, would make a better Emperor.*

"I—" Ignatius faltered. "That doesn't mean—"

"No sire, it doesn't. But it's something we need to pursue."

"I assume you'll be moving to the serum next."

The serum. Buspirathol. Truth drug. Layla's skin crawled.

Turine frowned. "Actually sire, I advised my people against that."

Ignatius cocked his head. "Why, Turine, that's not like you."

"Perhaps Her Grace has rubbed off on me."

"Well this is a banner day then. Because I, in fact, would encourage you to—"

Layla tugged at Ignatius's sleeve. "Is it absolutely necessary?"

He turned to her, as if startled to see her there. She stood with him and held his arm.

"My lady—"

"The mark of a man is his ability to choose what's right over what's expedient," she whispered into his ear, tippy-toed, repeating long-ago words to him.

He pulled away and put them forehead to forehead. "I need to show strength."

"Be creative. Reach down. That's real strength."

"He tried to *kill* you."

"And I don't want my life saved under the aegis of torture."

"It's not torture, Layla. I would *never*—"

"Oh?" she asked, backing up, eyebrows arched. "And which one of us has personal experience with fire burning through our veins, violating our own will and reason?"

General Turine cleared his throat, studiously contemplating the wall art.

Ignatius smirked at Turine's discomfort, then nodded once at her. "My lady."

"My lord," she said, drawing it out.

"No promises."

"Remember you have a reputation already. You have a psychological advantage. It can have a far greater impact."

He took her hand and kissed it. "You are," he said, "by far the most beautiful conscience I've ever met."

"Proud to be your guide, dear. Please just consider it."

He nodded again, and straightened his uniform. "Well said, my lady. General, dismissed."

Turine walked out. Ignatius still stood, staring listlessly out the door.

"You of all people," Layla said. "Advocated serum."

"We use it here."

"I know. You see it as a necessary evil. But you didn't even hesitate. What's really going on? Something has you shaken"

"Yes," he said. "Layla, when you first walked in…" He let out a long breath. "I had just gotten a message from Viceroy Stanlo. There are rumors out of Solita. That Benedik is alive. And that he's the one stirring up the protests across the Empire."

Benedik!
Now

While Benedik was stationed on Narconia, assisting in rebuilding efforts after the Mazarans razed the planet on the way to Lyria and Felix, Ignatius was stationed on Dega, watching the Swan Nebula tunnel for any signs the Mazarans would violate the cease-fire, a retreat that years later led to armistice. As Dega was an isolated tundra in the middle of a wasteland, Benedik, on Narconia, was tasked by his esteemed cousin to help him procure a birthday gift for the woman Ignatius *clearly* loved but was too damn stubborn to actually pursue.

Narconia was a hotbed of outrageous creations flooding the market, preying on an insular and conservative society, so task falling to Benedik, he had chosen a doll. A belly-dancing doll. Nothing special on the face of it, except a warning that the doll was technically banned on Narconia. Well, one simply could not tell a room of bored-to-tears naval staff not to do something.

Thus it happened that over two dozen Valharan officers spent half an hour transfixed by a half-naked belly-dancing doll. He had pictures.

Right now, back at a rebel base on Solita, Benedik was transfixed by a similar sight. Only, it wasn't a belly-dancing doll. It was one of Delilah's dancing minions, who planned on securing a spot for herself in a traveling troupe, all the better to perform for Viceroy Stanlo in his palace.

Benedik was pretending to be drunk again, and he graced Delilah with a sloppy thumbs up. The two of them had come to an understanding after he had thrown up on her. Benedik had been 'Just Drunk' and wouldn't *think* to disrespect her by making a move.

Delilah understood. And obviously quite relieved she wouldn't have to go that route to control her wayward playboy charge. Plying him with drink and stroking his ego was good enough to keep this hopeful future emperor in line.

"I think that's adequate," Delilah said, as the dance finished up to applause. "Stanlo's a lecherous idiot. Good for us."

The dancer wouldn't really need to do much for this operation, which was curiously disappointing. Far from cloaks and daggers, her task merely was to case the reception spaces to ensure the listening device they had planted just the day before was in place. The Altainans—the *Renebians,* because there was still no way those were Altainans—had provided the technology through their regular cutout, a dour long-faced man with eyes like saucers. Benedik had attended the meeting as well, at Delilah's insistence, because she assumed the "Altainans" would be happy she had co-opted him. But the device didn't appear to be working, hence the check.

Delilah clucked to a subordinate. "Check again." As he scrambled off to test the device, she turned to Benedik. "Low risk. But still would like to avoid sending someone in if I can avoid it."

Benedik, in persona, shrugged in an *I don't care* gesture but produced a lazy smile anyway in an attempt to be polite. Delilah rolled her eyes. "Right, then," she said, standing, hand slapping at her thighs. "Got anything?" she called in to the next room. "Listening device working?"

The lackey reentered, head shaking. "No joy."

She cursed and stalked toward the room, gesturing for Benedik to follow her. "Damn Altainans. Hope they didn't screw us."

"Still not clear on why you need a listening device anyway," Bendik said, as Delilah began fiddling with the device. "In a public room, no less. What's the plan there?"

Stanlo's palace. Freedom. There would be no way to con his way into *that* mission, unfortunately. Could he smuggle some sort of note in the dancer's bag merely saying, "Save me?" Her things would have to be searched by security, naturally…

Delilah was still talking, deep in her convoluted explanation of how bugging a reception room would aid her cause of revolution. Whoops. She trailed off when she saw Benedik's blank stare.

"Sorry. I didn't actually expect an answer," he said, and added a hiccup for good measure. "Got any more to drink?"

She rolled her eyes and eased her way out the door, bellowing a command to a passing stooge. "Hope you're not too soused to follow through with your promise," she said, returning, "when you take the throne."

"Self-rule for Solita," he said, tapping his head. "I remember."

"It's all gone better than I ever could have expected," Delilah said. She shook her head as the stooge brought him his drink. "The Emperor is angering practically every group you could think of. It'd be quite sad if it weren't a perfect storm for us. Tell me, has he always been this incompetent? We don't quite pay attention to the matters of the Imperium proper way out here."

Incompetent? Harsh charge to lay at the feet of a man who never wanted any of this to begin with. The kid who had punched anyone who had dared to disrespect Benedik, and Ephraim, especially. The teen imbued with purpose; he had always known he would join the army, and more than the compulsory years at that, serving for the glory of the Imperium, bringing Valhar kicking and screaming to a modern merit-based force as opposed to the play-refuge of scions—scions like Ignatius and like Benedik. The commander who had discovered common ground against a common enemy, and the Captain-General who had brought peace to the Whorl in the form of the Mazarans leaving it for good. A man who loved a woman fiercely, whose quiet regard for her accelerated the respect of every Valharan soldier serving on dega toward her and her troops. And the Emperor, *his* Emperor, his lord-and-liege, who was trying to balance tradition and history and liberty and prosperity and the sovereignty of his nation.

Incompetent? Ignatius was a man he would love and serve for his entire life. A man Benedik would die for.

That made his stomach turn in unpleasant corkscrews. What was he *doing*?

It all came down to the same thing. He shouldn't have tried to save his own neck. He shouldn't have been a coward. Let the militants ransom his life, and pay the ultimate price for the sake of Ignatius's rule. That's what he should have done.

If only he could throw it back into Delilah's smirking face. Tell her his Emperor exuded more power and grace in one whisker of his thick beard than she could ever hope to emulate with her steely eyes and complicated plans.

But that would be suicide. And at this point, too late for it to be a noble one. He needed to keep going, to undo all the wrong he had facilitated.

Thankfully, he was still playing drunk. So Delilah probably thought he had dozed off without answering the question. He fake-jumped as she touched his shoulder. "Yeah. Totally incompetent," he slurred.

"Well," she said, though with a cat-butt purse to her lips, "you'll be a vast improv—what was that?"

Benedik went alert. Shouting. *Shooting*. A breach. A rival faction? No, why would a revolutionary group have violent rivals? Government forces? That would be groovy. Although—he looked around. Betrayal was never a fun business. Could he ditch these folks so easily? It seemed to compete with his main personal philosophy: Don't Be A Dick, Benedik.

The urge to take up arms and fight in defense of these people he had lived and supped with all this time was strong, if ultimately self-defeating. Luckily, he was saved from that impulse by Delilah, who grabbed him by the lapel and forced him down a hall. "We can't let you be discovered." Good—no wait. *Not* good. If those were Imperial forces, he needed to be *found*, damnit. He squirmed out of her grip.

"Let me fight!"

"Oh, no. Hell no. You're too drunk to—"

"I'm an army captain. Used to be, anyway. I'm just dandy!" he yelled, racing past her. Delilah was probably pinching the bridge of her nose as she followed. The thought of the familiar gesture made him smile.

No, damnit, Benedik. *No*. Don't feel affection for the evil lady.

The argument was rendered moot as the hallway filled on both ends with armed personnel. Benedik and Delilah both dropped their weapons and raised their hands. A black-clad man near the front of the formation spoke into a personal communicator. "We've got Gruesse. Repeat. Jackpot." Delilah and Benedik were separated as they were both restrained and led away in opposite directions.

***

Benedik sure had spent a lot of time in handcuffs the last few weeks. And not in the way he liked.

He had been barrelled into a deceptively nondescript transport, not *too* roughly, maybe even carefully, yet the cuffs stayed on. He looked out the window to gather the fate of Delilah's crew, but said window remained darkened and opaque. Hopefully everyone was unharmed. And maybe they'd avoid a treason charge; no one had ever actually taken up arms against Stanlo. He had checked. Conspiracy and sedition though: those would be tough. And he wasn't going to lie for their sakes.

Although considering he was still restrained, perhaps he was in as deep as they were.

The viceroy's palace loomed ahead, highlighted by the glow of twilight's gloaming. Benedik craned his neck for a looksee out the front viewport. It was an ugly, squat sort of thing. Much like the viceroy himself. Maybe, with his freedom seemingly in Stanlo's hands, it was best to keep that observation to himself.

A short while later, Benedik rubbed his now-free wrists and sat sedately next to Gaius Stanlo, Viceroy of Solita. There literally had been a seal on his study door affixed with the appellation, which wasn't too surprising. Stanlo always seemed like the type of person who wanted multiple titles after his name: "Gaius Stanlo, Viceroy of Solita, Protector of the Tunnel, Keeper of the Flame, and All Around Swell Guy etc etc etc."

As this was Benedik's first visit to Solita—well, *visit* was an awkward term for "kidnapped and placed into a cryotube and held hostage by sexy militants" but why quibble—Stanlo had procured for him local comfort food upon which Benedik alighted eagerly, though not correcting the viceroy's assertion that Benedik must be famished from the meager rations likely afforded him while captive. Best keep the narrative of downtrodden, neglected prisoner, until he had a chance to stand in front of his Emperor, personally, and explain.

"I apologize for the restraints," the Viceroy said, smiling indulgently as Benedik took another canape between his fingers and threw it into his gullet. "Though your face is well-known through the systems, my men were understandably surprised to find it *here*, on Solita, of all places. Horrid way to treat a rescued hostage, and that is on us, but we needed to verify your identity first."

Benedik nodded obediently. "Of course, my Lord." He hesitated. "Although—"

"I feel terrible, simply terrible. The missing persons report has been going around for weeks now, and we certainly did our due diligence, but we had you right under our nose all this time. I certainly hope Emperor Ignatius won't be *too* cross with me. We did have some intelligence indicating you'd been taken by Altain and then contracted out to another entity, but I could not have imagined our own, Solita-grown rabble rousers were that entity. Fact is, however, it will give me reason to finally come down hard and end this self-rule nonsense for good." Stanlo's neck glinted with another indication of his station: the chain of office given to each viceroy. Most didn't wear them, though. Stanlo truly was one to shed feathers from his plumage everywhere he strut.

"Reneb," Benedik interjected.

"I beg your pardon?"

"It couldn't have been Altain. Well, it *could*, but it just doesn't smell right. Reneb makes more sense, my Lord. You see—"

"I prefer *Your Majesty*, myself, young viscount. And keen as your sense of smell may be..." Stanlo executed a rather prim shrug. "We'll let the interrogations sort that out."

I'll bet. Likely truth drugs as well, which was not going to go well for a certain Lord Benedik of Gruesse. But looking at His Majesty Gaius the Great's face, which by now resembled a cat face-deep in a bowl of cream, it was rather certain that he knew more than he was letting on.

Like the fact the insertion team had known Benedik was there all along. *Jackpot*, as he remembered.

He was so screwed.

As Benedik silently congratulated himself for keeping composure and *not* verbally spewing all his sins into Stanlo's ears—*well, done, my sweet love,* his Alina-voice declared—His Majesty clapped his hands once and rose. "Come," he said, "I have something to show you. Perhaps you can repay me the favor of your rescue by personally squiring something to His Imperial Excellency."

"There's top secret work afoot, my boy," reported Stanlo as he let Benedik into a room he could best describe as *hermetically sealed*. Top secret indeed.

"Twisted talons!" Benedik exclaimed as he looked around the space. Holographic projections everywhere, screens with status updates, maps, uniformed military milling around. Benedik picked up a flimsy and peered at it. He got just a glimpse of an alphanumeric code before the Viceroy ripped it out of his hands.

"Come," Stanlo repeated, annoyance creasing his features before he turned with a flourish, cape billowing, and walked on.

"We come to the matter of information, young viscount," he continued, showing Benedik into a smaller space, still ringed with screens and information. "You are likely not aware, but the Altainans are plotting to destroy our under-construction Solita tunnel with an antimatter weapon. We suspect they are going to enter via the Redma tunnel near some pathetic republic territory named Kaborlah."

Benedik located a chair—an ornate thing, quite incongruous with the sleek workspace of Stanlo's strategy room—and sat, heavily.

"Does the Emperor know?" he asked.

Stanlo gave him a quiet, appraising look. "The Emperor is who brought it to my attention. And charged me to retrieve all the information I could, while he puts together a fleet to sail for Kaborlah. Hence," he gestured expansively, "all this."

"But," he continued, "some of our most sensitive information is sent via courier. And that is where you come in. First and foremost, the Altainan weapon is hitting a few snags in development. This will buy us time. As far as we know, it is still in Alliance territory. Beyond that, however, we have an idea of how it works, and those schematics are what I would like you to convey to our Emperor."

Benedik grabbed for the plans and scanned eagerly. He missed doing science work.

It was an antimatter weapon that collapsed charged black holes and cut cosmic strings. It did so by increasing Belking radiation, up to a point at which energy loss was too great.

Those cosmic strings were key. They created the constant source of energy shooting through the subspace tunnel to keep it open. In a completed tunnel, one string held the ends open, and the other one looped through normal space. When closed in a loop, they caused vibrations that churned the fabric of space-time, negating positive the energy of space in their vicinity, acting like a negative mass within the wormhole, stabilizing it. But make the vibrations more chaotic, they would pull energy, and therefore mass, away from the string, making it smaller and smaller...

"Great Bird," Benedik breathed. "They've gone and figured it out. I expect it's even easier since our tunnel isn't complete?"

Stanlo nodded. "It's all down to that team our Empress Hadria sent, along with their families, over a generation ago through the Swan Nebula tunnel. Their descendants, more likely. They will take at least another ten years to make their way to the endpoint of our tunnel to do construction on that side. Everything depends on their survival, of course. But it gives the Altainans time. Time to plot, time to destroy, before our team reaches their destination."

The *dedication* of those families. Serving the empire through generations. Benedik closed his eyes, shoulders taut with shame. *I just wanted to serve you, cousin. But I'm not anywhere close to these people. I'm not worthy to share space with them.*

"How did Altain even think they were going to get in?" Benedik asked. "I see from this we're hoping to take Kaborlah to fortify our border more, but surely we'd detect an intrusion..."

"The rebels," Stanlo growled. "Like I said, we believe they contracted with Altain to kidnap *you*. Surely that wasn't the extent of their contract. Their payment, perhaps?"

"Still think it was Reneb," Benedik said, tapping his chin. The whole reason he had played along with this mess. Beyond mere survival, or an instinct to protect Ignatius from a difficult decision, the Reneb connection was how to unravel the threats to the realm. It had to be.

Stanlo shook his head. "We may agree to disagree on that, but the fact of the matter is, there are many who would want to harm a close relation of the emperor. I'm from an imperial line myself, you know. I've heard the family stories. Of course, aren't we all, if we go far back enough?"

Well, not really. The nobility was a rather insular group. Inbred, in fact. But unspoken in Stanlo's assertion was that by "we all", he meant only the people who mattered to him, not proles.

Suddenly, he just wanted to go home.

Beyond the weariness was a fierce protectiveness. The Empire was in *danger*. He needed to get back to his liege. Another Benedik philosophy: Never Ever Start A Fight. But, if you should find yourself in one, you better damn well finish it. And this was war.

"How soon can I leave?" he asked quietly.

"As soon as you're ready, Lord Benedik." Stanlo called a colonel over, who pressed a small disk in his hand with a bow. "There. It's encrypted so only the Emperor can open it. Radio silence on the way there, please. We think it's best to keep your survival a secret, for now, to ensure your safety on the journey. Oh, and Benedik—for when he opens it—Emperor's Eyes Only."

"But you just showed me—" he protested.

"Eyes only."

Benedik nodded. "Yes, Your Majesty." He took the disk and pocketed it, and looked around out the room's window into the expansive chamber beyond. "This is all very impressive," Benedik allowed. "To have such an expansive intelligence reach—"

"Well," Stanlo said, smiling with his teeth, "people do often underestimate me."

THEN

Then

"You should delegate more, dear," I tell Ignatius, as we promenade under an exuberant night sky. "Benedik would be great. You need someone to slap you upside the head once in a while."

"He'd enjoy that too," Ignatius says wryly. "Benedik is the best of us, honestly. By the Blessed Falcon, sometimes I wonder, if he had been chosen for emperor over me..." he smiles. "You and I would be happier, for certain."

I regard him, the man I'm to marry, with the weight of an Empire on his shoulders. Ignatius has always been important, always aristocratic, always powerful and reserved, but it didn't *consume* him, not the way the throne does. And he made the effort to be the silly, *normal* Ignatius I'd known, almost as a courting measure. But it's clear that over time, that will subside. As the months and years wear down in his reign. As the need to woo a bride—a need to convince me to *stay*—diminishes. He'll age, in front of my eyes.

How much of love is bound to the memory of a person, when you flashback to the joviality? He'll never again be that same youthful commander I met on Felix, we'll never be the giddy secret courting couple, smirking with the tiniest twitch of our lips with no one the wiser. I'm protecting, loving, based on who he was, the times we shared, the nostalgia of a crush, fighting for the man he used to be. He will always be somewhat formal, reserved, even with me, alone. What was silly, jovial: that boundary has moved. No more drinking songs on tables. That weight will always be there.

He clears his throat and he transforms. Not into something intimidating, but commanding and sure. His eyes, liquid pods of honey brown, flash with resolve. "Benedik thinks he can't get it done. I need to plan for when this all blows up."

We walk the frozen lake via starlight. The northern lights dance, the galactic core rises into the cold night, and the expanse of stars wink like silent witnesses, though in reality, every one of those suns are thundering loud cauldrons of fire. How many more things out there only appear placid and staid in order to lull observers, but instead are lumbering giants ready to buffalo and smash through someone's world?

"Poor Benedik," I say. "It's been a couple of months. I'm sure he was hoping to wrap this up and get home. None of us expected *Reneb* to be the problem planet."

He's made great progress with the Altainans, but now he's reporting the Renebian government plans to join Lyria in war.

And where Reneb and Lyria go, so does Altain. So Benedik's gains would be for naught.

Ignatius grunts in agreement. He takes my arm and leads me around a bevy of slumbering swans. "The Benedik of old would have been fine being this long from home, although he probably would be itching to at least visit another destination. But I think he misses Alina."

The city of Novaria has perfected the art of true dark sky, placing itself far from other population centers, here in the crook of a continent's arm, limiting nighttime light pollution, the soft glow of homey bungalows, stately mansions, and even tall buildings filled with bachelor pads illuminating Novaria with a whisper, not a roar. From Ignatius's ramshackle balcony, it looks like a cozy village, not a capital city.

It is still midwinter. The balcony *would* have been a better touch, because I could retreat back to that hidden tunnel inside the spare closet to warm up before braving the cold once again.

Come to think of it...

"Weren't we to walk the greenhouse tonight? Revisit the hallowed site of our engagement?"

He clears his throat. "We were." He pauses to look out over the lake. No lunar reflection in the ripples; the blank slate of the new moon is why we can see the night sky so perfectly. Without it, the pool is as dark and foreboding and unfathomable as that murky watering hole I had refused to dive into as a child on Kaborlah.

He turns back to me, face set in an expression I've never seen before. I've seen Ignatius be commanding. Intimidating. Disappointed. In love. Curious. Sad. Regretful.

But I've never seen every one of those aspects playing across his face at the exact same time.

"Did you get a message?" he asks softly. "About two months ago?"

An icicle goes straight into my spine, briefly numbing me, and then feeling returns in a riot of pins and needles but hopefully, *please by the Goddess, hopefully*, my face remains placid with merely a slow blink.

Unfortunately, the stillness of my face is likely enough a giveaway, and Ignatius's expression goes cold. Another example of misleading calm, as in his eyes are fire, rivaling a sun's corona. His taut shoulders and clenched jaw make him vibrate, like the cosmic strings of a subspace tunnel. What will happen if it snaps?

But I'm not afraid of him.

I could never be afraid.

"What are you talking about?" I ask politely, striving for calm.

"Something you deleted."

I turn back to the lake. "Ah." I sigh and allow my shoulders to drop. "The super suspicious one with all those numbers, huh." My lips quirk into a sad smile. "Yes, I deleted it, Ignatius. I didn't want any part of whatever that is."

"And you didn't tell us about it."

Breathe in, breathe out. Stay calm now. "Look, Ignatius, I love you, I would never betray you, but whatever that phishing expedition was, I'm staying out of it as much as I can. That meant not answering it, not aiding anyone, not even *keeping* it, but it also meant not reporting it."

Ignatius scoffs, a quick bark tinged with bitterness. "Layls. Come *on*." His sonorous voice plays musically in the night. "You knew the message was from Ransom. You knew he had an in into the palace and you didn't tell us. That *is* aiding them."

"And why," I ask, voice laced with derision, "do you think it was from Ransom?"

He clenches his jaw. I know then. He set me up. He tried to test me. Goddess-damned bird worshippers. "The buspirathol," I say flatly. "You would have had to tell your minions—was it Turine?—about what happened to me for them to craft that message." I shake my head and blink away tears. Does he expect me to grovel? Beg for forgiveness? I committed the crime of indecision. He, on the other hand, actively betrayed my trust.

Ignatius has gone still, awareness etched in his frozen face as if a neuron disrupting bomb exploded in the moment between *righteous anger* and *dawning realization*. That's right, bastard. After all I've given up, after the lengths I've gone to be true to him, after the hatred and suspicion from my own government, he's gone and proved himself no better.

"Layla." His voice is halting. "I didn't tell anyone about what Ransom did."

I scoff. "We're just going with abject denial—"

"I will admit I approved of Turine's plan to determine what you would do in such a case. I thought you would tell me, Layla."

"Send me home. You obviously don't have a mole in the palace sending me messages, and with me gone, you don't have to worry about security breaches. And I don't have to be subjected to this bullshit. Send me home."

Ignatius's face, normally all str'ng cheekbones and sharp lines and whip-smart steel eyes, goes haggard and lined. "I'm afraid I can't do that, dear," he says. Oh, *now* it's dear, is it.

My brows knit together. What? "You promised." The note in my voice is a curious sort of combination: hope, because I don't *want* to go; anger (obvious); and fear, because what would make Ignatius go back on his word? "You have absolute power," I point out. "You can do whatever the hell you want."

"Layla—"

"Are you going to back down on this promise too? Are you going to not be at all the man I thought I was going to marry?"

He splays his hands out helplessly. "I—" One finger comes up as his eyes light. "Marry me. This week. Let's just get married."

I pull away. The emotional whiplash of the last minutes has left me drained. "Yeah no. Consider this engagement off." This is ridiculous. *Foolish.* I don't belong on this planet, with its balls and curtseys, with its glimmer-eyed assassins and overzealous generals, with *nobility* and titles and an *Emperor*, who has absolute power but acts like he doesn't. "I'm not a citizen of Valhar. And now there's no plan for me to be. I now consider myself being here as a political prisoner. Send me home."

Ignatius speaks volumes with his pinched lips and reluctant swallow. Soundless sentiments I've seen so many times on Altain. Phrases like *security risk*. Words like *vulnerabilities* and *leaks*. He'd been so willing to let me go home at the beginning of all this. Even if there were a chance I'd take up arms as an enemy soldier. What's changed? I'm closely monitored here and I'd be closely monitored there. I wouldn't have anything to do; I'd be sitting on my hands. The only thing Altain would do is ask questions about what I saw while I was there over the months but...

"I know something, don't I?"

His lip twitches. Microexpressions. I know him so well. This one says, *Clever girl.* "Are you sure you're no longer my fiancée?" he asks. "Layla, it's safer if we're still engaged—"

"Look, Mr. Absolute Power, I don't care what your deal is. We're done."

"If we marry, you're no longer a foreigner—"

"Oh, I get to marry you to avoid being a prisoner is it?"

"You're overrea—"

"Don't finish that statement."

"Quite right," he says weakly.

"I'm never going to forget you told Turine about the serum. Send me home."

"I didn't—" he sighs almost painfully. "You're not going to believe me right now. He raps a fist on an outcropping. *Goddamnit*, it says. "You'll stay here. If you're no longer my betrothed your status is clearer than it was before. Political custody. Comfortable, but in different quarters and much less freedom. Damnit!" he says out loud, this time. "Are you sure, love?"

"Yes."

(No.)

"If that's the way it has to be," I add, "then so be it."

(This took a turn I hadn't been expecting.)

"Don't do this," Ignatius pleads, voice turning small.

"It's been a blast," I end.

(Shit.)

5/3/26

People always ask me how I can have a relationship without intimacy. As if physicality is a prerequisite for connection. Frankly, it's ridiculous. I've never noticed a difference, in the before and the after.

But Ignatius and I spent five years in a quasi, non-acknowledged, non-exclusive, non-committal, non-intimate relationship before he finally proposed to me in the palace gardens. A romance in theory. An almost-imagined, fantasy crush. All in my head.

Is it a wonder it's all gone to shit the first time an actual relationship is put to the test? We *have* become physically intimate, and it's all still just a sham.

6/3/26

I slam my fist against the walls of my new prison—excuse me, my new *accommodations*—and wince as I bruise my hand. Soft, that's what I am. I'm soft. Not by Altainan standards, but Valharan. Would Ignatius have let himself be caught by circumstance, staying quiet as a mouse, not making waves? Don't think so.

But here I am, the princess, locked away in the high tower for displeasing the king. I entertain a melodramatic daydream of breaking out, rappelling out the spare-closet balcony, commandeering a fighter, and high-tailing it back home, a hero to my people.

If I had the druthers, my best course of action would have been convincing Valhar I was loyal to them, being able to run free, and still helping my nation surreptitiously. Or at least now, figuring out what I've seen that has spooked Ignatius, then making him believe I'm coming back to him, and then getting the information back to my nation and helping them defeat the Valharan Empire.

But I can't do it. I should have played them. Some spy. I'm too loyal to Ignatius. Even though he proved he's not loyal to me. All signs pointed to that message being a trap, but I couldn't believe it because it would mean Ignatius himself betrayed me.

Where's the woman who stood up to her superiors over Felix, and later at Dega, then continued in Cygna City, arguing. *We can't just let this be the way we do things, or we don't survive?* I hear Anastasia's voice in my mind going, "Get some backbone, darling."

8/3/26

The walls of my gilded cage press in close, like a compactor plans to crush me into a cube of trash. And that I am. Rubbish. Refuse. Discarded. Tossed aside.

It's the utter desperation for companionship that's led me to this point. Those gorgeous eyes, deep unerring pools that have left me bereft, undone. Someone serious, a man, not a *boy*, someone important and steady and Goddess be damned, I'm an *idiot*, because I, of all people, am not serious, am not important, am not made to be an *empress*, of all things. A pathetic sack of neuroses, a silly girl who got caught up in the romance of it all, and now I'm *here*, disgraced.

The word comes to me unbidden: *lonely*.

I don't know how to make friends. Coworkers like Sri and Mena come and go like blips, people thrust toward me by the weight of circumstance. As for Ransom, the less said about that codependent relationship the better. And toward my brothers and sisters in arms, I had an undying sense of responsibility, but I didn't cleave to them the way the rest of them did to each other. The detachment of command suited me much better than as a fellow footsoldier. Rare is the person who makes my soul sing. Truly, my only friends came hand-in-hand with romance, and isn't *that* ironic, considering how few and far between paramours are. And so: Ignatius. And so, with the loss of him, abject loneliness.

Idiot. This is what happens when you leap. No plan, no contingency. *Marvelous, isn't it?* I ask the specter of the woman who crowed about her spontaneity to Ransom.

9/3/26

Lying here on this exquisitely tiled floor with the gold-leaf walls, my world spins like a fun-house gyroscope. I ball into a c-curve, still and alone in my room, a sepulcher to my utterly ruined heart.

21/3

Sixteen days in, and I find one of those stupid beetles. Don't want to squish the shit out of it, but none of the windows here open. I'll let him wander free. Ignatius deserves it. Maybe the bug will come visit me from time to time. Maybe I'll name him Manny (as opposed to Buggy.)

I'm fine. Really, I am.

24/3

I'm so tired. It's not like I'm in solitary confinement. People come by with food. Some even with conversation. Maybe it's a soft way to interview me. No matter. Nothing *bad* is happening, which is why I don't understand why I'm experiencing effects like exhaustion, nausea, a heaviness throughout my midsection.

25/3

I had his silly drawings physically in this journal, but I've just relegated them back to the net. First time in a long time I haven't had them right here, where I can rub them between thumb and index, the pads of my fingers delighting in the coarse structure, rough like he appears, the drawing a manifestation of his true self, whimsical and completely, utterly attuned to my inner life.

I don't imagine to the same vivid extent during the times I'm happy. He hasn't had the occasion to draw for me in the time I've been here on Valhar. But now loneliness has caused the chairs to dance, flowers to sprout up all around me, yawning and unfolding as they stretch and yaw, moonlight to dapple dewdrops onto the uncaring floor, growing and overtaking me until I'm floating in bubbles that carry me up, up past the palace spires until I starburst and rain back down into this city I want to love.

Paiana 26

The first time he comes to me, apology in his eyes, we never speak. I'm used to serving up my body for lovers regardless of how I feel, and so I let him.

The second time he comes to me I slap him.

"You can't sleep with prisoners. That's just not done. At least in civilized societies like mine." I point at him with what Ignatius once jokingly called the Kaborlah finger, that bent-back index of warning.

His eyes stare out in that perpetual thoughtful crease, this time with a mournful twinge as he touches the spot I struck. "I love you," he says. "Even if we're not together right now. I love you, I'd marry you in a heartbeat, and this is my way of showing you."

I scoff, the weight of countless relationships where the guy just *doesn't get the point* crashing to the floor between us. "It's not *my* way. And you should know that. *My* way of showing love is *not tricking your girlfriend by sending her messages from her long lost spymaster friend.*"

"Fiancée."

"Honestly, Your Excellency"—I spit the title—"I didn't feel like much of one. And *you*. You don't get to come here and pretend like nothing has changed. You're always getting things the way you want them. Nothing changes for you. Nothing shifts for you. Meanwhile I have to upend my whole life."

"Nothing changes?" The words reverberate through the ornate room. True to form, Ignatius never has to yell. The bass boom of his voice can roll like thunder when displeased. "Do you think I'm happy with this?" he continues. "I want you as my wife, my Empress, by my side. And I don't get to have that. Because of your *duty* to your nation." He turns away, one big clenching stressed-out man, such contrast to his dress: shirtsleeves rolled up, top button undone, hair askew. Like he's trying to say, in sartorial code, *here I stand, harmless supplicant for your affections, just your big ole goofy Nate,* and screw him, anyway, because for once, he isn't getting his way.

I fight my affection. "Yeah, duty to my nation. That's what we call *honor* and *integrity*. Isn't that what the entire Valharan noble system is based on? What kind of honor is abrogating a peace treaty behind a republic's back? Sneaking around?"

"My *honor*," he flings back, "involves protecting our nation. We need this tunnel because—"

Blah blah. "You're not the man I thought you were. Everything I loved about you, every memory is tainted." I throw the ring, which I've kept in a fit of sentimentality on my finger. It lands with a plink behind him on the marbled floor.

The look he gives me is devastation and loss.

But I get my way. He leaves. And there goes my entire source of sympathetic interaction, and I'll get to spend the rest of this "war"—because despite all this drama, Altain *still* hasn't declared one way or another—between four walls. Wait it out. In a way, it's for the best. I won't feel I'm betraying Altain by running free in the palace. I've been trying to have it both ways. Being a political prisoner makes more sense given my rank and my citizenship.

When love and duty collide, they are literally worlds apart.

Now

*
Now

Ignatius came home late that night, not unusual of course, given the demands of his position, but there was that look in his eyes that always made Layla squirm under the intensity of his gaze. He was struggling. That much was clear.

She loved Carlus, but sometimes she cursed him for putting her husband in this position. Thrust onto the throne, fighting challenges to his rule, fearing for his wife and child.

She accessed that stiff upper lip she had spent years growing in, and Ignatius wiped away his sad smile.

"How's moving in going?" he asked.

She stretched out on the ugly crushed velvet camelback sofa and made idle patterns as she spoke. "The Cruise Director isn't happy I'm putting a hold on renovations. With a war on, it just didn't feel right. But we're going through and tagging the historical materials I've found in the nooks and crannies. And updating the furnishings. And, you know, designing the nursery. Anyway, she should be happy we finally agreed to move to the larger digs."

"Baby forced our hand."

"Yeah," she said noncommittedly. She eyed the heavy drapes on the far exterior wall. Maybe Alina would like the challenge of making a gown out of them. Imperial chic. People would buy them in droves, flower-and-paisley pattern and all.

It was still too early to move. Imagine if they had moved for the sake of a baby the first time around. Coming home to a nursery after losing him, in that lonely shuttle...

Announcement or not, it was too soon. Too uncertain. Life undulated, a sine curve that seemed regular as a heartbeat but then, like labor, the contractions came and squeezed the life out of you and sped things up so fast you could hardly catch your breath and that's what loss was like. A *bam*, a crash, a cymbal-ringing thunderclap of pain and then the beats returned to normal, everything around you functioning as it should except you, still lost in the undertow.

She wouldn't breathe until the kid was out. And then what? Would this heir-eliminating assassin target a living baby?

Ignatius busied himself, checking his secure console for any messages. He must have not been at work. Exercising likely. He had the look of someone freshly showered. In any case, he was a valve in need of release. Sure as she could divine the weather from the cloud patterns back on Kaborlah, she was a barometer, reading the enormous pressure on him. The protests on the outer planets had devolved into what Mariah callously had referred to as a PR nightmare, and what Layla called a humanitarian disaster. Overzealous territorial governors and colonial viceroyalty advocated shooting into crowds and shutting down the press. The nations of the Alliance took the effort to condemn the violence even while engaged in war.

Right as rain, he pulled up a file showing a montage of the latest demonstrations in the far-flung territories—chanting crowds, some asking for the end to war, some agitating to crush the Alliance, some demanding the return of the Senate, some begging for enfranchisement—all at cross-purposes, the only unifying factor a dissatisfaction with Ignatius's reign. Some peaceful, holding hands. Some breaking glass. Local police, losing their tempers and reacting badly, imperial forces following Ignatius's dictum of peaceful engagement and trying to restore calm.

"This doesn't happen here," Ignatius said, pointing to a still frame of a screaming protester facing armored troops. "It happens where *you* come from."

"Well," she said, "until recently, everyone just did what you said. All this is exposing the cracks in your perfect society." Ignatius snorted, knowing a rant was incoming. "It's tempting to think your way is superior," she said, softly. "People are taken care of. No violence, no strife. Not at this level anyway. One community, one overarching culture, working for the common good. But you know, sometimes the road to true freedom and happiness is paved in strife. And no, before you ask, my home nation hasn't figured it out either. Maybe you all will."

How many injustices had happened in this Empire of his without anyone the wiser?

Without marches endeavoring to right the wrong? Would the nobility look back on those days and think them the golden era of Valhar, not realizing it was golden only for them? Valhar was finally on the path of the other planets in the Whorl—confronting all the bad in their midst. It was horrible and painful, but before, it had all been silent. It took pain to get change. Even when the pain hit people like her husband, it was a good thing in the end. Pain, like the contractions that would bring her baby into the world.

Also painful: running out of breath when she climbed the ancient stairs in the palace; and heartburn; and sciatica that once left her immobile on her bedroom floor (*that was a fun call to security.*) In the next few months, she'd probably have the classic beached-whale-in-a-bathtub experience.

"Ignatius," she began, turning to her spouse, who was now digging through a drawer filled with porcelain cat miniatures with a look of horror on his face. "*This* is what you've been dealing with?" he interjected. "Ugh, I'm sorry, Layls. Torture."

"Funny," she said. "Anyway, I wanted to talk to you about Benedik's memorial—"

His secure console chimed.

Ignatius creased his forehead. "A recorded message from Stanlo. No, dear, you don't have to leave. What's mine is yours." He pulled up the image of the Viceroy, while unceremoniously scattering the feline collection onto the (thankfully carpeted) floor.

"Sire," Stanlo began, "I've located young Lord Benedik."

Layla shot up so fast she misjudged her center of balance and stumbled back into the lumpy sofa.

Ignatius, for his part, didn't immediately start demanding answers of the inert screen, which must have taken extraordinary restraint, because Layla wanted to start screaming and shouting and crying all at the same time, even though the video couldn't answer her back.

"I can't get into too much detail in this format, sire, but information is on its way in a very reliable package. But it looks like those rumors about Lord Benedik's extracurricular activities were real. I'll let you deal with the intel in your way and wisdom, Excellency."

"Oh, Benedik," Ignatius said in a querulous voice, as in the background, Stanlo relayed flight information.

Layla made her way over and lay a hand on his arm. "Surely not?"

"Obviously, I don't want to believe it. I *can't* believe it. It's Benedik."

"Exactly."

"But, my lady—first a man with ties to Dracini and Abilio takes part in an operation against you. Now this. Collusion, Layla." He rubbed his eyes. "I feel like a terrible person for even thinking it. But I'm wondering if I'm making the classic mistake of acting like a man, not an emperor. A cousin, not a ruler."

"But it can't be, love. *Benedik*."

"Can it not? Someone, somewhere is pulling the strings against me. Not all of it. I have to believe some of this"—he waved his arms around—"was a natural consequence of war and change. But you know, and I know, someone with access to me and high up in the royal pecking order has a hand in all this." He briefly blinked back what looked like tears.

"Ignatius," she said, gently kicking those damn cats into a corner, "focus. First, we now think Benedik's alive?"

"All I have to go by is what Stanlo is intimating. I'm not planning on celebrating just yet. Or making any announcements."

"So, you're not jumping at the assertion your cousin is alive, but you're operating on the assumption he's part of some anti-regnal conspiracy? Nate, I know you've been under a lot of stress but—"

He held up his hand. "I'm not an idiot, Layla."

"I dunno," she mumbled. "Seems like your persecution complex is getting outta hand."

"I'm covering. My. Bases. Look, you know I love my family. I just eliminate possibilities one-by-one so I can get back to being a cousin and a nephew and whatever else without toxic clouds of suspicion hanging over every interaction."

"You should trust your family *with your life*. Just like we knew for a fact it wasn't Carlus."

"Layls, Carlus is the whole reason I'm this way! I love the guy. I trust he never has ill intent. But he screwed up so bad, his own *father* died."

"Seems to me," she said, hands on hips, "that you lot need better emperors. Save it!" she said as he began to squawk. "What're you going to do next? Send me to the gallows for perceived disloyalty?"

"Great Claws, Layla—"

"I seem to remember you siccing Mariah and Turine on me two years ago."

"I seem to remember you throwing a ring in my face," he said, dryly. He rubbed his eyes and sighed. "Look, I regret all you've seen of this Empire has been upheaval. From the beginning of my reign, with my cousin's abdication..." he shook his head. "You know what kind of leader I am. What I'm capable of being. The good I can do. You've *seen* it. But here, with this set of circumstances, I'm chasing one bad option after another and I *hate* it. I swear to you, Layla, you'll see the old Ignatius when this all finally settles. If." He sighed again. "What's it like?" he asked. "Loving a ghost?"

She rolled her eyes. "I'm to believe men are even more pathetic in their afterlives than in situ when confronted with their foibles." She knelt to pick up those stupid ceramic pieces—might as well enjoy the lack of a protruding bump while she could—and pursed her lips in displeasure as her husband went to ring Turine's people. Alas, when his mind was made up, her role ended.

Ignatius cleared his throat, and spoke into his comm. "It's time. Bring Abilio and Dracini in. And keep an eye on Henri and Alina, will you? Limited surveillance for now."

Layla rubbed her stomach ruefully. This kid was going to have a roller coaster of a life. Her own life had been out of control since she was born in a wind-swept hut on a forgotten backwater world.

Do this, do that. Go here and then there. Subsume your own interest. Play a role, don your smile. Subordinate yourself: to your parents, to your commanding officers, your president, your husband. Don't stand out, not until it serves their needs. Watch your adopted home implode.

* NOW

Layla had insisted she observe Ignatius's interview with Abilio, which, of course, Ignatius fought vigorously. He was right, really; this aspect of his reign was none of her business. She was a diplomatic counselor. But, this was partially about conspirators against *her* life, and an interview of a family member. All in all, there was nothing that was *more* her business.

So that was how she ended up watching through a two-way mirror as Ignatius interrogated his uncle. She looked around the observation station, shivering. Instead of one of the palace's fancy meeting rooms, or Ignatius's office or receiving area, they were in a cold, sterile place, which reminded her of the room off the People's House in Cygna City where Hari the counterintelligence officer interrogated her with his bionic eyes.

Why were these places always in basements? She had been taken to this location inside the Imperial Palace two years previously, and somehow, the location made her feel a keener sense of betrayal than any of the events that had led up to her being there in the first place. Poor Abilio must be feeling even worse. At least she had done *something* that put her in that situation.

Ignatius, to his credit, wasn't acting like some ridiculous kangaroo court barker and instead sat in a chair next to Abilio, feet angled toward him, as if they were scrunched together on a chaise lounge. "I'm sorry to bring you down here, Uncle," he said regretfully. "My security chief insisted, and my lax attitude toward procedure has been giving him an ulcer."

Abilio took in a breath and let it out, nice and slow, and looked at Ignatius warily.

"Sire," he said formally, "with respect, why am I here?"

Layla watched as Ignatius took the measure of him, eyes calculating the weight of history, family, and fealty. "Uncle. I need your honesty. About your intentions for my throne."

Great Goddess, Ignatius. Beside her, Turine gave a sharp nod of approval. Layla stifled a groan. Turine. It always came down to Turine, didn't it. Mariah was a tad overzealous, but Turine was the source of most of Ignatius's bad decisions when it came to mistrusting family vis-à-vis security.

"I can't imagine how you mean."

"I asked you for your honesty, so I'll give you mine. Viceroy Stanlo has accused your son of outward subversion of my rule. I would like you to tell me what you know."

Abilio stiffened. "How dare you," he said. It came out as a snarl. "You're about to announce my son's death and now you're accusing me of what? Sending him around the empire rousing rebels? Somehow? In the afterlife?"

Ignatius did not have the grace to look ashamed, although that brief pause in his throat before he swallowed told Layla—and Layla only—everything she needed to know. How was he going to play this? No hard evidence of anything. All smoke and mirrors. What was he going to say? *We have on the word of the viceroy your son is alive?*

"I'm in a difficult position, Uncle. I have circumstantial evidence pointing to possible involvement of your family in sedition. And I understand how this looks to you. How unreasonable I must seem."

"And you won't even share this so-called evidence, with me, *nephew*."

Ignatius shot him a look heavy with the weight of shared history. "No. Look. You're family, Abilio. But my wife is in danger. My *child* is in danger. And so I'm taking no chances, no matter how many feathers I ruffle."

"My child is *dead*."

Ignatius's eyes hardened at his uncle's statement, but there was also a look of shared mourning. But not just for Benedik. The shared fear of losing the ones they loved.

Her stable, stoic Ignatius was terrified for his wife and child.

Ignatius hadn't yet responded to Abilio's declaration, possibly gauging the sincerity of his response. He must have found what he was looking for in Abilio's eyes, because eventually his shoulders slumped and he worried a reluctant groove into the wood of the lone desk in the center of the room. "I believe you," he said. "I believe you would do nothing to harm this family. But between your position as a top choice for this throne, and your ties to the Earl of Dracini—of whom I'm less sure—I need to consider a suspect while we figure this out."

"And how long would that be?"

"As long as it takes, Lord Abilio. Which also means if you have any information—anything at all—it would behoove you to alert Us." He held up his hand as Abilio opened his mouth. "Take your time. Think about it."

Layla closed her eyes. Ignatius was past the point of reason. She needed backup. She needed Antonin Kurestin to knock some sense into him.

Benedik!
Now

Viceroy Stanlo had provided Benedik with a private shuttle and pilot and had restricted comm access to the cockpit, which was never left unattended except for the occasional privy break. "Top Secret," Stanlo had explained, when Benedik had protested this insulting lack of trust in his capacity to remain quiet. "Not taking chances."

Now Benedik was rendered speechless on the approach to Novaria, drinking in the blues and whites of his homeworld and the snow-capped mountains ringing the capital city. Novaria had been in the first throes of winter when he left, and well into spring now. Vibrant greens dotted the landscape. As the craft made its descent, his heartbeat picked up pace. Certainly he had taken trips away from home longer than this, but between the awaiting Alina and the knowledge he very nearly had never made it back, this homecoming left him verklempt.

"Now we're here," Benedik asked the pilot, who had just finished up the various check-ins for landing clearance, "can I at *least* check the news feed?" He had already slept through the beginning of the war, in cryo-transit to Solita all those ... weeks? Months? Ago. Who knew what else he had missed while he was doing his best imitation of a popsicle, turned pawn.

The pilot shook his head, and Benedik grumbled.

The Viceroy's craft was small enough to break atmosphere without the need of a transfer hub or space elevator, and his credentials provided access to an isolated landing pad, where Benedik found a small flyer awaiting him. Stanlo's shuttle pilot flicked an access card at him and then unceremoniously taxied away in preparation for space flight, without so much as a by-your-leave. All right, then.

Time to fire this baby up. It was a rare opportunity to fly one of these himself. Thankfully, it was armored. To the heart of Novaria. Benedik finally, gratefully, elatedly pulled a news digest up as he prepared to get his craft in the air, taking in absentminded glances while running through the flight checklist. Hmm. War didn't seem to be going well. Damnit. Protests and uprisings—Benedik quelled the encroaching guilt. A memorial service for the emperor's beloved second cousin—wait, what?

Well, Stanlo did say he was going to keep Benedik's survival a secret. His family evidently giving up on him rankled nonetheless.

Maybe he ought to teach 'em a lesson, then. After all, it was only proper to make an appearance thanking guests for attending one's big day. Its being his memorial should be no exception.

***

His dreams of waltzing into his own funeral unannounced were dashed when he glimpsed the security on the perimeter. Right. Cousin Iggy was the ruler-ascendant of the glorious empire. He'd need to play this just right in order to maximize drama without getting tackled by a suspicious rent-a-cop. And Imperial Security, closer in, would just call Ignatius. If they recognized him, that was. They might just skip the niceties and shoot him dead.

A buzz of anticipation began to build within him. A scheme, a scheme! A raucous tale of derring-do. What could he do? Biometrics meant no impersonating someone else on the guest list. Could he knock out a policeman and ... no, that was super illegal. His rap sheet was long enough, after this little misadventure.

Benedik was weighing revealing himself and swearing people to secrecy (with some bribery involved) versus joining the crowd of mourners ringing the chapel and making his move after his family exited the service (but a shame to waste tears on a living man), when a cobalt-blue liveried imperial guard walked straight over to him.

He was a very young man. When did the guards start accepting teenagers? He blinked and shook his head. No, he had to have been at least twenty, but, well, that still made him like a *kid* and oh damnit when did Benedik get old?

Kid was nervous too. Was he a real guard, even? Well, in any case, he flashed the correct credentials as he approached. "My Lord," he murmured, "it's you, isn't it, Lord Benedik?"

Benedik looked down, taking stock of his appearance. Impressive deduction, actually. He had access to proper hygiene facilities while quartered with the Solita rebels, but his beautiful flowing locks had become shaggy sans hairdresser. And his normally clean-shaven face was now bearded (he had tried to push the narrative he was literally replacing his cousin, who in fact sported an impressive beard.) Unfortunately, beard-maintenance was also not in his repertoire of skills, and although he *could* have shaved on the flight back, there was no real comfortable place to do so.

"How?" Benedik thus asked.

The kid showed him his equipment, which was indeed imperial issue. "Scanning the crowd, my Lord. Facial recognition and gait analysis. You stood out. But I wanted to check, before causing a scene." At the kid's gesture, Benedik consented to a retinal and fingerprint scan.

Benedik grinned wryly as everything popped up green. "Can you keep a secret?" he asked.

He said he could guide Benedik to his family for a discreet reunion and cancellation of the service. Or, if Benedik sought a dramatic entrance, he could lead him this other way. The guard began walking without waiting to hear if Benedik chose the sedate option or the dramatic option.

Fair.

The kid was apparently important enough to pass all the checkpoints without a second look, even with the straggler behind him.

And so it was, Benedik appeared before the outer doors of the Restful Chapel of Downy Blessings in the middle of His Excellency Emperor Ignatius I's eulogy to his Beloved Second Cousin and Friend, Lord Benedik Garaphalon Dargas, Viscount Gruesse.

The sniffling and shuffling of the outside crowd provided the soundtrack, like the light strains of a wedding processional. Benedik primped and scuffed, an anticipatory bride. The sunlight shone down, illuminating his long golden hair. Oh, damn it all. Split ends. He should've just cut it himself, if he couldn't find someone else. Ahem.

Lord Benedik, beloved cousin and friend, stood outside the doors of the holy chapel, and with one last muttered prayer to the Great Bird, flung them open and entered the center aisle.

No one noticed.

Wait, Ignatius looked up for a millisecond. A slight pause, not even a stutter, and he continued droning on.

"Benedik was, above all, loyal and true. Always one for a quick laugh, his serious and angry look surprised those who thought they knew him, but that was the face he wore, when someone insulted a person he loved." Eh. Ignatius was the one who'd punch people. Benedik was good for a cutting remark, mostly.

"He also had a propensity to shock, a flair for the dramatic, a subversion of expectations, and dear God, Benedik, I see you back there. Would you please stop this subterfuge and come up here and reassure your mourning family?"

Oh. Er. *There* was the chorus of gasps he had been waiting for. Although the slight difference between his bursting in there yelling *I'm alive! I'm alive!* versus being scolded by the Emperor as if Benedik had *faked* a death or something meant those gasps were less appreciative and more scandalized.

He sheepishly made his way forward, and fell into the arms of his family.

The reunion was all together too short, there in the cold reception space in the chapel. A crier went out front to proclaim the news, and Benedik ducked his head as the cheers from the crowd reached all the way into the interior room. Someone patted him down, and Benedik squawked as they found the datachip given to him by the viceroy. Ignatius, however, was already there, looming in a corner watching Benedik kiss his wife, slug Layla on the shoulder, submit to a vigorous hair-rub from his dad, and engage in an incredibly teary—and very unusual for him—hug with his father. "It's for your eyes only, sire," Benedik said, and Ignatius nodded gravely and pocketed the chip.

"I'm sorry to all of you," the Emperor said, "but we need to cut this short. Benedik and I are overdue for a chat." Benedik couldn't parse the looks the rest of his family were sharing. He was seriously missing something.

What he *wasn't* missing was how awkward his upcoming conversation with his cousin was about to be.

"I'll go over with you," his Uncle Tonin said, detaching himself from a nearby wall like a lone barnacle leaving its abode. He shared another cryptic look with Empress Layla, and crossed his arms in anticipation as he looked at his son. But Ignatius said nothing, just shook his head to himself, and beckoned him along.

"Ya didn't seem surprised to see me," Benedik said to his cousin as they exited the flyer at the backdoor private palace entrance. Ignatius grunted.

Ugh. Ignatius and his stupid propensity for knowing everything. He must have had him pegged from the moment he landed. How? Maybe Stanlo's pilot was authorized to provide the manifest when Benedik was finally free and clear, though that did make moot the customs- and inspections-free privilege afforded to a craft flying viceroy flags.

Oh, and that guard seemed very calm considering he had found a dead man. Benedik sighed.

"The kid was in on it, wasn't he."

Nothing but a tight smile and stiff posture. Ignatius went past the hallway that would lead to his personal study and headed instead toward the business portion of the palace, where, in the distance, that damn general—Turine, was he?—waited.

To Benedik's surprise, Uncle Tonin sped past them, turned, and interposed himself between the Emperor and his destination. "Uh uh. Nope. Not gonna happen, boy."

"Father," the Emperor said, and if there was a slight petulance in his voice, Benedik was not going to point it out, no sirree.

"Son, you take your younger cousin, there," Tonin said, inclining his head toward Benedik, "and *talk* to him. Like a decent human. In your study."

Ignatius drew himself up to full height, looking as if he was about to pull rank.

"*Lord* Antonin—" Oh. He was.

Uncle Tonin, cool as a watercress, merely raised his brows. "Oh, hell, no."

They faced off. Benedik slunk to the side, not wanting to be caught in the crossfire. To his shock, Ignatius broke first, thrusting fists into pockets and turning sharply to Benedik.

"All right, then," he said. "Come along. *You*, father, get to talk to Turine. Good luck."

The Palace was a familiar childhood haunt to Benedik, as he was a descendant of an Emperor—Titus, his great grandfather. The elegance, the opulence, the history, the *power* in those walls. Simply the most beautiful inanimate object he had ever laid eyes on. The study, where he used to sit at his Great Aunt Hadria's feet, enjoying caramel candy melts, was as warm and familiar to him as mother's milk.

No longer so nostalgic and inviting now, as his cousin, framed in a window, turned to face him, his countenance shrouded in shadow like a powerful villain from one of Benedik's childhood comic books. He donned earpieces and glanced at a portable reader in his hand...ah, Stanlo's secret information Benedik had couriered.

After he finished his review, Ignatius set the pieces down carefully on his desk. His hand rested there on top of the reader. The look back up was controlled and slow.

Ignatius straightened. Benedik clasped his hands behind his back.

"When I was a young man," Ignatius began, "and you, much younger, my father sent me to an apprenticeship in the mountains of Tyrii. They mine ore there, blasting through the layers of rock to retrieve the deposits. Such a small addition to our gross national production. Nothing compared to the resource mining on our settlements. One may wonder why they still do it. But they are a proud people. Proud to serve their nation, this empire." His unusually throaty voice scratched, but still held power.

"I learned it all. Smelting, especially. Roasting and reducing. Hot, claustrophobic work. I wish I could say it made a man out of me. But you remember me then, dear Ben. Passion burning. Fueled by a molten core. Only years later did the lessons of my father take. The fires of Tyrii forged me into the person I am today. You?" He made straight eye-contact. "You are seaborn. An undulating wave. A ululating symphony, a riot of expression. How free you are. How I've envied you."

Benedik's eyes widened as Ignatius's words broke off in jagged shards. Oh, oh shit. What the feathery fucking falcon was going on here?

"As carefree as a river. My babbling brook of a cousin. When does it turn? From fresh springs to the toxic wastewaters of Tyrii? What," the Emperor said, "have you done?"

A fist slammed onto the desk. Benedik jumped, then gulped. "You wanna see?" Ignatius asked, the sound emanating from him now rough and coarse, a furious whisper of venom. "It was eyes-only, so you don't know. But I'll show what you've brought me." Benedik managed the smallest *meep* which Ignatius seemingly took to be assent.

First up was a vid of Delilah, strapped to a chair, voice flat. Truth drugs. Nasty stuff. Explaining the Altainans kidnapped Lord Benedik, en route to the back border of the empire after negotiations fell apart. Shot his people and put him in a cryotube, and brought the ship, sans Benedik, to the Swan Nebula to squirrel it away. And Altain handed Benedik to her rebel group.

Tears pooled in her eyes as she answered each question, but they didn't fall, as if she didn't have the capacity to cry. Benedik's face contorted. Using this shit was barbaric. But Stanlo would, of course.

Ignatius paused the recording. "So," he said, "you were kidnapped." Benedik nodded vigorously. "Anything more you want to tell me about it?"

Oh, danger. But he would never lie to his liege. "They wanted to ransom me, sire. Demand from you independence, an abolition of the viceroy's rule over Solita. It's the tunnel, see, sire. The opportunity for trade, economic success. They want to own it and administer themselves."

"I never received any demands," Ignatius pointed out.

"I convinced them. Sire, you would have been in an impossible position. And I know you would have chosen the Empire, sire, which is fine! I am nothing, not in Your Presence. But it would have broken your heart."

"And so you joined them," Ignatius said softly.

Gulp. "Ignatius—" Benedik began.

He picked another file off the menu and pressed play.

"Hope you're not too soused to follow through with your promise when you take the throne," came Delilah's voice. And Benedik said—

"Self-rule for Solita. I remember."

"It's all gone better than I ever could have expected. The Emperor is angering practically every group you could think of. It'd be quite sad if it weren't a perfect storm for us. Tell me, has he always been this incompetent?"

"Tell me this is faked," Ignatius said. "Tell me, please, cousin." The pleading. Oh God, Benedik couldn't take the pleading. If only he could lie to him.

Benedik shook his head. "The audio is real," he rasped out. "But I wasn't—I was investigating—"

"You said it would have broken my heart, to have received a ransom demand for you. But you *have* broken it, Benedik."

Benedik teetered as if he were on an amusement ride he couldn't escape. Oddly specific, yes, but there was that time, when he was little, on an ancient carousel, and it had spun faster and faster...

Come to think of it, it was a pink pony he was riding. *That* was where the aversion had come from.

"Sire," he said, fortified. "Please. I was running a con. Something wasn't right. With this entire situation."

"You fomented rebellion!"

"I just wanted to serve you!" All he ever wanted to do was serve his Empire. Yes, he was nontraditional, but being an envoy, a *courier*? He could do more.

He could be more.

"So you tried to play secret agent?" Ignatius bit out. "Instead of just letting them make their demands so we *all* could have helped? I damn near arrested Abilio last week. Did you know that?"

"What? My *father*? My liege, I respect and love you, but what the *hell* does my father—"

"If only you knew the half of it," he replied. "Let me ask you, cousin. Did you sleep with Delilah there? She spoke fondly of you."

"What?" Benedik repeated. "No! That's so sexist, anyway, I can't even—"

"Would you have? If you weren't married? Not because you wanted to," he said, at Benedik's protest, "but because it would help sell your scam?"

Benedik nodded, mute.

"Bet it complicated matters, remaining faithful?" Ignatius waited for another nod. "So you spend all that effort to avoid betraying Alina, yet you betray me?"

"She's my *wife*," he said, finding his voice once again.

"And I'm your Emperor."

A beat. Shared glances. Benedik's eyes lowered.

"The outer territories have descended into violence. How many lives? How many lives have you inconvenienced? Maimed? *Extinguished*? You. Blithering. *Idiot*." His roar was a cymbal crash of thunder.

"Let me clear my fathers' names," Benedik pled. "They have nothing to do with this. I was *kidnapped*. This wasn't premedita—no, sire, I'm not trying to duck responsibility. Just making a case that this is my sole doing."

"There were assassination attempts against Layla," Ignatius said quietly. "I can't clear him from that. Not yet. Nor Dracini."

"Sire—" Belatedly, the content of Ignatius's statement caught up with him, and he blanched. Had he put Layla in danger? Was that his doing, and how?

Ignatius, ignorant of the dread spreading throughout Benedik's person, looked at a far wall. Anywhere but at him. "Our decision stands. And you're lucky We didn't throw you straight into the dungeons.

"You have dungeons?" Benedik asked, lightly, trying to even his keel of regret.

"If it weren't for my father," Ignatius said, ignoring him, "who has for some reason decided to meddle…"

"Sounds like a you problem then." Benedik grinned, a sickly thing, probably, not convincing, but maybe—

Ignatius didn't take the bait. "No, Lord Benedik. You don't get to be my friend right now. You are my cousin and my subject, and you have done violence against this realm."

Yes, he had. His Emperor was correct. Benedik sank to one knee. "Sire," he said, bowing his head, "please, forgive me. I was wrong. I only wanted to serve you, sire. I failed. I will accept whatever shall be done. I simply request forbearance for my family. For my fathers, for Alina. Even if you can't clear them at this time. In the end, if you must, I will take on their burdens too."

"Oh, get up, Benedik." Ignatius's face, still stern, at least didn't have the sheen of anger there had been throughout the conversation.

Benedik rose. He was reborn. Renewed. The light of his Emperor's love shone down on him, washing away the worries of the past. He would stand tall against all that would seek to harm him—

"Oh, God, Benedik, are you monologuing in your head right now?"

Benedik became aware of his struck posture, chest out, head toward the heavens. A blush stole across his cheeks and he straightened. "Uh," he stammered, "no. Just in thought. Um, Altain. Altain wasn't the one who kidnapped me and delivered me to Solita."

"But that's what the interrogation said."

"I mean, maybe Altain *kidnapped* me, who knows, but I don't think they were the ones to give me to the rebels. And I wager whoever did kidnap me and delivered me were one and the same. The Solita rebels had a cutout that claimed to be Altainan, and he said Layla reached out to Altain and that's how they found me, but of *course* she wouldn't reach out to Altain. Obviously, he was lying, lying about how they found me because I think they took me in the first place, but if Layla *did* reach out to anyone, then how would Altain know? Reneb, or I'll eat my hat. There's more, about wanting to keep the tunnel safe, which obviously wouldn't be Altain, and—"

Ignatius had already turned away from him while Benedik's gums were flapping. Sigh. He did this sometimes, as if putting him on mute. But looked like he had piqued his interest? He watched warily as his second cousin spoke into the secure comm.

"Go get Park, now."

*
Now

Layla had been fetched by Tonin, who had simply shaken his head and said, "I'm about to box that boy's ears."

"Nice to have you back, Tonin," was her response, and he, rather undignified, stuck his tongue out at her.

When she arrived, Ignatius was in conference with Turine, and Benedik sat just outside, lounging in a bergère marquise chair and damn Valhar for getting her so invested in understanding ridiculous furniture.

Benedik favored Layla with a deprecating grin. "Either they're in there discussing the intel I gave them, or they're preparing the gallows."

Tonin put a hand on his shoulder. "Not if I can help it."

"See, it worries me you even have to *say* that."

Layla made a face at Benedik, but it was only to hide he was right.

Ignatius's private study was roomy, but the amount of people jammed in there made it resemble a clown car. Turine stood ramrod straight in the corner, both scowl and feet firmly planted. Ronin Park, brought in last minute by a staffer, glanced around bemused, both at the people in the room and the room itself, which as far as Layla knew he had never visited. What he was doing there was a mystery to her, and likely to him as well. Tonin at this point had decided he was to be the adult in the room—and thank the goddess for that—so he took over one of the guest chairs, like he owned the place. And Benedik—Benedik slouched against a wall in a very un-Benedik manner, looking downcast and contrite.

Oh Benedik. What did you *do?*

"Well," Ignatius began, leaning forward at his desk and twiddling his thumbs, "I had intended this to be a private meeting between myself and Ambassador Park." No one responded. He sighed and flashed a small smile, noticeably brittle. "Far be it for me to question the wisdom of my advisors. Benedik, start talking."

Benedik startled and then haltingly began outlining his whereabouts and activities of the last few weeks as Layla gasped, Tonin looked at his nephew with fond exasperation—and a bit of worry, Turine's face grew darker, and Park kept up a face of polite interest, which was a tell in itself.

Benedik wrapped up with the belief that Reneb was the one behind his kidnapping and deliverance to Solita, not Altain, and his reasoning. Oh. *Oh.* Wait. So all that back and forth with Carlus about reaching out to the Screaming Goose to find him—

"Park. You *asshole*," came Ignatius's voice. Layla's eyes widened at the epithet. Apparently he had reached the same conclusion as her. "You knew where Benedik was the entire time."

"They were thinking of *killing* me, you dick!" Benedik added. "Whoever you are. Who are you?"

"Ronin Park. Ambassador from Reneb," Ignatius said with tired mien. "One of the pack of us from the Dega base, and from the Mazaran negotiations. Was Reneb involved before or after Layla got ahold of our friend 'Charles'?"

Park nodded and took the empty seat next to Tonin, gingerly seating himself as if readying for a confessional. "Um," he said, running his hands through his jet black hair, "before. My planet did the kidnapping itself. Layla's intervention didn't do much, except cause the RIS to pay off the mercs so they didn't provide information to Car—Charles."

"With *Mazaran* tech?" Benedik asked, aghast. "I was in a stasis unit!"

"Hey," said Park, "to the victors go the spoils."

Ignatius took deep slow breaths, in and out, but he apparently was not succeeding in finding calm, so each inhale and exhale came with a *woomph* sound, rather like a snorting rhinovore. His eyes closed briefly and then his voice came calm and collected. "Why, Park? Why would they do this? And you—"

Park shook his head. "I tried to warn them off, but there's only so much I can do from here, Your Excellency. The RIS was contracted by the Solita rebels, who promised Most Favored Nation status with the tunnel when they win independence."

"The tunnel the rest of the Alliance is trying to destroy?" Layla asked.

"Yeah, and as you know, Reneb's not fully on board with that idea. Look, economic viability is our primary motivator, so the ability of having privileged access to whatever resources you all might find on the other side..."

"And your source of information on the Altainan antimatter weapon?" she continued.

"One of the rebels, I think. Whoever we were dealing with on Solita. He didn't tell us, but accidentally let a few things slip that led RIS on the path. I didn't know," he said. "I didn't know what they wanted with Lord Benedik. I certainly didn't know they would end up using him to destabilize your regime."

Ignatius stared at him a long while. Benedik, obviously bothered by Park's last sentence, tried to speak, but Ignatius held up his hand. "You know, I called myself paranoid for assuming the worst of people I love. How could I think they would betray me? But here we are. Maybe nothing premeditated—both of you—but a grave disappointment nonetheless." He looked to Tonin. "You see? The backstabbing I deal with? Do you understand now, Father?"

Park said nothing. Benedik raised his hand. Ignatius let out a tiny groan. "Yes, Lord Benedik?"

"I'm sorry," Benedik said. "I was just trying to fast-talk my way out of it, you know, as I do, but it kept getting deeper and deeper and frankly weirdly efficient."

Layla waited for Ignatius to acknowledge his apology, but he shook his head and tapped his fingers on his desk in a *what am I going to do with you two* manner. She hazarded to speak. "Unrest," she ventured. "It *was* weirdly efficient, wasn't it. The Solita *militants* did that?" Ignatius looked up in interest.

"They were a handful of punks in a safehouse, Layls," said Benedik. "They thought they were in league with Altainans but if it was Reneb instead..."

Park shook his head. "Wasn't us. Not stirring up unrest, at any rate I promise, sir," he said, turning to Ignatius. "It probably *is* the Altainans. Sounds like their psyops."

"Layla?" Ignatius prompted.

She nodded. "But they usually have some sort of entity on the inside. Agents provocateurs, not Altainans themselves. And coordinated by a local rebel group. Not only does it not seem like the Solita rebels, it doesn't even seem like they're *capable* of something like that."

"I'll work on that, sire," General Turine said.

Ignatius, with the smallest hesitation, nodded. "Fine. We're done here. Park, set me up with a real-time encrypted vid call with your ruling family. I know you have that technology. I have some words for them. Benedik, your accursed data chip also had some detailed projections on the Altainan antimatter weapon. I'm sending you back into Altainan space to go find the damned thing."

Benedik made a tiny sound, a cross between a whimper and a wail. "Are you kidding me? How the hell—it's a huge Whorl—sire, going to Altain *started* this whole mess."

"You owe me," Ignatius bit out. "You want to prove your loyalty? Use that irresponsible free-wheeling mind to figure out where their weapon is."

Benedik sank to one knee. Ignatius rolled his eyes as if Benedik had done this more than once today; given his hangdog look it was quite possible. "I understand your desire to stop the Altainan weapon. May I go back near Solita please, in that case? Maybe I'll hear something, see a way they could sneak in. Just, please, sire, let me clear my father's name. Dracini too. I don't know how. And I know you've got domestic affairs well in hand. But I think I can learn about the weapon, and at the same time, maybe tracking down the organized chaos in the outlands will lead me back here to those attempts on Layla."

"That seems like a wild chase, Lord Benedik."

"No more wild than searching all of Altainan space for the weapon." Benedik rose and took up his place once more near the back of the room.

Ignatius sighed. "I don't see how going out there will help in one bit, but I acknowledge the point that we don't *have* a good starting point. So fine. You go kill two bears with one sword. But how the hell are you going to track down Altain's agents provocateurs? Stanlo tells me he has the entire Solita cell rolled up. They can handle the interrogations out there."

Benedik nodded to Park. "The rebels were in contact with a cutout who said he worked for Altain. They brought me along once, like a proof-of-life thing. Big eyes. Huge motherfucking peepers. Like they were staring through your soul." Layla turned at a sound behind her but it turned out to just be Turine pretending to stifle a sneeze. Hey, maybe he had a sense of humor after all. "Acted as an advisor at some points," Benedik continued. "I think he was the guy that told them to ransom my life." He turned to Park. "One of yours?"

Park shook his head emphatically. "I know who you're talking about. I thought he worked for the rebels."

Well now, *that* was interesting.

"Yeah," Benedik said, "then that's where we start. And ... I might have something that can help." He pulled a slender commlink out of his pocket. "I stole Miss Delilah's way of contacting the guy before I got picked up by Stanlo's people. Shoved it where the sun don't shine."

Layla reared away from it with a wrinkled nose.

"No! Not that way. Down the front of my pants. Didn't get noticed in the initial pat down at his palace. *Your* guys found it," he said, nodding to Ignatius, "but to be fair, this time it was in my pocket. Kind enough to return it. I figure, I head back to the vicinity of Solita and start calling it, right? Layla, you sneaky wench, what do you think?"

Layla crinkled her nose at him for a different reason this time. "Maybe we can refine that plan a bit. You and me. And, maybe Mariah."

"Okay," Ignatius boomed. "Mariah's out of the vicinity at the moment, doing a small task for me, but I'll send word for her to contact the two of you. It'll keep her out of Ephraim's hair anyway. *He's* dealing with the fallout of Lord Benedik's sudden survival and appearance. Now, all of you, I tire of this tediousness. Get out."

Okay then. Layla shared an eyebrow raisin' with Tonin as they shuffled out. He inclined his head toward his son, as if to say, *I'll talk to him.*

***

Later that night, a rare spring storm blew, the violent and crackling reminding her of the tempests of Kaborlah. She lay in the sunroom of her new residence, lights off, watching the strikes of lightning and holding her breath every time she felt the strikes of her child. Nothing anyone else could feel from the outside. Still early yet.

The slow pace of her pregnancy continued to be a paradox of time, as everything else outside moved so quickly. Now she understood when Amma would say each gestation felt a thousand years long.

Ignatius came in, pausing briefly in the sliver of light to avoid startling her, then knelt beside her and put his head on her stomach. "Can I feel?" he murmured as she worked her fingers through his hair.

"Too soft right now," she whispered back. "And it seems so far away and impossible now, but trust me, I know from my sisters, one day there'll be this outline of a foot coming at you and it'll freak you out."

He snorted softly, the reverberation tickling her and making her giggle. "Have you thought more about the surrogacy?" he asked. "The womb transplant?"

Not this again.

"Hell. No. Look, I've been thinking. I get the whole *the baby would be safer this way*. And I *was* being unreasonable about the adoption thing. It's really naming him or her as heir, if we do that. As you pointed out, we should do that all the time. It's just, I don't want to run scared. I don't want them to win. I don't want to spend our baby's entire life locking them up because we're afraid."

He put his face onto her shoulder and kissed it, biting slightly. "Mmm, I can honor that, love." Another kiss on her neck.

"How'd the rest of your day go?" she asked. "I know it started rather—"

"Ignominiously? Although knowing for sure Benedik is okay is—" he sighed. "My father slapped me upside the head after you all left the study."

"Wait, what did he say?"

"I mean *literally*. He smacked me."

"Oh. Um. What did *you* say?"

"I said *owww, daaad!*"

"Huh!" she said in glee, and Ignatius chuckled into her shoulder. "Told me I had driven my entire family away, and I needed to get a grip. And if I had a problem with him telling me so, he could 'go and f on off back to the Swan Nebula.'"

"Does that mean you're done messing with Abilio and Henri?"

"Yeah," he said. "Still not sure about anyone *not* in the family. And I still think Benedik's mission could be helpful." He paused. "I'm sorry, Layla. For all of this. It's just—"

"You're worried. For me and the baby."

"I'm *so scared*," he whispered, and his voice broke. A wetness on her bare shoulder, and an embarrassed grunt, and she pulled away and spun him around to face her. The sheet of rain on the window almost served as a foil to his attempt at stoicism.

"Layls, I think Felix is going to fall soon. We can't hold it, and then the Lyrian wormhole is wide open, straight toward us."

She breathed in a ragged sigh. And who the hell knew what the Alliance would do, if it could take Valhar. Would it eliminate the imperium? Would they force Ignatius and her off-planet? No wonder Ignatius had gotten so bad off.

"Hey," she said, tipping his chin down at her. "Look, you asshole. I'm stronger than you think."

"Ah, the Empress Layla appears," he said, with a small grin.

"Yep. And neither the Alliance nor a little light assassination attempt is going to scare me."

He started to say something, probably snarky, but was interrupted by a ping from his comm. He looked at it and his face paled.

"Work calls?" she asked.

"You need to come too," he said, and she gathered herself and hurried along beside him.

"Tell me the Altainans didn't beat us to the punch," he boomed as he entered the war room.

Turine cleared his throat, his color wan. "Sire, erm, well, I can't *tell* you that. We don't know for sure."

Layla looked at the main screen and gasped. "Oh Goddess Alive!" One hand fluttered to her mouth as the other squeezed Ignatius's hand. On the screen was her childhood home. Kaborlah. Fires burned on the southeastern continent, a bulwark of wreckage orbited, and, in the space around the small planet clashed Altainan and Valharan forces.

"Our force showed up, and quick as lightning, here were the Altainans. One of our dreadnaughts spun out of control and crashed into a solar mirror, which in turn fell into pieces over the planet. The debris there"—he circled a point on the screen—"has hit land."

"Can we hold the planet?" Ignatius asked.

Turine gave him a baleful look. "No, sire. Their numbers are too overwhelming. They were waiting for us. Not too early to tip us off, not too late to give us first mover advantage. *Somehow*," he said, looking at Layla, "they knew."

"I don't like your insinuation, Turine," Ignatius said. "Correct it, now."

"Sire," he acknowledged, tipping his head. "Well, the important thing here is that this weapon of theirs may have slipped by in the chaos. I think maybe it's right for Lord Benedik to head that way in his investigations."

"No," Layla fired back. "The *important* thing is that Kaborlah is not only suffering from an asteroid-level impact but an energy crisis too, with one of its solar mirrors gone."

"I wouldn't call it *asteroid*-level," Turine protested with that air of condescension that made her want to rip his hawkish nose off and slam it up his ass.

"But the impact far outstrips one mirror gone. The greenhouse effect from this is going to cause the cloud cover to get even *thicker* over Kaborlah, which means less solar energy which means less of *everything*. Agriculture suffers too, which means not only do my people not get fed but they don't get the money from exports."

Ignatius turned to her with a microscopic quirked brow. In code: *My people, huh.*

Although maybe one day they'd find out they *thought* they were communicating silently but really one person was thinking, *I love broccoli* and the other person was responding, *Yes, indeed, the purple couch is the best.*

"What are you thinking, my lady?" Ignatius asked, bringing her musings full circle.

"I'm thinking I need to go with Benedik."

The eruption of protest from *both* men solidified her resolve. "I need to help that planet," she said.

"And what, Your Grace," Turine said, "can *you* do?"

"First," she said, "politically, I seriously doubt those Altainan ships are going to land any time soon and clean up their mess on Kaborlah. They're patrol-and-blockade, not humanitarian relief. Putting aside the fact we were attempted conquerors—and Kaboralah doesn't necessarily think in galactic terms like that or care—a visit from a daughter of Kaborlah on behalf of Valhar would do a world of good. And from there, I can try to manage this crisis."

"If that Altainan weapon has passed, I really don't give a—sorry, sire—I just don't think an *Altainan* territory is our priority."

"You're not thinking large enough, General," Layla retorted. "Kaborlah is an important choke point. We might be able to direct the ripple effects from this to our advantage."

Really, the political aspects were nothing to her. Instead, first, she did think she could provide some relief and visibility. But, more importantly—beyond Kaborlah, beyond her family living there—she wanted to help hunt that weapon. "I'll also be safe, away from Valhar," she pointed out.

"You don't need to oversell it," Ignatius said with a small smile. He kissed her on the cheek. "Go. Go get your family."

"I wasn't—"

"But you should, Layla. Like we discussed. Or at least: ask them?" He furrowed his brow. "C'mon. They're *family*."

Ignatius, of all people...

She said nothing, but gave a small shrug of non-commital acceptance.

As they walked out, Ignatius bent to come closer, leaving lips brushing her forehead. "I'll fix this, love. I'll fix all of it."

She closed her eyes, inhaling his scent. "Nate, remember your silly beetle war? You started it. You threw one into a pitcher plant for the greater good—to make me laugh, to ease my nervousness so you could propose. But it had unintended consequences, and no matter how many times you gently trap one of them and let them free, you can't put the chaos back into the bottle. You *can't* fix everything."

Silently, he grabbed her hand and they continued on toward their rooms, and toward momentary peace. She turned a moment, feeling someone's gaze on her back. Turine stood down the hall, alone, staring at her with narrowed eyes. He opened his mouth as if to say something, then sighed and headed back into the war room.

Formless plans began to take shape, murky and unknowable, but with her and Benedik's different ways of thinking merged together, she imagined she could do far more than merely finding this weapon.

Because she knew what she had to do.

Kaborlah, on fire. Felix, about to wrest free and leave the Valharan front vulnerable. Her family—all of it—in danger.

Yes, she knew what she had to do. She had to stop this war.

THEN

Then

An unseasonable warm front blows through winter-lagged Novaria, and I've spent many sun-drenched days walking the outdoor gardens, my bodyguard by my side. Prison guard, more like, though I can see how there's room for both. Mariah's not bad company. She's fiercely loyal to the regime, but that doesn't preclude a sort of camaraderie. Not that we'd ever be bosom buddies, although a pathetic part of me screams, "Choose me! Love me!" *Neutrally polite* may be the closest equivalent.

Which is why her disposition this morning has me wary. Mariah's never *jumpy*, but today she's electric. Anticipatory with a hint of reluctance. My walk down the hall stops short as she suddenly blocks my way. "Okay, time for the straight shit. Why were you contacting a foreign government?"

Huh? "Are you talking about the thing that landed me here in luxurious custody or something entirely different?"

"I don't know how you did it," she says, "but *someone* pinged Reneb's databases from here trying to pinpoint Carlus's whereabouts. The universe of people who have any idea he's even in the vicinity of that planet is minuscule. I know it includes you. The General told me you were present during a discussion—"

"I've known far longer than *that*, Mariah. What the fuck? I'm not a hacker. I can't break past that walled-off garden intranet you gave me and—"

"It's precisely why we couldn't send you home. We knew you'd turn around *so* fast and give up that info—"

"For the Goddess's sake, Mariah, I told you I've known for almost a year! As soon as he left." We face off, hands on hips. Something about what she said—something doesn't sound *right*, but I can't quite parse it while two meters of redhead glares at me, teeth bared.

"The General wants to see you in the basement," she says, waving dismissively at me and changing direction. The palace has what appears to be at first a straightforward layout. Especially in the public areas. Well laid out corridors on a grid. The residence with a small enough footprint—it rises up on a spire—that one can access each apartment without immense amounts of searching. But tapestries and false fronts hold all manner of functions within the palace walls, accessible only to approved personnel. Thus Mariah leads me toward a mural depicting cavalry-laden battle, scanning her eyes at a specific location and allowing doors to appear and slide open.

The basement. I know all about basements. Mariah: is she reluctant? Gleeful? Her behavior today has me flummoxed.

To my utter lack of surprise, it's an interrogation room.

Battle-ready, I take stock of the situation. Not the stark chamber I feared, but then again, Ransom's office was also designed to be comfortable. Chairs set up for an "interview." Turine, armed crossed, glaring. Does that chair over there have hidden restraints? Oh, it looks like it. A younger man, putting on a more obvious "bionic" eye than Hari used to use, a clunky cybernetic monocle. Maybe no serum, today. Maybe.

I move to sit. A needle jams into my arm, and I yelp in shock and terror. "Merely a jab," Mariah murmurs. "Blood test, to check for any preexisting conditions."

Well, so much for the "no serum" hope. At least they're making sure it won't kill me. Inadvertently doing so might be *just* the pretext for Altain to declare hostilities. Turine nods and Mariah pushes me down into the chair. She pockets the vial of my blood for later. The young man sits across from me. One red eye widens. Focus whirls.

Turine leans in between us and places the vial of buspirathol on the low table, as some sort of: talisman? Warning? Promise? "Dame Layla," he says that snide tone, "be aware—"

He pauses as a door opens and—I can't describe this any other way, hyperbolic as it is—a whirling thunderous tempest of a man storms his way in. A vein bulges out of his forehead. His eyes are wide with rage, cheeks red, spittle collecting on his lips.

Ignatius, the man-turned-storm in question, takes the same stock of the situation I did—room, personnel, furniture, bionic eye, and, as his eye falls to the vial, he goes still. Absolutely still. And the entire room pauses with him, static set pieces depending on the Emperor to breathe us into life.

And then he expels air out of his nose and the tableau bursts into action.

"Sire!" Turine calls, leaping to his feet.

"You will not interrogate the future empress," Ignatius growls.

"We're taking precautions," Mariah begins, holding up her hands in supplication.

"I'm not marrying you anymore," I mumble, but not so low he didn't hear me.

"Fine," Ignatius says to me. He turns to the young man with the bionic eye. "You will not interrogate the only love of my life."

The participants freeze again, some with mouths ajar, some shallow breathing. Ignatius looks at me as if daring me to defy his sentiment. Which I do anyway.

"Not very objective of you, Your Excellency," I observe. "Not very adherent to your duty."

Instead of displaying anger at my ungraciousness, his countenance softens. "Some things," he says, "are more important than duty." He takes my hand. "The trick lies in knowing when that is. Greater men than me have floundered this test, but I like to think you are my guiding lantern. My lodestar."

"Sire," Turine interjects, "please reconsider. I respect your abiding affection for Dame Layla, but she represents our best chance for determining who our mole is."

"Like whoever tried to ascertain Carlus's location on Reneb?" I ask. "C'mon! Even if I had that level of technical skill, I wouldn't need to look it up! I'd just, I dunno, find some way to ask Park!"

Turine rears back in a shock I don't understand, and it isn't so much a surprised sort of thing but more dread. "That's not ... that's not what I mean," he finishes lamely.

We all regard him with varying degrees of squints, but Ignatius is the first to speak. "Huxley," he says, addressing Turine, "the mark of a man is his ability to choose what's right over what's expedient." He turns to me. "I'm going to send you home. If you want to go. I let other people sow my opinions and that's not right. I made a promise, and moreso, I trust you, with all your heart. You are free to go." He cocks his head as he regards Mariah and Turine, ready to demolish any objection. As I expect, they choose silence.

Would I go home? I look around the room. The same thing would happen at home. Out of curiosity. Out of an abundance of caution. All for the sake of security. What's the balance between security and liberty? If we give up liberty to keep us safe, what's the point? What are we trying to protect? At least Valhar doesn't pretend it's anything but interested in the continuation of the regime.

And if it happened at home, no one would be coming to swoop in and save me.

Okay, so maybe I should be embarrassed I needed my Prince Charming to rescue me from the dragon, but it leaves me with a warm feeling. I'm worth something to someone.

But still—

"You betrayed me. The serum. That was private. That was for you."

A curious little chuckle emanates from Ignatius's throat. Not actually amused. Almost filled with malice. "Mariah? Care to explain?"

"It was me," she says begrudgingly.

"Excuse me?" I ask flatly.

"I have—I had—a source in your man Ransom's office. He told me."

Had?

She answers my silent question. "He's been found out. Unrelated to all of this. Otherwise I would not be explaining. All right?" Her tone is defiant, but at a sharp look from Ignatius, she bows. "My lady." Amazingly, it is said without sarcasm.

"I was almost certain I hadn't told anyone," Ignatius says softly. "Almost. I admit, I don't think I had grasped how important that particular confidence was to you. I'm so very sorry about that. So I hesitated when insisting I hadn't shared. But I finally got to the bottom of it."

"That—"

That changes things quite a bit

"And the two of you!" he roars. "You bring her to the basement? Why?—Why shouldn't I have you two in the stocks immediately. How dare you treat my—my personal guest—like this?

We will speak. On this. Later."

His shoulders heave. And I am faced with a decision.

Now I understand the cold-and-hot routine of Ignatius's when we saw each other for the first time during the state visit. Because who knows what the right thing is? Am I going to now turn to him and say *yes I want to stay. I want to get back together?* Is that what I'm saying? And who would believe that?

No. I'm not going to return to the status quo. Niggling anecdotes in the back of my head bug me again. Ignatius nervous about sending me home even though I already knew about Carlus. Someone trying to find his location. A mole. Reneb threatening to join the war which would then pull Altain and all the rest of the Alliance planets into it too.

"I can help find the mole," I blurt out, not even knowing where I'm going with this, but needing to get control of my own life.

Mariah tilts her head. "You don't have any unusual access to your government." She says it in not her usual surly way. Abashed. Chastened.

"I have external contacts."

"And no one's going to think you're not connected to Valhar," adds Ignatius, now in problem-solving mode.

"Not trying to hide a connection."

"But," says Mariah, now, pacing, "you can't move freely. As far as anyone knows, you're engaged to the emperor. You're famous. And why help us?" she asked, stopping and glancing at Turine. "Why muddle up your loyalties like this?"

"Fine," I say, exasperated, "make it some sort of official visit then. Obviously Lyria and Altain are out, so..." I snap my fingers, "Reneb. Park is high up in the government there. And maybe then I can quickly jump in on Carlus. As for loyalty, whoever gave away the tunnel information, gave it to *Lyria*. I don't give a flying fuck about Lyria."

Yes. It's coming together now. "You need someone to untangle the disparate threads of what's going on around us," I continue to the skeptical stares. "Benedik is still tied up on Altain. Mariah, as you've pointed out, there are very few people who are working with the full set of information here. Send me. Maybe I'll find your mole. Maybe I can stop Reneb from declaring war. I'm your best shot."

Another pause. We all look at Ignatius.

"Take Mariah," he says. He and Mariah share a small look. I imagine it says, *We're still not okay. But I need you right now.*

Mariah pulls out her tablet. "When, sire?"

Turine splutters, an almost waterfowl-like action that I have to breathe through to ensure I don't start laughing. Bet *now* he knows what it feels like to be caught up in events outside your control. "But you're a political prisoner. You have no legal status here on Valhar. We can't send you as an envoy."

"Fine," I snap. "Ignatius?"

"Yes, dear."

"Marry me." Wait, did I just say that?

Ignatious looks caught between hysteria and relief, but it's okay, because only I can tell. To everyone else it's a momentary eye-widening and curling grin. "Certainly, my lady. When would you like to schedule this?"

Oh, I'm not ready for this. Am I really going to go through all this again? "Have Ephraim find a fortuitous date on your calendar," I say simply. I turn back to Turine. "Ok, I'm the future empress again. Happy?"

"You're not married yet," Turine sighs, "so your status is murky."

Ignatius crosses his arms and cuts his eyes to Turine. "General, I'm declaring her a full-fledged subject of Valhar. I can do that. You know why?"

"Why, sire?"

"Because *I'm* the Emperor."

Then

Ignatius asks me if I'm moving back in with him and I freeze.

"I know we're engaged again," I manage, "but maybe we should ease into this?"

He gives a sad whisper of a smile. "I would ask if you'd at least consider the guest space in my apartments, but it occurs to me I should reassure you I'm not holding you to the betrothal."

I try to be playful. "But you have to. I'm a full-fledged Valharan subject now."

He takes my hand. "Who cares." The words slide out in the melodic tone I miss oh-so-much. "You'll always have a home here. No matter what."

The sentiment, loving and unprecedented as it is, has such a tone of *finality* and *farewell* that I'm caught speechless. Maybe he'll think I'm overcome with gratitude. But no. Unlike him, I'm a terrible khed player, emotions warring across my face. And he sees it.

"Together," he says. I look at him in confusion. Rallying cry?

"That was my mistake," he clarifies. "Possibly the biggest I'll make in my entire life. We're going to disagree a lot. Strong personalities. Different cultures. Me, ascendant in a way I had never thought possible and you, figuring out how you fit in. Our relationship, brand new and so old at the same time. But we're in this together. This is our team. You tell me to pack this thing in, hand over my seal of office, and it's done. And if you don't, I will always hear your advice on my rule. I can't heed it all the time, but hopefully you understand that—"

"Of course I do," I interject, and Ignatius gives me such a look of hope I melt, and I *had* been looking at him askance like *is he seriously moving forward as if we're really truly back together?* but now am I actually *listening?*

His grip on my hand tightens and he clears his throat. And then Mariah comes up and interrupts our moment.

Her eyes are wary, and she considers me with a little scrunch in her forehead. What now?

"Sire." She hesitates. "Lady Layla."

"Mariah," we both say in unison.

She looks around the hallway and then nods at the door to my room. "Let's go inside."

We file into the small room, Mariah not giving it a second thought, Ignatius with a grimace—the last time he was in here I slapped him and threw a ring in his face—and as for me? I don't know. It kind of feels like home, this room. This room, representing a time of captivity, but also, a time when things were *clear*. No sudden citizenship to a nation I haven't sworn oaths to. No maybe-engagement to a man I want to marry with my whole heart but who heads a political system of which I disapprove, who is leading the Whorl into war because of nationalist politics. No Turine, looking like he wants to throw me in the dungeons—(wait, *are* there dungeons?) No Mariah, who—

Who is holding a single-use tablet out in my direction.

"What's this?" I ask, not wanting to look down until I have at least *some* warning of what I'm about to see.

"I went ahead and ran the analysis on the blood sample we took from you in the basement."

"Wait, you ran the test *after* we decided against this course of action, Mariah?" Ignatius scolds. Mariah shrugs, unrepentant.

I know it. I know it before she says it and maybe it's *not* what I think. Maybe I'm dying, or something, instead, but as I look back at the tablet, Mariah begins apologizing for telling us under these circumstances, and I keep reading, head buzzing.

"Layls, what is it?" Ignatius asks.

I look up. My voice is thick, and I have trouble getting the words out. "I'm pregnant."

Then

Dear Diary,

It's the year 1126 and we have an oops baby. Sex is the worst.

~Layls

Is that why I feel like I've been hit by an armored transport? My stomach churns, and it's not because of hormones or morning sickness or whatever happens in pregnant bodies. And it's not even because I'm contemplating the big picture of having a *child* or the *timing* or anything like that.

Really, I'm thinking of the fact there's something *inside* of me. An intruding life force, taking from me without my knowledge and permission. It gives me a full body cringe, like a parasite has invaded my body and oh heavens, I'm going to be a terrible mother aren't I.

Ignatius is taking this better than I am.

"You are going to continue the pregnancy?" he asks, scooting in closer to me as I sit on a window bench, frozen.

I nod.

He clears his throat. "Ok. I'm glad!" he hastens to add. "I just wanted to ensure you were aware. The existence of a child could be dangerous to the stability of the empire if he or she is illegitimate." He frowns. "I'm not trying to manipulate you into anything, or drop passive aggressive hints. It's not your job to worry about the stability of the Empire.

It's not your home. But, personally, I'd feel better if we can legitimize the baby."

"Isn't it already out of wedlock?"

"Conception doesn't matter, not that much. Status at birth. And before you ask, I can name them my heir, but there are still too many stumbling blocks. Full adoption would be the only thing that works, but for you to retain parental rights, we'd need to be married by birth, so we're back to my main point."

"So wait, now I'm pregnant and you want to marry me?" I roll my eyes.

"I've wanted to marry you this entire time," he says, quietly. "You know that. But I've been giving you space. The pregnancy gives me a reason to ask you. Especially since we've already intimated we're re-engaged."

"Okay, so you think *I* should agree to marry you because I'm pregnant?"

"We're not normal people, Layla. Think on that strong sense of duty and honor you have. Helping to keep an entire society stable—that's pretty honorable."

"So now you *are* guilt tripping me." But I soften that with a smile, not intending it to be a blow.

He gives a small, sideways smile and kisses me on the forehead. "Think about it. For me."

I already know the answer is yes. I too have wanted to marry him this entire time. This *entire* time. But following my heart and not my brain got me into this whole mess in the first place. I had thought it prudent to draw back a bit.

But, maybe now I have an external reason as well as an internal. I just hope I'm not being a love-soaked idiot.

Sleep on it, I tell myself, imagining myself shushing the ghosts of liberated women from the past, who are booing at me for letting a child tie me to an Empire.

Then

Jurna, 1126

Life comes, raises the stakes, makes us work hard for even the simplest, purest love. That is the order of things. As I learned as a smart girl on Kaborlah, when you shine bright, you get worried down to a dull sheen, all the better not to blind those around you. And now I know, wherever love blazes, the universe fights to wear it down to the embers. But those embers are the important part. They are the guardian light that will hold fast our promises.

Love makes you freeze in place, while a sculptor takes the whole of you and chisels down until you get to your essence, and then a spark from within grows and grows, a little molten planetary core, until it overtakes the sharp edges and the broken bits and superheats it, breaks it down, reshapes everything into a you that's more you than you've ever been. But it's new and it's a bit sillier than you've ever been, trusting, a motley patchwork, exterior shell threadbare in the most uncomfortable places.

Do it. Do your worst.

Make me reckless. Make me maudlin. Make me a believer. Make me jump into muddy waters. Make me a fool.

Goddess, make me a fool.

We are married by candlelight, icicles glinting off the searching gaze of the moon. Me in my red lengha, with tiny sparkling mirrored sequins, churies dangling on my wrists, the smallest tiara on offer, mehndi snaking up my hands and arms. He is repledesent in his uniform. Flurries tickle my nose. I'm no longer cold here in Novaria, on this winter's night.

I may never feel cold again.

Then

It is in the sun-filled breakfast room in our apartment that Ignatius and I have our final planning session before I depart for Reneb. Obviously I've moved back in with him, and taking the time to implement a few changes before my mission seems less feminine frivolity and more a survival mechanism. There are so few windows in the Residence. Ignatius has one in his private study, as do I in the room that will become my little office, but what I want is floor-to-ceiling panels of glass, showing me the expanse of falling snow, or the flowers I'm assured will bloom soon. A security risk in any case, but there is part of the building edifice facing inward, not toward communal gardens but curled in toward a windowless part of the palace. And there, in that curl, is a forgotten glass-surrounded stairwell, originally connecting Ignatius's—*our*—apartment and the larger one upstairs to which Beatrix had wanted us to move. Despite the lack of view, the light there hits just right in the morning, and I prevailed upon Ephraim to take down the non-load-bearing wall closing off the staircase and converting the landing. I thought it would take weeks or months, and instead it's taken mere days. And so, with the considerable alone time I have without Ignatius, I've, piece by piece, made it my own.

Maybe if Beatrix ever succeeds in moving us upstairs, I can turn that one into a glass-covered balcony with which to watch the sky.

We dine in my comfortable upholstered chairs—simply chairs, no fancy names—with a cheerful table graced with flowers, open and light and everything yelling *spring, spring spring* to shout away the Valharan winter. I could *live* in this room. I could stay forever. But time is running short. Reneb could declare any day, and so off I go to plead our case. We've signaled Park, best we could, without alerting the whole darn Whorl. Hopefully he'll bring it to his government. *Valhar is coming to parley. Please, just wait.*

"So," Ignatius states, "I think you're comfortable at this point with all the little nuances of our government to speak on my behalf on Reneb. And I want to make this clear. You have full freedom to do or say whatever you think best out there. Your voice has the same authority as mine."

"That's quite a measure of trust." I continue eating my paratha-and-egg breakfast. I've slowly been overcoming my shyness, sharing with the dining staff some of my personal favorites from Kaborlah, and if any dining companions are taken aback by the way I scoop some food up with my hands or with a piece of bread, they haven't made it known. (The palace staff were originally wary of wooing me with Kaborlahi food—before I asked for it myself—afraid of being appropriative. I peppered my response with a smile, bitter and true: *No one wants to appropriate Kaborlah. It's refreshing, for once.*)

Today, the chef has gotten it just right. More frittata than omelet, flat instead of fluffy, perfect combination of cilantro and onion. Paratha still hot from the cooking oil.

"Trust," Ignatius says, "is something I have in abundance. Wholehearted, unabashed, trust."

I put my food down, discreetly wiping my hands on my napkin. My eyes shift as Mariah enters the room, silent as a cat.

Mariah is to be my guide and protection on this journey, and we continue our uneasy, tension-filled truce. Before, despite our similar ages, I thought of her as the salty old-hand to my eager newcomer, which was fine. Coexistence, and all that. I don't want her respect, and no longer am seeking her friendship, but I thought, in the first weeks of my engagement, we could remain professional: bodyguard and assignment, doing the needful to get through the day.

"Oh, good," Ignatius says when he spots her. "I've been trying to find a moment all three of us were together and alone. If you're going to visit Carlus, you should know this."

Mariah sits with a thud, and I detect barely disguised alarm.

"Sire," she says, "it's not your story to tell."

"She's the Empress, Mariah. She deserves to know."

She pulls out a sucker and pops it in her mouth. "Sire, even you didn't necessarily *deserve* to know." Her voice emerges muffled. "You knew because Carlus went to you first."

I look back and forth between them. There's always one more secret, isn't there?

"We're not sending her in there blind. She needs to be working with full information—"

"Sire, if she's out there negotiating with Reneb, and she knows *and they don't*, that puts her in a very dangerous position. There's too much potential for a slip."

I see how this last has affected Ignatius, and I interject before I'm thrown back into the dark. "This is the thing you were so worried about, isn't it? The reason you didn't want me to return home, despite your promise? You were afraid I had seen something. That I had figured something out, about Carlus."

He sighed. "Turine was afraid you'd give up that he's on Reneb. Which is bollocks, since you've known, along with Park, but that's not something he realized."

"Yes, a fellowship of trust *I* wasn't aware of either until recently," Mariah throws in, arms crossed. She kicks petulantly at a table leg, making our porcelain teacups rattle.

Ignatius ignores the display. "Anyway, it's not something I wanted to explain to Turine, and there *was* this additional worry of you learning the rest of the story, and..." he shrugged. "As I've said, I was wrong. I'm sorry."

"And so?" I ask. "Are we done with secrets between us?"

He throws up his hands. "Unfortunately, I think Mariah is right. It will be too much of a distraction. But as your schedule permits, if you work with the Renebian government first and then find yourself traveling to see Carlus, Mariah can—"

"No. *Fuck* no," she says. We turn to her with mirrored expressions of shock. Mariah is always quite contrary, and is rude to me personally, but when it comes to the Emperor, she tempers her words with a veneer of submission.

"Look," she continues, "you know what Gustav cultivated me for."

"Yeah," I answer. "Murdering people."

She gives me a *look*. "Ensuring the continuation of the Empire. That includes, regrettably, some killing. *But the point is*, this is stability-of-the-Empire stuff. Sire, if *you* want to tell her when we get back, I can't stop you. But I won't have that on my head."

"She's the *Empress*, Mariah."

"And you're the Emperor, and if you didn't already know the secret, I wouldn't have otherwise told you."

"That's a dangerous claim to make, Mariah," Ignatius warns.

She shrugs. "So throw me in the dungeons for disloyalty. It's too explosive a story. And once you tell her, I'm going to be so far up her ass all day and every day, it might be worth it for you to stay silent instead."

"Yeah, so will Turine," I mutter.

"Turine doesn't know," Ignatius says. I look at him in shock. "Not this one. That's how closely held it is. No secrets between us," Ignatius continues with a smile, "so the truth is I have information I want to give you but Mariah won't *let* me."

Mariah rolls her eyes as Ignatius snorts to himself, amused by his own pout. But I'm still processing what I just heard. Even Turine doesn't know?

What did Carlus get himself into?

INTERLUDE
(Carlus, Crown Prince of the Valharan Empire)

THEN: Year 1123, Swan Nebula, at the end of the Whorl-Mazaran War

The runner comes to Carlus with news, and though he remains outwardly strong—after all, he *is* the Crown Prince—his stomach drops as if he were on an orbital dive.

"Your Highness," the runner says, kneeling. "I—" He looks around, as if just now observing the presence of the Mazarans, who gather around Carlus like the assorted carapace of a vulnerable corpus. He pales.

The long-limbed Mazaran leader fixes his large unsettling eyes upon Carlus and inclines his head. He wields control with stoic superiority, surely secure in his personhood above the scrappy scratching denizens of the Whorl.

We're all humans here buddy, Carlus thinks with intention, as if the leader's bulbous head indicates a talent for telepathy. *No better than the other.*

Perhaps with the exception of one Prince Carlus, who three years ago had done something he had thought *was* noble, but instead had made him no better than the metaphorical insect, fit to belong on the underside of one's shoe.

"Please," Carlus says to the Mazaran leader, with the best diplomatic voice he could muster, "I shall like to speak to my man alone."

The leader acquiesces with his customary smug demeanor. He is thin and reedy. Built for space.

It wouldn't take much for Carlus to snap his neck.

"Now," Carlus says, clasping his hands together, "what news?"

The runner's color doesn't improve with the Mazarans' departure. And then he speaks the words that shatter Carlus's world.

"Your father, sir."

They did it. Those bastards did it. They all but admitted it, afterwards, because of *course* they had eavesdropped. And in turn dropped hints that it was for the best, as Carlus is the *amenable* Valharan, after all.

Carlus stares into the bottom of his whiskey bottle. Full in cups he is, despondent and devastated. He has ignored several pings. Cousin Ignatius, likely. Wondering where he is, reminding him this is the night before the likely-fateful armistice talks with the Mazarans. That a social presence is required.

He can't. He can't fake conviviality.

"Your Highness," comes his cousin's voice in his head, "what—"

Carlus whacks the voice away but encounters flesh. Not in his head after all.

Ignatius, Commander of the Valharan forces on Dega. And that must be ... ah, Commander Kamil. *Dame* Kamil. Never met, but much learned. Especially from a certain besotted cousin of his. And who—

"That's Ronin Park," Ignatius says easily, following the direction of Carlus's eyes. "Assistant to the Reneb principal in the talks. Your Highness, what has happened? What can I do?"

"My father," Carlus croaks. He holds up a hand before Ignatius can kneel in fealty. "Alive. Incapacitated though. They believe he won't recover."

Commander Kamil gives a start. "I—" she looks to Ignatius for guidance. *Oh she's fully in, that one.* "This may change the tenor of the talks. I need to get to my principal—"

"No!" Carlus commands. *Good God man, what possessed you to blab in front of the Altainan?* Despite his woozy head, he throws *presence* into his words, willing them to understand. "We must keep this quiet. Gustav IV is still the Emperor, and thus he will remain."

"He's right," Ignatius says. He looks at the other two, beseeching. "You know how important this is. No one must know. Carlus can run things until ... until Gustav is better," he concludes, with a swallow.

And so a conspiracy is born. Not easily, not without discussion and wobbles. But in the end, Carlus is in the debt of three key people, and he will never forget.

Nor will he forget this was all his fault from the beginning. He who brought the Mazarans to the Whorl. A chain of events directly culminating in his father's illness. Who will likely never recover. Who will likely die, leaving the throne to Carlus.

Betrayer. Traitor. Faker.

Usurper.

THEN

Then

It feels weird, being at the orbital transfer station again. It was mere months ago I arrived here, still anonymous, before a short hop down to Novaria in a crowded nondescript passenger shuttle. Now our arrival is at a separate facility, completely empty except for the people assisting us. I half expect the damn room to be covered in gold leaf, but it's all cool metal and functional furnishings. The spin of the station, giving us gravity, is much less pronounced out here on the edge. Farther in where the public area is, the coriolis effect leads to stomach lurching moments. But I surprise myself by being caught in a bout of nausea from the slight spin, and then there was how I felt after takeoff from Novaria, and...

Right. Pregnant.

Mariah leads me impatiently down the corridor, moving as if she's clearing the way through an invisible crowd, barking at me from time to time to keep up. I've always thought an empress glides, tall and stately in shimmering robes of state while handlers fuss and preen, but here I am, stubby legs rushing to keep in time. I would say *at least there's someone with us carrying my bags*, because although I'm definitely not *too good* to carry my things, I'm feeling especially weak and fragile. Maybe it's really an effect of early pregnancy, maybe it's all in my head. But yes, good there is someone here to help, *bad* that the assistant gets to witness his new, very unregal, Empress-Consort huffing and puffing away.

This section of the transfer hub is *huge*, and who for? There likely are more VIPs than I originally thought who get to use it, and possibly the staff cleared it out for my benefit.

When we finally reach the berth my jaw drops.

"Mariah, it's a fucking *beater*," I say before I can stop myself. I catch a glimpse of my baggage steward widening his eyes. Sigh. *Language*, Layla.

Mariah doesn't miss a beat. "Okay, *Princess*."

Don't say "I'm actually the Empress, bitch." Don't say it...

"Look, bitchhh—" Oops. Shit. Think fast. "Betchhya 100 creds this piece-a space junk won't even make it through the Lyrian wormhole," I say, recovering. "Mariah, please tell me this broke-ass ship is creatively designed to look like a piece of shit and it's nicer than we think?"

She sighs, rubbing the bridge of her nose. "I hate to be charitable, but I do know your objection is actually about safety, not because you're spoiled. So yeah. It's like a fucking tank." By this point, the porter has dropped the bags and skedaddled, thank the Goddess. "But otherwise, okay, it actually is as bad as it looks. Safe but shitty. Pretty sure it's going to smell like feet and stale fish. C'mon," she says, beckoning me. This time I do grab my bags as we head up the ramp.

"I don't even rate a luxury shuttle," I mutter, not actually complaining but just, you know, *observing*. But apparently Mariah hears.

"Don't want to attract attention coming into Reneb. That government will be more willing to deal if they can keep this all hush hush."

Ah. "So we're rolling up to Reneb like a shifty white shuttle with FREE CANDY written on the side?"

Mariah, wonder of all wonders, actually *laughs* at this, a bell-like sound. Her face turns grim as we enter ship's aft. A cramped living space, no kitchen to speak of, only a reheater. I think I spot the location of the pull-down bunks astarboard. Cockpit, of course, forward. Mariah will likely do most of the flying when needed, although the vast majority can be automated. All in all, pretty standard fare for this class of ship, but it smells like mothballs.

Mariah wrinkles her nose. "Right. Let's see where to store our bags, or if there's any bunk privacy."

I take a moment to grimace through another wave of nausea—at least I know the baby is safe and healthy in there since it's making itself known—and then, from Mariah's direction, comes a muffled curse.

"What?" I ask as I walk that way. I find her in the makeshift bunk growling at a pulled-down, standard size mattress. We both twist our heads around, looking, hoping, *praying*, but eventually we stare at the truth laid out in front of us.

There's only one bed.

"Right," Mariah says. "We're sharing."

"Ugh." I make a face. "How about I take the floor."

"Okay, prin—"

"Don't okay princess me! I offered to take the *floor*."

"Knowing damn well I can't accept the offer which puts *me* on the floor."

"What, is that a royal etiquette thing? No one has to know. Seriously. Floor. I'm fine."

"What? Worried I'm gonna get your heart racing?"

"No, it means I don't want your sweaty body heat curled up against me all night! Floor."

Mariah points a dangerous finger toward me. "What's your problem?"

"What's *your* problem? Choosing where I want to sleep—which doesn't inconvenience you in any way, shape, or form—makes me what? Spoiled and entitled?"

"You wanna know what my problem is?" She walks up to me, menace written on her face. "You're a culturally insensitive bigot."

"A bigot," I repeat. "I'm sorry. Is it bigoted to expect we sleep separately? I wasn't aware of that particular Valharan tradition."

"It's not about that."

"Really," I reply. "Pray tell, what, then?"

"You show up, a newcomer, and you decide you're going to play both sides of everything. Sure, I love you, Ignatius," she says in a squeaky voice—I do *not* sound like that—"but I'm a Republic soldier so you must respect my oaths! Hee hee. There may be threats to your whole regime and way of life but it's against my soldierly religion to share them with you! Hemp hem. You're as bad as fucking Reneb. They pull that sort of shit too." She looks me up and down. "No wonder the Emperor thought you'd be decent at negotiating with them. Just try not to give away the entire farm in your bass-ackwards quest to please them, ok?"

"Putting all that aside, whatever that whole thing was"—I wave my hands in a circle, summing up Mariah's rant—"nothing to do with bigotry *or* beds. Maybe we should add logical reasoning to the curriculum for palace servants."

"Bitch."

"Hater."

"Democratic elitist."

"Imperialist harpy."

"You're the Emperor's wife. I swore to protect you. You know what? I'm even taking the floor, which you *have* to have known was the only viable outcome of all this because you're the *fucking Empress*. But we're *not* friends. No matter how desperately you seem to want companionship. Save it for hippy drippy Lady Alina."

"Mariah," I say with a sigh, "what can I do for you to be at least be *civil* to me?" She takes in a breath, ready, I'm sure, for another tirade, and I stop her with a growl. "Like, summed up in the fewest words possible, or something."

She leans in close and beckons me to bring my ear to her mouth. I comply, warily, and shiver as her silky voice reverberates with the words. She counts them off as she speaks.

"Choose. a. fucking side. Bitch."

Then

The length of the trip is such that Mariah and I do settle into a sort of rhythm, hot bunking so both of us can have comfortable sleep, trading piloting duties so it's not only her manning the controls when needed, and basically staying out of each others' way. She doesn't seem to anger at the long naps I end up taking, choosing then to sleep on the crash couch—our argument about the floor *may* have been slightly dramatic, but that thing is so uncomfortable it might as well be tile. The inexplicable nodding off at random moments worries me until Mariah explains its a natural thing for early pregnancy. Funny. I don't remember my mother or sisters ever resting this much, but honestly, when I lived on Kaborlah, my head was always in the clouds—or rather, out with the stars.

Ignatius, being the goofball he is only with me, keeps sending me dispatches from the palace, acting as if everything has fallen apart in my absence. *Day 12,* he writes in one missive, *the beetles have taken over the palace. I am writing from our fallback position. Even now, I can hear the scribble scrabble of their little feet, marching, endlessly, toward my oblivion. If this is my last, know it has been my honor to love you.*

I smile as I reread the letter, which precedes a flurry of later missives depicting in great detail the rise of the Beetle Empire, and flick my fingers to add the words to my little black book. Mariah, fresh off sleep and grimacing into her bulb of coffee, cranes her neck to catch a glimpse.

"What's that stupid thing you're always scribbling in?"

I tuck it in my pocket. "My diary."

"Dear Diary," she mocks.

"Shut up."

"What do you do with it? Talk about cute boys? Draw heart-shaped flowers?"

I sigh. "I write specific things, like a day-to-day journal, but I also write stories and poetry and go back and recount watershed moments of my life like I'm writing a book and keep things like..." I trail off. Ignatius's drawings and his letters to me are between us. "...mementos," I finish.

"Hmmph," she responds. "Seems arrogant. To put that much effort into recounting your life."

Actually, I think I'm keeping these memories for you, kid. Whoever you are. Whenever you are. I think I've always known. I've never seen my own amma as more than my life-giver. I want you to think of me as more. As complex. As rude, and coarse, and misguided, and loving, and brave. So I visit and revisit my words, adding more context, more story, struggling to put life and love into some semblance of order.

But I don't tell her that, and I don't want her snooping, so it's time to upload. At least the net is protected so only I can access it; my book doesn't exactly have a lock on it. I wave my hands and wipe away the words, accumulated over the last few months.

"What's the point?" she asks. "Not like you're rereading it."

"Actually, I do. I download off the net and back into the book a lot when I want to remember something from a specific era in my life. And, there's value in reflection, even if the words are never seen again."

"There's also a value in not writing down state secrets, and I'm not sure you're being discreet."

"It's always that with you, isn't it."

"With all the emphasis you place on duty and honor"—she spits out the words as if they're poisonous—"just want to make sure you're consistent."

Great. We were doing so well, and now we're back to this bullshit. At least we're just a few hours to Reneb. Finally. The distance of the Valharan Empire from the planets of the Alliance cannot be helping the *us vs them* dichotomy of Whorl politics. A matter of days to get around the respective ends of each faction, a matter of weeks in between, both in actual light years *and* in the placement of wormholes. The Lyrian Hegemony is the closest to Valhar, but really its colony Felix is the planet just past the inaptly named Lyrian wormhole; Lyria itself is much farther away. Thank goodness, because now we're at war with Lyria, I don't think passage closer to their home planet would be viable. Felix, luckily, is rather autonomous, and the colonial government there doesn't seem to have the same level of vitriol for Valhar that Lyria proper is exhibiting.

I've never enjoyed visiting Reneb. Too industrial chic for me. Not that the whole planet is covered in cities, of course, but I've mostly been to its capital, Draylin, and its cloud-scrapers are *literal*, reaching far enough up to induce my vertigo the minute I even try to perceive their height. The tallest spire of the Imperial Palace might rival some of Draylin's shorter buildings, but I've never paid it much mind, unlike here, where it's all *in your face*.

The Renebian system of government is rather opaque to outsiders, but it's not an insult to call it an oligarchy. From what I can gather, which isn't much, the richest families form a sort of ruling council, and by agreement, a prominent member of one family acts as head of state. And so I am received by the majestic, mahogany-skinned matriarch of the Tarlanian clan, Emma Tarlanian, who spouts the usual Alliance propaganda about the danger of a new, unsanctioned, subspace tunnel within the Whorl (*when did I start thinking of it as propaganda?*) and Reneb's duty to its close friend and neighbor, Lyria. "Mind you," she says, "we're not required *yet* to jump into this conflict. Our defense treaty activates when Valhar attacks one of the Alliance, which, intelligently, you haven't yet done. But assisting Lyria might be the moral thing to do."

Such horseshit. We've been going around this for hours. Maybe I should try the same tack Benedik is with the Altainans: pointing out economic hazards of war.

Wait. Economics. Reneb. What motivates Reneb? And what are the main interests of the Tarlanian family?

I lean back. We've been meaning to investigate the activity near the Swan Nebula relays anyway. "I'm sure you've heard some entity has been snooping around the comms relays the Mazarans left behind in the Nebula. Near your mining concern, I believe. Perhaps we can help you investigate."

"It was the Altainans," Emma says flatly.

"Why in the heavens? What could they possibly..."

"You're the Altainan," Emma says. "We rather hoped you'd be able to guess."

I shake my head. "No, I'm sorry. I don't know. And with the current tensions in the Whorl, I don't understand the benefit of possibly provoking the Mazarans. What if they accidentally activate a signal, and the Mazarans don't like we've reverse-engineered their tech?"

"Quite," Emma growls. I look at her more closely. This is the most honest expression I've seen from her.

"The Altainans will sure be busy if they join you in war," I say, slowly. "No worries about them continuing whatever nonsense they're courting with Mazaran technology. Your mining station was the first hit during the invasion, wasn't it?"

Emma raises her brows and runs one elegant finger gently through her tight curly hair.

Security. Economy. I steeple my hands. "You *are* aware if we're at war, our cooperation treaty with respect to the Mazarans is null and void. We are under no obligation to bail you out if they come blasting out of that tunnel again. And you know, last time, it took the Alliance *and* Valhar to push them back."

"Is that a threat, Empress?"

"No. An opportunity." Think Layls. Not exactly the Goddess's gift to negotiation, but I have Ignatius's power to make whatever concession I'd like. "We don't go to war, and you have a strong ally at your back. *And*, we can be the first to alert you if we detect a Mazaran ship, since we're the only ones left on Dega Base. And..." *Think*. "We can add our defense technology to your mining site. You might be the best at comms and medtech, but the Valharan Empire has warfighting as our superpower. That offer," I continue, "won't expire even if we end up at war later. We're not going to swoop in and remove the defenses, but we obviously also know all the weaknesses and loopholes therein."

"So you're saying let the Altainans do what they will, but you'll have our flank in case of blowback."

"Basically," I say. "Although in return we'd like first-hand information on what the hell Altain is up to out there."

"That seems like a new deal, Empress. What do *we* get in return for spying on the Altainans?"

I frown. Maybe let her think she's running me over. "Limited free trade agreements," I say. "Since we're all protectionist and all, it'll be a departure if we remove restrictions on any level."

She laughs. "Love that you acknowledge the protectionism. Still an Altainan at heart." I smile wryly in response. "No, my dear. Limited could mean so little to as not make a difference. How about equal claim on the resources you find through that subspace tunnel you're building?"

"What tunnel?" I ask gamely.

"Surely you're still not denying it."

"Look," I say, "let's jettison the money side of things. You stay neutral in this war, we keep you safe from the Mazarans. We upgrade defenses on your family's mining station. *You* keep an eye on the Altainans for us. Oh," I say, inspecting my finger, the swirls of the mehndi finally fading, "if you're so inconvenienced as to be pulled into a war against us because of your collective defense treaty—because one day Lyria *will* argue we've violated their sovereignty in some way—we'd be willing to overlook that transgression and keep up relations. In that specific case only, of course."

"A special friendship?"

"Maybe friendly acquaintances. Valhar doesn't trust Reneb *that* much, and I'm sure vice versa. We'd be fools if we did. But," I say, leaning in, "if you draft a statement of neutrality *now*, we'd be willing to give you lot a bit of wiggle room *later*. Shades of gray instead of black and white. If you do the same for us, of course."

She considers, rapping her fingers on the table. Finally she reaches out her hand. "Deal."

Now

Benedik!
Now

"Tell me, sire," Benedik said, pulling at his collar "why we're sneaking around the back way?"

"Your father sent you to fetch me?"

Benedik nodded.

Ignatius sighed. "Then, there's something afoot. And I intend to see it through."

The crepuscular rays from the setting sun lit the spires of Acamar Palace, the meeting place of Parliament when it was in session. Its entire mien screamed "government building," squat and stocky, brutalist and foreboding, beige and brooding.

The Emperor, of course, had his own secure entrance to the place, but where Ignatius was leading him now was through the basement kitchens and up a set of stairs. Ignatius, in full regalia, brought only one guard, but crept as though expecting an attack. The mixed messages made Benedik's head spin. And hadn't Parliament been disbanded?

"Why couldn't you bring Ephraim?" Benedik asked in a whine.

Ignatius spared him a glance as he fiddled with the device he had taken out of his pocket. "Ephraim's a busy man. And I thought you would enjoy this. Whisper now."

They were close to the side chamber of Parliament, where smaller groups tended to gather rather than the main public space. "Your father said Dracini and Corval had made their move, correct? Anything else?"

Benedik matched his low tone. "He appeared to be under time constraint, sire, sorry. That's all I have."

"Dracini would use the full chamber, but with Corval's moderating influence, they probably were smart and used something more innocuous. Biley, go ahead and take the camera. Room is small enough we should be able to get everyone." The guard, Biley, hesitated. Ignatius looked like he was about to roll his eyes, but of course he wouldn't, because he was *dignified* and *restrained*. "I'll be *fine*. But if you must, give Benedik your holdout weapon."

Only two days after Benedik crashed his own funeral, and he was already tired of the same old Valharan bullshit. And a cousin, whom he loved and would serve until his last breath, but who delighted in being secretive and mysterious. But he took the weapon and, without a proper holster, placed it in his pocket, hoping the safety would hold.

At the very least, the last 48 hours had appeared to dissipate the neverending tension his father and dad said had fallen over his entire family. The Altainan declaration of war had created a pooling of dread within their bodies, like a permanent and deep furrow between their brows. And the hits had kept coming: Benedik's disappearance and possible death; threats to Layla's safety; numerous challenges to the Emperor's regime—and the Emperor's heavy-handed response to both; disbanding Parliament; and casting aspersions on Benedik's father. Looked like Abilio finally had the Emperor's trust again. That would have been enough for Benedik to back off on his mission back toward Solita, but alas, *Benedik* hadn't quite won Ignatius back over, and anyway, someone needed to accompany Empress Layla. They were to leave within the next day, as soon as Layla got the all-clear to travel.

Thank the Bird for Alina, who had merely punched his shoulder and said this was excuse to make his homecoming welcome twice as sweet whenever he got back to Novaria.

"Surveillance installed, sire," the guard said as he reappeared.

"Sire, *what* is this abou—"

Ignatius hushed him and pulled out a portable display. "Just watch, Ben."

"And so," Dracini said on vid, "we take back our own power! The wishes of the nobility will not be ignored. If we want a Parliament, we *call* a Parliament!"

A few cheers and roars of approval. But many more were seen on the vid muttering to their neighbors and shaking their heads in confusion. Did they not know they had been called to Parliament? Perhaps not.

"Not everyone is here. A rump conference?" Benedik whispered.

Ignatius nodded. "Your father and I thought this was going to happen. Dracini believes in increased Parliamentary power. He *would* call a Parliament in defiance of Our will."

"My father believes in increased Parliamentary power too."

"And that's why Dracini confided in him," Ignatius said, grinning. "As for Corval?" He tipped his chin toward the screen. "Probably still bitter about Carlus's abdication."

"First order of business!" Dracini continued over the din. "A petition for His Excellence Ignatius I to reconsider his ascension, and a request for him to step down in favor of the more experienced."

Whew. *That* didn't have the effect Dracini had intended. The room silenced, shocked faces on all.

Benedik's mind raced. Perhaps Dracini's head will still be attached to his body after this. He had taken care not to word his statement in a seditious or treasonous manner.

One of the Lords raised his hand. "Excuse me, Lord Berilus," he asked, referring to Dracini, "who exactly do you envision taking his place? You?" The man looked around nervously. "Mind, I'm not *endorsing* any of this. I'm just wondering about motivations, is all."

Dracini bristled. "I would *never*," he bit out. "I would be supporting the candidacy of Lord Abilio, Earl of Gruesse."

Benedik's eyebrows climbed.

"I too support Gruesse," Corval supplied. "The circumstances of Emperor Carlus's abdication are suspect. I'd like to make a fresh start."

"Idiot," Ignatius breathed.

"Indeed," said another Lord. "The last imperial dynasty, too, was cut off due to charges of illegitimacy. As it happened, the charges were false! Isn't Viceroy Stanlo a descendent of that family?"

"Where *is* Gruesse, anyway?" someone cut in.

Abilio stood, and the room hushed. "I am here. However," he said, cocking a brow, "I was not told you were intending to hold a Parliamentary session, Dracini. I gather others here were similarly misled."

A few murmurs of agreement.

"Plausible deniability, my future Emperor," Dracini said.

Benedik winced. Oof. So much for language that would keep his head on his body.

"*Idiot,*" Ignatius repeated in a whisper.

"Well," Abilio continued, "to clear things up. The removal of Carlus would not have benefitted me in any way, because I had made it known to key voters during the election that I would not like to take the throne." He spread his hands. "If commanded, I would have done my duty, but it is hardly an ambition."

Really? Ignatius, too, looked gobsmacked.

"You've never indicated as much to me," Dracini argued.

("I could have *told* people I didn't want it?" Ignatius whispered, half to himself.)

"There was no need," Abilio informed Dracini. "Speaking to those voters—and I will provide you with names if required, as I note they are people you must have thought too risky to invite here today—they already had decided to support Ignatius. I concluded my election was rather unlikely and ceased my anti-campaign."

"Regardless," Dracini spluttered, "the time is now—"

"No," Abilio said.

"Excuse me, Lord Abilio?"

"I would refuse a nomination. Absolutely not. This is a case of vindictiveness, nothing more, and I will not stand for it."

Benedik did a silent fistpump of glee. Ignatius's shoulders shook in equally silent laughter.

Corval, who likely had *not* pinned all his hopes on Benedik's father, took over for the stunned Dracini. "Regardless," he said smoothly, "we *must* send a message to the Emperor. This utter disregard of our right to rule goes against all our traditions and the young whelp must be brought in line. Comes from that spineless father of his—

(Ignatius squared his shoulders)

"—now *there* was a mismatch. A Princess and a lowly baron?"

"Tell him yourself," Abilio said.

"Pardon?"

Benedik looked around. "Cousin?" he whispered. "Where'd you go?"

"You want to lecture your liege?" his father continued on the vid. "Do it in person. He's here."

Silence! In the chamber.

"Gruesse, you scab," Corval hissed.

"On the contrary, Lord Michel," Ignatius boomed toward Corval as he burst through the front doors, big balls probably clanging all the way. Rustles throughout the room as most sprang to their feet. "We-the-Emperor knew you and Dracini would make your move tonight. Never forget. We have eyes *everywhere*."

Technically not a lie.

"Now," he said, pulling up a stool next to the lectern and settling in, crossing his legs, "let's chat, shall we?" He made a patting motion and the audience sat, cleared throats and nervous shuffling rippling through the crowd.

"We've been watching the two of you for quite some time. Ever since Our-wife-the-Empress was attacked in the Corval Earldom with personnel formerly in service to the Dracini nobility. The Empress, who We may add, is *with child*. Now, who could *possibly* benefit from wiping out Our line? Perhaps having Us drowned by grief, unable to lead? Hypothetically, of course. In reality, you hurt Our family, We destroy you."

Corval looked around and let out a wimpy chuckle. "Sire, uh, I would think others would benefit from that more. Like, uh, Lord Abilio?"

"Abilio actively campaigned *against* election. We've certainly never had reason to suspect *him*."

Ignatius, you little shit. Benedik put this mouth to his fist while watching the whole thing on vidscreen in the back hall, trying to hold on his snort.

Ignatius raised his voice. "Now, to all the rest of you. This is an illegal gathering. Imperial police are here outside the building to arrest you for convening Parliament without your Emperor's leave to do so."

In the back hall, Benedik looked at Biley. Biley looked back at Benedik and nodded. Benedik let out a low whistle. "You ain't playing around, Iggy."

A few grumbles, from the usual suspects. "Sire," someone said, "our families will not stand for this. They will raise arms if I'm harmed."

The blatant *disrespect*. Is that what it had come to, while Benedik was gone? No wonder Ignatius was about to spit nails when he had learned of Benedik's deception.

"Oh?" Ignatius raised an eyebrow. "Anyone else have something to say about that?"

A commotion in the ranks. "Sire! We didn't know. We were invited by Corval under false pretenses! Please, sire."

"So, it looks like some of the prominent families would rise, but not enough to take Us on. Is that right? And all of Valhar will see what you tried to do. Because it's all"—he pointed up to the camera—"on surveillance."

Dracini paled, looking for somewhere to run.

"Wait, Lord Berilus. We're willing to discuss a pardon."

Dracini stopped, a sneer covering his features. "My liege, why would you do that?"

"Because We *listen*." He smiled ingratiatingly, and leaned forward as if a kindly mentor to a wayward child. The effect: prime-of-his-life Ignatius and Dracini—who probably still thought himself devastatingly handsome but who was really more akin to a skeezy old man—made Ignatius seem even *more* powerful, like he was deity-made-flesh, here to assist them all in atoning for their sins. "Now then," he said, patting his knees, "all this started when We disbanded Parliament, thus dismantling your voices?"

Corval stood, putting himself in the line of the Emperor's fire. "Financial responsibility for the entire Empire. Our sole power. You fired us for exercising that right."

"No, Corval. Parliament also has *fiduciary* responsibility to represent the people of Valhar in their best interests. All of Parliament passed a resolution approving of war. The loudest voices believed We were not expending *enough* for the war effort, so those selfsame people refused to levy taxes to pay for it. A contradiction, and an abrogation of responsibility. We disbanded you for failing in your duty to Our people, and performed *Our* duty by securing alternate funds. So simple. You give Us funding, We reinstate Parliament, and We won't throw all of you into Rigelus prison for violating Our direct command against assembly."

He looked around as a chorus of "yes, sire"s rumbled throughout the room. Ignatius nodded to himself then suddenly called out. "Benedik!"

Benedik jumped. Ignatius waved a lazy hand, beckoning him in the room. "Take notes for me," he said softly when Benedik eventually found a seat near the Emperor. He ignored the glares Dracini shot alternating between him and his father. So much for asserting Abilio wasn't the snitch. But no, his father acted shocked Benedik was present, as if he really had nothing to do with all this. Good man.

"Let us all chat," Ignatius repeated. "What do you all have for Us?"

***

An hour. An *hour*, listening to their petty grievances and recording it all in a format Ephraim would be able to decipher later. Ignatius had listened with a benevolent smile, actively participating in the discussion without stooping to sops like *We'll see what We can do* and instead actually proposing solutions and promising future follow-up on a timeline.

Of course, while walking out, Ignatius shot one last volley behind his back: "And don't forget. We have evidence of your treason. And We're not afraid to use it."

He just couldn't help himself, could he.

But now, it was time for home. Blessed home. No snarky Emperor-cousins, no political grapple ball, simply him and Alina. Still newlyweds, really, especially given the time they'd spent apart from the beginning of their courtship. A table set for two, a meal befitting four, one unabashedly fruity cocktail with multiple tiny straws. Just the thing he needed, as he walked through his door—

"What in galactic bird brain shit are *you* lot doing here?" Benedik glared at the scene before him.

"You're late," Mariah said.

"You're never. As in *you're never to ambush me in my own home.*"

"Relax, love," Alina said, sidling up to him and giving him a kiss on the cheek.

He glared at Ephraim. "I'm late because I was doing your job, mate. I thought you were 'so busy.'"

"I *am* busy, Benedik," Ephraim responded. "This isn't a social call."

Figured as much, given the additional presence of Empress Layla and that Park guy.

"We need to talk about our trip," Layla said. "I wanted to consult with Park to strategize how to find this cutout of yours."

Benedik regarded the Renebian ambassador. Although he was a FOIL—Friend of Iggy and Layls—and surely he had crossed paths with him here or there, he wasn't someone Benedik knew on sight. Well, until two days ago in the Emperor's study. Now Benedik could never forget him.

"Ah, bringing me face-to-face with my kidnapper, then. How avant-garde."

Layla ignored him. "While I have you, Park, can we go over what we're doing with this cutout?"

"Solita rebels thought he worked for the Altainans. Maybe he does, but he certainly doesn't work with my government, who thought he worked for the Solita rebels. Did I get that right?"

Benedik bristled. "So you assholes kidnapped me, but maybe the one directing the kidnapping is some other party."

"*Could* be Altain," Layla mused. "But that doesn't really fit. I do think they're probably behind the protests and unrest, though."

"And," Mariah added, "it was the cutout that promised Reneb Most Favored Nation status if they gained independence, so Reneb would've been screwed out of that anyway. Was it worth it, Park?"

"Mariah..." Layla cautioned.

Park finally looked at Benedik straight on. "So, *how* are you finding him? Last I heard, you were going to call him on the localized comm module and...what? Ask to borrow a cup of sugar?"

Whatever. It wasn't *that* bad of a plan. But apparently everyone in this room thought he was *stupid*. He sighed and decided to get serious.

"Apparently the cutout told the Solita rebel leader that the comms signal was untraceable. Think that yacht of yours can do it anyway?"

Park startled. "What yacht?"

"Come on, ambassador. I'm more plugged in than you think I am. Your yacht. The one you proposed to let us use as a make-nice gesture so we don't declare a separate war on your planet."

"It's not"—Park cleared his throat—"It was merely a suggestion. I'm not sure my government is going to approve."

"Oh, they will." Benedik shared a look with Layla. "I think the Emperor was properly irritated on his call with your executive. Now, can your yacht with its fancy tech track the commlink or not?"

Park sighed. "Let me look at the thing."

Benedik did so, and Park mulled over it. "Schematics?"

"Here," Mariah said. "We did a full scan before giving it back to Benedik. *Why* we're letting him take custody of it is beyond me—"

"I *found* it."

Park hummed. Then he snorted. "Yeah. Yeah, that's easy. No offense to you Valharans, but...untraceable, unbreakable, all that? Much easier than you all think it is. Two ways. If it's in use, you should be able to track its signal. This thing is only going to work with infrastructure built to support it, so if he used it on Solita, it is likely overlaid on Solita's system, piggybacking on normal comms waves. Just takes a few minor adjustments. But even if he's not on Solita, or not using the comm, I should be able to track the handset if you get close enough."

Layla scrunched her face. "It was built to *specifically* work on Solita?"

Park shrugged. "Yeah, I don't know what that's all about."

"The Wooly Wampus would be suspicious, for sure," Benedik contributed.

Layla and Mariah stared. "The...what?" Layla managed.

They looked as perplexed as he was. "You know," he said. He looked around for support. "Wooly Wampus? He's green and fuzzy, fights bullies and solves mysteries?"

"Nope," Layla said.

"Never heard of him," said Mariah.

"*I* have," Alina said. "It's a Valharan thing, which most of you—and yes, Mariah, especially you—would not know about. So maybe stop snickering at things you don't understand. Right Ephraim?"

Ephraim gave an apologetic nod. "I grew up with it too."

"Now," Alina said firmly, "I think you've done all you can do for now. Considering how soon you're leaving, perhaps we can spend time with our own families, alone, hmm?" She stroked Benedik's arm lightly. "I'm sure my husband's hungry."

"Thirsty, too," he supplied. Ephraim turned an interesting shade of red.

His amazing wife shepherded them all out the door and then turned, leaning her back against it.

"Okay, maybe I shouldn't have told you to relax. Sorry. They showed up and wanted a meeting and I thought it would also be nice to catch up without all the *stress* of the last few months."

"No," he said, crossing the room and clasping her hands. "Not your fault. I've been the punching bag for a number of years." Damnable bullies. The Wooly Wampus would have words for *those* four, that was for sure.

"But that's not *fair*, Benedik. You need to stop letting people treat you like that. You're brilliant. I don't think anyone else would have thought to ask the ambassador if his ship could track the comms, for example."

"It's my role. Everyone in the family's got one. I'm the lovable scamp who acts before he thinks."

Alina considered. "Well," she acknowledged, "that's about right. But you're still worthy of respect. Don't let family dynamics lull you into being the whipping boy. You're worth more than that."

"Am I?" *Was* he? "No one knows what to do with me." He began to pace. "After Carlus left, I had to quit the Imperial Service. And now, what? Our empire is in crisis, and what have I done to ameliorate conditions?"

He sat in his dining chair, and Alina pulled up beside him, hands in her lap, watching intently. "Even this trip out to the hinterlands is a complete boondoggle," Benedik continued, even though he hated the whine in his voice. "He was trying to send me toward Altain to get me out of his hair. Now, I'm babysitting Layla."

"Mariah's babysitting Layla."

"So I'm even more useless."

Alina rolled her eyes, then cupped his chin. "Stop being a testicle."

He barked a laugh, then took her hand. "Layla says men are allowed to be sensitive and soft and saying otherwise is misogynistic."

"Layla needs to keep her Altainan opinions to herself once in a while. Oh come on. Of course you're allowed to—ugh, why do I let that woman get under my skin. This is a Valharan marriage. My *job* as your wife is to keep you from becoming maudlin."

He gave her an eye-crinkling smile. "Who knew you'd turn out to be an old battle-axe?"

She crossed over onto his lap and straddled him, pulling at his kerchief, loosening his collar. "People think *I'm* silly and useless because I'm a noblewoman with a fashion line, and because I don't get caught up in all those political machinations other women do to gain a mite of respect and power on our world. Screw them. I know better, and that's all I need."

He pulled back, looking at her seriously. "You don't feel like you're being insulted and infantilized, sitting at home while I run off to places unknown?"

She frowned. "That question was the insulting one. What do you think I do all day—twiddle my thumbs? No, don't backtrack. Look, I don't need to be *utilized*. I'm not a commodity. I'm happy in my *silly* career."

"You're angry when you're cute."

"Ass."

He pinched hers in response. "I know not the same thing, but does that mean I don't have to be the ultimate servant of the Empire all the time? I..." he faltered, looking down. She kissed his nape, softly pecking up and down, her gorgeous teak skin setting off his newly-tanned arms like a gleaming gemstone gracing an unpolished band. "I can be me and that's okay?"

"Yes, love," she whispered. Her breath tickled his ear. "That's what I've been trying to tell you. Now, chipper up. This battle-axe wants to grind."

*
Now

Layla

The last-minute calls to the war room were getting old. What now?

Layla and Benedik entered, fresh from a planning session. Ignatius turned to her and nodded in acknowledgement. "My lady. We just got this visual sent over from Dega Base."

On screen, a Mazaran scout ship emerged from the Swan Nebula tunnel.

"What's our delay here?" Ignatius asked.

"Sent priority, sire, so only a couple of hours. Dega Base chose not to engage." Turine inclined his head. "Per the terms of our armistice agreement."

"Good," Ignatius said. "Contact our defense perimeter outside the Nebula border and reiterate they are to stand back." He checked his timepiece. "Our message should get to them in time."

"Are you sure that's wise, sire? They have enhanced signature shielding ability, so we won't be able to track them after they emerge from the Nebula. And even if we could, their advanced FTL means they could jump faster than we could catch them."

"We have an agreement with them. We'll let it lie, for now."

"Maybe they're just visiting?" Benedik ventured.

Layla barely stopped herself from pinching his arm. The war room participants either turned to glare at the two of them or shuffled their feet. *Thanks, Benedik. No, really.*

"More likely intelligence gathering," Ignatius said dryly. "Hopefully not as a prelude to war. As for agreements: let's contact the Renebian government. I'm sure Dega Base already warned the Tarlanian mining station of what was coming their way, and the station can directly alert their government, but I'd like to touch base as a courtesy."

"*And*, they might be able to track the Mazarans and let us know in real-time where they're going?"

He smiled at Layla. "Exactly. I'll keep Ambassador Park's office on alert for any messages passing through there for us. The information-sharing between our planets better be robust, or there will be much to answer for."

***

The Renebians, properly chastened regarding their hand in recent events, did indeed endorse Park's gesture of offering up his yacht, which was immediately repurposed to be considered the emperor's sovereign property.

Once, years ago, Layla had promised Reneb understanding. If only she could reneg and wring their collective necks. This is what happened when an enterprise rooted in business concerns took on the functions of government. Moral authority went out the window.

No. 'Out the window' was *not* the phrase she wanted to dwell on right now.

"Are we sure this is safe?" Layla asked. Wind buffeted her on all sides. "I mean, what if there's a gust the moment we're supposed to get in?"

Benedik grinned and stretched out, hands coming close to swiping Layla, causing her to yelp and scurry closer to the tunnel off of Ignatius's former spare closet. "Where's your sense of adventure, Layls?"

"I left it on the ground, *where I belong.*"

"Hey," he said, poking at her, "the two of us, *together*, doing the Imperial odd jobs we're both good at. What a lineup! You, and me."

"And Mariah."

"And Mariah," he agreed, as a small craft appeared, coming in close in an excellent display of precision flying.

A portal opened as Mariah's voice boomed over the shuttle's speakers. "Get in, losers. Time to go hunting."

"Just loud enough so the whole city can hear you," Benedik yelled back as he leapt over the railing and landed with a *thumpf* inside. He stood and gallantly extended his hand. "I've got you, Empress. No reason to fear."

This was fine. Just like diving into the watering hole in Kaborlah. Just like training in jump school. Like ejecting over Felix. Like leaping into love.

She closed her eyes, and Benedik caught her.

The entire Escape From the Imperial Palace subterfuge was necessary because they wanted to keep Layla and Benedik's travel secret from the royalty watchers, who undoubtedly would love to gossip and speculate about the Empress, a returned-from-the-dead noble, and a flight off-planet. Luckily, Park's former ship had been moved to the secure, isolated section of the orbital transfer station, and docking, disembarking, and finding the correct berth went without incident—or prying eyes.

"I call the floor," Layla said as she went up the ramp but no one responded. Whatever. *She* thought it was funny.

And ironic, because this ship was gorgeous.

Benedik boarded behind her and whistled. "*Okay,*" he said. "All this for an ambassador? Lookit. Multiple private rooms, wraparound sofa, is that—is that a *fish tank?*"

Mariah popped her head out from the cockpit. "Reversible thrusters, enhanced internal dampening, low-emission propulsion drive, solar wind assist. Damn thing should have racing stripes."

"How about the encrypted instant comms? Connects to Park's office and to most Reneb government facilities, right? I'd like to check that out."

Mariah nodded. "Next on my list. Turine's probably going to want to have someone reverse engineer this bad boy. We've been developing our own version of secure point-to-point using quantum entanglement but Reneb's been doing this for decades."

"Huh. Surprised they would let the tech out of their sight."

Mariah shook her head. "Nah. Just like they can't actually do much with the defense enhancements we gave 'em a few years ago. This will jumpstart new avenues of research, but like with all the Mazaran castoffs floating around the Whorl, actually replicating foreign technology is harder than it looks."

As Mariah got the ship out of Valhar's gravipause, Layla got an update from Park. "Reneb says the Mazaran ship's heading their way," she relayed after. "But slowly. They can use their advanced FTL, after all, but so far they appear to be content at sublight."

"Why are they going to Reneb?" Benedik asked.

Silence. Layla shared a look with Mariah, who had just entered from the cockpit. "I have theories," Layla said cautiously. "But that's neither here nor there right now." Benedik looked like he wanted to push the matter of *what the hell does Mazar have to do with Reneb*, but he relented.

*
Now

Getting close enough to Solita to find this guy was all well and good, but it would probably have to wait until they were on their way *back* from Kaborlah. While they were there, Benedik could start sniffing around for the supposed Altainan antimatter weapon.

Hopefully approaching Kaborlah wouldn't be a disaster. They'd make sure they transmitted as Renebian-flagged as they approached the wormhole, and then, hopefully they could just ... explain.

Okay, long shot. But Layla was still a citizen. Maybe she could pretend like she was acting on Ransom's message, one she had somehow obtained too late, and she, distraught, was just trying to get home with the help of the Renebians.

Home. Kaborlah.

She could never quite hide she wasn't from Altain Prime. Among Altainans, she stood out in her facial features, the even darker-than-Prime tone of her skin, her shorter stature. Provincial. And once they saw that, they could read her. Different cultural mores. Language. Everyone throughout Altain, at least the educated, spoke Whorl Standard as their primary language, but beyond that, Kaborlahis spoke a patois that only barely resembled the original language of Altain Prime. From time to time, programming or books would use the Altainan language instead of Standard, and some Kaborlahis, the ones not fluent in Altainan, were left out.

Centuries ago, before Altain claimed to be a republic, they tried to beat the Kaborli language out of her people.

And then, to add further insult, she didn't quite feel the desire to *defend* the damned planet. She didn't hate Kaborlah. But she hated her family. She had wanted to leave and never look back, and now she was returning on wings of mercy, trying to see what she could do to salvage the situation.

Her home was beautiful. But her toxic family dynamics weren't. Her lack of prospects, there on a world lost to time. Her empty stomach and her leaking roof.

She traced the location of her home planet on the inset display. Here, there be dragons.

She started at Benedik's loud and strident voice. "Hullo. Lord Benedik here, asking for Mr. Large Eyes to pick up?"

Layla rolled her eyes as she crossed the living space to snatch the commlink out of Benedik's hand. From time to time in the past week, Benedik had been activating the little commlink he had pilfered from the rebels, *identifying himself* and talking into it trying to reach the cutout and Layla just...

"How did you even survive primary school, Benedik? I'd imagine you tripped over your own feet a lot."

"Because the other kids tied his shoes together," Mariah contributed. Layla snickered.

The route to the Redma wormhole toward Kaborlah didn't exactly pass through the Solita system, but Mariah didn't think they'd lose too much time in transit to shuffle a bit closer and see how things were holding up out there. As long as they didn't get close to the new tunnel, the Solita Defense perimeter wouldn't concern themselves with the presence or the occupants of a small ship like theirs.

So she had been tolerating Benedik's periodic check-ins with the commlink, but eventually, they were going to get close enough that someone might actually *pick up*. She palmed it and placed it in her pocket, hoping Benedik would forget about it for awhile.

"Any more news about the coup?" Mariah asked.

"First of all, not a coup." As Layla had been saying for days now.

"Dracini tried to *depose* the Emperor.'

"No, he was just going to ask him to resign! It's total bullshit, but it isn't a *coup*. C'mon Benedik. You were there. Back me up."

Benedik mumbled something about respect and headed down to his bunk.

"More violent riots, people's properties torched on the outer territories too."

Layla sighed and put her head in her hands. Too much.

Mariah looked at her as if expecting a response. "You know innocents are being affected too? People living on the edges of the cities—nothing to do with any of this."

"That's horrible."

"Yeah, it is. Maybe when we get home you can make a broadcast telling them all to cool the fuck down and go on home."

Layla raised her head. "How long have you been waiting to make that ask?"

"Months."

"I'm not going to tell people to stop protesting, Mariah."

"Rioting."

"I *do* condemn wanton destruction. But I'm not going to dismiss their grievances."

"Coward."

Layla huffed. "Look, if I *were* to make a statement, it would be about how maybe I can get my husband to *listen* to them."

"People died, Empress!"

"*Protestors* are dying. In large numbers. When the local forces try to stop them from assembly."

"Doesn't give them the right to mess with innocents."

"Nope. But also doesn't invalidate their movement."

"*Seriously?* How can you justify violence?"

"War is violence, Mariah."

"This isn't war. This is people role-playing civil action and screwing it up. How can you even be okay with any of thi—"

"*Because revolution is messy!*"

Pause. The pounding in her temples went on forever.

"So," Mariah finally said. "You support revolution."

"They are in a fight for freedom."

"Damn Altainans stirring them up. Outlanders have no idea how good they have it."

"Really? You can say that with a straight face? C'mon, Mariah." There was a reason the unrest was the most potent in the outer territories. Corruption, secret police, economic stratification. Ignatius had been trying to address it, in his way, but he was fighting multiple wars on multiple fronts, and three years and a distracted emperor wasn't long enough to combat entrenched systemic oppression. The Altainans had lit the match but the territories were the tinderbox.

They stared at each other through the heartbeats. Then Mariah turned away in disgust. "Who are you?"

"Someone who believes in freedom."

Mariah scoffed. "Empress, you swoop in from another planet—one we're now *actually* at war with, let me add—and immediately start bitching and moaning about our system. And it reeks of arrogance. Colonialist arrogance."

"*Colonialist?*"

"You Altainans would take over the Whorl if you could. Make everyone conform to your values. Arrogant. Privileged. And hypocritical. You married *into* this. You chose to uphold a system you apparently abhor. What gives you the right—"

"Mariah we had this out years ago. It's time to move on."

"You should have turned him down. When he proposed. Like you did the first time. You weren't willing to compromise on dual citizenship back then, but you are willing to gain riches and wealth on the back of 'subjugated peoples'. Spare me." Mariah stalked back toward the cockpit.

"We actually proposed to each other," she mumbled.

A throat cleared behind her. Benedik had returned. Layla's cheeks grew hot. "Um, I know that wasn't the point..."

Benedik raised both hands in surrender. "Don't worry about me. And besides, you know, I know all the stuff you do behind the scenes."

"Maybe she's right."

"No, Layls, she's not. Well, okay, she made a few good points. Come to think of it, a lot of what she said seemed spot on actually—"

"Thanks, Benedik. Really," she said, not entirely sarcasticly.

"I know Ignatius plans on making changes,.." Benedik said. "But slowly. Maybe more slowly than you and I would."

Layla nodded.

He continued. "Besides, I don't think it would bode well for your marriage if you demanded—what—like he quit as emperor or something."

"He offered."

"Really?"

"A long time ago. Not viable. Especially then. Two emperors in the space of as many years? Talk about shocks to stability. And then what? Someone else just ascends to the throne. Maybe you, maybe your father, but even if it *were* you, I think you'd end up making the same calls as Ignatius. And your father is traditionalist enough that much wouldn't change under him. Other than more Parliamentary control."

Benedik shivered. "You tell your husband to stay put. Don't want to be emperor *or* the crown prince, believe me."

Now

The Mazarans had become the main driver of foreign policy for almost eight years now. Each side believed the other had forgotten the horrors of that war.

But maybe the problem was they remembered all too well. The entire insular Whorl was traumatized by the bloodlust of outsiders. The Alliance thought they were protecting the Whorl from more. Valhar thought the exact same thing, with their opposite actions—

"Hullo! This is Benedik for Big Eyes. Anyone there?"

Layla whirled around, one hand going to her pocket as the other reached out to Benedik in a STOP! gesture.

"I'm not an idiot, Empress," he said sourly. "I'm needling you for fun. We're still too far away from the planet to actually make a connec—" he paused.

"What?" Layla asked. "What?" more urgently.

"It went through," he said. "There was no failure tone. No answer either, but *it went through.*"

"Shit!"

"I *am* an idiot."

"Guess we *are* close enough to Solita, then?"

Benedik frowned. "Close enough there's some comms infrastructure working with it. *Not* close enough to actually reach someone on the planet. So, he's out here somewhere."

They looked at each other and both immediately ran over to the yacht's comms equipment.

"Tracking the handset," she said. Benedik read out the relevant serial number.

"I can't—" she fiddled at the controls, tried different search parameters, but it was useless. "I can't get a lock. The signal disappears somewhere around *there*." She pointed away from the system. Interstellar space in the outer dust cloud. They had taken the main system wormhole that had brought them much closer in.

"So the cloud is obscuring whatever's out there? But not so much we couldn't make a comms connection or track the handset there."

Layla nodded. "I'll get Mariah."

"So here's the deal," Mariah said, pulling up a system map. "You have that signal ending on the very inner edge of the cloud. But I'm willing to bet wherever we need to go is much farther in."

"How much farther in?" Layla asked.

"Who the fuck knows? That cloud is a light year across. If we just bumble our way in, you know how long it would take us to traverse it, even at FTL speeds? The other option is here," she said, pointing farther into the system. "There's a microwormhole no one apparently uses because it just connects back into the damn dust cloud. We'd have to get over near the orbital radius of the fifth planet, but we're already heading that way, so it's only negligible travel time there, and then it shoots us back out *here*—" Mariah pointed to an area deep into the cloud.

Layla studied the map. "Is it all along the same vector?"

"If we think of the signal emanating along a straight line, yeah. It's in the right direction of the wormhole. And if we're wrong, we can retrace our steps, shoot back into the system, then fly back out to the edge of the cloud where the signal disappears, and search there. Although we're really cutting into our timetable at that point. Because then we'd have to get back to the *main* wormhole to jump away to the Gracy system and then head for the Redma wormhole."

Damn. They were supposed to be getting to Kaborlah. The wrong thing may make them too long here in Solita to make a difference out in the Altainan territory. But the right choice would be *relatively* zippy, even if traveling farther in-system to reach the microwormhole would take time. And something fishy was going on here.

"Make the jump," Layla said.

Mariah gave her a thumbs up and went toward the cockpit—then stopped.

"You wanna fly, Commander Kamil?"

Layla stared at her a moment. Insult, or gesture of truce?

"I find I forget you had a life beyond pretty dresses," Mariah explained softly.

Layla grinned. "Well, in that case, hell yeah."

She was silent while traversing subspace. It had been a while. She could almost imagine Mariah smirking at her inexperience, a *hah, so much for being a hotshot* jape, but it would be even worse if she somehow harmed the ship, like a kid scratching the paint on Abba's new ride. Eventually, however, her nerves settled and she deemed it safe to speak.

"This handles like a dream."

"Told ya."

"Baby likes it too." The kid was kicking in a rhythm. She thought she would hate it—this idea of a living *thing* inside her body—but actually, it was nice. A secret connection.

The wormhole jump was the smoothest she'd ever piloted; granted, she actually had not done many of them, as her time as a military pilot involved being hauled around in carriers. But still. Park traveled in *style*.

She studied the map once more. The terminus of a microwormhole could come far into a system, because its gravitational pull wasn't strong, and any wobbles it would have on a system would have stabilized over the millennia since it was a natural phenomenon. The larger wormholes were often technically in systems but far enough out they didn't counter a sun's pull. The man-made subspace tunnels were more intense. The one out in the Swan Nebula had captured the rogue planet Dega, which now orbited around it. The Solita one was technically out in interstellar space outside the system, past the dust cloud, even, though on the other side of the system from where they were. Traveling to it was no easy deal using Whorl FTL technology, although the damn Mazarans with their advanced drives would just consider it a hop and a skip away.

"Okay," Mariah said briskly. "Scanning. Benedik," she called back, "you got that equipment up and running?"

"Yeah. Transferring feed to the cockpit now."

"There," Mariah said, pointing to the console screen. "Jackpot."

Layla did some quick calculations. "Only twenty minutes by sublight. We lucked out. Or rather, whatever's out there is purposely close to this wormhole."

"But in the opposite direction of most traffic, such as it is," Mariah said, tracing her finger. "Anyone traveling FTL through deep space would head *this* way to get to the nearest systems." She tapped a section of the screen. "Some of the most studied icy debris and comets have orbits that cross close to *these* points. This is close by, but with no danger of anyone stumbling across it."

"And in one of the thickest concentrations of debris in the cloud," Benedik said, arriving. "Was reading some abstracts."

Some abstracts. She teased Ben a lot, but the thing most people didn't realize was that he was a complete nerd. All part of the mystery of Benedik Dargas. "Is that why our sensors still can't pick anything up?" she asked. "All we have to go on is tracking this handset's signal." She studied the commlink Benedik was holding. "Actually, that's pretty impressive. Do you think there's something out here that connects to Solita's comms relay? Somehow?"

"What the fuck do the Solitans *have*?" Mariah asked.

"*That*," Benedik concluded, "is what the Solitans have."

In front of them was the largest behemoth of a ship Layla had ever seen. Ugly, too. Long, cylindrical center, with pylons curving around it, leading to spinning sections that must be the habitable environment.

Mariah scanned it and swore. "Layla, it's a particle accelerator."

Layla's eyes went wide. The fucking odds... "The Altainan antimatter bomb?"

The three of them stared. Benedik had his head cocked. Mariah kept mouthing words, likely profanities, silently. Layla didn't know what she looked like. But what she *felt* was sad. Her home did this. Brilliant idea, but violent and deceitful.

Benedik finally reoriented his head. "It's not functional. Right?"

Mariah looked at the board. "No contacts. No one's sniffing us wondering who the hell we are. Damn thing looks dark. So," she said, turning to Benedik, "*not* functional."

Hmm. "Activate that commlink again, Benedik," Layla said.

He stared at her. "You want me to *call*?"

"No one's hailing us. Nothing looks *alive* over there. Might as well."

Benedik shook his head. "Layls, I don't think it's a good ide—"

"Consider it an order." Her voice remained flat, channeling another, forgotten Layla. Channeling the person she used to be.

He whistled. "Well, *shit*, Empress. Okay." He cleared his throat and lifted the commlink to his mouth. "To the unidentified cutout associated with the Solita rebels. And with Reneb. And um, Altain. This is Lord Benedik Dargas, Viscount Gruesse. Acknowledge. Over."

Nothing. Not a failure tone either.

Benedik grimaced. "We're gonna need to go over there and check it out, don't we."

Mariah responded by handing him her extra weapon.

Layla looked back and forth between them. "What about me? We got an armory on board?"

Mariah snorted. "Nuh-uh, Princess, you ain't going."

This bullshit again. "I'm not a wilting flower."

"You're the Empress and pregnant with the heir. Hell. No."

"I can order you."

"I can ignore you."

"My commands have the weight of the Emperor's own voice."

A scoff. "What are you going to do, *tell* on me? I'm your security. You're. Not. Going."

Of all the—

Benedik lay his hand on her arm. "Empress, you have every right to order her, and I will stand beside you back home to vouch for her dismissal of your word. But she *is* your security, and she's right. You are mother to the heir. We need to keep you—both of you—safe."

Layla sighed. Damn. He was right. She was being a pouty toddler.

"But I don't like the disrespect you've been giving our Empress, Mariah," Benedik warned. "I'm watching."

Layla piloted the yacht close as Benedik and Mariah went EVA and torched their way in. Damn. She was hoping they'd take the tiny skip in the ship's hold so she could sneak on with them.

She kept the direct comms channel open to monitor their progress and busied herself. Nothing too taxing or important, at first, to calm her nerves worrying about Benedik and Mariah over there. Downloading the diary of her last fateful trip with Mariah might be a useful distraction. She looked at the end product, her notebook bursting with words. Messy and imperfect, like life, like marriage and romance and sex and family and heritage.

The comm burst to life. "It's a ghost town," Mariah reported. "We found Benedik's guy, though. Dead." She relayed how Benedik closed those huge eyes—Benedik's phrasing—for the last time.

"I guess that's to be expected," Layla said. "Anything useful on him?"

"Obviously found the commlink, but otherwise no," Benedik said, joining in, voice sounding more low and hoarse than usual. Maybe it was the commlink, maybe the circumstances. "I'm not keen on bringing a dead body on board with us, so I got a picture of him and a hair sample and we'll send imperial agents out later."

"We can probably inform Stanlo on Solita and let them deal with it," Mariah said.

Something trickled in the back of Layla's mind, an insistent tapping going *you know this. No really, pay attention.* What? She wanted to prod and query the voice, but no time. "Wait," she said, taking a stab at what her brain was trying to tell her. "Don't tell Stanlo *anything*. Does he know we're here?"

"It's Park's yacht. Who knows what sources the viceroy has, but we're not exactly broadcasting your presence."

"What about *here* here, Mariah? Near this derelict collider?"

"Don't see how. Sensor shadow, remember? Can't see this unless you're right on fucking top of it."

"Keep it that way, Mariah. Radio silence on all of this."

A pause. "Yes, Empress," she said.

What was trying to work its way up her consciousness?

"They could have snuck past Kaborlah, but someone had to let it in the Solita Defense Perimeter," Benedik said after they were underway back through the microwormhole. "Which makes your insistence on not informing the Viceroy's office really reasonable."

Yeah, but that wasn't *quite* it. Layla shook it away. It'd come soon enough. "I'm still stuck on it being derelict and abandoned," she said instead.

"Making an antimatter weapon is just theoretical at this point," Mariah pointed out. "Turine was pretty surprised the Altainans could manage it. I bet they were trying to get it to work up to the very end and eventually gave up."

"Think it could still generate nuclear power?" Layla asked. "I mean, that'd solve Kaborlah's energy crisis. We could find someone to tow that sucker right back on out past the Redma wormhole."

"And give it back to the Altainans?"

"Well, Mariah, you *said* they couldn't get it to work." Layla bit her lip. "Yeah," she resolved. "That's what we're going to do." That meant they accomplished *both* their missions in the same day. Couldn't coordinate all that from here, though. "I'm calling Park and seeing if he can get a message to Ignatius." She considered. Maybe. Radio silence didn't quite apply to encrypted comms, but if she used Park as a middleman, who knew if the Renebians themselves could hack in? She'd have to play it by ear.

✱
Now

The minute Layla managed to raise Park, he exploded.

"Where the *hell* have you been!"

She raised her eyebrow in what she had come to think of as an Imperial Gesture. "Pardon?"

Park blew out a breath. "I'm sorry, Your Highness, Your Grace, whatever the fuck you are. But we've been trying to get you the entire day."

"We've been out of comms reach. We're good now. We're near the Solita system's inner core, but heading out to their main wormhole."

Park waved her words off, obviously not caring one bit where they were or where they were going. "The Mazarans made it to Reneb. Took their time. And as expected, Carlus went out to meet them."

"*Carlus?!?*" Benedik broke in.

Shit. "I'll explain later. Hush." She ported the call to a networked device and padded down to her stateroom.

Park waited with tapping fingers and started back up as soon as she gave him the all-clear. "He called me immediately," he said, now with a hush. "He wanted to talk to you. I don't think he's told the Executive yet."

"What? Surely you all are monitoring him."

Park winced. "He's not exactly on Renebian comms. He's on the Mazaran scoutship. Alone. Which can call our comms, sure, but we don't have the backdoor into the system."

A tension ache coiled behind her eyes. "Park, what the hell."

"Maybe I should back up."

The coil had sprung into a full headache by the time Layla sat to debrief Benedik and Mariah.

"Apparently Altain tried to reach out to Mazar over two years ago," she began. "After Lyria first confirmed the existence of the Solita tunnel."

"That makes no sense," Benedik said, scratching his head.

Mariah made a gurgling grumbling sound, seemingly from the back of her throat. "The relay. Near Dega. That the Renebians said Altain was messing with."

Layla nodded at her. "Exactly. They were trying to send out an SOS, as it were. But they couldn't get it to work, so they sent an envoy out to them to chat. One year there, time for diplomacy, one year back, and here we are."

"To do *what?*" Benedik stuck his hands on his waist and glared at her, as if she had all the answers and had purposely withheld knowledge. She went to lightly poke at his extended hips and he slapped her hand away. "Let me flounce. It's one of the many little joys in my life."

"Ben, from what Park told me, Altain wanted Mazar to collapse the Solita tunnel. Unlike Altain, they have the technology. I guess the weapon we saw out there was their backup plan in case the Mazarans didn't come through."

"And they knew we knew about Kaborlah, so they went ahead and snuck the weapon in and hoped they could fix it in time. But..." Benedik massaged his temples. "The *Mazarans?*"

"The Mazarans," she continued, "are perfectly happy keeping the Whorl a cul de sac. Serves their interests, you know? They're our only link to the outer galaxy."

"Just as Valhar's been saying this entire time," groused Mariah.

"Quite right. I concede the point. I don't like anything that advantages the Mazarans. Anyway, that scout ship? It has a weapon that can close the tunnel. Works much along the same lines, but, you know, in a smaller package."

"Wait." said Benedik. "The Altainians reached out to the Mazarans to protect us from the Mazarans?"

"Better the front door you know," Layla said, "than the back door that can admit who-knows-what. Maybe the Mazarans in a less cooperative government, maybe some other threat."

"Or this is about keeping Valhar down in the guise of enforcing treaties." Mariah shot her a look of challenge. Layla wasn't inclined to argue.

"That too," she said, acknowledging Mariah's point. "And if we trust Park—which, I'm choosing to do right now?—this was Altain and Altain alone. Just like their own antimatter attempt."

"Altain will need to answer to its allies for the secrets it has been keeping," said Mariah.

'Altain.' So abstract. It was Roya. Roya and Sri and Ransom, not only trying to blow a tunnel but asking the *Mazarans* to help.

"Okay, Layls," Benedik said, "and Park knows all this because..."

She gulped. Well, this was awkward. How to begin?

"Benedik, Carlus lives on Reneb. That's where he fled after abdicating. And he met the Mazarans when they landed. Mazar apparently thought this was an Alliance-wide op. Reneb was the closest allied planet."

Benedik gaped. If he noted she didn't quite answer the question, such as *What the hell does Carlus have to do with any of this?* he didn't say.

Mariah looked to the side. "Layla, Park's calling again."

Layla shot out of her chair. "He got ahold of him."

Benedik trailed after her, looking lost. "Who?"

Layla ignored him, answering the comm. "Park, whatcha got?"

"He reached out again, so I'm hooking you into the call. Stand by."

The screen split, and the second image resolved into the interior of a futuristic ship, with former Emperor Carlus's face smiling into the camera. "Lady Royal."

"Charles."

He craned his neck as if to try to see around her. "Benedik? Is that you, cousin?"

Benedik stiffened, and almost went into a salute. "Sire—er, Cousin Carlus. Hi?"

Carlus smiled softly, eyes crinkling. "Long time." His voice was a near whisper.

"Hate to interrupt this touching reunion," Park cut in, "but kindly, where the hell are you, Carlus?"

Carlus cleared his throat. "Right. Well. Park updated you on why the Mazarans came? They stopped on Reneb, hoping, I guess, to get further instruction from Alliance leadership. The Altainan envoy chose to stay behind on Mazar, of all things. Or maybe he had no choice. Anyway, of course, the Renebian executive was gobsmacked. I meet them, start bluffing, acting like maybe we can collude to get my throne back and effectively be a Mazaran puppet. And then I ... erm ... stole the ship."

"You stole the ship," Layla repeated.

Carlus broke out into a full grin. "*Yeah*, I did. And the stealth capability on this is smashing! The Mazarans are basically back on Reneb, completely bollocksed." Carlus's easy speech and manner struck her. Someone bred to be formal, looking free.

Mariah crossed her arms. "We need you to bring that thing back to Valhar." She didn't seem abashed in the slightest, giving stern orders to a former emperor. But that was Mariah for you.

"Yeah, I expected you'd say that," he said, looking a bit green around the gills. Or maybe that was the glow from the fancy panels in his cockpit.

Layla held up a hand. "Hold on. Those aren't necessarily the Emperor's orders. Park, what did Ignatius say?"

"He's out of reach, Layla. Out in the mountains, I think?"

What? In the middle of a crisis?

"He knows something's up," Park hastened to say. "I didn't dare tell him the whole story over even a secure commlink. This is too, uh, explosive. But he says he trusts you, if there's need for you to step in. So, really, what do *you* say?"

"I'm still so confused," Benedik whispered.

She lay a hand on his arm. "Ben, I'll give you the full story in a bit." Her other hand fiddled with the book in her pocket. Maybe letting him read the entry about her trip to Reneb would be the easiest. Explosive as it was—

Explosive.

Carlus had once sacrificed his oaths to protect Valhar. Could she do the same?

"Carlus."

"Layla."

"That weapon. There's a weapon on the ship that can collapse a tunnel? Do you know how it works?"

"Erm, supposedly." Carlus glanced around and appeared to fumble through compartments in the cockpit. "I don't know the specs, but I'm pretty good with weapons tech and can learn, while I'm here on the lam."

"Carlus, hold tight. Don't head for Valhar. If you want to stay somewhere near Valharan forces, make your way, on stealth, to Dega." She braced herself.

Oh Goddess Alive, was she really doing this?

Ransom's voice came to her unbidden, telling her any direct action against Altain would kill her citizenship. More. The face of her sister, who burned her bridges and couldn't come home. The unmoored feeling of being a foreigner on an alien, unfathomable world, where she'd never be fully accepted. *Or trusted*, she thought, as Turine's face swam before her.

If she did this, it was possible she could never go home again. If she did this, she'd cut off an entire slice of her life. If she did this, she would turn her back on the idea of a free society, and yoke herself to an ancient system.

What was right? What was wrong?

But she looked at Carlus, and she knew the answer.

"Thing is, Carlus," she continued. "Everyone. I think I know how to end this war."

She explained the plan, and waited for objection. Instead, she found herself waiting as jaws literally hung open.

"Um, wow," said Benedik eventually. "What about Altain? They won't be happy with you."

"*Screw* Altain," Layla said. "They've lost me. I'm done." Lies. She wasn't done. She wasn't ready for this.

End the war, lose her Altainan citizenship. The idea should not have hurt as much as it did, but it *burned*. Constrain her choices even further than she had before. Commit to one loyalty—to the *monarchs*, not the defenders of freedom.

"You're out of your damn mind," Mariah said. "But, if you think you can pull this off..." Mariah shrugged, and it was a deliberate gesture, not an unconscious one, overwriting the tension they had between each other. As if to signal: *we're not okay, you and I. But maybe, for now, we'll act as if we are.* "You're the boss," she concluded.

Layla looked to Carlus next.

"You're the Empress," he said simply. "I'll do as you command."

*

INTERLUDE (MR. CHARLES CARAVOSA OF RENEB)

Now: Year 1128, somewhere in a nebula in a stolen Mazaran scout ship

Carlus Augustine Phillipe Dracus Caravosa, second of his name—now Charles; husband of Nadia; father of Natalia, Filomena, and Ian; son of the great Gustav IV—certainly had many names.

None of them rivaled the names he regularly called himself.

And what would one call him if looking at him now?

Lined. Weathered. War-weary. Care-worn.

Ill. Terminally, in fact.

Carlus had never been an impulsive man. Nor headstrong. That had always been Ignatius's department. And Benedik's. Certainly Carlus had an immense capacity for *stupidity*. He had demonstrated that quite well—albeit secretly—when he first encountered the Mazarans.

Jumping the Mazarans and stealing their scout ship had been all three: impulsive, headstrong, and *stupid*. Terminally stupid, in fact. But the knowledge of death sometimes changed the way one lived. And made one wonder what his legacy will be.

The Empress had given him an assignment.

The Empress was no physicist.

Carlus had more than a passing familiarity with the subject. Benedik too, in fact; it was a skill Carlus shared with that little shit, who pretended he was much dumber than he really was. Weapons, war, and wormholes. The love languages of Valhar.

And Carlus saw the flaw in the Empress's plan. Not immediately, not when he was still on the call. But later, when he realized, he also knew:

It wouldn't have changed a thing.

He would have said yes anyway. He would have said yes a thousand times. For Valhar. For his Empress. For his redemption.

Carlus knew what he had to do. His hands caressed the holo of his family, projected from his tablet.

I love you, he mouthed.

THEN

Then

Reneb

As we leave the Executive Mansion, we find Park waiting next to a small luxury flyer.

"Your Highness," he bows. "I'm to convey you to your next appointment."

I resist the eye roll and allow him to lead me to the backseat, where he joins. Mariah takes up residence up front, fingering her weapon with unease. She had put up a stink when asked to turn her weapons over at customs. We managed to compromise on one of her wimpy little backup stun guns.

"Our man Charles lives rurally. Rolling hills and babbling brooks. Just sit back and enjoy the ride." Park shoots me a grin.

"How long is the flight?" I ask.

"Only about three hours. It'll fly by."

Three hours. I shift uncomfortably.

I end up making him pull over three times so I can take a piss. The final time, I grin nervously. "Overactive bladder. What can ya do, right?" Mariah smirks but thankfully doesn't say anything. At least my nausea has calmed.

I try to change the subject. "So, Park, I never really got to talk to you when you gave me the news last year. How in the hell did you convince your government to even take Carlus, much less keep his residency here secret? What's in it for them?"

Park harrumphed. "What makes you think we needed to get something out of it?"

"Oh, come *on*."

He sighed. "Fine. Carlus argued he'd negotiate with the Mazarans on their behalf if they ever came back through the tunnel. Implied he'd have their ear."

I scrunch my forehead. "Why would he do that? I don't remember him having any particular connection to the Mazarans?"

He shrugged. "Beats me. But it worked, so here he is."

Wonder if it has anything to do with the secret I'm not allowed to know. I try to gauge Mariah's reaction, but she's looking straight ahead, stiff-backed, no different than usual.

Carlus lives on a country estate, complete with vineyards and grazing cows and gable roofs. So different than what I associate with Reneb. Can't take the Valhar out of the man, it seems. Aristocratic as ever.

At first glance, Carlus is the same as I remember him from the Mazaran negotiations. Big, burly bear of a man. Ignatius's beard makes him look patrician; Carlus's makes him look like a lumberjack. A bushy mustache too. Jolly. In another life, maybe he would have been a tavernkeeper, but in this life, he's a formal, impressive presence.

"Well!" he calls in a boom not unsimilar to Ignatius's, but less seductive and more jovial—maybe I'm biased here—"It's been a long time, and so much has changed."

He comes closer and takes my hand, peering at me. "Park was kind enough to alert me of your marriage. Congratulations, my Empress." He then bows, and I back up a bit in shock.

"Yes, uh, thank you," I say. "It certainly doesn't seem real."

His laugh is more like a deep grunt with a *ha* at the end. "Well, say what you want to say about the spectacle of royal weddings, but the long planning time and the pomp of it gives one time to prepare for the life change." He shakes his head. "From Commander Kamil to Empress Layla. I'm chuffed." He's too regal to ask the obvious questions.

"It was a shotgun marriage," Mariah says, bowing quickly to Carlus and pushing past us to, I don't know. Check the house out for threats or something. My jaw drops but I clamp it back up quick.

"Ho!" Carlus says, staring after her. "Mariah is the same as ever. Well, enough of that. Come along everyone. Empress—you are not yet comfortable with that title, are you?"

I shake my head.

"Well, if you were still engaged, I would have just referred to you as Lady Layla, which is hardly appropriate anymore, but Lady..." he snaps his finger. "Lady Royal. That holds proper respect, in Valharan tradition. Is that pleasing to you?"

Yes," I say. "Thank you. How shall I refer to you?"

"Just Carlus!" he says, with another grunt-laugh. "Or Charles, as I am to so many around here. No more titles or honorifics. I dare say it has been freeing."

And on second look, he's not quite the same Carlus I met on the Mazaran ship. Maybe it's because our positions have changed. But it's beyond that. During the Mazaran negotiations, he was shell-shocked. Gaunt and sunken face, despite his girth. I hadn't really noticed, given his strong presence, but now, seeing the contrast, it's clear I had met him at a bad time in his life.

Too bad the main reason to quit being Emperor is death. Because it'd be nice to look forward to Ignatius no longer having this duty, this life.

I'd never met former Empress Nadia before; when I was on Valhar for my damehood ceremony, after pushing the Mazarans back but before the armistice, then-Crown Prince Carlus and Princess Nadia had been stationed offworld. She's a freckle-faced brunette with an easy smile, and I'm again struck by the peace permeating the walls of this home. Not a very modest abode, certainly, but still, personal and warm. Carlus's kids don't even bother meeting their guests, the two youngest choosing instead to chase each other outside. They're rather young. They probably don't remember being royalty or being taught propriety. Good for them. Princess Natalia, the eldest, would have been the next in line for the throne, but here, she wears stained overalls over muddy boots, lying by a creek watching tadpoles.

Will you be denied this life, my child? My son or daughter? Will you be relegated to knee socks and smocked shirts? Have I condemned you, by the circumstances of your birth? Or should I be pleased, that you shall never know hunger the way I did, that you will not be some unloved dirt-smudged child on a lush-yet-empty world? How will I deal with the inevitable rebellion? With understanding and grace? Or with anger at your entitlement and privilege?

"Now," Carlus says later that afternoon, after a casual lunch, "what did you want to see me about? I assume this is more than a social call."

I look around the table at the assorted personages. Hmm. "Mind if we take a walk?" I ask.

There's a large pond on his property. It's warm here on Reneb, and there's no mountain looming over us. Carlus and I stroll, arm in arm, and he silently diverts me from a flock of ducks sunning by the water. But I'm hit by the duality: the memory of Ignatius and I walking the frozen lake, the accusation I hid a message from Ransom, the ensuing hurt and sadness.

"As you know, Lyria recently declared war," I begin.

He nods. "Any danger of Altain and Reneb joining in?"

"There was. Hopefully averted, for now. The main reason for my visit, actually."

"And the secondary reason?"

I pause, and turn toward the water. "Also to do with the Lyrian declaration. They had specifics on the tunnel. That's why they went ahead and called for war. Evidence. Plans. Timelines. There's obviously someone within the Empire feeding them information."

Next to me, Carlus goes still.

I want to reassure him we don't suspect him, that I'm only after information, but I know to be patient. See what comes of it.

We resume walking.

Eventually he speaks. "How can I help?"

I begin carefully. "There are those, in the Whorl, who would think you an easy mark. You were pushed out of power through no fault of your own, an accident of birth that could have been corrected with paperwork."

"And so, what?" he asks with a chuckle. "That gives me reason to betray my people?" He smiles to himself in a private joke I cannot hope to understand.

"It's a pressure point. Not saying it's a correct one, but someone in the Alliance wanting information may have tried you first, before eventually landing on whoever the mole was."

"Or the mole could have done this unprompted."

"There is that," I concede. "But it was worth an ask."

"Hmm." He frowns and tugs at his beard. "Obviously the Renebians fish for information—Park included. But nothing like *that*."

"Any visitors?"

"An associate of Gaius Stanlo's. Relatively recently, in fact. Didn't give a name but had the seal of office as bona fides." He shook his head. "Pointless visit, really. Well, about the legitimacy issues. He wanted my thoughts. Do you know about Stanlo's background?"

I haven't even met the guy. I do know, from my recent briefings, that he's the Viceroy of Solita and therefore the closest planet to the under-construction tunnel.

It turns out, as Carlus explains to me, that Stanlo is descended from a former emperor, whose progeny had been thought to be illegitimate and therefore lost the throne. An ancestor of Empress Hadria was elected in their stead. But history shows us Stanlo's ancestor had been secretly married, and that the claim of illegitimacy was a perpetrated fraud from a rival.

"So Stanlo was looking for advice on succession laws?"

"Effectively," Carlus said. "I think he was rather put out he wasn't under consideration by the electorate following my removal." Carlus scoffed. "Not that it would have mattered. He's not that qualified, nor smart, nor prudent. My father had sent him out to Solita to take over the viceroyalty to basically get rid of him. Perhaps shortsighted, seeing he should have known the Solita tunnel would become relevant in Stanlo's lifetime."

"But alas," he continues, "that won't help you find your mole. The Solita tunnel is a boon for his little kingdom. He wouldn't blab the plans to the Lyrians."

I think back to those briefings. "And General Turine trusts him. They're thick as thieves, Mariah says."

The former emperor shrugs. "Well, then there you have it. I took a picture of his envoy, if you're interested. I'll shoot it over to your tablet when we get back to the house." We resume our silence, still arm in arm. Genteel. Refined.

Carlus looks like he's in another world entirely. Lips thin, staring off into nothing. He looks down at me from time to time as if he wants to say something, but then clams up. Eventually I can't take it anymore.

"Lord Carlus?"

He looks at me in surprise. "Not a Lord anymore," he grunts.

I frown. "Maybe not on Reneb. But you are, you know. Regardless," I continue. "What exactly is bothering you? Can I help?"

He lets out a sigh, a rolling boulder of a thing, and for a second I'm worried I've displeased him by prying. But instead, it looks like he's searching for words.

"Nothing is bothering me, exactly. Lost in thought." He lets out a breath and stops, guiding me to a small bench. "I never did thank you. For keeping the secret of my father's illness."

"It was nothing," I say.

"Oh? From what I understand, you're a patriot. Or at least were," he acknowledges, looking at my wedding jewelry with a raised eyebrow. "You never told your superiors that Valharan leadership had changed hands. That there was a vulnerability there to exploit. An emperor not able to rule, a crown prince in his stead. You never sold me out. Why? You hardly knew me. Park I can understand. He's self-serving. He could have parlayed a relationship with me into moving up in his government."

I had never really thought about it before. The *why*. I search my memory, trying to place myself back on that ship, back in that stateroom. "Ignatius asked me to keep it secret," I eventually manage. "It was important to him. And to you, of course. And so..." I lightly tap my fingers on my legs. "I didn't give it much conscious thought, but that's why. It felt exploitative to run and tell my superiors."

"Mariah doesn't know," Carlus said. "That I blabbed on the Mazaran ship. Obviously she was aware of my father's condition and that I had taken over for him, but I never told her I had told Ignatius, much less two offworlders."

"Yeah, I gathered that. She was plenty surprised I have even a passing relationship with you."

"*You* are a surprise. I thought you'd never agree to marry Ignatius after the first time he proposed. Yes," he said, smiling at my startled look, "I know he asked a few years ago. I also know you turned him down."

Should I explain? Does he know already? "Erm..." I begin, "I wasn't willing to give up my Altainan citizenship. Because, well, you know." I wave vaguely at him. "The law about that."

"Ah," he says. "I gather my cousin repealed it?"

I nod.

He grunts. "Well, I don't approve. Split loyalties are never a good thing in a populace, much less in a ruler and ruler-consort. You see, you need to choose a *side*, Lady Royal."

"How?" I ask. "How am I supposed to do that?"

"Choose who guards your heart. Who doesn't betray you."

"Everyone betrays everyone," I say, maudlin.

"Don't I know it," he whispers. He looks off into that distance again, eyes playing out some sort of tragedy. "Lady—Layla. Here's what you need to ask: whose heart is in the right place? Whose betrayal is borne of a bumble, not malice? And that's how you choose."

I shake my head, still not able to parse it.

"I will tell you something," he continued. "Something Mariah knows. Something your husband knows. Something I suspect you *don't* know, given the way you approached me about the possibility of a mole in your government. Am I right in assuming you've been left in the dark?"

I perk up. "I know there's something I don't know," I say, wincing at the idiocy of that statement once it leaves my mouth. "But I don't know what it is. At all." Right. Smooth, Layla.

Luckily, Carlus just chuckles. Then it tapers off, and he's back in that liminal space he's been residing in for the entire discussion.

"My lack of legitimacy was a cover, Layla. It's true. I was born out of wedlock. To save face, my parents intimated the woman who bore me was a surrogate, not actually of my flesh, but turns out, my father had a long affair with her. But you'd also be correct in saying it's an overreaction to strip a man, already vested as ruler, of his crown for something like that. After all, I was my father's acknowledged son. With but a bit of paperwork, there'd be no problem at all. However, as I said, it's not the reason I was ousted. I was asked to abdicate," he says, stilling hands that had begun clenching and unclenching in an unruly ballet, "because I betrayed my empire. My family. Really, the entire Whorl."

And then he braces himself and tells me.

Then

It's common knowledge the Mazarans visited our Whorl before the invasion. There was no base at Dega at the time, so no alerts to scream at us, *A stranger is arriving!* But from time to time, we get travelers. Pilgrims. Merchants. Generation ships. Explorers. Some stay, and become part of our tapestry. Some trade in information and goods and are then on their way. The system, until five years ago, suited us just fine.

We knew about the Mazaran Empire, naturally. Heard about their steady expansion into the space just outside the Swan Tunnel's far terminus. If the Mazarans visited, we'd be wary. But obviously, they didn't advertise themselves as such. How would we have known?

But what I didn't know, and what Carlus has just told me, is that while the Mazarans were sniffing around, taking the measure of the Whorl and its politics, they found the isolated, self-serving, and militarily proficient Valharan Empire. They found Gustav, who was fiercely protective of not only his people but who believed progress was in reaching a hand out to the rest of the governments on the other side of the nebula. And they found Carlus, the crown prince, who was wary of diluting his culture by allowing in the soft colonialism of the self-proclaimed democratic planets.

Jackpot.

And in the end, he assured the Mazarans that were they to invade, he could sway his father toward isolation so the Mazarans could take the rest of the Whorl, ostensibly leaving Valhar alone.

Treason. Not for betraying the Whorl, but for making deals behind the Emperor's back. After all, unlike the power invested in me, *Carlus* had no claim to speaking with his father's voice.

"Our culture venerates warfighting. No, we don't fight it needlessly, but we will rise to the challenge with joy. It's all glory and honor. But I saw that conquering force, and I knew they could win. Subjugate us. Loot and pillage and take our history and our peoples and smash them to bits. And I decided I wanted to avoid war and to isolate our empire. I decided to throw the rest of the Whorl to those wolves, so we could live safe behind a brick wall. I made a deal with the Mazarans, behind my father's back. I thought I was keeping us safe. Turns out, I was just a coward."

I don't know what to say.

The *cost*. Dear Goddess, the lives lost in that ill-fated march of conquest and subjugation. We pushed them back. We battled them to a standstill. But we didn't *win*. The whole threatened war we're having right now over the Valharan tunnel is a direct result of our scars from the Mazarans. And I'm not sure if we'll ever heal.

And Carlus had simply told them we were ripe for the taking.

I close my eyes, feeling the soft breeze coming off the sedate pond in a bucolic corner of the world, where peace and happiness rule but regret and self-loathing plot. I see Carlus's far-off eyes, even when he's looking straight at me.

Everyone betrays everyone, I had said.

But whose heart is in the right place?

I can't sit here and say Carlus made his decision out of the goodness of his heart. After all, his decision would have condemned multiple planets in the Whorl, saving only his Empire. But he wasn't evil. Just *wrong*. So incredibly, terribly, wrong. And selfish.

But what is evil, truly? If it's selfish men making selfish choices out of cowardice, then maybe I can't say he didn't commit evil. But he, himself, is not evil. He's just a man.

I still don't know what to say. I can't address the substance of what he said. I can't provide absolution. Instead, I ask, "What happened next?"

"You and Ignatius convinced my father to come out swinging on behalf of the rest of the Whorl. And that was that."

A flash of insight. "And what happened on the Mazaran ship? During the armistice talks?"

He gives a double take and then peers at me closely. "Yes. You know that's when I found out my father had suffered his heart attack. And when I made the decision we'd keep it quiet, and I would just rule from the sidelines." He gulps and looks off again. "That's also when I found out the Mazarans were the ones who did it."

Everything clicks into place and my head goes in my hands. Gustav would still be here today. I hardly knew him, but my heart still squeezes tight, thinking of the loss of that, by all accounts, good man. *Carlus* would still be on Valhar, the Crown Prince. And I—where would I be? Would I have even met Ignatius or would the Mazarans have not pushed so fast to Felix? And if so, later. Without Carlus's Law, would I have accepted that proposal the first time around? Never even *met* Ransom, or even the president, apart from maybe some sort of military ceremony?

I wouldn't be the fucking Empress, that's for sure. I wouldn't be here, confused, a child in my womb, wondering what love and fidelity even *are*. Or if I could ever be truly accepted for who I am. I wouldn't be so lost. So torn. Perhaps a quiet ex-soldier, living a quiet life with a minor duke out in the foothills of the Corval mountains.

"I skipped the dinner that night," he whispers. "I got drunk. Drunk enough to torpedo the peace talks. Ignatius stopped me. No, he didn't know," he says, at my shocked look. "Having him there was what helped calm me. I didn't tell Ignatius, not even after you and Park left that evening. It was one of my many regrets. If I had told him then, I would have saved our nation pain and upheaval. As it happened, I couldn't hold the secret. I told Ignatius later, after I had already begun my reign. He told me to go to Mariah. Mariah told the Prime Minister. From there, we decided I had to leave."

My silence is damning.

"You must think me a monster, Lady Royal."

"No," I assure him.

"A fool, then."

I lie. "No more a fool than the rest of us, just trying to figure out how to do right."

"If I could redeem myself somehow, make those bastards pay—a lifetime couldn't correct this. You see now, why it was eminently possible someone could have come to me asking for information on the tunnel, had they known. The same guy who already sold out his Empire once. However, I believe it is still a closely held secret. Not even Park, or the rest of the Renebians. Only Ignatius. Mariah. Henri. And, I have to assume, the spouses, including you. And so, the only person who has come to see me recently is that representative of Stanlo. I'm sorry I couldn't be of more help."

I squeeze his shoulder as we stand to return to the house. "You've been wonderful, Lord Carlus."

"Just Carlus."

"Charles."

He grins. I smile back, despite the latent anger I'm trying to lock away. Condemning this man won't bring back lost lives. And, he did sacrifice. He did what he thought was right—wrong as it was—and he suffered the consequences.

But something is still squiggling in the back of my mind. Something that doesn't make sense. It isn't until we've already left to head back for the capital city that I find it. Carlus's treason may be an incredibly closely held secret, but his asylum on Reneb is also known only within a small circle. Even more so, his exact location.

How did Stanlo's man know to find him here?

Now

BENEDIK!
Now

Empress Layla was mad. Barking. There was nothing more to it.

Benedik loved it.

His mind wandered as he flipped through Layla's little black book. Carlus. On Reneb. Who would have thought? Truthfully, he never understood why Emperor Carlus had to flee after abdicating. It's not like he was *ousted*. He just didn't think it was a good idea to stay in power if he wasn't technically a legitimate son of Gustav. Backward view, really. He should have been able to stay on. But at least it spared Valhar the debate. And leaving the Empire made sense, so there wasn't a former Emperor hanging about getting in the way of the new one.

But no reason to go into *hiding*.

Layla said reading her entry on her visit to Carlus would clear a few things up, and it *was* nice to see Carlus was living happily and in peace. But he kept getting distracted, because Layla's plan to end the war was...

Well, it could work.

Maybe. Something niggled at him and he opened his mouth to speak—

"Okay," Mariah said, plopping down onto one of the crash couches with a lollipop in her mouth. Layla didn't give it a second glance, but Benedik stared.

"What? Helps me think." Mariah flashed him a rude gesture.

Layla smirked. "Not an unusual sight around the palace."

"*Anyway*," Mariah continued, "let's plan this out. After Carlus does his thing, it'll be live-broadcast, so then you make your little speech and we hope for the best?"

Layla nodded. "Ignatius thought it was best I do it. There's a damn good chance this is actually going to paint a bigger target on our back, but my being the face of it might be less of a shock, and therefore may temper the response. If the dangerous and smug Emperor Ignatius of the dangerous and smug Valharan Empire makes a *ha, we win* speech, pride alone may make the Alliance powers not listen. And besides, I'm the one out here talking real time to Carlus."

Ignatius was finally back in the capital, but due to the sensitivity of Layla's plan, she didn't want to risk Park or the rest of the Renebians getting wind of it. Using their comms system between the yacht and Park's office was out. Layla had sent an encrypted note over to Ignatius the slow way and they had received the reply some time after, blessing her plan and providing guidance.

Not for the first time, Benedik reveled in not being in charge. But there was a certain *removal of responsibility* that nagged him.

"We should head that way. Meet up with him."

Mariah and Layla stared at him. He bristled. Oh yes, silly Benedik, right? Never knows what he's talking about.

"Look. He's all alone out there. This is *Carlus*. You know, as in former Emperor?" He modulated his voice to be soft and low. "And he's family. He pulls off this scheme of yours, Layla, what do you think is going to happen to him? The entire Alliance—"

"Our ships are out there," Mariah interrupted. "The Valharan sentries. They know no details, but they know to let him through. They'll cover him."

"It won't be enough. He's going to get detained. I'm not talking about *fighting* the Alliance, you two. But getting him free? Negotiation and diplomacy? All the stuff we're supposed to be *good* at?"

"It's weeks away, through Alliance territory," Layla mused. "Ben, we're the farthest away. We should get someone from the capital to head out there."

Benedik chewed his lip. She was right. Damnit. He had a brief vision of requisitioning the little skip in the hold, heading off on his own, but alas, it wasn't rated for wormhole travel.

The inaction clawed at him, spreading prickles up and down his arms. He stretched a palm, as if he could will the unease out of him.

Damn. "Any idea what you're going to say yet?" Benedik asked, switching tracks.

Layla winced. "Not yet? I mean, I kinda used to do this for a living, but this particular statement is going to be…"

"Epic."

"Infamous."

Benedik inclined his chin. "Point conceded. I'll let you work." As Layla nodded and made her way to the rooms, he looked at her journal. A real sign of trust, allowing him to flip through.

So, where was he. Carlus, happy. Nadia and the kids doing well—thank the Falcon. *Flip*. Walking a pond. Okay. *Flip*. A visit from a Stanlo minion. Hmm. He had a lot of questions about Stanlo lately. Keep that in mind. *Flip*. A secret Layla knew was a secret without knowing the actual secret? Hmm.

Benedik shot out of the chair as if ejected. Heart hammering, he paced, cursing quietly to himself.

I made a deal with the Mazarans, Carlus had told her, *behind my father's back.*

It couldn't be. It just couldn't.

Carlus. Oh, Carlus. He had looked up to him, his much-older second cousin. How? What?

Oh, Blessed Falcon, this was why Ignatius could believe ill of Benedik himself. He had already seen treasonous idiocy from family members.

How. Could. He.

Benedik thought himself an easy-going man. Others thought him flighty. Fanciful. Quick with a kind word, first to forgive and move on. But Carlus betrayed an *Emperor*. Even if he became one after—actually, that was even more unforgivable. Benedik could read between the lines. The Mazarans tried to *kill* Gustav to put the more amenable Carlus on the throne. Eventually did kill him, at that, Benedik gathered. He, like most of the extended family, knew Gustav was incapacitated that last year of his life. But he didn't know this.

Gustav would have possibly still been alive, on the throne, to this day.

Damn him. Family or not. Looked like Layla forgave, but she wasn't Valharan-born. Not an original member of the family, no matter how much he loved her. Benedik, a born and bred Valharan royal, could not let this go.

Well, forget it. No diplomatic mission to spring him from the clutches of the Alliance after all. Carlus could fend for himself.

Clarity. Layla thought this would give him clarity. Benedik blinked back tears. No clarity here. Confusion. Fear. Betrayal.

Benedik mourned the man he thought he had known.

He was the only one in the common space when the comms console pinged, and he thought about just smashing it silent. Instead, he gritted his teeth and answered.

"Carlus."

"Benedik!" Carlus's smile, wide and genuine, turned Benedik's insides into ice.

"I'll get Layla," he said simply, and began to walk off.

"Wait! Cousin! How are you? It's been so lo-"

Benedik pivoted to stalk closer to the console. He brought his face in, so hopefully the effect was him looming over Carlus in whatever accursed Mazaran cockpit he was in. "You are not my kin," he growled. "You are not my emperor. You sold out our family. Our people. Your father. The entire Whorl community. You don't get to talk to me. Ever again."

"Layla told you, huh," Carlus said, face grave.

"No," he mocked. "It came to me in a *fucking vision*."

"Ben..."

"No."

Layla chose that moment to bound up the stairs, and the sound of her footsteps stopped short behind him. Guess she noticed the standoff. Benedik turned to her, still cold. "I wish you had never shown me," he said.

Her mouth opened slightly, but no response came. Only then did he notice her red-rimmed eyes. What was *she* all mournful about?

She pushed past Benedik to the display. "Carlus. Are you in position?"

"Sure am, Lady Royal. I know how the weapon works and everything. We going to broadcast across the Whorl?"

"If you think that's best."

"Okay, then." Carlus flipped a switch and gritted his teeth.

Despite his anger, Benedik felt chills at the historic moment he was about to witness. This was it. This could swing the war. Maybe in a good direction. Maybe bad. Layla's plan was not guaranteed to work. They could be bringing the entire Alliance down on them. He wasn't so naive as to believe Valhar had been subjected to the full scope of firepower in these opening months of the war, and there were unaffiliated planets that could also join up against them.

He reached out and squeezed Layla's hand. Layla squeezed back, harder than necessary, then sent a note to Mariah to join them in the common room.

"Attention, denizens of the Whorl: This is the former Emperor Carlus II of Valhar. A few days ago, a Mazaran scoutship emerged from the Swan Nebula tunnel. Pursuant to our armistice agreement, neither Valharan nor Renebian forces engaged. They arrived on Reneb, where I have been living for the past few years, and spoke to me.

"Yes, they spoke to me. They spoke to me because they believed me an ally. They spoke to me because over eight years ago, they enlisted me to keep Valhar away from their attempted conquest of the rest of the Whorl."

Layla and Benedik shared a look. "I didn't ask him to share all that," she whispered. Benedik frowned.

"What I learned," Carlus continued, "was that they had been invited back into the Whorl, back into our *home*, by the Altainan Republic. This scout ship, which I have liberated from the Mazarans and am now flying on my own, has an embedded antimatter weapon that can close subspace tunnels. The Solita tunnel, still under construction, could be shut down by overloading the tunnel's energy output, causing it to collapse upon itself. Now, I ask you: Why would the Mazarans want to help Altain in this endeavor? Because they view another tunnel as a threat. It is an escape route out of the Whorl. It opens up further opportunities for resources and trade. And the Mazarans don't control it. Because mark my words: they got the better deal out of this armistice. They have their thumbs down on us, and we were too naive to realize.

"Now, I said the Mazarans had reached out to me years ago to ensure my cooperation. Citizens of the Whorl, they received that cooperation. And then, as I was not the one in power in the Valharan Empire, they caused my father's death. I have sinned. I was wrong. And today, I seek redemption, and I will avenge the harm done upon my family."

The picture switched to that of Dega, and the Swan Nebula tunnel. Next to Benedik, Layla's breath came out in stutters. Ignatius had promised them he would ensure the Valharan forces on Dega would not intervene, and they hung back, arrayed in formation at a safe distance.

"Behold! The route to Mazar. The Swan Nebula Tunnel. The *Mazaran* tunnel. And I am going to close it."

Carlus turned off his sound but kept broadcasting from his exterior camera.

He was awfully close to the tunnel.

"What is he *doing?*" Layla whispered.

Oh. Oh no.

When Benedik had listened to Layla's original briefing, something had seemed off. He had stayed silent, planning on speaking up after searching his memory. But then he had read that journal entry, and all thoughts had disappeared. But now ... oh.

"Layla," Benedik said quickly. "I looked at the projections of how to collapse a tunnel. You can close one under construction rather easily with a weapon like this. But a completed one..."

Mariah cussed fluently. "He's going to collapse it from the inside."

The three of them shared shocked looks, and then Layla lunged for the comm.

"Carlus! Carlus, what are you doing?!"

Carlus's stony face came back on screen. "Layla. Lady Royal." He nodded to the others. "Cousin. Mariah. This is the only way."

"No! Carlus, I didn't mean for you to sacrifice yourself!"

"It's the only way," he repeated. "I'm dying. You know this."

"So spend your time with your famil—"

"I'm doing this, Layla, and you can't stop me. Go love *your* family, Layla. Make more babies. Live free." He cut the connection.

Mariah pummeled the arm of her chair repeatedly, a violent *rap-a-tap-tap* of anxious distress. "You can stop him," she said. "You're the Empress. You speak for Ignatius. You can order him not to do this."

Yes, Layla *could*. Benedik looked to her. What the fuck was she waiting for? But Layla shook her head.

"He's made his choice."

"What?!?" Mariah went for the comm. Layla put her hand over hers and mouthed no. Benedik, in sort of a detached fugue, watched her lips tremble. "Don't dishonor this, Mariah. He's going to stop this war."

"This. Was. *Your*. Fucking. Idea." Mariah bit out. "Know this. *You* killed him."

Layla gasped as if there were no air in the cabin. Benedik winced at the tears falling from her eyes. (He wiped his own away surreptitiously). "I know."

Benedik tried to speak a few times, and finally worked past a croak. "Give it a rest, Mariah," he said softly. "Layla's right."

Mariah squinted and blinked a few times and then wandered over to a chair, gingerly lowering herself down.

Layla and Benedik watched, hand in hand, as the Swan Nebula tunnel flared for the last time.

"What about the forces on Dega?" Benedik whispered.

"Already evacuated," she said. "Ignatius made sure of it."

The light grew brighter than it ever had before, and then shrunk darker than he had ever seen.

Benedik kept staring. Surely there'd be more. Surely the end of an era—and the end of a great man—would not come in a whimper but a roar. Surely, at least, a starburst, a riot of color, tendrils of light, as a salute, a sending-off of his beloved kinsman, Carlus II of Valhar.

He stood frozen, waiting. No one spoke.

But that was it. It was done.

Layla, still shaking while on his arm, took deep breaths, in and out. She removed her hand and wiped her tears with her sleeve. "Right," she said. "My turn."

In the end, Benedik couldn't quite remember the words of Layla's historic speech. She broadcasted all over the Whorl, just as Carlus had done, just as Altain had done months before when declaring war, informing them there was now only one way in and out of the Whorl, and if they tried to stop that, they'd be isolated for ... well, for centuries. There needed to be a team on the other terminus to build a subspace tunnel. With no way out of the Whorl, no new construction. And so, Layla concluded, the deed was done. The Solita tunnel construction would go forward. And the Whorl needed to lay down their arms.

That was the gist of what she said. But Benedik spent the speech in his room, Layla's words piped in, as he kept his head between his knees.

His cousin. His Emperor. Lost to him. Then found. Then repudiated. And now gone forever.

I should have been there.

The illogic of it didn't matter. Maybe if he hadn't argued with Ignatius's original impulse to send him to Alliance territory. Maybe he would have ended up on Reneb and could have stolen the craft himself. Or he could have at least seen Carlus. One last time, in the flesh.

Layla had gotten to visit him and Benedik hadn't.

He still held Layla's notebook, and he stared again at the pages, trying to make sense of it all.

Everyone betrays everyone.

But whose heart is in the right place?

Not really the most pithy of statements, and yet. Benedik flipped backwards.

An associate of Gaius Stanlo's.

Wait.

He ran out of his stateroom, almost leaping up the stairs, and grabbed a surprised Layla. "The associate. The Stanlo guy," he babbled.

"Benedik, what the heck?"

"Your recollections. The man that met with Carlus. Before you visited. Carlus said he'd send you a picture. Did you get one?"

She frowned. "Yeah, I think so. Is it not in the book? Or no. Why would it be?"

"Layla, do you have it? Can you get it?"

She nodded and pulled out her tablet. "I can find most anything. Um…" she fiddled around a bit, and threw a projection in the air. "Here."

The enormous eyes of the mysterious cutout stared back down at them.

Layla looked at him, question in her eyes, and Benedik nodded. "Yeah, that's the same guy I met. There you have it. The guy that the Solitan rebels thought was an Altainan agitator, who is the same guy the Renebians thought was a Solitan rebel intermediary—was Stanlo's agent all along."

*
Now

Layla

Her earlier tears for the loss of citizenship—for a *fucking* piece of paper for some artificial border—now mocked her. Selfish. Myopic.

Evil. She had let Carlus do this. She could have stopped him.

How did she know what was right? How?

She had thought she was making the biggest sacrifice today by cutting her ties to Altain forever, but then, Carlus put her to shame.

"Stanlo," Mariah said, interrupting her thoughts. She paced around the room, lollipop in her mouth. "Let me at him."

Mariah hadn't forgiven her, not yet. But she took her duties as protector of the realm seriously. Layla gave her a contemplating look. "Arrest?"

"No. I'm going to kill him, and bring his head back on a spike."

Well, when in Valhar...

"All right," Layla said quietly. "Nate gave me the authority, right? Go for it."

Mariah stumbled. "Wait, what?"

A giggle threatened to work its way out of her gut at the look on Mariah's face. But it wasn't funny. *None of this was funny*.

"Okay," Layla conceded. "Maybe we shouldn't execute him at first sight. I'd like to yoke him back with us and bring him to the Emperor. But if he resists, cut that motherfucker down. Just maybe don't bring back his *head*. That's kinda gross. We can find another trophy."

Mariah blinked at her. "Whatever happened to juries and due process?"

"This is Valhar, bitch. And I'm a Valharan Empress. We do it our way."

Mariah huffed happily. "Nice to finally meet you, Empress."

It was like a coming out party, but with dancing on the ashes of her past.

Well, credits to chips Stanlo had arranged for the attacks on her and the baby. Fuck. That. He thought his ancestors had been cheated out of the throne. He had wanted to be under consideration when Carlus left. Goddess Alive, the motivation was clear and had been *staring her in the damn face* this entire time. "But there's a lot of moving parts here and I don't quite get how Stanlo fits into it all."

"Allow me," Benedik said, bowing. He pulled out his tablet and threw a projection into the air: a network of faces, with a crisscross of red lines. Benedik twirled his hands excitedly as he spoke, evoking a frenetic savant.

"I was up all night," he explained. "Right. Here goes." He presented the chart with a flourish. "How Stanlo usurps the throne without killing. See, that's the thing with a Valharan emperor. The people won't tolerate regicide. No sirree. I said as much to the Solita rebels. Anyway, the key is that cutout. He talks to the rebels, pretending to work for Altain. He talks to Reneb, pretending to work for the rebels. But he's *Stanlo's* man. Stanlo is behind my kidnapping. Think about it. Stanlo knows how opportunistic Reneb is. They want that sweet sweet free trade with Solita. Stanlo knows the rebels wouldn't trust Reneb, so he misrepresents the interested party as Altain. Works since Altain is already operating in that space, trying to stir up revolution, right?"

"Right," Layla said. Logic the hell out of the situation, indeed.

"Right. So the rebels get ahold of me. Threaten to execute me unless Ignatius approves home rule. Think about it. If the Emperor says no, I die. Stanlo crushes the rebels in response, and looks strong. If Ignatius says yes, the rebels *still* kill me. Maybe *they* don't, but Stanlo would make sure I die. Either way, Ignatius looks weak and I die. In fact, if the Emperor agrees to home rule, Stanlo could easily veto that and lead the other nobles to anger. Chaos is the game. So people mobilize against Ignatius. That happened, didn't it? If he's removed, my father would refuse the throne. Apparently he would have refused anyway, but in Stanlo's estimation, he would refuse out of heartbreak. Carlus was ineligible, because of his illegitimacy, as are his children. *You*," he said, pointing at Layla, "were to get eliminated, as soon as he learned you were pregnant. Because otherwise, your baby would actually be automatically emperor or empress after Ignatius stepped down, and I doubt my father would mind playing regent. And in the end, who's left? Stanlo, who is *legitimately* a member of a former royal family."

Layla raised her hand. "Um, what about Anastasia?"

Mariah snorted. "He probably forgot about her."

Benedik grinned. "Quite right. And, besides, as Ignatius's mother and a woman to boot, she'd be unlikely to be chosen if the election came down between her and Stanlo."

Layla stood and studied the chart. Plausible. More than plausible.

Benedik squinted his eyes in thought. "He must have been pissed off that I was still alive and kicking and messing with his plan. So he needed to get to me...fuck. The surveillance device. That the cutout gave us. It was supposed to allow us to spy on Stanlo, but he used it to spy on *us*. The rebels, that is. And he recorded me completely incriminating myself."

"Which discredits both you and your father," Layla concluded. "You know, Carlus told me Stanlo was an idiot, but—"

"He still is," Mariah said. "And I'm going to end him."

As they arrived back in the Solita system, Mariah started to give instructions for Layla while she and Benedik went down, and Layla objected immediately.

"Oh no. Oh *hell* no. This time, I'm coming. Look," she said, before Mariah could get a word in. "You want to take down a king? You need an empress. And if we end up killing his ass? It's under *my* orders. How the hell else do you expect to get *out* of his chambers after killing the *viceroy of Solita*?"

"I know you speak for Ignatius, but the defense forces? Might not listen to the word of the Empress anyway."

"But they won't kill us on sight. That's the most important. Even if I need to get Ignatius to actually belatedly approve." No hurt pride there. She *wasn't* the Emperor. Regardless of how much he trusted her.

After the tunnel collapse, Ignatius had sent just four words, on open comms. *Oh, well done, love.*

Nothing about his grief over Carlus, or questions on how that came to be—understandably, given the venue. They'd have to mourn together.

It was evenfall as they arrived at the palace, in the little skip from the yacht's hold. Layla chose Benedik to stay behind this time. (*Please check on the sexy militants,* he had pleaded.) For all anyone knew, he was still on Valhar, in gobs of trouble. Walking around free and coming to Solita would have engaged Stanlo's danger sense.

A visit from the Empress made sense. Her Whorl-wide address had been from the yacht, flying around the Valharan Empire. The Solita tunnel had just become more important than ever before. Yes, why wouldn't she take the opportunity to drop in on the Viceroy of Solita, the new hotness in nobility?

Still, Mariah had fretted about Layla's safety. What tricks did Stanlo have up his sleeve? After all, this was his home field. Could his security forces be trusted to defend her if it came down to it? Or would they pile up against her? What hope would just one Mariah have against dozens of guards?

Well, on that last point Mariah had stopped and contradicted herself. Just one Mariah, she said to Layla, was more than enough *thank you very much*.

Layla wasn't inclined to dispute the point.

"Your Grace," Stanlo welcomed her, bowing low. "Allow me to lead you to our secure war room, where we can discuss—"

"No," Layla said. "Your personal study, please."

After some polite protestations, Stanlo relented and led them into a very *Valharan* room, fancy this and fancy that everywhere. Yet despite her dislike of Valharan decorating, this room differed in that it was plain ugly. She was talking flying cherubs and sainted kings. By the Goddess, did he imagine himself one of them?

She wanted to study the inlaid stone mosaic in the marble tiled floor but looking down to the ground wouldn't exactly portray strength. So she forced a look of polite disinterest as Stanlo bustled about ordering refreshments for his visitors.

Some light fare and steaming mugs for the guests, daintier china for the host. Mariah politely passed Stanlo's to him, at least attempting to honor Valharan tradition. Layla sniffed her hot cider when it arrived, but didn't drink. Unlike the rest of the royal family, she hadn't been effectively immunized against popular toxins.

Here, there be dragons.

Stanlo looked at her pointedly and took a large sip out of his own cup, and then gingerly placed it on its saucer. "Your Grace," he began, "thank you for blessing us with your presence. Your actions with respect to the Mazaran tunnel were simply marvelous. And now our Solita tunnel will be on the map, permanently. We're humbled to be the gateway to a new realm of exploration."

"And with regards to your tunnel," Layla responded, "when exactly did your treason begin?"

His smile froze. "Pardon?"

She stood, walking to the walls and looking at those ugly fat flying babies. "Well, at first, we were more taken with the idea of you eliminating the royal family one by one. Benedik, kidnapped and ransomed. Ignatius, pushed out for being ineffective. Abilio, by grief. Anastasia, by oversight. And myself and my child, by murder." She took the fork from her small plate and stabbed at a grinning cherub, theatrically.

"Erm, *Your Grace,* I don't quite know—"

"Hard to prove, of course. Your man, the one with many fake affiliations, is dead, on the Altainan antimatter ship out in the Solita dust cloud. But funny that, the antimatter ship. That thing was wired for Solita comms. You were more than aware of where it was."

"The antimatter..." he spluttered. "Why in the devil would I risk *our tunnel—*"

"Why chaos, of course. Certainly, it's a boon for *Solita*, but if you're angling for emperor, it's less important to you. The tunnel leading to war helps your case that you're a more stable choice as emperor. Oh, my. You're the mole that leaked the plans to the Lyrians over two years ago." She collapsed back onto the chesterfield, her head thumping against the headrest as she pretended to think. "Why, you let the Altainan antimatter weapon in. That's the only way it could have made it through the Solita Defense Perimeter. They had to rush it, because you *knew* we were going to try to take Kaborlah."

"You've gone daft. Your Grace, you have no proof of any of this ... this fantasy you've made up on the spot."

"Actually, I didn't *just* think it up. I was shitting you. And I do, in fact, have proof. My man in the Altainan government can vouch for your hand in these matters."

She had made the call immediately to Ransom, using the encryption he had taught her so many years ago. Biting the bullet, as it were, but instead of letting him rant and threaten her, she explained the ship was to be returned to Altain and expressed her hope it would be used to assist Kaborlah's energy crisis. Ransom's face had thundered but he saw the opportunity, nonetheless, in confirming Stanlo's actions.

To her surprise, Stanlo stopped protesting, stopped discussing the tunnel at all, and instead was muttering to an absent Benedik. "You were supposed to die, you blithering blond idiot." Then Stanlo appeared to notice her again, as if for the first time, and his lip twisted. "Congratulations, Empress." He pulled a blaster out from his desk and aimed it at her. "But you're too smart for your own—" He stumbled as a knife suddenly appeared in his chest, thrown from across the room by an alert Mariah.

"God, how cliche can you get?" Mariah complained, rolling her eyes. "Were you just about to start the whole *and now you shall die* villain bullshit?"

"Oof. If he doesn't die by your knife, Mariah, maybe it'll be via snark attack." Layla frowned and knelt by him, looking helplessly at his wound. "But I don't think he was going to *kill* me. Shouldn't we call emergency—"

Stanlo breathed with stuttering gasps. "Better die ... assassin's knife ... not hanged." He groaned and weakly pushed Layla's hand away.

"You wanted to do things the Valharan way, Empress," Mariah said gravely. "Either I get rid of him or we call a medic. Can't have it both ways."

"So, we could save him?"

Stanlo's heaving became more rhythmic, yet deeper, more distressed. But his eyes glittered. "I'm more dangerous to you alive."

"I can't believe I missed," Mariah muttered. "Out of practice. That should have been a fatal wound. Empress," she said, "you know our intent. You know what *he* wants, and the Emperor wouldn't want the quagmire of his being alive. We should put him out of his misery, unless you enjoy leaving him in agony?"

Layla looked at the man, as if for confirmation. Mercy was good. It was right. But it felt akin to putting an animal down, and Layla wasn't sure she liked this new Valharan way of hers.

"Do it, you soft ignoramus," Stanlo managed to get out. "Don't know ... got a drop on me."

("Oh dear," Mariah said, "because I put something in *your* drink.")

Layla squared herself up. "Yes. Of course. Do it, Mariah."

Mariah might have muttered "finally" under her breath, but if she did, Layla couldn't quite blame her.

Layla began to look away as Mariah did her duty, but changed her mind. This was on her. She should watch. Without a wince, or indrawn gasp.

Somehow, everything was easier when he became just a body. It wasn't like she'd never seen people die; hell, she had seen so much worse. Some due to her orders or her mistakes. But this wasn't a battle in a war. Or maybe it was.

Newly emboldened, Layla tapped the corpse lightly with her foot. "You drugged him? Wasn't he immune to most—"

"Buspirathol, baby. Not as effective as injecting it, for the truth properties, but it does make one rather loopy. Anyway, I'm more annoyed I didn't get it right on the first throw. Bam. Straight to the heart. Legacy of my former career. Sloppy of me." She looked down at his body. "Well," she said briskly, "time to engage with his security forces to make sure they don't shoot us."

"Let's search the office first," Layla suggested. "In case we find anything else incriminating."

Mariah nodded sagely. "Ah, yes. *Valharan* due process."

In the end, the security forces let up after Benedik piped Ignatius through the Renebian comms on the yacht, ordering them to stand down and announcing Stanlo was executed for treason. Hopefully Park got a kick out of listening to *that* in his office.

(*I think we should offer conditional amnesty to the rebels too, sire*, Benedik had piped in. *Considering they were duped by one of our own. Our responsibility, as it were.* Ignatius had demurred).

Layla made sure Benedik conveyed to Ignatius that it was all wrapped up. Everything was solved. The culprits faced justice and she was positive it was safe for her to return. She hoped he knew her well enough to detect the lie. Mariah, certainly, gave her a knowing look as Layla spoke. They'd have to conference back on the yacht, away from prying eyes.

Palace security had given the two of them wide berth, but understandably balked at the idea of them bringing Stanlo's body with them back to the ship.

"I mean," Layla said, "he's no less dead because we can't drag his carcass back with us. It's not like we need proof of death."

Mariah smiled a wicked smile. "Ah yes, Empress, but you're a true Valharan now." She produced a pair of pliers out of one of her myriad pockets. Layla gave it a proper *what the actual fuck* look. "You bag a predator, you take a trophy. With your leave, of course, Your Grace."

"Yeah," Layla said, mystified. "Go on. Give me a proper Valharan education."

*
Now

A week later, they arrived at the Imperial Palace, a triumvirate straight off the musical hit charts: The Princess, the Dandy, and the Assassin. The trio made their way through the halls toward the war room, their progress unimpeded, by decree of the Emperor. Layla held her head high. Benedik strutted. And Mariah held two objects in her hand: a seal of office, and a tiny cloth drawstring bag.

Layla strode through the doors first, breaching them with a force that startled the men within.

Ignatius stood from the center conference table and spread his arms magnanimously. "Ah, my lady! I've been relaying your exploits to the general officers here. Welcome home."

General Turine likewise stood, giving her a nod of respect. "I hear Viceroy Stanlo tried to kill you."

"Eh," she said. "We killed him back."

The frozen smiles on their faces were worth it.

Mariah tossed Stanlo's chain of office on the table. It landed with a clang. The cloth bag went after it, into Ignatius's hands.

He opened it, and pulled out a baggie of teeth, still bloody from extraction.

"A token." Mariah bared her lips in a predatory grin. "Empress wouldn't let me chop off his head."

"Well." Ignatius held the bag up in wonder, "I certainly admire the pragmatism." He looked around. "Shall we conclude this in a more private setting?"

The four of them, plus Turine, walked to Ignatius's study. "Thank you for attending me, General," Ignatius said. "I see you've spent the walk issuing some directives on rooting out further abuses. I appreciate you."

"So," Turine began as they entered Ignatius's personal sanctum, "now that all that business is sorted—"

"Oh no, General," said Layla. "Not sorted at all. Few loose threads to worry at, are there not?"

"If that's true, then we should all get back to—"

"Sit, Turine."

Turine looked to his Emperor for support, but Ignatius merely patted his hands as if to say *You heard the lady. Sit, sit.*

"Pragmatism," Layla said, "meant we searched Stanlo's offices." She nodded at Benedik.

"Ahem. Lord Benedik here, for traitorous asshole. Repeat, it's Benedik." He moved the small disc away from his mouth.

They knew a voice wouldn't start emanating from Turine's britches, but the low ping from his pocket—a message alert— was enough.

"Quantum entanglement. Just one set in existence, am I right? Leased to you, General, for beta testing on the order of three years."

Turine's mouth worked a silent soliloquy. "Yes," he finally said, pulling the twin device from his trousers. "I gave the second device to the Viceroy." He looked around. "Is that a problem?"

"So," Ignatius said, "you had a secure method of communicating with a man who turned out to be a traitor?"

"Sire," he protested, "it means nothing. A communication method, nothing more—"

"It's not the only thing we have on you, Huxley," Ignatius said softly. "I had Mariah check up on you before she left on this trip. You see, you didn't push for truth drugs for the captured driver in the attack against Layla. That didn't sit right with me, so I went and talked to him myself. I still didn't suspect *you*, but I knew something was happening. I eventually got enough details to have Mariah go around making a few visits to the Volg and Free Press without threatening arrest and offering clemency. Mariah found ties to the Palace itself."

"Sire," Turine said stiffly, "you never told me."

"Because, frankly, by that point I *did* suspect you. And I was right. The same day of the fateful tunnel collapse, I was back out in the Tyrii barony, working my contacts. The miners. The smelters. Some, incidentally, who are members of the Volg. When they found their leadership were contacted by *you*, they were properly horrified, ready to help me in whatever I needed. Their faithless leaders, they found, had hired out some contracts to go after *my wife. My child*."

The room fell silent, but in a watchful way. Like it was pulsing with the force of Ignatius's anger and distress. Layla imagined beads containing words and recrimination scattered haphazardly on the floor, and visualized them gathering together like ball bearings caught by a magnet, then all streaming back to Ignatius.

On cue, Ignatius let out two breaths in quick succession—likely intended to be self-calming but which came out like dragon puffs—and spoke again. "Turine." He paused again, working his jaw. "How could you? How could you turn against your Emperor?"

"Sire," Turine began, although the word sounded swallowed, more akin to a gulp of fear. He stopped, looked around. That same far away look Carlus wore. "I want you to know. I had nothing to do with the Dracini insurrection. I agree with him that pushing Emperor Carlus out because of his illegitimacy was highly suspect—"

"Turine, you idiot," Mariah broke in, "that's not the real reason Carlus abdicated. Come *on*. He just broadcasted it to the entire damn Whorl!"

Turine looked like a credit had just dropped in his brain slot and activated it. "Ah. Right. That would explain..." he rubbed his head. "Sire, I never intended to betray you. This is to protect you. That woman," he said, pointing at Layla, "has been a problem the moment she arrived on this planet. Back when she was part of the Altainan delegation. I saw it during the Senate incursion. She stopped you from pursuing all means necessary to stop the mayhem, and what did that lead to? More protest. More chaos. A demonstrable threat to your rule. Sire, she can't be trusted."

"So you tried to *kill* her? So, you allied with the man who would plot to *bring down* my reign and put himself on the throne?"

He shook his head. "I didn't know!" he exclaimed. "I had no idea of Stanlo's plans. Truly," he insisted, looking around once more, this time wildly. "He came to me for help, in finding Carlus. We agreed on the legitimacy issue—I thought. He wanted to talk to Carlus and understand."

Benedik snorted. "So you broke into the Renebian records for Stanlo's benefit, to find Carlus, which you let Mariah think Layla did."

Mariah and Ignatius looked at him in surprise. "What?" he said. "Layla let me read more of her diary."

Layla nodded.

"And I asked for his advice on Lady Layla here," Stanlo continued. "He suggested a few things. I didn't know it would serve his plans for destabilization."

"Including trying to frame me and my father to throw the scent off you, I suspect," Benedik growled.

"This makes no sense!" Layla exclaimed. "The Volg *like* me."

Everyone looked at her with varying degrees of pity and disbelief. "What?"

Mariah snorted. "You're Altainan. You want *full* democracy, Empress. The Volg represent the merchants. Their name's a misnomer. They want to be minor lords. Not one of millions. You know this. C'mon."

"Wait..." Layla said, mystified. "That day when Roya visited the Lords' Parliament—they were protesting *Altain*?"

"Great God, save me from an idealist as Empress," Mariah complained, putting her hand to her head.

Ignatius hadn't cracked a smile at their antics. He continued to stare at Turine, thunder on his face. He commed out. "Arrest Turine. Get him out of my sight."

"Sire, please," he pleaded. "I'm loyal to you! I've done all of this for you."

Ignatius shook his head and turned away.

THEN

Then

It isn't until we're off Reneb in our shitty little corvette that I turn to Mariah and say, "Hey. Just so you know, Carlus told me everything."

Mariah doesn't take her eyes off the controls, but they tighten and her fingers go stiff. "Well. He must trust you," she says, bite in her voice.

I change the subject. "While we're out here, I want to stop by Dega Base."

Now she *does* turn and look at me. "We're supposed to go to Reneb and come right back."

"And I'm telling you we're making an unscheduled stop."

"Layla, I don't think—"

"Am I not the Empress?"

Face off. I win. Mariah grits her teeth and makes the course change.

The frozen rogue planet Dega orbits the large, swirling, Swan Nebula tunnel. Not like the cold of Valhar, but even *colder*, ice and frost everywhere, no sun to warm anything. Before the dome, it would have been impossible for life on Dega to survive at all, but over the centuries, survive it has. But even now, it's desolate, bare, eerie. But, *but*. Right above it is the Swan tunnel. Blue fluorescence, angry tendrils of energy hissing out of it, and it's like the Goddess opening up the heavens.

Once, Ignatius Kurestin commanded the Valharan forces on Dega. Now, it's Antonin Kurestin, and my goal is to bring him home.

Tonin is tall and skinny with a reedy mustache. He doesn't carry himself the way his wife and son do. There's a self-deprecating stoop to his walk, and an unassuming air. At first glance, one would think him inconsequential. But I know better. I know the influence he's had on Nate's life. I know Anastasia loves him with a passionate fire. Sometimes, it's the one who is the most still who can move mountains. Tonin might rate a second look. Then one sees. Integrity flows from every pore. Loyalty. Family. Duty. It's all there. He just doesn't have to be loud about it.

Tonin greets me with the same warm smile and hug his wife graced me months ago. Then he bows to his Empress, and I stop him, hands on his shoulders, attempting to lift him. "Please, don't," I say.

"You're going to have to get used to it," he says, grinning. His eyes soften. "I'm sorry to miss the wedding. Although, as I hear it, *everyone* missed the wedding."

"The timing was unexpected," I say. "But I'm here for a related reason. Would you consider coming home? To Valhar? Ignatius misses you," I add.

He turns away. "I knew that's why you were here. Look, Empress Layla, my duty is here. My duty is to be away from the throne. My ilk aren't welcome."

"I don't understand."

He sighs and regards me with a faint note of pity. For what? For not understanding his culture? "I'm not a high noble. For me to have a hand in the Emperor's affairs is unseemly."

"But Henri Dargas and Ephraim are *commoners*."

He nods. "They have defined roles. Prime Minister. Personal Secretary, or majordomo as we call him. It makes sense. It's within clear boundaries. Father, man-who-raised-him: that's harder to parse. My duty—"

"Duty means nothing without love," I insist. "Your love demands you be by your son's side. And besides, Ignatius wants you there."

"If my Emperor commands it, I will come."

I throw up my hands. Men. Aristocrats. Of course Ignatius isn't going to *command*—

We're interrupted by one of Tonin's aides.

"Lord Antonin, there's an Altainan shuttle going through the subspace tunnel." I look at Tonin. He looks at me. We both hightail it over to the command center.

And yeah, there it is. Altainan design, Altainan flagged. Going to Mazaran space.

"Know anything about this?" Tonin mutters to me.

I shake my head.

Then

I leave Dega with a promise extracted from Tonin to *think about it*, at least, and that's the best I can do. Hopefully I've jogged something in his mind. Ignatius won't talk about it much, but I know. I see his feeling of abandonment. He needs his dad.

It's a few days later, taking the long way back to Valhar, that I feel a stabbing pain in my lower stomach. It stops me cold.

No. Could it be?

The pain occurs again, and then I feel a dampness between my thighs. If I'm being dramatic, I'd write *I scream*, but I don't. It's not like that. It's not like watching someone you love dying right before your eyes. It's so much more pedestrian than that. Mundane. The worst monthly you'd ever have, maybe. But the utter banality of it? That might just be the most heartbreaking thing about it all.

Kid, I'm losing you.

Just, *nothing*. Like you never existed. Washed away. And I didn't ask for you. Pray for you. You were unexpected. Unwelcome. And now you're leaving and...

I don't want you to think you were unloved. You're not. You're loved. You don't have to go.

One thing people never talk about miscarriages is how *long* one can take. Ten days, I bleed. I look to see if there're any clots, if I can get a glimpse of you in a clump of cells, but it's normal. Breakthrough bleeding, just a longer duration than usual.

I don't do much during these days. I sit in corners, staring into nothingness. I don't tell Nate. I will, but in person. This isn't the type of thing you spring on someone in a fucking letter.

Mariah sits next to me and hands me a lollipop. I pop it into my mouth, absentmindedly.

"I didn't even want this baby," I confess.

"You're still allowed to grieve."

I didn't expect such empathy from her, so I remain silent and unsure.

She *rubs my back*. "It's not your fault. It's so common."

I work up the courage to say what's been eating at me this entire time. "I chose to go on this trip. If I had stayed home, maybe we could have been near medical attention."

She scoffs. "And what? You think they'd been able to stop it? This isn't something external that happened. Cells divide wrong. Things don't take. It *happens*. And going on a trip? Look. Pregnant women are badasses. Sure, they get exhausted and pukey, but they can handle a fucking business meeting on another planet. The Emperor even was worried about sending you off because you're apparently fragile now, but I set him and his claptrap back in his place right away. You," she says, punching me lightly, "you are stronger than you know."

What is happening here? I want to ask the question. I really do. But it isn't my place to dig. So I breathe in and out, as Mariah comforts me.

THEN AND NOW

THEN

I come home. Tell Nate. We grieve. He tells me I'm free.

You can't be rid of me that easily, I say. *I choose you.*

And we dream. About a marriage where Gustav is still alive. He'd be Lord Ignatius and I'd be Lady Layla. War between our peoples is averted and remains that way. An uneasy peace, but a lasting one. I can liaise with the Altainan flyboys that come out here for an exchange. He can agitate for enfranchisement.

And in this dream we still have *you*. Maybe an entire chaos of kids, with no predetermined future. Not Kaborlah rats, nor royalty. Just all of us here, with *choice*. And *intention*. And *freedom*. Two star-crossed lovers, who defied fate and managed to have it all.

You, my darling, and your brothers and sisters. You all will be the vanguards of a new Whorl, one in which power doesn't announce we are prosperous and free and therefore make it so, while billions lean and strive for an impossible dream marketed to them by political systems. One in which we don't see it as duty to be pawns, striking down our fellows in some unwinnable khed game of knights and clerics.

Maybe some of it is unachievable. But maybe the rest is attainable.

It's only a matter of time.

NOW, they lie together on the balcony, watching the morning rays bathe the palace. Ignatius plants a kiss on the top of her head. "You did good," he says. "A true leader. I'm proud."

"I just had to go full Valharan to pull it off."

"Is that so bad?"

"It's not a victory to deny one half of my existence, Ignatius. This is a wakeup call. We need to change this paradigm." She props herself up on one arm—as much as she can, these days, feeling more and more like a top-heavy weeble wobble. "Time and time again I've chosen you. Nothing ever changes for you. Meanwhile I have to fold myself into little triangles to fit into your life. It's time for you to choose *me*."

He tugs her back down again, gently, and she puts her ears to his heart, as if she can suss out his intentions, his courage, his dedication. "Think carefully about what you want the next fifty years to look like," she says. "This isn't some sort of ultimatum. I will gladly choose you all over again, over and over. I'll be by your side. But whichever way you go on this, do it with *intention*. Think on every implication. For you *and* for our little family. That's all I ask. As long as you do that, I will abide."

He pulls away slightly and cups her face, regarding her with a furrowed brow. "How exactly are you thinking?"

"Honestly," she says, "I wish we could stop being royalty, but I know *that's* not an option."

"I've always said I would, for you."

"The Imperium is not the life I wanted with you. You can't be you. As a ruler you never get to relax. You never get to be my Ignatius. And I never get to be your Layla. It's frustrating," she finishes lamely. "But maybe there's a way we can do it, take the pressure and idolatry away, without traumatizing your Empire."

"Would you marry me all over again, knowing all you know now?"

"Absolutely."

"Well," he concludes, "then we'll be fine, whatever we choose."

"I'm almost tempted to invite Carlus's kids back here, permanently," he continues. "Have little Natalia take over as Empress. Nadia could be regent. We could be free. You, me, and..." he rubs her stomach. "Little Carly."

Layla raises her brows. They might need to work on that name. "I wouldn't wish that fate on Natalia. Forget the legal hurdle, still, about the legitimacy of the family. Why would we *do* that to her? I'm just happy they all can come back and visit now, from time to time."

And Benedik took off today from Valhar, Alina in tow, to pay his respects to Carlus's family. Layla wishes she could go.

But the Alliance won't grant her safe passage.

"Truly, we wouldn't do that to Valhar. Just like we've said all along. That much change in power is too much." He sits up. "I'm thinking on what you said earlier. Formalizing city and community elections. In five years, elected governors. In five more years, representatives in a House of Commons. What do you think?"

"The nobles will be *pissed*," she says.

"Those fuckers tried to depose me, and I came back and trounced them. I don't care."

Layla holds in a peal of laughter. Besides, with Carlus's Whorlwide pronouncement, Ignatius's reputation is likely to be wholly rehabilitated. After all, Carlus put their Empire in danger. Ignatius is the war hero who helped drive the Mazarans away, despite the then-Crown Prince's actions. And his Empress was once his Alliance counterpart. "It'll be continual chips away from the power of the nobility and the Emperor," she attests. "Then self-rule for the colonies. The Viceroyalty would not be pleased."

"What was it you told me once? That it's the price of admission to the overarching Whorl community?"

Yes. Without a free vote, levies and taxes on their goods will continue. The Valharan people need a say in their government for the democracies of the Whorl—hypocritical as they may be at times—to accept them.

If Valhar even wants that acceptance.

The night before, returned from Solita, she found her Altainan citizenship papers and printed a copy. She set them on fire. Altain indeed came through, officially expelling her from the Republic. And it still stings. And it still hurts. And she feels thrown away. But what of it? With a child, a husband, and a new beginning: maybe, just maybe, she can wholly embrace the Valhar in her, and leave the past behind.

She lays a head on Ignatius's shoulder, deep in thought, as the sun rises over the seat of the Valharan Empire.

Afterword

Thank you for reading! If you enjoyed The Star-Crossed Empire, please help others find this book by leaving a review on Amazon or Goodreads. The recommendation of readers like you is a valuable piece in the career of every independent author.

The story of the Galactic Whorl will return in later standalone installments of the Whorl Chronicles series.

To keep up to date on new releases, please visit my website and sign up for my mailing list.

mayadarjani.com

You can also keep up on release news and other extras by following me on Twitter (@DarjaniMaya), TikTok (@maya.darjani), and/or Instagram (@mayadarjani).

Acknowledgements

This is my second published book on this new independent publishing adventure. The second this year, in fact! As always, I'd like to thank the mentors and programs that made me into the writer I am today, including the mentors of Author-Mentor Match and RevPit.

However, I'd also like to acknowledge the indie sci-fi publishing community, which has embraced me and my silly books: fellow SFF authors, enthusiastic readers, and book reviewers. I'm floored by the encouragement, promotion, and advice I've received this year. The SFF Insiders community, in particular, has been an absolute gem of a resource.

As always, the online writing community is essential for so many new writers in both helping them navigate the wild world of publishing—both indie and traditional—and being metaphorical shoulders to cry into. In fact, many of them became the metaphorical paper bag into which I needed to breathe, often. ('Maya gets anxious about random things' is a common theme.) The LGP server, the Baguettes, and my tiny group of snarky Scifi Placeholders keep me happy and whole. Special thanks in that regard to Yvi, Lindsey, and Arumi.

Thank you also to Rajani, who gave me the first enthusiastic and encouraging review of my previous book, Ancient as the Stars, and had the dubious honor of reading an early review copy of Star-Crossed Empire. During her read of SCE, she helped identify points where I still had pacing issues or clunky exposition. Thank goodness for her. Writing a dual timeline novel is no joke! I'm thankful for the fresh pair of eyes.

R. Lee Fryar read a version of this ... oh, way back in 2020, I believe, and she, as she always does, gently helped me course correct on many writing craft aspects. Melissa Work, my eventual AMM mentor for a later book, read the beginning of this book in 2021 and provided me with some of the most loving statements about my writing that I have ever received, and I will always treasure it.

And to my family, who has always been supportive and loving: thank you.

About the Author

Maya Darjani is a writer, photographer, stay-at-home mother, and former lots of things: counterterrorism officer, legislative correspondent, freelance journalist, and executive assistant. She writes genre-bending fiction about badass women, dual loyalty, and the false promise of patriotism. Maya has been an Author-Mentor Match mentee and a RevPit winner. Her debut indie novel, ANCIENT AS THE STARS—a Firefly x Expanse space adventure with humor, snark, and lots of heart—launched June 2024, and her Vorkosigan-inspired romantic space opera, THE STAR-CROSSED EMPIRE, published in November 2024.

Also by Maya Darjani

Broken Union
Ancient as the Stars
Loyalty to the Max